D1112226

THE CATCH

ALSO BY KIM WOZENCRAFT

RUSH

NOTES FROM THE COUNTRY CLUB

THE CATCH

KIM WOZENCRAFT

DOUBLEDAY

NEW YORK • LONDON • TORONTO • SYDNEY • AUCKLAND

PUBLISHED BY DOUBLEDAY
a division of Bantam Doubleday Dell Publishing Group, Inc.
1540 Broadway, New York, New York 10036

Book design by Fritz Metsch

Library of Congress Cataloging-in-Publication Data
Wozencraft, Kim.
The catch / Kim Wozencraft. — 1st ed.
p. cm.
ISBN 0-385-48516-6
I. Title.
PS3573.098C3 1998
813'.54—dc21 98-5629
CIP

Printed in the United States of America

October 1998

First Edition

1 3 5 7 9 10 8 6 4 2

FOR RICHARD

You may be a state trooper,
You might be a young Turk,
You may be the head of some big TV network,
You may be rich or poor,
You may be blind or lame,
You may be living in another country under another name

But you're gonna have to serve somebody, yes indeed

—"GOTTA SERVE SOMEBODY,"
Bob Dylan

ONE

Annie felt as though she had just closed her eyes when she heard Kurt stirring. She lay still, listening in the dark, as he sat up, swung his feet over the edge of the bed, stretched, drank some water. The empty glass clinked loudly on the sandstone coaster. She heard him step into a pair of jeans and pull on a T. The bones in his neck popped when he stretched again, this time standing.

She opened her eyes and saw 3:03 glowing blue-green in the dark. He was running on four hours' sleep. She rolled onto her stomach and plumped some pillows, crawled up them to look out the window. A quarter moon hung low to the east, midway through its night journey. The lilac blossoms, white, were long gone from the two trees outside the window. She missed them. The lettuce and kale in the garden were enjoying the cooler weather; they'd perked up two weeks ago, after drooping through most of August. A lone giant sunflower stood reverently in the southeast corner of the yard, its head hung in prayer.

She put her head back on a pillow and closed her eyes, heard Kurt digging in the pitch-black closet for his boots. Kane, the big Alsatian shepherd who'd been sleeping in his corner, rose and stretched, letting out a soft, whining yawn. He'd been with them since a few months after their wedding, almost six years now. Kurt had named him from the Welsh for "beautiful," and he was that—solid white, with deep brown eyes—as well as smart.

"Are you taking him?" Annie asked.

"Oh," Kurt said, "you're awake. Yes."

She sighed in response. He walked around to her side of the bed, sat down, and began kneading the back of her neck. She realized how tight her shoulder muscles were, considered whether they'd been that way even in sleep.

"I hope to make it home by dinner," he said. "I'll call you." He leaned down and pushed aside her hair, kissed her gently.

"Leave him, please."

"Annie. He's very helpful."

"Ah." Her tone was flat, not quite mocking. "That's what's important, isn't it."

He didn't respond. She pulled the covers to her shoulders.

"I've been working on this thing for months," he said. "People are counting on me."

"I thought we agreed."

"And we need the money."

"There are other ways."

"Where? The shop?" He shook his head.

"You haven't given it a chance."

She sighed once more.

"After this, I promise, I'll be free to give it what it needs." He took her hand, stroked it softly. "Really get into it, make it work. Bear with me here. One last shot."

"You said that last time. And the time before."

"You want me to skip it?" His voice, rising. His voice, which held such care, such quiet music, his voice, which could calm her so capably when she was fighting her own thoughts.

She pressed a finger to her lips, the shushing gesture lost in the darkness. "I don't want to live with this fear," she said quietly.

He pulled her to him. "Annie. I love you. I love what we're building here. I love our family. It's important to me to provide, and to do it well. I love you."

"I don't want to live with this fear." She wasn't sure he'd heard it the first time. He was the optimist, and disapproving tones sometimes went right past him, causing him to miss words, even entire sentences.

"Soon you won't have to," he said. "I have to go, or I'll be late." He stood up. "I have a plane to catch."

She pulled herself up to look out the window again. The night was clear.

"Give the boys a hug and a kiss." He paused at the door, patted his thigh to signal Kane. "When this is done, we'll get away for a few weeks. Maybe go down to the ranch."

He went quietly down the stairs, carrying his boots. Kane swung past the bed on his way out, touched Annie's hand with his cold, wet nose, his way of saying good-bye. His toenails clicked on the wooden stairway; the front door opened, then shut softly. She heard the gate latch and, a few moments later, the rumble of a large, powerful engine and tires crunching gravel as Kurt eased his truck down the long drive toward the road.

She felt the emptiness of the bed, wondered if she was lonely or relieved. Then Timothy awoke with a cry of pain. His two-year molars were coming in early. She crossed the hall to his room, bundled him against her, rocking and soothing. He wouldn't settle. She carried him to the rocker and put him to her breast.

He quieted instantly, slipped away into a bliss she could not imagine yet was part of. Before the children, she would have been out there to help Kurt—perhaps not eagerly, but willingly. Tonight, though, his leaving was a broken promise that filled her with fear and resentment.

She rocked ever so gently, barely moving, and gazed at the faint reflection of mother nursing child that glowed, grayish-white, on the night-darkened window panes.

TWO

Kurt stared past Bill at the sod strip, or what he could see of it in the dark: a little over five thousand feet long, good grass covering. But an early hurricane, which had flattened several towns in the Florida panhandle, had been gentled by the time it reached the Catskills, bringing three straight days of soft, steady rain that had turned the strip pulpy. The clouds had moved on, but the strip was still wet, and there were worrisome spots. He tried to step back from the moment, press down his anticipation, and consider whether it was foolish to continue.

In the larger sense, no doubt it was. He'd been smuggling for more than ten years; had to figure the odds were beginning to stack against him. Okay, so the feds' interdiction rate sucked—they busted roughly ten percent of the given number of loads in any year. Fools and amateurs got caught in the act. Little to fear there. The problem was, those they arrested often dropped names, and usually the names they dropped were legends in the business—whether the guys doing the ratting had ever even met them or not, much less done deals with them. The authorities had most likely heard his name from Maine to Miami to California to the Northwest Territory. It was the Breakfast Cereal Theory of Informant Behavior, put forth to Kurt by Dr. Philip Tetlow, an itinerant psychiatrist whose clientele likewise traveled extensively and were often in need of nerve tonics: the flakes always gather in the four corners of the box. The trip Kurt had done with the doctor in 'eighty, the year before he met Annie, had been one of his best, though only moderately lucrative. They'd brought in a relatively early load of Maui via Doc's yacht, *The Final Analysis.*

Kurt hadn't seen him much since then, Dr. Tetlow having chosen to remain adrift on the high seas after an indictment came down with his name on it.

Kurt looked at the runway. What runway?—it was a strip, and that's *all* it was. He'd stumbled across it one afternoon shortly after moving up from the city in 'eighty-two, a few short weeks before Alex was born. While Annie lugged her huge belly from room to room, unpacking boxes, straightening, nesting until she literally felt the first sharp pains of birth, Kurt wandered the back roads, scoping out his new territory, trying to make the countryside familiar. The world was strange and wonderful in those days, when he wound through the woods on narrow country lanes, amazed that a baby was growing in Annie's belly. He had wanted to be a father forever, it seemed to him. He counted the days, though only to himself, knowing that Annie was putting more than enough pressure on herself to be prompt about the due date. He had massaged her feet every day of the pregnancy, twice a day as they neared the birth and her weight became onerous. He thought she had never been so beautiful as when her belly swelled and grew round. He would rest his hand on it each evening, waiting for a kick from the baby inside, leaning close to say, "I love you. I can't wait for you to come out and play. We'll have so much fun." And late in the pregnancy, Annie could feel a difference inside when Kurt spoke to Alex; she knew Alex heard his father's voice.

A big smile came to Kurt's face when he first saw the strip; opportunity had once again presented itself. He would find out who owned the property, how often they were around, if there were caretakers. That was part of what he did; he scoped out airstrips and opportunity. He kept the landings random, spread out, unpredictable.

But the optimism he'd had when he first discovered the strip was not in him tonight. He wished Annie hadn't seemed so fearful and disappointed. Her doubts created fresh ones in him. He had the feeling he shouldn't be here.

Too late now. He pressed his boot into the sod, gauging the texture with his leg muscles, looked up at the night sky, stars dimming as dawn approached, and back at the runway. Shake it off.

Johnny Nocenti, a red-headed Italian out of Brooklyn, was out checking the strip, stepping as gingerly as a winter fisherman testing the ice. A few feet away stood Bad Bill Schapp, a totally insane three-hundred-and-fifty-four pound *mensch* from Staten Island. Everybody loved Bad Bill, and Kurt counted him among his most trusted friends. Bill would take the bulk of the load to the city. Kane loped in wide circles around the two of them.

"I dunno, bro," Johnny said. "Still feels awful mushy."

"Nothing we can do about it," Kurt said, approaching. He pressed a button on the radio stuffed in his back pocket and was reassured by the burst of static. They were all hooked up, each man with a hand-held and each vehicle with an under-dash mount, waiting for word from the pilot.

"We could get it rolled first thing in the morning," said Johnny.

"Why be sensible?" said Bill, squeezing his words between his teeth. "Let's see if we can get ourselves killed."

"He'll be here in an hour, two at the most." Kurt glanced over at his truck. Hovering ghostlike behind the windshield was the narrow face of Gary Smith, drawn tight with fear. The burst of static over the truck radio had no doubt alarmed him. Gary was quiet, as raw-boned and lanky as America's sixteenth president. Married. Three kids. Broke. He was a caretaker at the lodge down the road, and didn't have the appetite for this kind of thing. It was his wife who had asked Annie to see whether Kurt had any extra work for Gary. She wanted to buy a piece of property. Now Gary was doing it. Kurt tried to think of something he could say to ease the man's discomfort, but there wasn't time. And it would ease up on its own as soon as the plane landed. Gary saw him looking and raised a hand, as if to say thanks anyway.

Other than Gary, those Kurt had gathered were his closest associates, men he knew he could depend on. His end would be roughly a million, he kept telling himself, as though he were in it only for the money.

He moved forward with Johnny, walking the strip. It took Bill a moment to throw his weight in gear and lumber after them, but he caught up before they reached the section they were most concerned about: a large ragged patch about a third of the way down, torn up by landing gear from local Cessna 150s and small Beechcraft twins.

Bill stubbed a toe at a chunk of sod.

"Golfers will please replace their divots." He sighed. Kurt chuckled at him and felt the coolest breeze of night, its iciness the signal that dawn would indeed arrive soon. Autumn, too. Already the night air was scented with the slightly moldy aroma of dying leaves.

"He'll get in all right," he said, aiming his words at Johnny. "And he'll be going out light."

"Feel this stuff," Johnny said. "He comes in like usual on this—"

"Hey," Kurt said, "we can stand here and worry about it all you want, but the fact is it's too late. He left the Bahamas on time. If he made it around that hurricane, he'll be here at dawn. He probably got a boost from the tailwinds."

"Knowing Ben," Bill said, "he probably just went through it."

Kurt was as worried inside as Johnny was on the surface, but refused to give in to his doubts. It didn't matter. After a certain point, you had to let it go. It was the scammer's maxim: what happens happens.

They called Ben Rubies "Ram It and Slam It" for a reason; Kurt had seen him land where few pilots could. He would set the bird down, no problem. But as Ben's ETA drew closer, the runway was feeling more and more pulpy beneath Kurt's boots. He was far from sure they'd ever get the plane back up. No. It was nerves. That's all. A case of the nerves.

A blast of static came from the radio on Kurt's belt; he grabbed it and keyed it quickly.

"What was that!" Spitting into the mike.

"Somebody's trying to reach us." The voice of Father Francis came back at him through the handset, calm, deep, and clear, almost singing. Father Francis was like that: the closer he was to calamity, the more serene he seemed. The summer before Kurt met Annie, he and Father Francis had bought a used motor home from a radical Baptist group based halfway between San Antonio and Waco and used it to haul loads of Oaxacan pot north to Staten Island. The bus, a 'sixty-eight Bluebird Wanderlodge, had a large, professionally painted logo on each side and, across the front, *Global Evangelism Television.* They were rarely stopped, but when they were, Francis Xavier Stevens, eight years back from Nam and still wondering what all the fuss was about, unswervingly convinced the cops that he was born again in the name of Jesus and on the road to spread the Good News. On one occasion, Kurt had managed to hold a straight face while Father Francis almost induced a narrow-faced state cop outside Saint Louis into a roadside baptism. Ah. The good old days.

Now he looked at the sky, just coming gray, and at the darkness of the Catskill woods surrounding it. Ben would be early; he was sure of it. For a moment he allowed his paranoia to go unchecked and became convinced there were agents out there, waiting to pounce. But Kane would have scented them by now. He thought of Alex and Timothy, home sleeping, where he should be, and of Annie, probably up, her eyes worrying the same paragraph over and over as she tried to read herself to sleep. He wondered if his love for her was desperate. He tried to remember if there was a point when she'd suddenly become insomniac; felt a mild swell of guilt and forced himself to quash it. He loved her: focus on the task at hand.

He looked again at the sky, his ears tuned, waiting for the sound of a plane engine and trying to convince himself that he had to be here. He had the workers, and he trusted them, most of the time. Maybe he should have run the trip from a distance. He wished his decision to be here hadn't sent her into a funk. He wished she were here. That was part of her resentment, too. She missed the action. She claimed motherhood was more than enough, and he adored the way she had taken to family life. He was still astonished at the depth of his feelings for her and for his boys. Didn't she know how important it was for him to provide for them? They'd fought about it more than a few times.

His thoughts were interrupted by a distant sound, a faraway hum that brought to mind a soundbite of Ginsberg's poetic, antiwar Ohm. NBC? HBO? Kurt tilted his head, tuned in. Ohm. There it was. Distant still, but quickly drawing closer. Oh, man. It was not Ohm. And it was gonna be louder than he'd ever considered. Oh, man. Of course it would. *It's a DC-6, you fucking fool,* four engines screaming as they drove four propellers hard and fast enough to carry ten tons of cargo through thin air.

"Bring 'em in," he said into the radio. His voice sounded calm after the raging of his thoughts. As he spoke, the roar of the plane's engines swelled until it seemed to rattle the very hills, shaking the entire valley. Still the noise came, kept coming, as though from far away. Oh, Sweet Jesus, it was loud. Kurt cringed and peered over the tree line. Louder. It was getting louder.

It had to be just over the hill. The sun beat it, cresting the ridge off Mohonk as the enormous noise driving the propellers drowned out the efficient engines of the pair of thirty-two-foot box vans pulling to a stop at the north end of the strip.

Father Francis was in one, Lonnie McGrath in the other. The two had grown up tough Irish outside Boston; joined the Marines together. Father Francis, a black Irish version of Jerry Garcia, leaped out of his van, pulled off his glasses, and lifted his eyes to the sky. He clapped his hands to his ears and shook his head at Kurt. Brother. McGrath unfolded out of his truck, smiling widely. Most of his upper front teeth were gone, the result of a rifle butt to the mouth during a drunken brawl somewhere in the wilds of Saigon—not with the enemy. He ducked down the runway, galloping wildly, shaking his head gleefully at the noise.

"All right, Colonel Kurts," he shouted. "How you gonna get yourself out of this one?" Kurt glared at him. The engines rattled his brain; adrenaline wracked his body. It occurred to him that he might be right in the middle of a very serious mistake. His biggest fear hit him square on from behind: he was insane. How simple. It explained everything. He pulled himself back from the brink.

The only thing to consider now was whether the pilot would be killed. Rubies was a balls-up flyer, a specialist in STOL: short take-off and landing. He could get in and out of strips like this one. Scam artist to the core, but that was okay. The need to con people was something Ben had no control over, and Kurt had factored this into his plans.

He jerked his head hard to the left, felt the joints crack, forced his mind back to the runway and the plane and the decision.

McGrath slapped him on the back—hard. "Well?" he said. His attitude gave strength.

Kurt jogged over to the truck and got on the radio.

"Little Red Riding Hood to Papa Bear," he said. More static, and then the maniacal hoarseness of Rubies's voice and the roar of the plane engines, coming over the radio too. "This is Papa Bear, yeah. I'm right on top of you!"

"We know!" Kurt shouted. "We know! We can hear you."

"By the time I get there," Rubies yelled, "the entire state'll be hearing me!"

"Easy does it," Kurt said; "it's been raining." He climbed out of the truck just as the plane cleared the tree line, badly overshooting the end of the runway.

"Oh, shit," he whispered.

Rubies slammed the nosegear into the very patch Kurt had been scared of. Its wheel sank into the sod, plowing dirt, gravel, and grass into a writhing snake of soil and jamming the front wheel to a stop. The fuselage snapped free of the nosegear. Rubies killed the engines; the plane skidded down the runway on its chin until the main landing gear folded, and then it slid on its belly. Kurt thought of fire, realized no, then worried that the plane would go off the end of the runway and crash into the trees. He watched, his muscles ready to explode as the plane slowed, slowed, the noise of metal skidding on dirt so strangely loud, it translated into a weird silence in his brain. The plane did a one-eighty, taking forever, and then, at last, rocked to a delicate halt, one wingtip brushing against an oak sapling at the edge of the woods.

It was suddenly quiet. And then Kurt heard the sound of Father Francis and Gary Smith. Running.

They were halfway to the woods when McGrath barked out, "WHERE THE FUCK ARE YOU GUYS GOING?" It was as though he'd beaned each of them with a rock to the back of the head. They halted, turned, and stared at him. A destination hadn't crossed their minds. The little gland in the middle of the brain that is ever-tuned to danger had short-circuited thought, zipping it past the rational area of their gray matter and hijacking their bodies in the interest of survival. The two of them stood still as sighted deer, staring at McGrath.

Kurt said to him, "Bring out the vans, load them first, and get 'em out of here." McGrath moved, yelling the basics at Father Francis and Gary. "Get in the trucks! Drive them out to the plane!"

The plane door opened and a khaki-clad Ben Rubies emerged as though slightly late for a business appointment. He walked briskly toward Kurt, stopped suddenly, ran back to the door.

He came out carrying a small suitcase and slapped Kurt on the shoulder as he brushed past him.

"Get me outta here."

"Where to?" Kurt fell in beside him.

"The airport."

"The red truck," Kurt said, pointing. "I'll be right there." He veered toward McGrath.

The conveyer belt was already in place; McGrath and Father Francis, inside the plane, were sending down the first bales of Colombian marijuana. Bill, Johnny, and Gary Smith loaded the vans. They were into it now, working quickly and methodically.

Kurt looked up at McGrath, who tossed a bale onto the belt and straightened up, jerking a thumb over his shoulder at the huge plane he stood inside.

"Whaddoo I do with this?" he said, grinning.

"Gee," Kurt said, shrugging, smiling back, "I guess just leave it here." They were confident now that they would get out all right. The offload would take twelve or thirteen minutes. Even if someone had called the police the instant the plane crashed, the load was out of here. It would take the cops at least half an hour to get to the strip. Timing was all, and Kurt had always had the gift. But even Annie would think he was cutting this one close. Foolishly close. He wished again that she was with him. She'd be right in there with Lonnie and Bill or out pulling jiggers on the perimeter. But ever since Alex arrived and then Timothy, she'd stopped running with him and become domestic. He loved that she took such good care of the boys, even though she'd grown more and more adamant that he get out of the business. She would still admit that it was nice having a fireproof safe full of hundred-dollar bills, never having to worry about grocery money. Or money, period. And she was still curious about the details, wanting to know but not wanting to know. She missed it, he was sure; missed the rush, missed the calculation and precision of the risk. Sometimes he felt unsure of what she expected of him. Especially lately.

Ben's right foot was tapping a staccato against the floorboard when Kurt got in the truck. The air inside the cab was gray-white, full of cigarette smoke. Kane was lucky to be riding in the back.

"Whaddaya gonna do with the plane?" Rubies asked.

"Whaddaya mean, what am I gonna do with it?" Kurt rolled down his window and motioned Rubies to do the same. "Got something in mind, Ben?" Rubies thought for a moment, and it occurred to Kurt that the guy was seriously trying to come up with an idea.

"Nah," Rubies said finally, lighting a new cigarette with the butt of the other. "It'll come up stolen. No way they can trace it to us."

"You said it's insured."

"Lloyd's of London." He laughed. "I'll get back to you on it."

At Stewart Airport, Kurt hugged Ben and left him in the coffee shop, puffing away on his umpteenth Camel of the morning. Near baggage claim and arrivals, one large lobby in the small commuter airport, he pumped some quarters into the pay phone and checked with the safe house. They were ready to load the semis.

He was on State 209, en route to the safe house, when he came over the rise just south of town to find state troopers manning a roadblock. Four squad cars and an unmarked. Major. A couple of semis were in line, and several cars and pickups. He braked to a stop at the back of the line, working to calm himself, readying his demeanor for the cops at the checkpoint ahead. He reached to pet Kane, in front with him now.

"Guess you can't expect to crash a plane and not have them start a serious search," he said. He chuckled to himself. Laugh it off. No way they could pin anything on him now. Maybe. The dog gave Kurt's hand a lick, as though he knew Kurt was trying to bolster faltering confidence.

Kurt eased to a stop at the checkpoint, his pulse wanting to explode, and rolled down the window. A New York State trooper nodded precisely and asked for driver's license and registration, please. Kurt had them ready.

"What's happened?" he asked.

"Escape," the trooper said. "Eastern Correctional." He tucked Kurt's license into his belt, nodded at Kane.

"Beautiful dog," he said. "Would you mind opening the back, sir?"

"No problem," Kurt said. He wanted to say no, not unless you can show me a search warrant, just on principle, but this was no time to get in a hassle. And there wasn't so much as a seed back there. He was nervous all the same. The uniforms did it to him, uniforms and guns, and it seemed as if the cops were all wearing these uptight little mustaches lately.

He got out slowly and led the way to the rear of the camper, cranked the handle, and raised the door. The trooper aimed his flashlight, took a quick look, nodded.

"Thank you, sir." He handed Kurt his license. "Sorry for the inconvenience."

"No problem," Kurt said again.

As he climbed back into the cab, he was shocked to see two men in DEA jackets standing next to a black-and-white barrier. He pretended indifference as he put the truck in gear, but his insides were taut. One of them turned to give him a steady look, and Kane let go a low rumbling growl as a trooper waved Kurt through the checkpoint.

"Chill, buddy," Kurt said softly, reaching to pat the dog. "We're all right." He pulled away slowly, wanting to get another look at the DEA guys. State roadblock to find escaped prisoner? Why were the federal narcs hanging around? He couldn't believe they were letting him go. There would be a tail. Had to be. Okay. Things were getting weird. Maintain. Just drive slowly away and maintain.

He let out a controlled sigh and watched his mirror carefully as he headed away from the roadblock and toward the Stone Ridge market, where he bought a couple of cases of Corona and a bag of limes and thought about changing his route. Maybe he should go straight home, get off the roads, but he had to warn his men about the roadblock. And he should check the product, gauge the quality. Most important was that he show solidarity with the others. He didn't know how long the roadblock would be up or whether the cops would move it, but he had to figure his guys would be ducking serious heat when they pulled out carrying loads. He thought about sitting on the stuff at the safe house, but that was always risky. He checked the parking lot carefully, convinced that there was a tail, but saw no sign. He spent the next forty minutes winding through the countryside on back roads he knew from hours and hours of driving them, getting to know them for just such an occasion as this. If there was a tail, he would lose it on Crossing Place Road, a single-lane dirt track that went right through a branch of the Esopus Creek. Sedans like the cops', even if the water was low enough for them to attempt a crossing, would get hopelessly bogged down in the mud.

He crossed the creek slowly, wishing not to disturb some teenagers fishing upstream. Pulled to a stop on the far bank and waited.

Nothing. No tail. Just plenty of paranoia, enough that he had to concentrate not to grind his teeth.

•

McGrath was all business and into it as he pulled the barn door closed behind Kurt and grabbed a clipboard off a stack of bales. Though the afternoon was unusually cool, McGrath had been at it since before dawn, perspiring through much of the day, and his shirt was soaked. Kurt was glad his buddy's sweat smelled of labor, not of fear.

"Looks good," McGrath said. "Check this out." He handed Kurt the inventory.

"There's heat all over the place," Kurt said quietly. "I just came through a roadblock on 209."

"They'd be here by now if they even had a clue," McGrath said. He pulled a packet of rolling papers out of his pocket, plucked a handful of buds from the bale, and led Kurt to a workbench on the barn's south wall. While they smoked, the others continued loading bales onto the conveyer belt, which carried them to one of two tractor-trailer rigs backed up to the giant barn. Cartons of institutional food were stacked just outside the trucks. The pot would be surrounded with cases of chili, sauerkraut, hot fudge, and who knew what else had been ordered for cover.

McGrath rolled a joint for the others and delivered it to Gary; then came smiling back to the workbench.

"There were DEA guys at the roadblock," Kurt said.

"We'll take the thruway." McGrath shrugged. "Fuck 'em." He grinned.

"Run a lead vehicle out front then, and have him keep you posted."

When the trucks were loaded and the drivers on the road, Kurt and the others set about cleaning up the stash house and barn, trying to gather all traces of illegal plant material. As he swept, Kurt tried to push back the feeling that he shouldn't go home. But he could make it for dinner if he headed out soon. He wanted to see his children.

He wished again that Annie were with him. She'd always been good in situations like this: cool like Father Francis but not as brazen as McGrath, and possessed of a determination that, Kurt was convinced, posted some kind of psychic *No Trespassing* signs around the perimeters of his operations. He'd teased her early on, calling her Annie Oakley when they were driving the back roads in the hill country of Texas, intoxicated with love and looking for craziness. He'd been impressed with her knowledge of the territory, the dirt roads and ranches and even a few caverns good for hiding out.

He missed her now, though he knew he had to stay away, ride this out, see where it went. He headed toward Olive Branch, again winding slowly along back roads. Kane rode with his head out the window, lapping in late afternoon sunshine and cool air. The first leaves were turning. So he'd left a big, supposedly stolen airplane on somebody's airstrip. No big deal.

The bartender at the Krumville Inn, who reminded Kurt of the Wizard of Oz, gave a quick smile of recognition and stood with his fists resting on the bar, awaiting Kurt's request. The wall to the left of the bar was plastered with labels from three hundred and two varieties of beer available. Food could be had, too, though there were fewer choices: fried chicken, French fries, hamburgers, onion rings, pizza. Stuffed mushrooms.

Kurt sat down and ordered a Chimay Cinc Cents, an ample bottle of ale brewed by Trappist monks at the Chimay Abbey in Belgium. He took a long swallow and another. Those *pères trappistes,* they knew what they were doing. A woman with black fingernails moved a stool closer and asked if he'd like to play eight-ball.

"Thanks," he said. "The table's occupied." He recognized the guys who were playing, a couple of local sheriff's deputies who hung out regularly at the inn whenever they worked the day shift. Kurt knew them enough to say hello, and they knew him the same way. There had never been any official contact.

He thought about finding out if the roadblock was really for escaped convicts. It was perfectly believable; there were five or six prisons in the area, at least. IBM and the New York State prison system were the major—practically the only—employers in Ulster County. But as he approached the pool table he saw alarm in the eyes of the deputies. It was as though they were shocked to see him out walking around, as though they were thinking, "There he is!"

He said hello but kept walking, headed for the front door. He knew it now: he was hot as hell's attic. He expected them to stop him as he pushed through the heavy oak doors, but no voice rang out. Kane did a little dance on the front seat when Kurt got back in and started the truck.

"Old-buddy-old-pal," Kurt said, "we've got heat." He wondered where to go, began inventorying what he was holding. Where the fuck were they? No one had been on him at the safe house. That's what they were waiting for, for him to lead them to the stash. If they'd picked him up at the roadblock, though, he'd lost them well before he got here. But there was no mistaking it: those deputies had been shocked to see him on the streets. Time to lead them away from his home and, on the way, clean up his act. Ditch the radio. Lose his address book, any notes, papers, everything but a piece of ID they'd have to accept. He felt certain he was about to be arrested, tried to shrug it off as paranoia. Things are cool. Things are okay. Just drive.

Then, when he passed the Tongore Trading Post, a Chevy pulled out of the small parking lot and established a two-car distance between them, maintaining it exactly. And then another car, also a Chevy, pulled off a side road and fell in behind the first. There they were. Not even attempting to be discreet.

"Shit," he muttered. "Shit. Shit. Shit."

Half an hour later, when he turned right into the vast parking lot at the Hudson Valley Mall in Kingston, the Chevys continued straight ahead. What were these guys doing? He should be dog tired, but he'd gone into overdrive: brain buzzing and body wired. Annie would be in a fine mood by now. Almost seven, he hadn't called, he wouldn't be there, and that was only the beginning. She'd probably heard about the crash and was worried sick. But he couldn't call. If the feds were on him like this, they doubtless had agents on the wires, monitoring calls to and from his home.

He parked the truck in the sea of vehicles and put Kane in the back, after pouring a bottle of water into a pan he kept for that purpose. He opened the camper windows.

"Don't worry, boy," he said. "I'll send someone for you as soon as I can." The dog stared at him with total trust. "Man," Kurt said, "I'm sorry, pal." He went back to the cab and pulled out the radio from under the dash.

He ditched it in a trashcan at a small side entrance to the mall and walked in. A blast of warm, polyester-scented air filled his nostrils, and immediately he was overwhelmed by depression. Who created all this ugliness? He didn't know what he was doing or why he was doing it. She was right; why hadn't he listened? He was only waiting. Passing time and waiting. He thought back to fourth grade, when he'd begun greasing his hair back and disgracing his blueblood heritage by hanging with the wrong guys after he saw an episode of *Dragnet* about juvenile delinquents. *Rebel Without a Cause* had been an influence, too. He'd begun a paper route for cash and started a gang, the Pink Rats, made himself president and treasurer for life. He coerced Jonathan Snyder, a Quaker boy who lived a few blocks away, into letting them use his family's great barn as Pink Rat headquarters. He painted a skull and crossbones on a metal box with lock and key, kept cash and cigarettes in that. And fellow Pink Rat Chris Reed taught him how to drive. At age nine, he could creep into his parents' bedroom, lift the keys silently off the dresser as they slept off the latest round of daiquiris from the latest round of parties, slip out the back door, and roll the car down the driveway. Once in the street, propped up on pillows so that he could see over the dash, perched on the edge of the seat so that he could reach the pedals, he'd start the engine on his father's latest Pontiac. Chris would be waiting in his own dad's car a few blocks away, and the two would drive around the neighborhood.

One foggy night when Chris stayed home, Kurt was motoring up Cliff Road and a police cruiser turned around on him. Its lights came on.

"Oh, God, they got me," he said aloud as he eased the car to the curb. He'd been arrested several times since, and always it was the same feeling: not so much fear as simply a major interruption in your plans, and you know there's gonna be trouble.

Officer Ide was amazed and, luckily for Kurt, amused. He delivered the child to his sleepy-eyed and thoroughly embarrassed parents, and never failed to remind Kurt's mother of the incident whenever he saw her. Kurt became famous. He would write on the blackboard: PINK RATS MEETING TODAY AT 4 O'CLOCK. BE THERE OR ELSE!

There hadn't been much serious trouble until junior high. In ninth grade he ran up against a student teacher in phys ed. Young guy from Springfield College, a real hard-ass. Didn't like Kurt from the start, and when Kurt showed up one afternoon to pitch without his sneakers, the teacher ordered him off the mound. Kurt kept pitching in his street shoes, black loafers. The teacher came at him, screaming, and Kurt gave him the finger. By the time the teacher grabbed him, Kurt was primed to fight, and he saw the girls' gym teacher herding her class behind the backstop as he went for the guy. He had the coach in a headlock, was punching him in the face, pounding, and then suddenly realized what he was doing, let go, and took off across the ballfield and over a hill into the woods.

They sent him to a shrink, who used words like *strong sociopathic tendencies* and gave his parents the choice of putting Kurt into reform school: a private one if they wished, a public one if they didn't. He wound up transferred to Thompson's Academy, a disciplinary private school, as euphemism had it. But he didn't need the evaluation to tell him what was wrong. It had always taken a call from the police department to get his father's attention.

•

He found a pay phone and dialed his lawyer's office. Mark Levine was a long-time friend and his lawyer since the first time he'd had legal hassles, at least as an adult. And he was good. He'd got the evidence suppressed on that case back in 'seventy-nine, when a trooper had searched the Global Evangelism Television van after neglecting to obtain a warrant. Without Mark's aid, Kurt and Father Francis might well be doing laps in the big yard of some state joint in Pennsylvania right now. And there was that time in Texas, the trip with Annie. Mark hadn't actually defended him in that one, but he'd hooked Kurt up with an excellent counselor in Austin, who posted bond in a matter of hours and went about the business of demolishing the state's case.

The answering service picked up, and Kurt left word and then tried Mark's home number. The machine came on.

"Mark," he said. "Kurt. I'm about to get popped. If you don't hear from me, check with DEA. And call Annie, please . . ." He went on with directions about Kane and the truck.

Hearing his own words brought the reality a little closer. He *was* about to be arrested. Fuck. But the load was out, gone. What could they have? Only a crash-landed DC-6, asshole. That's what they have. You were out of your mind to try to pull that one off. But they didn't get the trucks, or they would have grabbed him before this. They were following him because they hoped he would panic and lead them to the load. He realized he was standing there holding the pay phone receiver while a recorded voice chimed, "If you'd like to make a call . . ."

Where was the heat? What were they waiting for? He would not let them catch him in a dark alley somewhere, though God knew they could take him to one once they had him. But at least he'd have witnesses while they arrested him. The man perusing videos in the store across the way had to be an agent, no question.

He swung away from the phone and walked into the first open doorway. Assaulted with flashing lights and weird utterances from forty or so video games, his brain went into a freefall. He jerked himself back, took stock. The arcade was loaded with teenagers, all sloppy jackets and huge high-tech sneakers, and he was saddened to realize how quickly his children would grow up. Someday, if he lived long enough, their youth would seem to him to have passed in an instant.

He walked numbly over to a token machine and tucked a five into the slot, listened to the clink of coins against the metal holding cup. He saw the number 3 next to a coin slot and shoved in the required tokens. The image on the screen rushed him: the seal of the Drug Enforcement Administration, patriotic blue and gold, the message beneath—*Winners Don't Do Drugs.* Speed metal blistered out of speakers; images flashed on screen; Kurt picked up the heavy steel gun attached with airline tether and began blasting away at bad guys.

Five or six teenage boys drifted over as Kurt pumped imaginary lead into the onscreen images. He was a good shot; the boys nodded approval. He glanced at one who was taller than he was, unconsciously picking a zit. The kid smiled and Kurt started shooting everything that moved, every image that popped up on the screen: an armed robber waving a shotgun, a teenage punk in black leather, a screaming woman holding a bag of groceries, two hoodlums demanding money. Kurt banged away, dropping them one after the other. The teenagers snickered; Kurt popped a Barney Fife–looking deputy and watched his score plummet.

"RELOAD! RELOAD! RELOAD!" the machine screamed at him, and he aimed the gun skyward and pulled the trigger three times. Bullets appeared in yellow, lower right screen. He aimed again and fired, a woman in curlers fell back through her apartment door, her screams rivaling Fay Wray's in *King Kong*. And then he saw the tall kid's hand drop from his chin and his mouth fall open, and all of them were backing away from the video game and he kept shooting, not even aiming anymore.

"ON THE FLOOR NOW, MOTHERFUCKER! THE REST OF YOU, GET BACK! GET BACK! GET BACK NOW!" Not the machine; this was real.

Kurt turned. A man in black was in his face, waving an automatic, totally wired, screaming like some half-drunk and wholly freaked-out junkie armed robber sticking up a bodega. Three others were right behind him, calmer, but all of them aiming guns at him. The boys took a few steps back, but not too far away; they wanted to see this. Kurt let the electronic gun fall against the machine, dangling from its tether, and slowly knelt on the floor. He eased onto his belly and put his hands behind his back. The carpet smelled like used sweatsocks. One of the agents grabbed his arms and wrenched them in a hammer lock. Metal bit into his wrists. Massive anger in the grip; and the freaky one planted a kick into Kurt's side as they yanked him to his feet, again pain in his wrists. Man, were they pissed off. No way they had the load.

The last thing he heard as the agents hustled him through the crowd outside the arcade was one of the teenagers inside: "Awesome!"

THREE

Dinner was too far away for them to make it without some kind of snack or a loud duet of the Tantrum in E Major. They'd lost track of time in the barn when Alex discovered a litter of kittens up in the haystacks. Just turned four, and he could scramble up the ladder before Annie knew what was happening, a skill he must have honed while playing with Kurt. That hadn't happened much lately. Daddy was busy.

In their chairs with bowls of applesauce and chunks of cheddar in hand and on face, they settled and watched quietly as Mommy set about making dinner. Mommy.

Carol came in, sniffing the air and letting her nose lead her to the stove, where Annie was working on a pot of spiced lentil soup. Carol was her sister, three years younger and, though they had their differences, also mostly her friend. Carol had arrived in tears at the beginning of summer and had been with them since, hiding from her husband. Annie had thought Ron a prick from the moment she met him, and it turned out she was right. Last spring, he took Carol out to lunch, told her he'd filed for divorce that morning, and that he was madly in love with her best friend of seven years. Annie thought drawing and quartering an appropriate punishment for that, or perhaps a plate of Steak and Ale appetizers in his lap. Carol had been more civil, or else too stunned to move. She told Annie it was like entering some kind of soap-opera reality. Now she took over stirring the onions and garlic, cinnamon, ginger, cumin, and cloves, freeing Annie to slice some carrots.

"There's a good film at Upstate," she said.

Annie didn't look up.

"Starts at seven," Carol said. "Laura will sit if you're game."

"I often feel like game—"

"Annie. Please."

"I can't."

Annie kept slicing, focusing on the carrots and the knife in her hand as though she were performing major surgery. "Carol . . ."

"*Tin Men.* Supposed to be funny."

Annie slid a wide blade of carrots into the pan.

"We'll come home right after."

"I can't." She put the rest of the carrots in.

"You can't just sit around here worrying about him." Carol handed her the spoon. "I take that back. But you shouldn't."

After five already, he wasn't going to make it for dinner anyway. Why not go? Because she didn't want to? Because she wanted to be home so she could know, the minute he was done with it, that he was okay one more time? Carol didn't get it. She didn't understand.

Annie wanted, someday, to be able to look at the lines in Kurt's skin and the gray in his hair and have some idea of the stories they told. She would go day by day and not notice, and then one afternoon they'd be sitting on a front porch and their children would be grown and gone and they would have each other, their history together etched into their faces. She remembered a day not long after they'd begun going out, when they'd stopped at a roadside café somewhere between San Antonio and San Marcos and sat on a lush, dusty balcony sipping margaritas. They'd watched as an elderly couple, an ancient couple, pulled a Caddy, that yellow color, into the parking lot. The man got out and eked around the car and opened the door. He helped the woman out, and then offered his arm. They hobbled slowly, shuffling toward the entrance. Annie could swear that when they looked at each other and smiled, they were laughing at their condition, remembering a time years earlier when it didn't take them half an hour to walk twenty yards. And she had seen something else. The man and the woman still loved each other deeply, maybe even more than they ever had when younger. They were together. There was something between them that had passed all the tests, something that had endured. Kurt had seen it too, and had slipped a hand across the table to touch Annie's arm.

"That's probably us, someday," he said. "Depressing, isn't it?"

"What about middle-age crazy, when you buy a red sports car and start chasing women who read *Cosmo?*"

"Remember this about me," he said. "Loyalty is my strong suit." He had looked her in the eye and smiled, gripped her arm, gently but urgently. He meant what he said.

When they met and married in the space of eighteen months, the connection was both physical and spiritual. Their relationship had leaped to its feet within hours of being born and had, until recently, grown as steadily as a young fawn in a pleasant green meadow. They had seen some things, done a thing or two in the tiny crack of time before household and children and, recently, Kurt's business had taken over their lives. She remembered the heat of an afternoon in Houston, outside was one hundred and thirteen degrees, humidity ninety-seven percent. In New York City they called that a steambath, and people paid money to sit in tile-lined stalls full of it. She and Kurt had bailed from an air-conditioned restaurant and gone out into the countryside, under a tree next to a deserted lake. It was a Thursday and he'd taken her hand and kissed her fingertips one by one and then pulled her to his chest. They were dripping with sweat even before he reached to unbutton her blouse. He cupped her breasts in his hands and said, "If we have babies, they're gonna have to fight with me over this." She'd been startled at the thought, having never seen a nursing infant except in *National Geographic* magazines. The high school librarian made sure to cut out all the photos of naked people and bare breasts before putting the issues on the shelf, but Annie's grandfather had an attic full of them, and he'd given her a subscription when she turned thirteen, so she'd seen it all in spite of the librarian's puritanical intentions. But she'd been raised to think that American babies drank formula from beneficent companies like Gerber and Beechnut. Breasts were there to be bound up in black or white lace, to attract men. They had nothing to do with nourishment or life. She must have looked at him oddly, for he added, "I'm kidding." They'd spent most of that afternoon naked under the tree, sharing salty kisses and fresh water, taking rest as they needed it. Once, Annie opened her eyes to see a red-tailed hawk circling in the distance, its wings tilting kite-like in the currents.

Lately, though, they were rarely together. It was what she had feared most when she said "I do." He had promised then to go legit, though he argued that what he did was as legitimate as any legal enterprise. They had the shop, Raffaella Antiques, which he'd started as a cover, and he could have turned more attention in that direction. But somehow he'd not made the switch. Business deals failed to pan out. He had dreams enough for ten people and couldn't help it if he got involved in one half-baked business venture after another. Friends, relatives, associates, kept coming to him with great ideas, wonderful ideas, stupendous ideas, looking for financing. They were all good causes. Annie told him he had his fingers in so many different pies, he was in competition with himself. But she believed in him and felt certain that he would find something. Eventually. He took regular donations of cannabis to the buyer's club in the city, where people who had AIDS and cancer could quietly purchase the herb to help ease their distress, whether it came from disease or treatment. He earmarked his donations for the indigent, and the man who ran the club was grateful, happily distributing relief to those who couldn't afford to pay even the club's modest prices.

"Annie?" Carol's voice was sounding more and more like their mother's, raw from tobacco smoke, angry, resigned.

"You go ahead," Annie said, waving off Carol's concerned look. "I'm fine," she said, stirring the soup. "Honest. Go ahead. I'd really just like to do some reading."

"I hate going to the movies alone," Carol said. She waited for a response. Nothing. "Maybe I'll take Tim and Alex for some ice cream or something. We'll drop in on Laura."

"I'll go with you tomorrow," Annie said. "I promise. Kurt will want time with the boys."

"Being optimistic again?"

Annie gave her a look but said nothing.

After dinner, she kissed Alex and Timothy good-bye and helped Carol get them into the Jeep. On the way back to the porch, she passed one of the pear trees in the front yard and plucked down a ripe one. She stayed outside after they pulled away, enjoying the delicate sugar of pear juice on her tongue and watching the sky go to orange and pink, then gray and blue. Sunsets were good here in autumn, though one of the things she missed about where she'd grown up was the Texas sky, as endless as summer seems to a child when it's only just June.

The empty house was heavy with silence. Annie wondered for a long moment what to do. She wished for an instant that she'd gone with them or taken up Carol's initial offer. She wished Kurt hadn't taken the dog.

She poured herself a glass of cabernet and wound up curled in the club chair in the corner of the den, holding what Alex called the snake book. She flipped through, found herself reading about the diamondback rattler. That was something she didn't miss about Texas: the variety of venomous snakes. But it seemed civil to her somehow that rattlesnakes gave a warning before striking. She'd pulled up one evening to a house she shared with two other women during her sophomore year at Rice University and found a rattler curled on the front porch, plucking fat brown June bugs from the window screen. She watched for a while, then climbed onto the hood of her car and threw a shoe at it. It startled, turned to her with eyes indifferent and murderous at once, then curled down the steps and away into the sparse brush at the edge of the woods. The next year she had transferred to New York University in downtown Manhattan, not because of the snake, but because she wanted a taste of the city her mother had talked about so excitedly all the time Annie was a child. The city no longer lived up to her mother's expectations, but neither did Annie. She laughed at herself and closed the book, put it on the corner table, and took up instead her volume on gardening and began browsing the plates. Back in spring, Kurt had thinned a couple of acres out behind the house—backbreaking work of the kind he most loved—and she wanted to think about which plants might bring some color to the area beneath the tree canopy. It would soon be time to put in bulbs.

She sat admiring pictures of tulips and daffodils, hoping the phone would ring and that it would be Kurt calling to assure her he was okay, everything had gone fine, he would be home in an hour or so. But she didn't expect it. Things rarely went off entirely as planned. That was part of the attraction for him: the last-minute changes, the clandestine logistics. She'd lived it herself, early on, going out with him on weekends, back when they were still just lovers, before they got married and had the boys. It had been scary as all get-out. Fun. A real life adventure after another five days spent in her windowless office at the Calvani Group, where she had gone to work straight from graduation. She tried to ease her conscience about taking succor from the stock market by directing investors to funds holding shares of environmentally aware companies. It was a stupid way to spend her life, she knew that much, and the recognition could and often did splinter her workday into its individual minutes. Don't you *dare* look at your watch. You'll go insane.

She hated it. She hated the stainless steel lobby, she hated the gut-sucking rise of the elevator, she hated the efficient and absurd chastity of pantyhose and the yeast infections that came with every package, the endless search for a pair of comfortable shoes that didn't look sensible. She didn't know what she wanted, but she knew she didn't want this.

She fell in with others in her office whose loathing equaled or surpassed her own, and their days were money-money-money, and then five o'clock or six o'clock or eight or nine o'clock—they worked hard—would arrive and off they would rush to Bistro du Moment, cloaking themselves in jadedness to fend off the décor. Forks poised over plates painted with designer food, they would ask the important questions: *Is it art, or mashed potatoes? Could we get another bottle of that red?*

And then one day in early April, on a date with a handsome and vacuous British trader, there for the month from the London office, she was introduced to the joy of powdering her nose. Avoided it all through college, instead sticking with pot and whatever 'drine was around at exam time. She hadn't realized until her date with Hal or Harold or whatever he called himself just how horrible it was to go through life as one of the dopamine-deprived. That must have been it, why she couldn't find happiness. Until now. Until the beautiful white powder hit the back of her throat and brought her fifteen minutes of . . . of what? Euphoria in a tiny glass vial. Euphoria by the minute.

It wasn't long before she told Harold, cute though he was, that it was over, go find a brain and see if you can squeeze it into that gorgeous skull of yours. Not exactly those words, but now here she was, alone again, buzzed at yet another stupid party, drinking, another stupid Absolut rocks in hand, and waiting for two of two things to happen. One: she would meet (be introduced to, fall in love with, marry and have children and live happily ever after with) the friend of a friend from her office, visiting the city from Paris. Two: before this friend of a friend showed—*if* he showed—she would be able to hook up with, dare she call him that, her supplier. She'd been there an hour. Both of them were late. She was sure that either one or both would have wonderful explanations. Who cared? She supposed she could go to whatever room at the party had been designated or overtaken, where doubtless there was a line waiting to do lines. Join the coke whores.

She was looking at people's shoes, thinking she should have a T-shirt made for occasions like this. Something in black, of course, with neat white letters in elegant cursive on the front: *Socially Inept.* A pair of calfskin boots entered her line of sight, accompanied by the lug-soled sandals of Kathy, her match-making friend. She looked up; Kathy's puckered expression told her this was not Thierry from Paris, the man she was supposed to be meeting. The final buzzer had gone off, the game had expired without either contestant even showing. This was a last-minute substitution.

"At last you two meet," Kathy said, and let go a nervous giggle.

"Kurt Trowbridge," he said, and extended a hand. Nice smile. His voice was gentle and resonant. Kathy patted Annie's arm and nodded approval at her newly minted couple—see you two later.

"Can I get you another?" T-shirt beneath linen jacket, blue jeans in a sea of black, Annie among the wearers. Black suede skirt, black cashmere sleeveless mock sweater, her skin still February white in spite of spring's arrival.

He escorted her to the kitchen door. So far, the apartment was handling the crowd. A black-and-white bartender poured from pretty silver and gold bottles and smiled politely.

Refreshed, they wound through the crowd and out to a small garden, a twelve-by-twenty lidless cube of nature, dusky right now, attached to the back door of the brownstone. Uncluttered; no people at the moment. There was a stone bench in a rear corner, beneath a small, struggling tree. They sat, and Kurt reached up and ran a finger along a limb, inspecting.

"Ginkgo biloba," he said, mildly surprised.

"I'd never have made you for a botanist," Annie said, dismayed at how hard she had to work to get some words out of her mouth. He was just a guy, at just a party; it was no big deal really. Why was it so hard. Why was it. Always. She was horrible at small talk. Horrible. Wasn't sure when she got that way, but thought it happened when she hit high school. *Socially Inept.* She wished Eric would hurry up. Where was he?

"There are some in China that are supposed to be around two thousand years old. Still going strong."

"That's far too long for anything to spend in a single incarnation." She tried a smile, but wasn't sure what shape her lips went into.

"I don't know." He chuckled. "It might be nice to just plant yourself somewhere. Sit there and think for a good long while."

Maybe that was what she needed to do. She nodded agreement and sipped her drink. He seemed nice, this guy, but there was a certain wariness in his eyes. He'd seen some things. She wondered what.

"Supposed to be brain food," he said, stroking a leaf. He turned his attention from the tree and shifted to face her, blue eyes cutting into her green. He wanted to get to know her; that was it. That was what his eyes were saying. Or was she misinterpreting, reading too much into his gaze? It ran in her family, the ability to misread men's intentions.

"Two thousand years," she said finally.

"Blink and it's gone, right?" He smiled and broke out a joint.

The smoke tasted of watermelon, and when the high came on, it was gentle, easy. Relief. Simply relief. Now they had broken the law together. Now they were fast friends. What was she worried about? Eric would show, eventually. He always did. And even if he didn't, there was always cocaine to be had, plenty, as long as you had cash or genitalia, and she wasn't that hard up yet. Mr. Jones hadn't moved in with her; she still had enough dollars for the habit. She could wait just a minute with the best of them.

She watched as Kurt let go a bit of smoke from his mouth and pulled it into his nostrils, seeming to enjoy the act itself as much as anticipating the effects of the herb. He flicked the orange tip from the joint after a couple of hits, put it in a small black cigarette case, and slipped it into his pocket.

"Thank you," she said. He leaned elbows on knees and turned to face her.

"What did Kathy—" she started, but decided she didn't want to know. Maybe he just wanted to fuck. There were always those. She didn't get that sense, but her record in that department was weak. How could you know? And it seemed as if the women who *did* know were the women who just wanted to fuck, too. As if there was some kind of wavelength you could tune into that let everyone else on that wavelength know you were there and ready to play. It made her feel hopelessly provincial, that she didn't want to just fuck. She wanted somebody to love. Somebody who would love back. Good luck, sweetheart.

She looked at him. His nose had been broken at least once, though this history hadn't revealed itself until she studied him. Red hair, and one didn't just have red hair; one was a redhead. Talk about connotations. He had a wide, intelligent brow, deep-set eyes. He sat watching her look at him, the hint of a smile on his lips, like *Go ahead, take a look, I'm here, I'm real, I'm honest, and life is full of adventure. We could check it out for a while, see where it goes.* She couldn't recall meeting anyone so open in a long while.

Eric, appropriately, chose this moment to arrive. He looked good, as always. Eric dressed. Black trousers, handmade shoes, matte silk threads in a heavy weave. He was the kind of guy who looked good in Italian suits. His accessories included a pair of emaciated girls, late teens, their bared bellies the color of cornsilk in late July, hair likewise. They wore black stretchy fabric wrapped around their chests and thighs, and black leather thongs on their feet. No makeup. No nail polish. They vogued and gave the patio a cool once over.

Kurt glanced at the trio and turned back to Annie.

"Sex 'R' Us."

"Be kind," Annie said. "Think of their trauma when they find their first wrinkle." She saw Eric whisper to one of them, and the two evaporated into the crowd that by now had bulged at the back door and was beginning to spill onto the patio.

"God," Eric said, approaching, consciously overacting, his voice full of awe. "I just love how their vacant eyes fill so dependably with raw desire whenever I aim a camera at them. It's so . . . so . . . so totally mundane." He turned to Annie. "Who's your friend?" Hint of British to his accent, as though he'd been in London.

She introduced them and there was momentary silence. Eric questioned Annie with his eyes.

"Excuse us," he said, and took Annie by the arm, walking her toward the door.

In a room somewhere, he handed her a small vial, spoon attached inside the lid, and she loathed herself.

She heard him quote a price, *as a favor to my friends,* and she sniffed a spoon. Glanced at him. *Knock yourself out,* and she did three more. Ah, there. Things were right. She opened the small leather bag looped over her shoulder and gave him the cash, tucked a fresh vial inside the bag.

When they returned to the patio, Annie felt as though Eric were delivering her to Kurt. She looked from one to the other, amused and angered at once. Eric questioned Annie's judgment with a raised eyebrow and slipped into the crowd. She tried to recall when they'd met. She couldn't. But her brain was there, buzzing along happily. Alive at last.

"Old friend?" Kurt's question was heavy with dismay.

"I'm sorry," Annie said, resuming her seat on the bench, trying not to sniff conspicuously, but there was no way not to. "He can be rude. I hope you won't take it personally." Sniff-sniff. He sat down next to her and said nothing. She thought this was probably the end of their date, but he didn't move. He looked at her, then at the door, then back at her.

"Feel better?" he asked finally. The question was sad but sincere.

She didn't answer.

"That's some serious shit you're doing."

She wilted, stunned to a whisper. Tried a laugh. Then, "Why don't you get to the point?"

He sat watching her. She flashed angry at the sadness in his eyes, but looked away as she recognized his words, identical with those she'd been hearing in her own head for several months now. That tiny voice that wouldn't go away, though she worked hard to build a psychotropic hut, taking handfuls of white mud mixed from cocaine and alcohol, shaping bricks of it, stacking them day by day, hoping to build a wall high enough to contain the voice of reason, the voice she sought to obliterate.

"I meant no offense," he said. "But you're a wreck." He shifted back, gazed across the patio.

"How nice to meet someone of superior moral fiber."

"Get pissed at me if you want. I didn't mean it that way."

"You said it yourself," she answered. "I'm a wreck."

He looked at people drinking and smoking and chatting and laughing on the patio.

"C'mon," he said. "Let's get out of here." He stood and offered his hand. A screen materialized in the buzzing, throbbing lump of gray matter inside her skull, rolling down white and sparkly just behind her forehead, sounds from the party rippling somewhere in the background. There she was in the darkened auditorium of Lake Worth Junior High School, watching gritty black-and-white. The narrator's tone—'sixties news establishment nasal bark—enhanced the menacing nature of his warnings. A syringe full of blood . . . Look, kiddies, watch the junkie shoot drugs. If you take LSD, you'll jump out the window, even if you don't really want to kill yourself. But maybe you do. Maybe you just don't know it.

She looked at Kurt's hand and then up at his face. He was only being kind.

"I think I'll stay," she said.

"Please don't be angry at me," he said. "Just a cup of coffee."

They landed at a patisserie in the Village, high brick walls, ivy-covered, uncomfortable wrought-iron chairs, but a deepening sky above. A gurgling fountain in the center of the restaurant's patio splashed against the gentle hum of evening conversations.

He sat with coffee and some kind of dangerous chocolate pastry, half pie, half cake, before him. Annie sipped some tea and felt a slow, heavy ache spreading up her spine and into the back of her neck. Her brain was getting heavier, soggier, grosser by the minute.

He asked if she was okay.

She nodded and sipped more tea. "I'm just going to run to the loo."

He leaned back in his chair and sighed.

When she returned, he had paid the check. He stood up as she approached the table.

"This was a mistake," he said. "I'll get you a cab."

She wanted to stay and talk to him; convince him that she wasn't really in as bad a shape as he thought. She had to make him understand that she was not strung out on anything; she did this because she wanted to. Her head was filling with bubble bath. She would go back to the party. First, more tea. Water, even. Get something possibly nontoxic and liquid in there.

"Go ahead," she said, sitting down. "I'd like to finish." Down to half a gram already, and the need was settling in her gut. It was always like this. Stay clean for a week, sometimes two, then take that first hit and it's off to the races until the cash machine says no. Time to get back to the party and see if Eric was still there.

"Let me take you home," he said, easing back into his chair as though trying not to disturb it.

"What do you do?" she asked, as though there'd been no interruption.

He sipped his coffee. Cold. Made a face.

"You don't look so good," he said. "I'll take you home."

"I just—" She couldn't finish the thought; couldn't finish the sentence. She ached. She wanted to crawl under the table and hide. She did not want to be involved with yet another asshole and she wanted more powder and hated herself for wanting it and sympathized with the need all at once.

He stood up and offered his hand.

"Don't be so hard on yourself," he said. "At least let me get you a cab."

It would take an act of God to bring her body upright. He stood waiting. She hoped that wasn't pity on his face. She took one last sip of tea and began the process of standing up.

Slowly now, easy does it, one foot in front of the other.

When the taxi halted in front of her building, an Upper West Side monolith, he pressed a napkin into her hand; in it was wrapped a small bag of pot.

"My number's there. Maybe . . ." He let the sentence fall away, squeezed her hand gently before getting back in the cab.

She went on autopilot, into the Korean grocery downstairs: orange juice, apple juice, and assorted fruits. Some yogurt and several bottles of water. Salad bar: sautéed spinach, yes, sesame noodles, yes, gad, skip that next one, whatever it is, and then the sight of all that food turned her stomach. She paid and left.

When she got inside her apartment—a studio, but good light—she put the groceries away. She went to her front door and locked both locks. It was Friday night. She swore to herself that she would not emerge until Tuesday morning.

She found a mirror and carefully, lovingly, tapped out the last of the cocaine from the vial. *This is it. Last time. Ever.* It occurred to her to rinse it down the drain, show some strength. She bent to take it in. Sat back, closed her eyes, leaned back her head, sniff-sniff, catch the drip, the last precious taste. It was not of cocoa leaf; there was nothing green about it. Chlorine and hydrogen, fresh from the refinery. Mmm, mmm good. She opened her eyes, stood up, and went to her closet to ransack, looking for stash that might have been left from another spent weekend.

•

God save me from the good old days. She closed the gardening book, took a sip of wine, and looked around the quiet living room, wondering at how oddly life went. Human beings out there running around, bumping into each other, ricocheting like pinballs. The first few days she'd spent in New York City, she would wake at night and lie in bed with her eyes closed, seeing sidewalks packed with people walking toward her. Packed. Masses. Hordes. People everywhere, rushing, rushing, rushing. She'd never seen so many people in one place at one time in her life. It was nice, now, when she ran in the woods out behind the house; it was nice to encounter a solitary deer or a few wild turkeys. Chipmunks screeched and rattled small branches to frighten her away from their hiding places. Yesterday, as she rounded a curve in the trail on her morning run, a huge great horned owl had debarked from an oak and swooped not ten feet in front of her as it took off through the forest.

A scuffling noise outside the window caught her ear and brought her back up straight in the chair. She thought first of raccoons, but darkness was just falling; it was barely seven-thirty. They usually came around much later. Maybe it was the bear cub that had been sighted at a golf course a few miles south not a week ago. It had spent the afternoon lounging in a tree, obliging photographers until almost dinnertime, when it clambered down and lugged away into the woods. Annie wished once again that Kurt hadn't taken the dog, who was wonderfully gentle with the boys, but afraid of nothing, a perfect companion for her children.

She listened. Took a breath and listened some more. Silence, washed by a gentle breeze rustling the trees. The shed door was closed and locked; the bird food would be okay if it was a bear.

Another scuffling noise, louder now, real, a crash—

The front door of her home splintered and hit the wall. Men with guns blew through the hole where the door had been.

"ON THE FLOOR, BITCH! NOW!" She rose from the chair as her insides went liquid and the room filled with them, all in flak jackets and black masks, crouching and dodging, aiming guns at her, at the staircase, at the kitchen door, everywhere. She stood, unable to move, until one of them got right next to her, stuck his gun to her head, screaming, "I SAID NOW! GET ON THE FLOOR!"

She felt herself folding downward, thinking, "Umpires from hell," and at the same time saw the incongruity of her thought. She knew she was trying to comply with the order, but they were all moving as though under water . . .

Something slammed against her, and one of them had her on the floor with his knee in the small of her back and a large handgun behind her right ear. Her thoughts stopped coming in words; there was only sensation: visceral fear, death whispering, the tether of life connecting her to her children. Her children. She reached for thought, for reason; the room was askew, black boots everywhere stomping the floorboards. She'd landed half on a carpet; the wool was cool against her cheek. She noticed one of Alex's tiny metal cars under the couch: the pink Cadillac convertible he'd plucked from a sale bin at the grocery checkout. She remembered the old couple, hobbling from their Caddy to the restaurant, heard Kurt's words: *Loyalty is my strong suit.* She held her breath. Please don't shoot me.

I have to see my children. I have to see Kurt again. Please don't shoot me, I love my family. She held her breath and thought she might pee from fear, but anger began leaking into her from somewhere deep in her center. It took hold as quivering yellow filled the edges of her vision, threatening to close off sight. Bastards. Jackals. She closed her eyes and made herself breathe slowly, regularly, with rhythm.

Think. Don't struggle. Think. She went limp.

The pressure from the man's knee eased up a bit, but he was still firmly planted. She smelled the miasmic odors of tobacco and gun oil coming off his hand, floating the few inches to where her nose was pressed against the carpet. Asshole. She shifted and he prodded her skull with the barrel of the gun. Thank God the children were away, thank God Carol was away, thank God Kane wasn't here. He'd have gone for one of them and they'd have shot him for sure. Wait. Wait. Cool now, cool. All the time looking around the room, hearing their crude laughter as they ripped open the couch, tore up chairs, kicked over tables. The house was filled with their anger.

Their jackets were printed with large white letters on back: DEA.

One of them came out of the kitchen with a carton of eggs and walked around the living room, breaking them, one by one, letting yolk ooze onto the carpets Kurt had brought from Afghanistan.

"Dear, dear," said the man, holding her down. "My, my. Just look at this mess." He snorted a cop-sick laugh.

Annie lay on the floor, felt sweat trickle around the curve of her neck and under her chin and the electric tingle of adrenaline in her fingertips. She wondered if they already had him. Closed her eyes, listened.

Oh. There were several in the kitchen now, starting on the dishes.

Toward midnight, she began to think they might just blow the search. Not that there was anything substantial in the house, but Kurt kept his personal stash here, and that could run into a few pounds if he was saving any particularly good buds for friends.

They let her sit in the club chair, handcuffs biting her wrists, as she watched the clock above the mantel, stared out the window, looked at anything but the cops, who were taking their time dismantling the place.

She almost spoke out when she saw the Jeep come up the road, slowing down as Carol caught sight of the flashing red and blue lights surrounding the house. Would she think Annie was injured and come in? Annie wanted to shout out, "No! Go on, get away from here!" She sat still and tried to pretend boredom. The Jeep passed; Annie imagined Carol eyeing the agents posted at the end of the driveway, staring like a curious neighbor as she drove past slowly, probably to loop back around to Laura and Mike's. She could not even think what she would feel like if Alex and Tim were to see her here, like this, in handcuffs.

Almost four hours now. They sliced with knives, prodding here, pushing there, knocked on walls, tapped on floors. She watched as their initial exuberance turned first to anger, and now, as the search wound down, disappointment.

The stash place, behind the bookshelves, had once been a crawl space where the settlers who built the house used to hide from the natives. Kurt had lovingly and carefully restored it. Annie wished she could have made it inside before the cops crashed down the door. She wondered whether, if they didn't find the stash, they would still take her in.

She shifted in the chair. At least they'd cuffed her hands in front. She was able to lean back. The adrenaline that had flooded her bloodstream was diluting; a wave of fatigue washed over her, head to toe. She closed her eyes and listened to strangers walk around her house. She wondered how they'd got a search warrant. They couldn't just come in and do this on a whim. Someone must have given them information.

Headlights flared in the window, flashing through her eyelids. She sat up, turned away, opened her eyes.

A radio crackled and a static electric voice mumbled something indecipherable.

"Great," one of the agents muttered. "Kessler's here." A few of the cops made attempts to straighten some furniture; others simply continued searching.

A man came in the door, attired like the others but without a vest. He was of average height, wiry brown hair. Bearded. His movements were sharp; his eyes took in the scene and registered dismay. He scanned the room again.

"Gentlemen," he said, shaking his head sadly.

"Gentlemen." He looked at Annie, and she realized he was embarrassed. "I'm sorry," he said to her. He picked up a ladderback chair from the floor and posted it in front of her, sat down. "They shouldn't have done this." On second thought, he motioned her up and removed her handcuffs, invited her to sit back down.

"My name is Joseph Kessler," he said. "I'm with the Drug Enforcement Administration. Your husband is in custody at the Ulster County Jail. He'll be transferred to the federal holding facility in Manhattan sometime tomorrow." He waited for her response.

Finally, she was able to croak out, "Is he okay?"

Kessler nodded. She noticed a small scar high on his right cheek, just below his eye. He was handsome in an offbeat kind of way, aware of it but not particularly amused by it. There was more to him than that.

Agents grumbled through the room, wandering about, waiting for inspiration or dumb luck to reveal the stash to them. Kessler seemed amused at their plight. Annie did not understand how all this could seem ordinary to him, but he was completely at ease. She realized she'd been staring at him and turned her attention out the window. She saw the pear tree, heavy with fruit, behind the half-dozen cop cars lining the drive. One car still had its lights going, a beacon to anyone who might pass on the road.

Here it was, the thing she had always managed to push away as an irrational fear. Here it was in her living room, not caring that when she'd said better or worse she meant it. Kurt loved her. He loved their children. He was honest and caring and decent; he worked hard. But here it was, the thing she would not admit possible, the thing she had, over the years, convinced herself would never happen. Kurt was careful, and, since the birth of the children, especially careful to protect her from details. Even she hadn't permitted herself to know. What was the phrase—*willful ignorance?* Here it was. Her husband had been arrested. She might be right behind him. Kurt wasn't doing anything wrong, just something illegal. It was only a plant; it was a gift of nature; he need not fear his karma. Who was she kidding?

"Where are your children?"

Her lungs went empty. She took in a slow breath, said nothing. Before them, it was different. She'd been willing to pay for the thrills with various denominations of risk. But all that had changed with their arrival. They'd brought new understanding of love. They'd brought new respect for life.

"I'm asking because I want to ensure their safety," he said.

That was what she wanted, too. To ensure their safety. To give them a home full of love. To be there for them as they discovered the world. Kurt was in jail. Daddy was in jail. She stared Agent Kessler in the eye until she understood that he was sincere.

"They're not here," she said. "Am I under arrest? Do you have our dog?"

He turned to one of his agents. "What'd you find?"

"Where you been?" the man said. "We waited long as we could."

"At dinner," Kessler answered.

"Hot date?" The agent flashed a conspiratorial grin and tossed a spice tin to his boss. "Greek oregano, it says. Dean and DeLuca."

"You cook?" Kessler asked Annie. "My ex-wife used to cook. I guess she still does." He opened the tin, took a whiff, scoffed at the agent. "Just what it says." He stood up, closed the container, and placed it on the corner table, picking up the snake book.

"I'm sorry," he said, thumbing. "If I'd've been here on time, much of this would not have happened. This mess is totally unnecessary." The chair and table looked odd to Annie, sitting untouched as they were in the ransacked den. When Kessler looked at her, she was startled by the calm intensity of his gaze. "Are you all right?"

"No one showed me a search warrant," she said.

Kessler replaced the snake book carefully.

"Interesting creatures," he said. "The warrant is boilerplate, nothing unusual about it. I'm sure your lawyer will get a copy, but I'll show it to you now, if you like."

She shook her head no. He sat down again, leaned toward her. She noticed spikes of brown radiating from the pupils in his otherwise deep green eyes. She averted her own and disliked the shamed schoolgirl who was gazing at the floor; got angry again, raised her eyes.

He studied her openly for a moment. There was nothing self-righteous or predatory in his appraisal. She shifted in the chair, wondering what he saw. Housewife? Dope dealer? Scum of the earth? Things she would not let herself see? She had married a smuggler. So had Rose Kennedy. She looked at Kessler, wondered again what he was thinking, what he thought of her—the smuggler's wife. She'd known she was a mess when she met Kurt; still, she'd looked both ways before crossing the street. And he was a good father, a good man, a good person. He loved her. He'd said the smuggling would stop when they married. And then when they were expecting Alex. One last trip would do it. She had failed to let herself stop believing. Maybe this would have been the last trip. Yeah, yeah, yeah. She'd gone with him that time in Texas, when he took her to the ranch shortly after they met, and they'd come within a whisper of catching a case that time for sure. It wasn't even that she so much wanted him to stop except for the risk of his freedom.

But none of that mattered now, and it didn't matter what this man sitting across from her thought or felt. It mattered what he did; that was all. She stared at Joseph Kessler and flashed on Kurt—in some godawful holding tank full of vagrants and drunks, maybe even a wife beater or two—and then, oddly, she thought of her mother, of all the time her mother had spent sitting at the kitchen table, smoking cigarettes and hating her father, maybe hating herself for failing to notice before the wedding that her mate was a beer-swilling salesman who was least desperate when he was on the road. Her mother had chosen a salesman, or bumped into him or whatever it was that had happened between them. Annie had chosen Kurt, and when she learned he was a smuggler, she chose to stay with him. And did it matter whether she had thought about consequences or whether she had simply fallen into the life? It wouldn't matter to the handcuffs. It wouldn't matter to the bars of the cell.

"You have a lovely home," Kessler said. He leaned back, relaxed, as though they were old friends. "I really am sorry about this." He looked around the room again and then at her. Right at her. She had the feeling he wanted to help her, but she knew that was the most dangerous thing in the world for her to be thinking at that moment.

"Where's the load?" Staring at her, like, tell me this now and I will make everything all right again. It will be as if we were never here.

She remained silent.

"He has fucked up big time," Kessler said. "Does he expect you to take the fall with him? Some of them do. They expect their wives to go to jail. Maybe they figure to save their marriages. It's always the kids who lose." Annie recognized suddenly that he was weary, that he had seen and been part of much that made him sad.

"Mothers go to jail," he continued, "kids get chucked into social services. For what? Honor? Loyalty?"

She felt heat in her face; she thought at first it was fear, then recognized anger. Fear was cold. Anger was hot.

"I can cut him some slack," Kessler said. "But I need a reason."

They could take her from Alex and Timothy. They could take her right now. Anger left, replaced by an iciness that did not rush at her suddenly, but entered like an IV drip, straight into her bloodstream, polluting it with dread. She sat upright and tried to appear calm before a man who could wreck her life forever in the next simple instant.

"Mrs. Trowbridge," he said. "There's a DC-6 crashed at a strip a few miles from here. We've already matched your husband's truck tires to the tracks left in the mud. He tried to dump the radio from the cab of his truck before we arrested him. But we got it, and it's made for talking to airplanes, tuned to the same frequency as the radio in the crashed plane." He lowered his voice to a whisper: *"Where's the load?"*

A crashed plane. But he'd said Kurt was in custody, safe. She thought of Father Francis and Bill; they'd probably been there. McGrath. The others she might not know.

"Was anyone hurt?" She surprised both herself and Kessler by asking, but she had to know. They were friends.

"Did you know any of the others, besides your husband? You must have."

"You said there was a plane crash," Annie replied. "I was just asking if anyone was hurt." She didn't know where the load was, or how big it was, or anything else except that there probably was one, somewhere. She didn't know, and she didn't want to know. But she wouldn't have told him anyway.

"Ah," he said finally. "I'm always reassured when I encounter yet another faithful wife." He extended an arm, business card in hand. "In case you need me." When she didn't take the card, he placed it carefully on the table. "I hope to hear from you soon. I'd like to help you, and I'm in a position to do it."

FOUR

She watched, too exhausted to hold on to her anger, as the cops holstered their guns and packed up their equipment and drove back to wherever it was they had come from. She stood for a long time on the wide front porch, staring after them, unable to believe that Kessler hadn't taken her in.

He had done her a favor. A big one. She wondered if he would want something in return, wondered how he was playing her. She hadn't got the sense that he seriously expected her to cooperate, and she had got the sense that he respected her for that. He seemed to be the most civilized man she'd met in some time. If circumstances had been different, she might have encouraged a friendship. Or maybe she just wanted to like him because she needed to: he could help her and possibly save Kurt from prison. She despised her motivation, if her appraisal was accurate, but was too disoriented, too confused to be sure of anything.

She watched them gunning off the long drive and out onto the county road, spewing gravel against the trees; she walked through the broken door frame into the entryway, wondering if Kessler had known his agents were going to destroy her home.

Laura picked up on the first ring—*Are you all right?*—waited for a yes from Annie and put Carol on the line.

"They trashed the place," Annie said. "Give me an hour. Tell Laura I'll call her tomorrow. Please. Thanks." She hung up and went at it wildly, righting furniture, stuffing innards back into the couch and chair and locating blankets to use as throws, vacuuming what they'd strewn about, trying to scrub away any trace of the invasion. She wasn't sure what to do about the eggs on the carpets. She blotted and dabbed and remembered a mixture of water, Woolite, and vinegar. She scrubbed. She was furious. She was numb. The dead bolt on the front door had been forced through the frame. She pushed the door as closed as she could, then positioned a chair under the knob to hold it in place. It would have to do for the night. She grabbed Kessler's card from the table, found herself staring at it, not so much at his name as at the words *Drug Enforcement Administration.* The name seemed ominous, an indication of serious power at work. Serious. She recalled the spring afternoon when the track coach had showed her to his office, an extension of the boys' locker room, really, and how the word OFFICE painted on the door seemed to function as warning: If you gotta come in here, you're in trouble. Coach Jones had positioned himself on a bench, his back against a painted cinderblock wall, and pulled her onto the bench in front of him. *Let me just see if I can get that kink out of your back. We can't have you running in pain now, can we?* That was how he'd started things, and once things got started, how he kept them going. Sometimes she had tried ducking out quickly after practice, going home and straight to her room to continue reading whatever book she was due to report on—but somehow she almost never did. Pain was part of running, Coach would tell her, his hands progressing steadily down her back; pain was part of sport. Overcoming it was not so much truly that as it was learning to get past it, to exert one's will over it. But there were things you could do to ease it, rub it out. A good massage was all that was needed. And all the while he was talking she was removing herself from her body, because she knew that in a few minutes one of his hands would leave her back and slip around her waist to the front and beneath the elastic band of her blue-and-white Lake Worth High School running shorts and she didn't want to be there when it did. If she was there, she was nothing but another fucking cunt, too stupid to recognize that she existed only as a wet place for men to stick their dicks. But if she took herself out of it, she could still be a track star. She could run very very fast and bring home ribbons and trophies to the smattering of moms and dads cheering in the stands. She couldn't recall her father making a single meet. A bunch of girls running in circles just could not compete against the sight of big strong men bashing each other on the football field.

She shoved Kessler's card in her jeans pocket; this man was a presence in her life now, in the life of her family, an unwanted presence and one that she could not force away. She could have quit the track team, she supposed, but she hadn't. She sat down in the chair she had spent most of the evening in, looked at her wrists where the handcuffs had been, realized her hands were shaking. Carol would be here with the boys soon. She reached for the half-finished glass of cabernet on the table. Reached to sip; wound up gulping. Went to the kitchen to pour another. What was it Father Francis liked to say? *Don't do the crime if you can't do the time.* A rhyme. How nice.

She hoped they were all okay.

Calm down. Just calm down. Wasn't that what she said to Alex when she was trying to help him through a moment? Take a deep breath. Slowly now. Calm down. She wondered if they had Bill and Father Francis, too. The unflappable Father Francis. She hadn't spent much time with him lately; their paths crossed these days only when they were orbiting around one of Kurt's trips, a few times a year.

Always calm, Father Francis. Always. She remembered the stunt he and Kurt and she had pulled that time near Austin. She'd been fearless then herself, foolishly so, it seemed now. They'd been staying at Kurt's ranch in the hill country, close to where she'd grown up. She had walked away from her job only a few weeks earlier, a voice in her brain cutting loose with the girl version of a long, heartfelt, soul-filled, drawled-out Texas-style *Yeeeeeeeh-haawe,* the kind only a real cowboy could make, as she exited that elevator one last time.

Texas. She could almost taste the sky. Texas was the place where you could be a respectable outlaw.

They were early in love then and invincible. She went with Kurt to a Ramada Inn outside Austin, where they met with a walking bundle of nerves who claimed to hail from Brownsville. Frenetic Fred, they'd dubbed him. He left them sitting on a bed in a poolside room, holding a pound sample of organic Oaxacan. Said enjoy, he'd be in touch.

When he'd gone, Kurt studied the closed door for a long moment before turning to Annie. "This thing might be sour," he said quietly. "Methinks I smell a rat."

"We can always lose the heat," she said.

"Listen to you, Annie Oakley." He threw his head back and came around laughing, wrapping an arm heavy with muscle around her shoulder. "Like you've done this since you were sixteen, or something." She still wasn't used to the weight of it but liked it. There had been a moment—was it yesterday?—when they were sitting out on a rock crop west of Austin, watching the sunset, and Kurt had rested his forearm across her thigh. April and it was hot already, and his skin against hers, the weight of his arm, the air around them humming with spring life, and he shifted closer and put his arm around her. When she leaned against his shoulder, he sighed a quiet *yes*. She was scared out of her mind to think that she had found the man she was supposed to, that he had found her, and who in God's name knew what would happen now. But it didn't matter. The fear didn't matter anymore. Nothing mattered. He'd been there next to her, and the sky gave them its colors as it melted into the horizon and for just that instant everything, for as far as she could see, even into yesterday and tomorrow, everything had been perfect.

He squeezed her gently and leaned for a kiss.

"I'm in love," he whispered. He stood up suddenly, crossed the tiny room to zip the kilo into a gym bag, and returned to sit next to her, sobered. "It's real, you know," he said. "This goofball turns out to be trouble, we get popped, we go directly to jail. Do not pass go, do not collect two hundred dollars. Although if we do it right and don't go to jail, we collect a lot more than a couple of meager C notes."

"I'm not worried about that," she said.

"I shouldn't even have had you here. He's seen you. He doesn't know who you are, but, you know, if they nab us, you're part of it."

"We won't get caught," she said, as though it were a given.

Maybe she didn't really think about it. Maybe she was euphoric, being free, feeling for the first time in her life that she was in love with a kind and decent man. There were scars, but he seemed unaware of them. On his forehead, just at the hairline, a half-inch thread-thin cicatrix, a trophy from a high school fight. His right shoulder had a surgical gash where they'd repaired a dislocated shoulder and broken collarbone after a particularly vicious wrestling match. His left hip had another surgical scar, this one wide and long; he'd shattered his hip in a motorcycle accident soon after winning the Massachusetts wrestling title his sophomore year. The Olympics had been on the horizon that night, until a car slammed into him from the left and threw him to Arizona State, where he hoped to heal sufficiently over the course of his four-year scholarship, maybe take a shot next time around. But the coach there was a jerk, and that was when Kurt had first joined his buddies on the team in crossing the Mexican border and carrying back some pot, as much to prove himself as to make any kind of profit.

Annie traced a finger down his cheek, thinking his scars were like tattoos. It was as though he'd sat down and chosen them, asked the artist to begin his work, and now the stories they told were etched into his skin like ink. She loved him, pure and simple. Whether or not her mother would or ever could, and that was doubtful. Whether Carol would or not. She loved the way he stood on the planet, aware of how small and helpless all the billions of humans are.

He'd shown her a way to escape the office, the job, the city, escape the illusion of security her mother so believed in and constantly pushed her toward. She had found somebody to love and someone who loved her. She wanted to run again, to play outdoors in the shade of oak trees. This time, she thought, with this man, things would be for keeps.

Part of her didn't believe all this was happening, but the part of her that had loved to play Cowboys and Indians when she was a little girl was banging a drum and chanting. She had always preferred to be an Indian, even after her parents, one time, on a trip north, stopped at a reservation somewhere in the flat dry dust that was all she knew of Oklahoma. The Natives were not restless. They were totally bored and completely pissed off, and were suffering the onslaught of cheesy white tourists only so that they could put food on the table. She was five or six then, and aside from the times she spent on her knees, faced with Christ on the Cross, it was perhaps her first experience with pity, the emotion in this instance accompanied by a vague and uninformed guilt.

Father Francis left later that day, en route to Boston with the load. Kurt and Annie stayed at the ranch for a couple of weeks, eating fruits and salads and drinking gallons of water, cleaning out residue. He showed her how to meditate. They drove west into the desert and pitched a tent, ate mushrooms next to a campfire. They made love and whispered of making babies.

•

Headlights again, flashing through the window. Annie started, opened her eyes; she'd been so lost in thought that she hadn't heard Carol's approach in the Jeep. She looked around the battered living room. It would have to do. Kurt had got off clean that time, he and Father Francis both. The grand jury refused to indict for the same reason the judge had refused to demand bail money. Where's your evidence, His Honor wanted to know. The cops' claim of eleven hundred pounds of marijuana in the back of the van could hardly be substantiated when Kurt and Annie and Father Francis had stolen it from them. She rose to go out to the porch; had to catch her balance. Fatigue and the wine and the crush of the night's events left her dizzy. Who knew? Maybe he'd be lucky again.

Alex was groggy but awake as Annie scooped him into her arms and carried him to the house. Carol followed with Timothy, who was out cold.

"Milk," Alex said with a sigh, and his head flopped onto Annie's shoulder and he was asleep.

"My room," she whispered to Carol, and led the way.

They put the boys on the bed, removed their shoes, and pulled the covers to their chins. Carol paused at the door of the bedroom on the way out.

"I can't talk about it tonight," Annie said quietly, still standing bedside, staring at the boys.

"Of course not," Carol snapped. "You never could."

"Carol—"

"Excuse me," Carol said. "But did I see your house surrounded by *police cars?* Am I mistaken, or has your front door been knocked halfway off its hinges?" She turned, stopped herself, let out a sigh, and faced Annie again. "Maybe if you could, this wouldn't have happened in the first place."

"If I could what?" Annie said. "Unburden myself? Talk to somebody?"

"Yes." Carol stood, waiting.

She didn't get it. Nobody would get it. For Annie to talk to anyone about what Kurt was doing would be to betray him. If she talked, even to Carol, others would find out. It wasn't that Carol was a gossip; it was just the way things were. Loose lips and all that. And Carol might one day find herself on a witness stand, sworn before God to tell a truth that would help put her brother-in-law in prison.

"There's nothing I could have told you that would have made any difference," Annie said. "So let's not fight about it."

"What are you talking about? Why are you still with him? Annie, he's not going to—"

"Shhh!" Annie said. "You'll wake the boys." She followed Carol into the hallway and closed the door behind them.

"I just don't want you to go to jail," Carol said. "Is that unreasonable?"

"Do I look like I'm in jail?"

"He won't stop," Carol said.

"He will."

"When they lock him up."

"They seem to have done that. Are you pleased?"

"How can you even say that?"

"Just asking a question. Are you happy that my husband is in jail? I'm sure Mom will be thrilled."

"Annie—?"

"I'm not naïve. All the years they spent fighting? Hating each other?" Annie rubbed at a smudge on the door frame, just for something to do.

"Please."

"She wasn't exactly crushed when dickhead told you he wanted a divorce, was she? You think she expects either of us to end up with a decent husband?"

"I think that's what she wants, yes."

"Well, I don't. And I have no intention of getting into the kind of triangle you always wind up in with her and some jerk."

"Annie, that's not fair."

"What's fair? You're going to tell me that you haven't fallen in love with creep after creep, one after the other? We both have. Until I met Kurt."

"Just looking for Daddy, I guess." Carol sneered.

"And she gets in the middle and the three of you have a roaring good time fighting until she reveals him for the horrible person he is, and the sad part is she's right about him, and the two of you chase him off and then she has you all to herself again. Who needs that shit?"

"Ever the optimist, aren't we?"

"I guess so," Annie said. She was the one who had always assured Carol that everything was all right, even when the noise of their parents' fights came up the stairs and seeped under the door, into their sky-blue bedroom.

"This is pointless," Carol said. "I'm glad you're okay. I'm glad they didn't arrest you." She turned off the hall light on her way downstairs.

Annie went back into her room, stood beside the bed, looking at her boys in sleep. She saw Kurt in both of them, maybe more so in Tim, the red-haired hellion who was so eager to grow up. But Alex, too. Not even in kindergarten, and already wanting to save the world from evil. She hoped at some point they would discover that being human had nothing to do with being a hero. Being human took more strength. She did not know whether or when to tell them where their father was. Kurt would probably want them to know right away.

The silence of night was broken by a lone katydid, whirring forlornly in the cold outside. Maybe the last one of the season. Out there calling into thin air, wondering on some insect level what had happened to the heat and thrum of August, when friends were on every tree limb, humming.

A dull ache gripped her chest. The Ulster County jail. Tomorrow they would take him to Manhattan. She wondered what exactly they had on him and how she would make his bail. She worried about Kane, wondered where he was and how long it would take to get him back. She was as tired as she had ever been in her life, but did not know how she would get to rest. The only thing she knew was that she wanted to spend what was left of the night with her children sleeping in her arms.

FIVE

Kurt sat leaning forward, practically bent double, his head resting against the seat in front of him, his knees stuck there uncomfortably. He held his cuffed hands behind him against the small of his back. If he moved, the cuffs bit into his wrists. Pinched. He felt like a stray mutt sitting in the rear of the dog catcher's van. He wondered how Kane was doing. He hoped Annie had him by now. There had been no phone call yet, but he hoped Mark had got his pathetic little message and reached Annie. He had no idea how she would react to his arrest, and that bothered him. Maybe she would pull herself back to his side and help him circle the wagons. Maybe she would abandon him. Stop thinking that way. She won't leave over this. She would never bail out on you like that. She's strong. She is standup.

An Ulster County sheriff's deputy stood outside the car, guarding the prisoner. The deputy rested his right hand on his holstered pistol and held the butt end of a twelve-gauge against his thigh, aiming it skyward as he scanned the darkness around the station, looking at everything but Kurt. Vapor lights fought against the arrival of dawn, casting a yellow pall on the two-story, faux deco, godawful-red brick sheriff's office and the short row of black-on-white department vehicles in the lot out back.

Kurt's eyes were full of sand from a day that had started in the middle of the night, that fucking Ben Rubies had pushed his luck right off the end of the runway, and then the unloading, and the loading, and the unloading, and the packaging, and the loading, and that drive, and whatever had possessed him to go to the mall, and the arrest, and last night in a holding cell and the drunks in the tank down the end of the row with all their mewling and puking, and now he was off to the Metropolitan Correctional Center in downtown Manhattan; he stopped thinking in words. He processed images while anger turned to a gloom that settled on him like the small morning fog he watched slip silently into the crevices between the hills on the other side of the highway.

A man came out, nodded at the deputy, stood sizing up Kurt. Kurt looked at him once, long enough, and returned his gaze to the headrest in front of him. Bearded. Green-eyed. Intense.

"Shouldn't be doing this," the man said, more to himself than to the deputy. "Got nobody to ride with me; I'm alone."

The deputy stood just as he had been, shrugged.

"Maybe I'll leave you in back." Kurt realized the man was addressing him and turned. This guy looked more like an accountant than a cop, and Kurt knew right away he was dealing with intelligence.

"Yeah," the man said, unabashedly talking to himself now. "I should leave him in back." As he started to shut the door, he said to Kurt, "Sorry about the handcuffs. It's—" He stopped, opened the door, reached for Kurt's arm to help him out of the car. Kurt stretched as much as he could with his hands cuffed behind him; he'd been so twisted and cramped that already his muscles ached.

The man urged him to the front seat. Kurt went without argument.

"You'll be more comfortable up there," he said, flashing his badge. "Special Agent Joseph Kessler, DEA. And I can keep an eye on you."

Kessler shut the door, strode around the front of the car, got in, started the engine, eased onto the roadway, and looped around toward the entrance to the thruway. Kurt wondered if the guy was performing, pretending absentmindedness. He wondered if it was a conscious thing, or if Kessler had watched too many episodes of *Columbo*. Doubtful.

When the bored, red-lipsticked woman in the toll booth held out a ticket, the agent badged her and she pulled it back, offering a nod and a smile with the clipboard holding a form for him to sign. As he accelerated away from the booth, Kessler slipped an arm up on the seat back and said, "Looks like you haven't really got a big problem here."

Kurt stared straight ahead.

"Unless something happens," Kessler said finally, "it doesn't look serious."

Unless something happens.

"I just want to remind you," he added, "that anything you say, I can and will use against you in court. So we probably shouldn't be talking about the case."

"What case?"

"This one. The case sitting next to me." Kessler pointed a finger and mouthed the word. *You.*

"I don't even know what the charges are."

"I don't either, yet. We've got some ideas, but we'll see what the prosecutor decides."

What could they have? Not possession. Not possession with intent to distribute. Conspiracy, maybe. That statute got stretched often enough. They had an empty plane at the end of a private strip.

"The load's gone, right?" Kessler said. "I mean, we get a call about a plane crashing and rush right up, but we get there too late."

"Why was I arrested?"

"You're right." Kessler chuckled. "They'll probably give you a parking ticket and fine you for abandoning a vehicle and leave it at that."

Kurt wondered what they did have, but he could hear Mark's voice in his head: *Don't say a word. Not a word.* He wondered if any of his crew were in custody.

"But if one of your buddies decides to roll . . ."

Don't look. He wanted to, but kept his eyes straight ahead.

"One of your people," Kessler said.

Now Kurt turned and met the agent's gaze. Whatever they had, hey, nothing he could do about that. But he wouldn't give them shit. They didn't have Bill; he was sure of that somehow. Bill was bulletproof, one of those guys who never got caught, and that was all there was to it. It didn't happen. Bill knew how to observe things, and he knew how to listen to his intuition. But even if they arrested him, no fucking way he would talk. He had no family, no strong attachments. Kurt was his family. McGrath and Father Francis were as standup as they came. Four years in the Marines.

Viet Nam. LURP. Lonnie had done three years' state time for possession, Massachusetts. You get caught, you do the time. End of discussion. He was the most likely of the four to get into trouble over something stupid like a bar fight, but would never cut a deal with the cops. Insane, totally fucked by his time in Nam, but he knew the rules and abided by them. Smith was a worry. Kurt would never have let Gary in, not before. Smith didn't want to be in, but his wife wanted him there. She ran him totally out front. But he'd been working for Kurt for almost five years, as groundskeeper and handyman. He was honest and reliable. If they popped him, he was dangerous. He had plenty to lose.

"Handcuffs bothering you?" Kessler said. "You look uncomfortable."

"It's okay," Kurt said. He wasn't trying to be tough; he wanted Kessler to keep talking.

"I'm sorry about those. I'd loosen them if I could."

"Let me guess," Kurt said. "Regulations."

"You been arrested before." It wasn't a question. "Your wife—Annie, right?—she was pretty much scared out of her mind last night."

He could feel Kessler looking at him again. He started to turn, changed his mind, stayed as he was.

"You saw my wife?"

"We ran a paper on your place. Didn't find anything. A couple of ounces of pot, but I'm not interested in that."

A search warrant. Panic clubbed him from the back seat; his vision went pink around the edges. The boys. Annie. He hoped it wasn't the same crew that had arrested him. Fucking maniacs. He couldn't breathe.

"I always feel bad in those situations," Kessler was saying. "I try to be as nonthreatening as possible. I got the sense that your wife is a kind and intelligent person."

"Nonthreatening?" Kurt heard the word coming out of his mouth, but wasn't sure he'd said it.

"These days, you know, some of these younger guys just coming in, they'll toss a place if you so much as look the other way."

"Did you arrest my wife?"

"If I hadn't shown up, they probably would have."

Kurt felt anger surge up from his stomach; the muscles covering it went taut. This guy was making himself out to be some kind of hero, like he had charged in and saved Annie from the bad guys or something.

"Your kids weren't there, in case you're interested. She wouldn't tell me where they were."

Thank God for small favors. Kurt sat silently, cursing himself, despising his stupidity, wanting nothing more than to hold his wife and children in his arms and tell them how sorry he was. He had never thought they might go through something like that. His business was his; what was between him and the law did not involve them. Fuck. He felt the cuffs on his wrists and wondered if they'd done that to Annie.

"A few of my guys did a number on your place. I apologize for that."

"Hey," Kurt said, monotone, "no problem."

"Annie was frightened. She probably won't tell you."

"Yeah, well, that's between me and her, isn't it." It bugged him that this cop would call Annie by her given name, as if they were old high school chums or something. Who the fuck did this guy think he was, a guidance counselor?

They drove a while longer, Kurt hunched forward, the cuffs digging at his wrists. He wanted to ask if they'd knocked or kicked the door down, but he thought he probably knew. He'd caught a couple of charges up in Maine some years back: criminal mischief and menacing with a firearm. Cause enough for a judge to issue a no-knock warrant. Not that the cops ever knocked, anyway. That was long before he'd met Annie, years before he'd decided to settle down. He and Father Francis and Lonnie McGrath had been out in the woods, on private property owned by a close friend of Kurt's. The sky was stunned with sunlight to an almost neon shade of blue, and leaf color verged on psychedelic. *Was* psychedelic. They'd been out walking, hiking around, enjoying the autumn, readying to head south for the winter. They heard barking in the distance, a racket, and headed that way, Father Francis leading. Soon they come on a pack of bloodhounds, baying and leaping at a tree, slobbering, going wild. And up in the tree, scared out of its wits, was a young brown bear. Just as Kurt and crew arrived, the hunters did too.

"Listen," Kurt said, "this is private property and you guys are trespassing. The owner doesn't permit hunting here."

The hunters were all heavily armed. High-powered rifles, pistols; a couple even had machetes. One of them pulled a revolver from the holster on his belt and held it, loose, his arm limp at his side.

"No. You listen," he said. "We tracked this bear here and we're going to shoot it. And if you try to stop us, you might get hurt. There might be an accident."

The guy meant it. Nothing to do but back down. Kurt and McGrath followed Father Francis back to their cabin, Father Francis slipping quickly through the woods, a man on a mission. He emerged from the cabin with an AR-15, an M-1, and a 9 mm. He distributed the weapons and got into the truck they were driving at the time, a 'forty-nine Chevy pickup, green as pine. They found the hunters' car easily enough.

All Father Francis said was, "Armor-piercing bullets." The three of them opened up on the vehicle, also a pickup, but this one almost new, a 'seventy-seven Ford, clearly well taken care of. They shot out the windows. They shot all up and down the sides. They shot through the hood into the engine block and the radiator. They shot until they ran out of ammunition. Kurt kept seeing that bear, the fear in its eyes, and the guy with the pistol threatening to shoot them, the dullness and stupidity in his.

The hunters filed charges. Kurt explained the situation to the sheriff, who was most sympathetic, but still Kurt had come away with a conviction. He'd paid a fine and restitution for the car. Father Francis and McGrath thanked him for fading all the heat.

"Sure I can't loosen those for you?"

He wondered if Kessler had seen his rap sheet. He made no answer.

"Just tell me one thing," Kessler said. "Off the record. I swear it. Don't you worry about your family? Somebody getting hurt?" He took his eyes from the road to assess Kurt. "This is not about a bunch of hippies having fun anymore."

No point arguing. It would lead to anger or conversation, and either one was dangerous right now. Kurt was tired. He just wanted to get through the process, make bail, and go home. Make sure his family was okay. After that, he didn't know.

"Any of your friends ever get strung out? You?"

Of course he'd been strung out. He didn't know too many people who hadn't been, at some time or another, on one drug or another, or on food, or on exercise, or on whatever it was they could use to get high or at least get their mind off whatever it was they sought to escape.

"I plan to get strung out when I'm in my eighties," Kurt replied. "On heroin. Just me and my wife, sitting on the front porch in our rockers, nodding and feeling no pain." Or maybe by then someone would have concocted a potion that had all of the pleasure with none of the hazards. How nice to be able to escape the inevitable pain of old age: the bone-deep geriatric pain that everybody for some insane reason seemed to think should be endured rather than relieved. Forget it. He would eat right. He would stay in shape. He would cultivate pleasurable activities and keep his brain engaged, remain involved. But when it came time to do those final years, when the quality of slumber deteriorated to the point that it was difficult to distinguish between waking and sleeping states? That was the time to take dope. Don't just endure the trip. Enhance it.

"The people who loaded your Six," Kessler said, "down in Cartagena or wherever, they sell that shit too."

How much did this guy know? The plane *had* been loaded in Cartagena, and by people connected with the Colombian cartels, but they had a lock on the market. Kurt didn't like funneling money to some fat South American dictator, but it was at times the only place you could get product.

"I had a kid brother was a junky," Kessler said. "Killed himself."

"That's a shame," Kurt said.

"Yeah."

"Was he a cop?"

"No. Just a junky."

Kurt stared out the window. Dawn coming up. Man, was he tired. The car rolled past apple and pear orchards set a hundred feet or so off the thruway. Nothing like a nice crisp McIntosh bathed in parfum d'exhaust.

"How'd you get into it?" Kessler said suddenly.

Kurt wanted to answer that he was just one of those hippies, but the less he said, the better. This guy could be easy to talk to, but it was too risky.

"Ah," Kessler said, "taking my advice. Smart. How 'bout I tell you? You started out smuggling a few pounds across the border to your friends on the wrestling team in Arizona, right? Bagged a wrestling scholarship and then walked away from an asshole coach who demanded you cut your hair. The suits demand I cut my hair, sometimes, too. They can be like that."

Kurt didn't reply.

"Europe then, the whole trip. Amsterdam. Then off to Morocco. The Middle East. India and Nepal. Making connections everywhere, getting serious about the business. And what about your pal Rosie up north? Thousands of pounds. How long's he been down now?"

Rosie. Fuck. This agent knew his history. But how much? Anger washed over Kurt. His pal. His brother. Marking time in Canadian prisons. Years now. Years and years. Refused to say he was sorry. Refused to say he wouldn't do it again. They hit him with their longest hash sentence ever. Rosie had written him about it. How he watched through the bars of his cell as the murderers and rapists and child molesters came and went: two years, seven, ten. They came and went, and some came back again and left again. Rosie did his time. Still hadn't apologized.

"You don't stop soon, pal, it'll be too late," Kessler said. "You'll wake up one day and your kids will be grown and your wife won't know you anymore and you'll be an old man in a cage."

Kurt grunted, tried to make it sound like a laugh. He wriggled in the seat, trying to get his wrists into a less painful position. Something was backward here. Something was fucked up. Here he was under arrest for smuggling a plant, and the guys who were out there selling weapons and war got ribbons and presidential commendations and all that kind of thing. He'd thought about going legit; he'd done business with plenty of legitimate companies, importing figs, pistachio nuts, ceramic tiles, English translations of the Koran, whatever he could use to disguise hashish shipments. Now and then he even turned a profit on the legal cargo. He thought sometimes it would be easy to go straight, go legitimate. He was a reasonably entrepreneurial fellow. Why not? Why not bring in a few tons of pistachios or figs—clean—without the danger, without the intrigue, without the risk? There was money to be made, and you could smile at the customs man without so much as a quiver in the spinal cord. You could take your paycheck and go home to your family and live a decent life. Why not? He thought of his old pal Chris from high school, Chris, who'd taught him how to drive at the ripe old age of nine. Chris was settled now, buying odd little pieces of property here and there and building Jiffy Lubes on them. Making reasonably large bucks. Had one of those houses in Wellesley with sufficient charm and the trim yard and fresh flowers in the dining room. Attached two-car garage, kids in private school, and he did the two martini thing before dinner each night. Chris had confessed to Kurt one night after they'd had a few that, sometimes, though he loved his wife and two children dearly, when he walked into his living room at the end of each brief and glorious day, sometimes he felt he was trapped in a Martha Stewart wet dream.

"Look," Kurt said suddenly. "I go out to pick something up at the mall and suddenly I'm under arrest. I don't know what for and it's been twelve hours and no phone call. I'd like a phone call."

"You'll get your call."

"When?"

"The way I see it," Kessler said, "you've got two ways to go. You been doing this fifteen years, more or less, made yourself some money. Probably a pile of money. Smart guys get out of the business. You get out now, if you beat this, the statute of limitations is up in five years, and you're home free." He looked again at Kurt. "My bet is you can't. You can't stop. You're hooked. Not on dope. But you're hooked. You know it, and so does your wife."

Why did he keep bringing her into it? Like he was in love or something.

"If pot wasn't illegal—" He stopped himself. Don't take the bait, man; don't get into it. He closed his mouth.

"Ask me," Kessler said, "you're acting like a fucking fool. You got a wonderful family, you're a smart guy, you put the same effort into something legit that you do into smuggling this shit, and you could be just as successful—without the threat of prison."

Keep your mouth shut, man; don't start talking to this guy. He's baiting you.

"I just came out the ass end of a very ugly divorce," Kessler said. "My old lady put up with me, or with me always being gone, for twelve long years. The cop thing, you know. Is he out there getting shot at, is he out there screwing around, Johnny's stepping up to the plate for the first time in his life, why couldn't Dad make the game, the fucking beeper going off at all the wrong moments—" Kessler's voice reeked of disgust, whether at himself or his wife, Kurt couldn't tell. "I got kids, two boys and a girl, and I love them the way you do yours, and now I get to see them on weekends. Maybe. When I can make it and they can make it. It's like we don't know each other." He reached for the radio, turned it on and off in one motion. "You know your kids? They're young yet, huh?"

Kurt felt buried.

"Anyway," Kessler said, tone casual now, and cool, "it's too late. You're busted, pal. You are in the system. Maybe we didn't catch you right this time, maybe we won't get this load; we'll have to go with the plane as evidence. That and whatever we cull from your buddies. Even if it isn't enough to send you away right now, eventually we'll get you holding heavy. Nobody with anything to trade does time anymore. Somebody will rat on you. Know how much time you'll get if we prove that was your Six?"

"What the fuck are you talking about?" Kurt asked. "I don't know anything about any plane."

"Yeah, right," Kessler said. "A shitload, my friend." Grinning now. "A whole motherfucking shitload of T-I-M-E. And you will, ultimately, get convicted. If not on this, then on some other trip."

Convicted. The agent's words hit like a fist to the belly. Kurt twisted in the seat, saw Kessler tense. He sat back quickly, showed that he wasn't making a move. The cuffs were hurting seriously. Convicted. Or killed. Or go on the lam. The guy is right. I'm a fucking maniac. And now I am on my way to jail.

Kessler eased the car onto the road shoulder and pulled to a stop.

"I can take them off if you give me your word there'll be no trouble."

"That's okay," Kurt said. "I just want to get where I can see about bail." Kessler stared at him for a long moment; Kurt returned the gaze. Kessler reached across and popped the seat belt.

"Face the window," he said.

"I'm all right," Kurt said. "You don't have to take them off."

Kessler waited until Kurt turned and then he popped the lock on the cuffs and ratcheted them closed before tossing them in the glove box. Kurt rubbed his wrists, trying to erase the red marks left where the cuffs had been gnawing on him. His left hand had gone numb; it began to tingle as circulation returned.

"I'll have to put them back on before we arrive," Kessler said.

The agent gunned back onto the thruway, driving with the confidence of someone who'd spent considerable hours at the wheel. Traffic was sparse, mostly semis hauling who-knew-what toward Manhattan. Kurt wondered where his own trucks were, and whether they'd encountered any trouble. He was reasonably sure DEA didn't have the load.

"You know, I respect you," Kessler said. "I know you have morals, you're a straightup guy. Ordinarily, the Albany office would have handled this case, but I've been investigating your organization for some time, so I got the call."

His organization. That sounded ominous. If anything, his was a *dis*organization. Kurt didn't reply, because all he could think to say was, "If you like me so much, then why'd you arrest me?" But if Kessler had been on his case that long, it was pointless to continue to pretend total innocence. It would only piss the agent off, make him that much more determined to put Kurt away.

"You could be very comfortable," Kessler said. "You could start over. Live straight and not have to worry about someone like me coming along to spoil your party. Give your wife and kids a decent life."

"We have a pretty decent life. Or did until you showed up."

"Look. I'm one of those guys who's never happy." Kessler was relaxed now, talking as though to a friend. "I know you're a heavy hitter. I want sources. I want to know where this stuff's coming from. I want to know who puts up the money."

Silence.

"If you're worried about getting hurt—"

"There's no reason for anyone to want to hurt me."

"Many a good man has taken his family and gone into witness protection."

Not an option.

"Doesn't it bother you that last night your wife was scared half out of her mind, and you were nowhere around? Anything could have happened. Anything."

Kurt kneaded left palm with right fingers, seeking pressure points that would ease the tension, saw Kessler looking, and then shifted in the seat and sat back to reassure the agent. He didn't want the cuffs back on.

"If you really loved your family," Kessler said, "you'd cooperate."

"I have nothing to tell you," Kurt replied.

"Think about your family. How your actions affect them."

"I think about them all the time." He wanted nothing more than to be with them right now. When the boys had spent an afternoon outdoors, you could smell grass and sunshine in their hair. He missed them. He wondered how long it would be before he could hold them again. It was always like that, being away from them: he counted the distance in hours.

Think about your family. Who was this guy? He remembered that first week Alex was home with them, when he insisted that Annie, sore from the birth and exhausted from midnight feedings, rest in bed or in the big club chair in the living room, her feet propped on the ottoman. He brought her meals and made tea and massaged her legs and feet. They would have visitors in the evenings. He did shopping, made party snacks, and welcomed friends who came by to welcome Alex to the world. Kurt had been surprised at the outpouring of good wishes, had basked in the warmth of their friends. One morning Annie had fallen asleep on the couch and Alex was awake with him, that was the first time they'd been alone together. He put little Alex on a blanket on the floor beside him and they had their first one-on-one. He hoped they would never stop. Alex lay on his back in a little white cotton knit cap, chewing his fist and watching Kurt intently, studying Dad. Dad. And Kurt, when he said, "I love you, little boy," he could have sworn Alex recognized his voice as the one that had come through to him while he was still in that other place, liquid place.

Think about your family? Who was this guy?

"I don't understand," Kessler was saying. "You claim to love your kids and wife and yet what you do puts them in jeopardy. How does that work?"

"They're in jeopardy because of you, not because of me. I haven't done anything." Enough of this self-righteous crap. He was ready to cut loose, let Kessler have it.

"You put your ideas about being a righteous guy before the well-being of your family," Kessler said. "To me, that looks selfish."

Lay off, man, just lay off. Kurt was loath to agree, but Kessler had a point. There were moments—lots of them—when Kurt wondered if, under the guise of providing for his family, he did what he did for self-gratification.

"Who you going to jail for?" Kessler asked.

"You know what I don't get?"

"No I don't, buddy, and I'll tell you something else." The agent was angry suddenly; Kurt was surprised at his vehemence. The state narcs, that time in Texas, they'd been so pissed, one of them had got up real close to his ear and whispered, "We could make it look like you tried to escape." And he'd been serious. Kurt tried to read Kessler, got no sense that he was that sort.

"I'm trying to do you a favor, pal. Trying to keep you on the streets so you can be with your family, but you gotta cooperate, you know?" He shook his head with disgust. "Get with it, man. Get with it."

Kurt leaned against the passenger door. How the fuck was he supposed to get with it? Give up his partners, his friends, his crew? Become a rat? No way. Out of the question. He remembered the face of Mr. Fontana, the grocer, glaring down at him when he was caught red-handed at the age of ten or eleven, and the pain of Mr. Fontana's huge right hand clenched around his biceps.

Kurt had lifted his shirt and pulled the packs of Double Bubble out of his waistband. Handed them over silently.

"Who are the others?" the grocer said, his words thick with Italy. "Who was with you?"

Kurt frowned up at him, refusing to cooperate, refusing to give up his pals.

"I'll call the police!" Fontana screamed.

Quaking inside, Kurt said nothing.

"Who are they?"

Kurt shook his head. Fontana looked hard at him for a long moment, and then, to Kurt's amazement, pinched him and let go of his arm.

"No more stealing gum," the grocer said. "No more."

"Okay," Kurt said.

"It's good you didn't tell on your friends." Fontana smiled. "You're a good kid."

Kurt had run down the sidewalk as fast as he could, to the park, where he would wait for his buddies to show and they would sit chewing gum from their stash and recounting the great escape. But he'd felt respect coming to him from Fontana, and it had made an impression.

He looked at Kessler.

Kessler smiled. "I know you've got another trip in the works."

The shock turned Kurt stony, but he managed to move his head as though to get the view out the window. Kessler had to be guessing on that one. The trip was barely formulated, not even completely planned. Who the fuck was this guy?

"Remember that wild ride from Beirut to Paris?" Kessler said. "Mid-East Air? Bumpety-bump? The forced landing in Athens?"

Kurt could only sit there, freed from the handcuffs but constrained by astonishment. Remember? Yes, Agent Kessler. You were there? Beirut? The Wild, Wild Middle East? His stomach tightened the way it had years earlier when an engine went out during a commercial flight he was on. The plane had nearly crashed. He remembered the few Europeans on board, carrying their jaded and superior sensibilities like overstuffed Gucci satchels; the Middle Eastern businessmen in suits and ties, how American of them all. He'd gripped his seat with the best of them as the plane lurched toward the runway, his fear somehow transforming itself into amusement at the irony of the situation. He'd just hit the big time. His pal Rosie had hooked him up with a Lebanese businessman in

Queens, a man highly respected by the New York crime families. That had made Kurt nervous, but he recognized that the family thing was a system, no more, no less, that in some ways was more honorable and legitimate than the one operated by Uncle Sam. Still, it seemed petty in its way, and barbaric. In the end, none of that mattered. Who controlled things controlled them, and organized crime controlled all matters pertaining to the importation of contraband into the U.S. You had to pay your dues, if not to the Taxman, then to Johnny Whoever from Brooklyn. And right after Kurt met the guy, Johnny Nocenti showed up and in his ever-reasonable tone said he had friends at JFK who could pull air freight without it passing through customs. They were Italian but not mobbed-up, not connected to anyone in particular; they knew Johnny through a shared cousin, knew he was trustworthy, and they were looking to take advantage of their catch. Did Kurt want to meet them? Voices in Kurt's head sang a hallelujah chorus, and he said, "Sure, Johnny, I'll meet them."

He had traveled to Lebanon, been given a Ping-Pong-ball sample of hash. That first night, at the Commodore Hotel in Beirut, he lay on the bed, holding the sample. The windows were open, the air warm and dry. The hashish perfume, sweet and earthy at once, filled his nostrils as he inspected the sample more closely. Good stuff, but they must have taken him for an amateur. This was high-grade commercial, which would do just fine, but best to establish right away that he knew his hash. This was not double zahara, the finest grade, and tomorrow he would tell them. He'd discerned already that they were middlemen, Christian, from Zhalé, a town controlled by the Phalangist Party. And the Christian Phalangists were hooked up with the U.S. government. He didn't like it: warlords and furtive government agents from his birthplace lurking around, trying to manipulate history with Siamese twins—drugs and arms—and spilling blood everywhere. What they didn't understand was that you had to keep rooting out the negative in any system, recycle it, replace it with positive. Otherwise, that system would collapse.

A knock on the door had brought him to his feet; he stuffed the hash into a desk drawer and stood for one barefoot moment—glancing from door to window and back, thinking about bailing but where would he run—before a key opened the door and he was facing a cadre of plain-clothes policemen. Had to be. They let themselves in and began searching, carefully, handling things with courtesy and restraint. Kurt stood beside the bed, watching them, listening to their language, which required a strong tongue, and wondering at how calm he felt. He supposed he'd been expecting them.

One of them, portly, with hair slicked hard against curls, said in English, "We know who you are. You're a big hash dealer from America. You have hashish here and you are under arrest." He waved the sample. "Big Man, Big Dealer," he said. "We know you have a lot of money here. Where's the money?"

"You've got me all wrong," Kurt said. "I just like to smoke."

They drove through dark streets to a building, French Colonial. He was placed in a room full of large, carved wooden furniture. The floor was tiled, the ceiling high, the bookcases loaded with texts in French and Arabic. He sat and waited while the man left to guard him stood quietly.

It was after midnight when the judge walked in, laughing and talking with a huge, serious man in a leisure suit cut of something that looked like linen. There was a younger man with them, early twenties, who spoke to Kurt in English, asked if he wanted coffee. Kurt nodded, and the young man left the room. The judge took a seat behind his desk and picked up the evidence, about a quarter-ounce of hash. He looked at Kurt, then at the hash, and handed the sample to the big man. The big one looked at Kurt and clucked his tongue.

"Where you get hashish?"

"Zhalé."

The big man sniffed the hash and turned his nose up, pretended to spit. "No good," he said.

"Pretty good," Kurt said. "Could be better."

The young man returned and put coffee on the desk, the judge spoke to him. Kurt wished he could understand Arabic. The young guy waved a hand toward the man in the suit and said to Kurt, "This is Mohammed Faran. He is the chief of customs in all Lebanon, and from now on you will do business only with him."

Of course. Absolutely. No problem. He wanted to get up and dance on the judge's desk.

"How many tons can you take, and what price will you pay?"

Next day, it was early afternoon as they drove toward the huge valley at the edge of the Syrian frontier. Outlaw territory. They passed through a number of dusty ramshackle towns. What women were visible wore chador, hiding themselves in black robes from Syrian troops prowling the streets with Kalashnikovs pointed skyward or toward pitted sidewalks. No one bothered the Mercedes.

Left to himself for a few minutes in Baalbek, Kurt stood among the crumbling but massive stone pillars of the Temple of Baal, watching a couple of guys charge a few intrepid tourists to ride camels around the perimeter of pre-Christian ruins. Perhaps when this was over he could go into the leisure business, call his company War Zone Vacations. Come to Baalbeck, Temple of the Sun.

In spite of the guys cashing in with the camels, the earth beneath him radiated something unusual, as though this place still held its ancient energy, undiluted by the passage of time. The stones, too; it was coming from the stones. He had learned about himself that, as any given trip progressed, he would become more superstitious. Begin looking for omens. His faculties served him well in that sense. He thought to make peace with the spirits of the place where he was working.

He strolled among the ruins, feeling the hum of ancient civilizations, the wrath and vengeance of the Old Testament and the mindset it generated: fodder for war. Religion grew food for the monster. He stared at stone the color of sand and time. The Temple of Baal. Baal, the bad god, namesake of idolatry. Worshipped by ancient Semitic peoples who paid homage with much sensuality—or with prostitution and child sacrifice, depending upon your historian. He stared, lost himself in the stones. His skin prickled with history, and he was at one with the spirit that sought to defy corrupt authority, the one that knew peace. He stared. *Look at you all,* the stones said, *all of you squirming on the face of the earth, torn between seeking to fly and wanting to dig clear down to the core of the planet with your bare hands. Lift your face to the sun. Smile.*

Later, as the Mercedes began the descent from Baalbek, in every direction as far as he could see, green and beautiful *cannabis indica* plants stretched their bushy arms skyward, waving in the afternoon breeze like corn in the fields of Indiana. He had always loved farms, and this one was a beauty, astonishingly large, green everywhere, radiating good health. He was never less than awed at the sight, and he had seen it many times since.

A few weeks later, he and Johnny were in Johnny's Staten Island garage, cutting open the crate that held the best and freshest Lebanese hash the U.S. East Coast had ever seen. It disappeared at connoisseur prices, and Kurt's reputation was established. Virtually overnight, he went from being a moderately successful wholesaler of other people's loads to being an upper-echelon international smuggler who got paid in suitcases full of money.

Three years and many loads later, he went to that party and met Annie. He was thinking by then that he should start looking for legitimate businesses to invest in, quit while he was ahead, but he was still fascinated by the game of outwitting the authorities and still firmly believed that the laws were stupid. The smart thing would be to get out before he got busted. It was beginning to feel like a sickness—*You go back, Jack, do it again, wheel spinning 'round and 'round*—his own personal disease, something he had to struggle through. It scared him, this need to keep returning to the table, upping the stakes.

And look where it's got you now, *fool.* Through the windshield, he saw the sun just beginning to peek over the top of Bear Mountain; its rays clarified the grit on the glass.

Beirut. He couldn't believe it, couldn't believe Kessler had been on that plane. How long has this guy been on my case? How much does he know? Say something.

"You need to wash your car."

Kessler smirked, like, *Is that the best you can do, bud?*

"Is Annie okay?" Kurt asked.

"She seemed okay when we left. That was late last night." A tone of sincerity bled through the words; anyway, Kurt thought that's what he heard. He counted the truck headlights punctuating the thruway morning.

"I'd like to make a phone call."

"When we get you to MCC." Kessler rounded his back, flexed his arms against the steering wheel. "I'll bet she was good. Those Texas gals. Did some trips with you, right? Before the kids?"

Kurt envisioned Kessler behind a desk and, on the desk, stacks of manila folders spilling paper everywhere. Information, details of this and that: all about him and his crew. About his wife. All of that because of this guy. This agent sitting next to him. Hello, Reality.

"But isn't that just it?" Kessler was saying. "You put your family into this world, and it's a world where people go to prison, people get hurt."

"It takes some sick motherfuckers to go in and terrify a woman, a mother, in her home." Kurt said.

Kessler shook his head. "You think I don't know I've got maniacs on my crew? That's what I'm telling you. The game's changed. It's fucking dangerous out there. Think about your kids, buddy. Think about your wife. If you don't, believe me, a woman like that, somebody else will."

SIX

Her muscles were sluggish with fatigue after a scant three hours' sleep, but sweat was essential. She had to send the tension somewhere: excrete it through the pores of her skin, respire it from her lungs. Breath in through the nose, out through the mouth. Four paces each way, four footfalls each breath. In with the good, out with the bad. In with the clean, the positive, the fresh. Out with the negative, the dirtied and polluted. Four paces, four breaths, and four words over and over, pounding her—Kurt is in jail / Kurt is in jail / Kurt is in jail. Stop it. Just run. Run and run and run. Focus on the sunlight, dappling through the trees.

She pictured him, a few hours south in Manhattan, sitting in a cell at the MCC, where all the famous criminals went: the swindlers and dictators, mobsters and terrorists. What fine company, and no judges until Monday. No bail until a judge could be found, and even then, who knew? Dr. Tetlow called it "Friday night justice," the way the cops tried to make big arrests after five on Friday, because it almost always meant the prisoners spent a weekend in jail before a judge was available to arraign. Cheap shot.

Just run. It's all uphill, pay attention now to the rock-strewn dirt road, feel your legs getting stronger, run and keep running. Kurt is in jail / Kurt is—

A loud snap, the crack and rattle of hooves kicking timber, then the thud of hooves on dirt. She stopped dead in the path, scanning the woods. There it was just ahead: a white tail bobbing among the trees. She stood, breathing hard, looked long as the deer disappeared easily into the greenery, running gently, with none of the desperation of the hunted.

Silence now, the deer already out of earshot, just silence. The wood thrush who'd arrived in May had disappeared. Annie kept hoping to hear his song one last time, but he'd left early in August without saying goodbye. In his stead had come a few lazy cicadas and lots of katydids, the latter chomping on evening as though it were dinner. The conifers, eastern white, spruce, and hemlock, towered in green, standing as they would, unchanged, through winter. In spring, their fingertips showed briefly light green, but by the end of June they were back to themselves.

Somewhere far off, a cardinal gave his long piercing whistle and chirped *the bird~ the bird~ the bird.* They traveled in pairs, the male lipstick red, the female mostly brown with only a touch of makeup, the better to conceal herself from those that would have her for lunch.

Annie stood looking at trees and the sunlight touching them long after the deer had disappeared. Those cops, the one with the gun. She'd never been so scared. Those awful men, invading her home like soldiers in some kind of demented war. Redundant, that phrase; all war was demented. Maybe he would help. Kurt was in jail. Kane was missing. He should be with her right now, scouting in the woods as she ran, looping around every so often to let her know he was about. That one, though, Kessler; he'd seemed decent and kind. Maybe she should try to talk to him.

Shake it off. Shake it off and go on. She took off, picked up the pace, feet falling on dirt packed damp from the rain of a few days ago. Steady uphill, up and up and up, the effort just what she needed. She could not picture life without her husband, life with the knowledge that he was somewhere locked in a cage. He was not bad. He did not hurt people. He was open and loving and warm. He was a criminal.

She ran, pushing herself, glad to feel the effort in her muscles and lungs, in her heart. She remembered Coach Smith. High school track. *The day you won your town the race . . .* She spat at the thought of him and pushed on, dodging rocks. The way up demanded maximum effort, made her work.

The old quarry road wound through acres of oak and pine, maple and birch. The morning was cool for September, somewhere in the forties, the sky a deeper blue without the haze of humidity washing it out. She broke into a sweat finally, and got her breath, got her pace. The black dirt road, not much more than a car-wide path, was still heavily shaded, though leaves had begun to fall. At the top of the ridge, she stopped, walked in slow circles, stood looking. Mohonk to the east, the Schwangunks to the south, the Catskills to the northwest. Hightop Mountain, looking like a moss-covered pyramid, sat at the edge of the Catskills, calling to mind a wise woman from one of the several indigenous tribes long ago driven from these lands. The Wappingers, the Mohicans, the Esopus. Manatees. Waranawankongas and Lenni Lenape. They had been here when the Great Bead Trader arrived on Manhattan Island with his band of intrepid explorers. Annie stood in the sun and breathed deep, breathed slow now, slowing down, feeling the sweat on her forehead. She looked at the mountain. The wise woman sat peacefully, her hands folded in her lap.

Annie wondered at her magnificence, then felt keenly her own confusion and worry. This was her mother's country, though her mother had thirty-four years earlier moved to Texas to marry the man of her dreams, or something like that, two years before Annie was born. In her mother's eyes, the trap was sprung: Mary LaForet from Wappingers Falls, New York, was caught and caged. It was 1955 and she was a housewife in a three-bedroom, carpeted, tract home in Austin, Texas. Misters Fox & Jacobs were buying up farmland and spreading their suburban blight across the wilds of Texas. It was the new frontier. For Mary, it was air-conditioned hell. She'd had the doctor knock her out cold shortly after she went into labor. Annie had been yanked into the world by a cold steel clamp fastened about her skull. Of course she didn't remember, but she was certain she must have screamed bloody murder. She wondered if the parish priest had forced her mother to kneel on the big concrete steps outside the church on a cool December morning and be forgiven by God (via the priest) for the sin of bearing a child. They used to require that, the Catholics, the powers that be in the Church. You had a baby, ergo you must have had sex. Shame on you. Kneel out here where all the world can observe as I forgive you. The husbands were in no way held accountable. They were only doing their bit for the Church, making lots of little Catholics to populate the pews and drop currency in the collection basket.

The drone of a plane fell earthward from the open blue above the woods, its obnoxious noise trespassing on the quiet of early morning. She stood, exposed to the whims of the pilot. It had been worse at the end of August, when the county sheriff and the FBI and DEA had buzzed the skies daily in helicopters and small planes, taking pictures on infrared film. Cannabis had a quicker metabolism than most plants, and showed up on the film as red or red-orange among the blue-green seas of other vegetation. The task force pilots circled Annie's hill regularly, but she was certain that was because it was a good-size chunk of woodland, not chopped up into one- or two-acre housing lots. She doubted any real suspicion on their part. They flew all over the county, maybe not as much or as often as they did in Humboldt, California, but often enough. The barbarous percussion of helicopter blades beating the air always took Annie back to the door of her parents' living room, where she used to pause on her way out and take a quick peek at the television. On screen were images sent fresh from Viet Nam: bloodied men and boys—boys who then looked her own age but now would seem children to her—boys with rifles, boys in helicopters. There was something so overwhelmingly ominous about the sound that whenever she heard it, even now, she half-expected it to be accompanied by the blatting of machine guns. She did not recall her parents having had much to say about the war. Maybe she just didn't hear it, but more likely they didn't talk with her about it. It was possible they didn't talk about it at all, being convinced that to speak against the government on an issue so serious as war was not patriotic. You could complain about taxes and bizarre research projects, but don't forget the Pledge of Allegiance.

And Annie, after eleven years of reciting it five days a week from September through May, decided early in her senior year that she wasn't so sure the words rang true. She'd sung *Oh beautiful for spacious skies* plenty of times, too, and *land of the free and the home of the brave,* and, like most of the roughly two thousand students at LWH, reluctantly lent an ear each morning when a faintly scratchy static heralded the morning's announcements. The loudspeaker through which the voices arrived was covered in something that wanted to be black leather and was hung front and center in the classroom: . . . *the senior class project brought in x amount of dollars; the prom possibilities are looking better every* . . . She had sold a reasonable number of Christmas candles, ugly glass jars with cheap white wax poured into them and your choice of green, red, or gold glitter sprayed on the glass. Junior year they'd sold trash bags. At least those were functional. She remembered pale industrial-tile floors, spent no small time studying them, light green and beige, the same colors as the floor at the place that gave out drivers' licenses. Every place you went that was associated with the state of Texas had these tiles in them. How many square feet? She wished her father were selling those instead of whatever it was he was selling this month. He said it didn't matter. He was a salesman; he could sell anything. So it didn't matter. What did? The prom? Annie listened as the principal, who wore his hair like Elvis Presley but never jiggled his hips, and who ordered the boys to keep their locks trimmed to certain standards—his—thanked the senior class treasurer. And then whoever it was who'd exhibited outstanding citizenship and therefore been awarded the honor of leading the pledge came on. Annie pulled herself to her feet slowly, under the glare of Miss Watkins, the token female coach of the girl's track team. Miss Watkins didn't want to coach anything or anybody. She wasn't an athlete nor was she interested in athletics. She taught geometry and dated Coach Smith. Annie placed her hand over her heart and kept her mouth shut. Miss Watkins let her own mouth drop open, to express her dismay, her utter and unabashed disbelief.

A few days later Coach Smith caught Annie in the hallway outside the room where he taught biology and told her to see him at practice that afternoon. They walked the infield, covered with a thick lush grass gone strawlike for the winter. He told her how it was. As a member of the track team she had an obligation to set an example for others.

By the end of the week, when Annie still wouldn't recite, the argument had come down to the level of "I know I can count on you to bring home points at a meet, and besides, you're going to State this year, I'd hate to lose you over this." Say the pledge or I'll have to kick you off the team. You love running and this is probably your last chance to do it. There aren't a lot of athletic scholarships around for girls; the money goes back where it came from: into football. You'll be raising babies soon. This is your last season. The flag will be around forever. You're making me crazy. I'll see you after practice in my office.

Last season. Raising babies? No way. Asshole. He was an unabashed jerk. She jogged away, leaped a hurdle that someone had left sitting near the forty-yard line on the infield. Her form was accomplished, but she knew what Coach Smith was looking at. Later, she'd gone to his office, as instructed.

The plane droned away in the direction of the Hudson, and Annie snapped back. Stepped forward to run, brought her thoughts back to pace. Downhill now, and leveling off, and then downhill again. She ran and breathed and ran and loved the sunshine as it slipped between leaves just going red and yellow and orange. Air bit the back of her throat; she swigged from a small bottle of water without slowing.

She ran and ran and here came Texas again, carrying the pale bronze of an autumn afternoon when she'd arrived home from school to a sudden and unexpected lecture from her mother, who sat at the kitchen table and read to her from a pamphlet. *"It is a known fact that one of the primary aims of the Communist Party in Russia is to infiltrate and destroy America's youth with drugs."* When her mother dropped the pamphlet to her side and pursed her lips, all Annie could wonder was whether she, Annie, was being accused of having joined the Communists. That was what her mother seemed to be saying, but Annie didn't know any Communists, had never even heard the word uttered, except on television and when they went to visit her father's parents so father and son could wind up in shouting matches. Why couldn't her mom talk to her about track, or her grades, or what she was reading? So Communists were plotting to take over America by destroying its youth with drugs. They were all the way in Russia. Might as well be Jupiter. Even if they succeeded, what would be the fun in taking over a nation of drug addicts? Annie sat listening as the Chasm expanded. No wonder her friends took dope. But she knew some seniors who had signed up for the Marines already and were watching Viet Nam wind down with dismay. Sophomore year and a total drag to be stuck in Dallas, too young to be a hippie, or maybe just not enough guts to thumb out to

San Francisco. She had answered honestly: No, Mom, I've never taken anything like that. And then dishonestly: No, none of my friends do either.

Still going to church even, Saint Somebody of Infinite Mercy, but all she saw when she got on her knees was the wall above the altar with this statue of an emaciated male body nailed to a cross with blood dripping down his face and blood dripping out of a hole in his side and blood dripping out of the holes in his hands and feet. And it seemed to her that though the book said this was salvation, it was really barbarism, meant to scare the parishioners witless. During all of her childhood, even into her first semester at NYU, once a year she knelt at the altar rail to take the smear of ash on her forehead meant to remind her she was dirt.

A few months later, her answers about taking drugs would have been insincere, but not outright lies. She'd smoked some pot by then. Only a couple of times. But the pamphlet had already been lost in a drawer in the kitchen where her mother hated to cook, and a silence so thick had fallen between mother and daughter that nothing would have been mentioned even had Annie's mom noted her daughter's bloodshot eyes and the heavy application of Jean Naté to cover up the smell of reefer. The argument had begun over career plans—Annie told her mother she wanted to be an artist instead of a legal secretary—and was still in place. Her mother, who had grown up second youngest in a family of six boys and two girls, remembered what it was like to endure World War II rationing and wanted her daughter to have a steady and decent-paying job. Annie could think of nothing more soul-killing. And her mother added the inevitable coda to the discussion: "Whatever you do, don't just rush out there and get married and have kids." Annie nodded and thought, "Don't worry."

She slowed her pace, fell into a fast walk, began noticing the mushrooms that had sprung up in the moist black soil of the road. She recognized the brilliant orange cap, spotted yellow, of the *Amanita muscaria,* fly agaric, felt the flutter of something like fright in her chest. Kurt had told her about these; she'd never seen one. Thought about picking it, drying it, eating it, but left it. It wasn't Russian, it was American; all it would do would be to put her into a stupor. She left it to grow and do whatever it did with its mushroom existence. *Kurt is in jail. Kurt is in jail.*

She kicked up her pace for the final downhill plunge, steep, rocky, and treacherous. She pushed it, picking her way, working not to stumble on stones, ducking the low branches of saplings, leaping as much as running. Speed was irrelevant here; what mattered now was agility.

•

Carol called her out of the shower to take the phone.

The voice, rapid-fire and sonorous at once: "I've seen him, he's okay, they didn't rough him up, your dog's in his truck parked at the mall in Kingston. Don't talk to anyone and meet me in my office at eight Monday morning."

"Mark," Annie said. "How are you?"

"Pumped," he said. "These bastards. How are you?"

"An agent told me they matched tire prints from the truck. I assumed they had Kane too."

"It's a bureaucracy, Annie. None of them knows what's going on. Can you get to the mall and find the truck? Kurt's worried."

"Is he okay?"

"I told you, he's fine. I'd let you know—"

"Of course. I'm on my way."

"I've got no paperwork on the truck, and none on the dog. I'll try to get some. Don't talk about the case—to anyone. If you need anything, call me." He gave her his cell phone number and hung up.

Annie dripped back into the shower and rinsed her hair, trying to massage some sort of rationality in through the bones of her skull. The thought hacked away incessantly at her. She couldn't escape it for more than a few minutes at a time. They had him. They had Kurt. How could she have been so stupid as to let him go on with it? Let him? She hadn't let him do anything. He did what he did. She'd made her wishes known. Or thought she had. Maybe he just hadn't heard her. Maybe he had. She closed her eyes, pressed her palms against her temples, a steady, gentle touch. It would work out. She would find some way to get him out and keep him out. She had to; that's all.

The boys were still asleep, Alex's head pushed up against Tim's stomach so that their bodies formed a kind of curled T. She wanted to be there when they awoke, to catch their sleepy smiles and eager hugs and welcome them to the day. Tomorrow, maybe.

The phone rang just as she was headed out the door.

A recorded voice, female, rather prim. Annie recognized the A T & T woman from Lewisburg, Pennsylvania. Each prison had its own phone system and particular operator voice. "You have a collect call from a prisoner at a federal correctional institution. Caller, at the tone, state your name—"

"Dan." His voice was flat with a mix of boredom and anger at having to go through the procedure. Seven years for pot. Two kids, five and eight, living in Albuquerque with their mom while he finished up his last fifteen months. One of several of Kurt's friends Annie had met only via telephone, because they'd been locked up since before she got married. They sent pictures at Christmas. They talked about lockdowns and horrid food and bad doctors; they talked about the young kids coming in so violent and all; and they talked always about missing their families.

She listened to the rest of A T & T's lecture about not using three-way calling or call forwarding or you *will* be disconnected, got the cue to press 1, and said hello.

"Oooh," Dan said, "maybe I should call back. Are you okay?"

"Monday evening," Annie said. "He should be back by then."

"Away?"

"Detained."

"Oh, man. Sorry to hear it. We've got no phones Monday. I'll try Tuesday."

She drove, worried almost sick over the dog, pissed at Kurt for taking him, angry at Kurt for going in the first place, angry at him for staying in the business so long and not listening to her, and angry at him for every infraction, minor or major, that he'd ever committed against their relationship. Angry at him, period. Not sure how to get un-angry. Single motherhood; hey, Kurt, there's a fun game. Single parenthood. A bitch in need is a bitch indeed. Dan's wife had taken their kids and moved away, gone into hiding or something. Shamed. Annie thought she might do the same. She wondered what prison and separation from them would do to Kurt.

She'd learned about it from her father—separation—and wondered who had taught him. They had not spoken for some years. She missed him terribly, but that was it: she'd been missing him for most of her life. She had no idea who he was or what he believed in, and doubted she ever would. And that was what would happen if Kurt was taken away: he would become someone she no longer knew, someone she missed.

Maybe Carol wasn't the only one who chose jerks. Maybe Jerk Destiny was encoded in their chromosomes somewhere, a gene sequence straight from Dad: love me, love me, love me, and if you don't love me, then love somebody just like me—someone incapable of communicating with you, who can't express his own feelings but thinks the reason he can't communicate is that women are somehow inferior, not capable of understanding him. Their brains are smaller, for God's sake. They must be dumber than men.

But Kurt wasn't like that. He was the first and only one who'd convinced her that she was lovable. And she knew, whatever else might be the case, that he loved her truly. It was in his eyes when he brought coffee and the Sunday *Times* for them to scatter all over the bed. It was in his arms when he wrestled with their children. It was in his hands late at night when the candle flame warmed the room and he rubbed lavender oil into her back, her shoulders, her legs.

The parking lot surrounding the mall was a giant black scab on the surface of the wounded earth. Annie drove slowly, circling the anchors—Kmart, JCPenney, Sears, and Hess's—God Save the Queen. She circled and tried to shake her mood and looked for Kurt's candy-apple red GMC. They should make a nail polish that color.

Three trips around, slowly, watching shoppers hop in eagerly and stroll out languidly, as though someone inside the massive complex were distributing the ultimate mood-leveling drug. She went around once more, convinced that she was somehow looking right at it and not seeing it.

It wasn't there. It simply wasn't there. Where was Kane?

She took the back roads home, wound past the animal shelter, saw four dogs imprisoned in four chain-link cages. Mixed breeds all, they yelped desperately for attention as Annie drove slowly past.

·

She was only a few confused steps from the Jeep when she had to stop and set herself for the boys' tackles. They'd been playing on the porch with Carol, and ran fiercely toward Annie when they spotted her. Alex arrived first, throwing his right shoulder square into her left thigh and wrapping his arms around her leg, trying, she was sure, to knock her flat on her back. Tim was right behind him, not yet ready to leap the way Alex did, but able to hit with no small impact. They each had a leg now, and their feet moved steadily as they growled and tried to take her down.

She sat and grabbed them both in a hug, began rolling on the grass. They squealed and giggled and squeaked out, "No, Mommy, stop! Mommy, stop!"

Annie watched as they jumped up and began running in circles around a tree, yelling and waving their arms wildly.

"Annie." Carol walked over, sat down next to her. Annie turned to her sister. Carol was heavily into makeup, always had been: she changed colors seasonally. She had almost modeled, an agency up Dallas, but Ron, her soon-to-be ex, vetoed the idea immediately, the creep. Today her hair was in a French braid.

"I'm thinking it's time for me to head home."

"Home to what?" Annie asked.

"To a place where I don't have to worry that the cops are going to show up and kick down the front door."

"Carol, they've done it. It's over. They won't—"

"No, Annie, listen to me. I'm scared. You can't live like this. You can't do this to them." They looked in unison at the boys, who were running in large circles around the front lawn.

"What do I do?" Annie said. "Walk away from him? It would kill them. You know how they love him. And so do I. Maybe you disagree with what he's doing or done or whatever, but he's my husband. Anyway, he understands now."

"Oh. Gee. And all they had to do was put him in jail."

"I'm not going to up and leave him because the law has come snooping around."

"What if we'd been here? What if the boys had—"

"Nobody got hurt."

"Luck. That's all. *You are a mother.* You have to think about your children."

"Don't you think I do?" The edge in her voice caught the boys' attention; they stopped in their tracks and looked over at her. "Sorry, guys," she called to them. "It's okay." She lowered her voice and turned to Carol. "Every waking moment, and a good portion of my sleeping ones, they are with me. Don't tell me to think about my children. Don't accuse me of not loving."

Carol said softly, "Well, that was always it, wasn't it?"

"What?" Annie snapped. "As in, if you aren't willing to sacrifice your happiness for me, then you must not love me? I've had quite enough of that, thank you very much. Pass it on down the table."

"He's not being fair to you. He's not being fair to them."

"Carol," Annie said, "we cherish them. Do they seem unhappy to you?"

"He's in jail. And they're going to put him in prison."

"You don't know that."

"You can't possibly think they'll let him off."

"Just because they arrest you doesn't mean they have a case. Innocent until proven guilty? You've heard the concept?"

"They're going to put him in prison."

Annie stared at her. "All I can say is it's a good thing you won't be on the jury, because you're ready to send him away right now, before he's even had a trial, for God's sake."

Carol glared at her, the glare she'd used all her life to express her anger at Annie, the source of which seemed to be almost everything Annie did and everything she thought and everything she felt and even how she dressed.

"He told you he would stop a long time ago," Carol said. "And he didn't. And now he's been caught."

"What is it? Is it that if I don't leave my husband the way you and Mom did that I'm somehow not being a good mother?"

"Look, he says he would be in the business even if it was legal—"

"I'm sure he would."

"Forget it," Carol said. "He wouldn't have anything to do with it. It would only be farming, anyway. Raising crops. And the money wouldn't be nearly as good."

"Unless the big corporations got involved."

"Annie."

"What?" The word came out angry, resentful.

"You're missing my point."

"No, I'm not. You're calling my husband a liar."

"I'm saying that he's a gambler. An addict."

Annie saw her look, measuring.

"Have you considered," Carol added, "that he might even be happy if he has to go into hiding and leave you all behind?"

She had, but would not admit it. She would never admit that to her sister. "We went for a walk one afternoon," she said, "Kurt and I. We'd found the right person to watch the shop, he knew antiques, he was trustworthy, and he was cool about dope. Alex was going on three, and I was four months along with Timothy. I thought Kurt was out of it by then. He'd promised before we tried for Timothy. He hadn't been sure he wanted a second child, but I persuaded him it would be better for Alex, better for all of us. And I wanted another baby, Carol. As much as I'd been afraid the first time around, the second I was that fearless. And once we'd committed, Kurt was into it all the way. Swore he was getting out once and for all, and he threw a lot of time into the shop, fixing it up, acquiring pieces. I thought he was enjoying it, and I thought that was the source of our income.

"And he *was* enjoying it. But then we went for this walk and he told me he'd just brought two thousand pounds into Louisiana. Not cocaine. Not heroin. Not alcohol or tobacco. I mean, Carol, come on. You smoke a joint yourself now and then."

"Only at parties."

"So?"

"It's different."

"What's different? If there weren't people like Kurt, bringing it in, you wouldn't have the luxury of firing up at that party. You think I should leave him because he brings over in bulk something you and millions of other people use a little bit at a time? Or is it just that you think I should leave him and that's as good a reason as you can come up with?"

"It's illegal. That makes it dangerous."

"So I should split and do what? Take the boys to Mother's?"

"I would."

"You can't say what you would or wouldn't do. But I believe you. You depend on her for everything."

"Wrong," Carol said flatly. "But I look at those kids and I know I would do anything for them."

"So would Kurt," Annie said. "And so would I. Including everything I can to keep their family in one piece. That is the most important thing for them. Their family. Why are you so eager to watch it fall apart?"

"I'm not, goddamit!" Carol lowered her voice. "He's risking your life and he's risking the lives of your children. Can't you see that?"

"Oh, come on, Carol, the cops aren't going to shoot us. I mean, yes, I was scared out of my mind last night. One of them held a—" She stopped cold, shuddered. There was a sore spot between her shoulder blades where the cop had planted his knee. He'd had a gun to her head. A gun. To her head. And it hit her, suddenly, that the only reason he hadn't fired was that he hadn't been sure he could get away with it. Her brain went leaden. He had wanted to kill her. That was the thing she had felt but refused to feel. He had *wanted* to kill her. He wasn't supposed to want to, but he did. He had.

She tapped her forehead. *Hello, in there? Anybody home? I know we're all sleepy and shocked and all that, but it took us almost twelve hours to really understand how close we came to getting killed last night. Let's stay on our neurological toes, shall we?*

"Annie?"

"It's over. They won't be back."

"How can you deny it? You think they'll just go away and not bother you anymore?"

"It's a court thing now."

"They broke down your front door."

"I'm not leaving him, Carol. I'm not going to tear apart my family."

They cooled, seeming to realize at once that neither was going to convince the other. Leave it on the table with the rest of their differences.

"I asked myself what I was doing," Carol said, "hiding out up here, trying to keep from giving Ron a divorce. Like, finally, why am I going to such lengths to hold on to a total asshole. Enough of that nonsense. She can have him, and good riddance to both of them."

"They'll live miserably ever after."

"He'll divorce her, too. I bet he'll have five or six wives, maybe eight or nine, before he's done."

"What do you all see in him?"

"It's not what you see," Carol said. "It's what you don't see."

"He picked you. Surely you think he has some discrimination."

"You haven't met his new sweetheart."

"She was your friend."

"She was never my friend. If she'd ever been my friend, even for just a few minutes, she wouldn't have run off with my husband."

"You should thank her."

"Maybe I should send her up here."

They laughed, wanting not to fight.

"It's something in the water down there," Carol said. "Us Texans—"

"We Texans—"

"Shut up," Carol said, smiling. "You're not a Texan anymore. No self-respecting Texan would say 'we Texans.' There's no such thing as a wee Texan. Us Texans do love to marry and divorce. I'll be the last in my club to go through with the paperwork.

"I'll miss you all," she continued, "but the truth is I'm scared. I can't stay here."

"Yes you could."

"I want things to be normal. I think my nephews deserve a normal life. My sister deserves a normal life."

"Like we had normal? Not for me." They were so much alike, she and Carol. They were so different. "You have to understand. Before I met Kurt

I didn't even think I wanted a family. I certainly didn't walk around hoping for one."

"Not that you'd admit to yourself."

"You know why? Because, hey, what's a family but bickering, anger, and incessant worry? Why should I have wanted a family?"

"Sometimes I think we grew up in separate households."

"I saw what I saw."

"Me too. I know Mom loves us, and Dad too, in his way."

"So do I. I hold nothing against them. I just don't want to subject myself to all the grief. Maybe you see that as selfish, but I see it like *Why be part of that?*"

"It's life."

"It doesn't have to be."

"What, somebody dies and you just skip the funeral and pretend it never happened?"

"No. You go to the funeral and you say good-bye and offer your love and consolation to the other living."

"I'd rather die than go to a funeral."

"At least there's a time limit. A few hours at a funeral is an awful lot easier to endure than half a lifetime of bickering and hatred."

"But here you are. Madame Earthmother, living in the country, raising a family."

"Who'd've thought." Annie chuckled at herself. "I'm out with the boys, the older women we pass always smile, their faces light up, and you can tell they're remembering their time with young children. I'll be like that, I'm sure. Some younger women give you these glances, you know, like *How can you possibly consign yourself to motherhood?* I catch nothing but fear and anguish from them, but it goes away. And I see them and think *There but for the grace.*"

"You see that in me?"

"No. But I think one reason you see so many jerks is that you're looking for one to marry."

"I think I'm through with marriage."

"C'mon. Only one divorce? What will your friends think?"

"It's the cowboy thing," Carol said. "That's what messes everything up for Southwest women."

"I got a good piece of advice from Granny. She said never let a cowboy get up on the roof of your house, because if you do, he will fall off it intentionally just to gain your sympathy. I never thought I'd have children, Carol, until I met him. And I guess the problem is that I'm still astonished at the joy of it."

"Is this a pep talk?" Carol smiled, saw Annie's face. "Sorry," she said.

That was her way. Always had been.

"So what are you going to do?" she asked.

"Get Kurt out of jail. We'll take it from there."

They looked at each other, and mimicked together: *"I have to talk to Kurt."*

Annie's laugh was genuine, but she knew herself enough to recognize that panic was wending its slithery way into the part of her brain that would give it free expression.

"There's a carnival in Rhinebeck," Carol said.

"They'll love it," Annie said, getting up and dusting herself off. Kurt was beyond help until Monday, and soon the boys would start asking for him and for Kane. Diversion was essential.

•

The women stood at a pale green rail with the rest of the grownups, watching Alex and Timothy go in circles. The boys sat, each in his own brightly painted pink-and-green dragon, the beast just the right mix of fierce and goofy to reliably catch children's attention.

"You're blessed, you know," Carol said after a moment. "Look at them."

Timothy had taken the cue from the kids around him and was steering enthusiastically, his fine hair glinting copper in the noonday light. Alex had figured out that it didn't matter which direction he turned the wheel on the dragon's head; the ride was going where it was going. Still, he liked it enough to smile and wave when he whirled past Carol and Annie.

"Nothing like a carnival to make you feel like a grownup," Carol said.

"Especially when it's a real-life one," Annie replied. She watched the kids going 'round and 'round and pushed back the panic. It would overtake her if she let herself worry for even one horrible instant how her children would fare if the authorities decided to throw her into jail with her husband.

A tap on her shoulder jerked her attention from the boys and sent her heart banging; she tried to say hello to the couple who lived down the road but found herself stuttering. The Aldersons laughed at her surprise and, in doing so, helped her recover. Laura, who worked part time at the shop, exchanged hugs with Annie. Mike, dark-headed, easily six feet two, was holding their daughter, Lacy, who waved wildly each time Alex came around in his dragon.

"Annie," Laura said seriously, "how are you?"

Annie nodded okay.

"Kurt's in the city?" Mike asked. Annie nodded again. "So what happened?"

"It's stopping," Carol said. "We'd better get the boys." Annie excused herself and went with Carol.

Lacy squirmed out of Mike's arms when she saw Alex approaching. She and Alex ran for each other, embracing and giggling deliriously when they met.

"Annie," Laura said, "tell us what happened. Last night, Carol and the boys, and we heard the plane, too." She fell in next to Annie, behind Alex and Lacy, who were tugging Carol toward an inflated two-story-tall lime-colored thing full of jumping, bouncing, laughing, pushing, yelling children.

A plane. She'd nursed Timothy after Kurt left, and hadn't got back to sleep until almost four. Now she remembered hearing something, dimly, just around dawn, a noise that seemed to go on and on through the fog of a sleep that had finally descended and was so delicious she couldn't bear to think of waking up.

Tim strained against her arms, wanting to be with his brother. Mike reached for him.

"C'mere, you," Mike said, his voice dropping from its usual soft baritone into a tough-guy growl. Tim responded immediately, letting himself fall from Annie's arms into Mike's.

Laura started to ask something, but Annie cut her off quickly, turning her attention to the green thing.

"Just look at them," she said, laughing at Alex and Lacy. They were into it, trying to copy the big kids' moves as they threw their bodies recklessly about the open-ended rubber room.

Laura took her arm and said, "Tell me what happened."

"The cops raided our place—"

"I know that. Carol was quite upset."

"It was awful."

"We heard the plane crash, Annie. Now tell me what happened."

"You did?"

"You mean you didn't?"

"I must've slept through it."

"You couldn't have. Everyone in the valley heard it. And everybody knows the cops raided your house, too. We heard Kurt was arrested. Talk to me!"

"They have Kurt. And they could have taken me in for a little personal stash they found in the kitchen, but they didn't."

"Is he okay?"

"They think he brought in a big load of pot."

"An entire *planeload?* Annie, are you—"

"Am I what?"

"Am I like—"

"Whatever is going on has nothing to do with the shop. I know that much."

"God, I hope so," Laura said.

Annie wanted to tell her how the drug agents had smashed her home and how frightened she'd been.

"I don't really know what's going on at this point," she said.

"I always wondered how you guys did so well with such a little shop."

"He didn't do it, Laura." She couldn't tell whether Laura believed her.

"This is horrible," Laura said finally. "What can we do?"

"The bail hearing's day after tomorrow. We have a lawyer . . ."

"I can't believe this. Are you okay?"

Annie, listening, felt that none of it—the rides, the garish music of the kiddies' midway, her friend's voice—none of it was real. She reached for the railing that separated her from the green thing full of children and held on until the dizziness passed.

On to the exhibits. The huge poultry barn was open and airy, its shade welcome after the time in the baking sun. It smelled of fresh straw, and the floor, smooth concrete, was spotless.

Timothy was enjoying a rest in his stroller, taking in the chickens and turkeys and clutching a lemonade. Alex and Lacy held hands and walked carefully down the aisles between the stacked cages, amazed at the plumage on some of the more exotic birds.

Annie bent on one knee to point out a pair of hens to Tim. They were white with black spots and had impressive topknots of the same feathers sprouting from their heads like water from a fountain. She was reminded of runway models in *haute couture.*

The turkeys, two rows over, were huge and alert; when one of them cut loose with a loud and demanding gobble, Alex and Lacy jumped back and scanned for their parents. Annie caught Alex's eye and smiled; he moved toward her.

"Loud, eh?" Annie said. He nodded and slipped his hand into hers.

She saw a man watching the exchange with an amused smile, and then realized he was smiling not at her and Alex, but at her. He stepped forward and offered a hand.

"Annie." As if they were long-lost friends. "Remember me?"

Eric. She stood smiling and fighting the ugly memories bombarding her brain: all the times she'd phoned him and all the times he'd come through for her during that weird year and a half when he'd sold her cocaine, sold her consolation, feeding the monster that was caged in her skull, talking so nicely to it. He always knew just what to say so that she wouldn't feel guilty about buying his drugs.

She introduced Eric around, and Laura took it on herself to herd the crew a few cages down, leaving Annie and Eric to talk.

He hadn't changed much: cropped brown hair, clean-shaven. His face was a bit drawn, as though he'd missed a night's sleep. He wore khakis and a white dress shirt, collar open and sleeves rolled, Topsiders, with a small camera bag draped over his shoulder. He had the air of one who was traveling solo.

"Still taking pictures," he was saying. "Doing okay with it, I suppose, though I'm bored with fashion. I'm thinking about war. May pop over to Beirut, take a few rolls. Trying to decide. You? Married, I presume? Your kids are beautiful."

Annie watched him talk.

"Your husband?" Eric was looking around, trying to guess.

"He's not here," Annie said. "How is it you—"

"I have a place near Millbrook now. Weekender, you know, and summers pretty much. I've been coming here for several years. It's like time travel."

"We're across the river."

"Woodstock?"

"No." Annie laughed. "Not quite hip enough for that action."

She was ready to move on, but did not wish to seem rude. *But why not? Why not seem rude? Why even worry about it?*

"So who'd you marry?" Eric asked. "Why wasn't I invited to the wedding? I'd've taken pictures."

"You met him," Annie said. "I think it may even have been the last time we saw each other."

"When?"

"At that party. You wouldn't remember."

"Happily married?"

"No complaints."

"What does he do?"

"We're in antiques."

"Lovely. So where is he?"

"He's in MCC," Annie blurted out, not sure why, except that she was put off by his high-and-mighty tone as well as his questions. Her answer worked; he appeared stunned.

"He's in jail?"

"You know the place?"

"Only through acquaintances." He'd been, maybe still was, a coke dealer. Of course he would know it. "I'm sorry to hear it," he said. "What for?"

"Marijuana, they say."

"God, can you believe they're still arresting people for *that?*" He put a hand on her shoulder. She couldn't remember him ever being so sincere, but he seemed genuinely sympathetic.

"I'm really sorry to hear it. How long has he been in? I know a very good lawyer, a great lawyer in fact . . ." He was digging in his camera bag. He pulled out a card and handed it to her. "Is there something I can do?" The questions came rapid-fire; he retrieved the card, wrote a number on it, and handed it back. "My place up here," he said. "Listen, I know it's been a while, but I hope you'll call me. Call me if I can help. Any way at all." He was closing his bag, preparing to leave. He leaned and kissed her cheek. "It'll work out," he said. "Call me. I'm not just saying that. Call me."

She watched him wind through the crowd and disappear out the wide-open doors of the exhibit barn. How quickly the mention of jail chased people away.

The afternoon was turning pale; time to think about heading home. She looked at Eric's card for the first time. It was a woodblock print of a bearded fellow in a tall, cone-shaped hat, grinning mischievously. Next to it, centered:

THE WIZARD OF ID
PHOTOGRAPHY, ENGRAVING
JUNGIAN ANALYSIS

A PO box in Manhattan and an 800 number were printed along the bottom. She tucked the card in a pocket and caught up with the others, greeting Alex's searching eyes with a smile. Timothy was sprawled in his stroller, asleep, his face the picture of peace. Annie envied him.

"Old beau?" Laura asked.

"Old connection," Annie replied.

"Oh. Sorry."

"Don't apologize," Annie said. "He was much nicer than I remembered him."

•

She might not have noticed the black plastic bag on the front porch except that she was concerned about the broken door. Carol, catching the look on Annie's face, steered the boys around toward the garage entrance. Kurt's truck was parked in the driveway.

"Daddy's home!" Alex shouted when he saw it.

"Daddy! Daddy! Daddy!" Tim echoed.

"No," Carol said softly. "Just his truck. He won't be home until Monday." Annie heard Tim's voice trail into the garage: "Is Monday this day?"

She knew before she stepped onto the porch what was inside the trash bag. She walked slowly closer, pressed a hand against it, shuddered at how cold it was, and did not fight the tears that stung her eyes. She pulled open the plastic. There was a single small bullethole, ringed in blood, in the white fur covering Kane's forehead. His eyes were open, gone milky. She pushed his eyelids down, pulling at the rims of his eyes to get them to stay shut. Goddamn whoever did this.

She had daydreamed often of the days Alex and Tim would spend romping through the woods, of how safe they would be with their big white shepherd. He was their protector. He was her protector. It was Kane who made her feel secure on the nights Kurt was away. She did not know what Kurt would do when she told him.

She had dug holes before, in the garden, but this was her first grave. Kane's body was curled at her feet. She reached to touch him but pulled back. She had known she depended on him; she hadn't realized how much she loved him.

An hour later, the sunset was threatening and there were rocks everywhere, laid into the earth like part of some 3D jigsaw puzzle. She wasn't a foot and a half deep. She rested the shovel and walked in the direction of the spring. She would have to call Mike Alderson. The rocks were too big.

SEVEN

The September sun had cracked over Manhattan like an undercooked egg, spreading warm and yellow and sticky over the entire island. It wasn't yet ten, and already the temperature had hit seventy-eight. From the feel of things, the humidity was hovering somewhere in the same neighborhood. Annie coughed futilely against a cloud of diesel fumes that spewed from the back of an idling bus just as she passed it.

Five sweltering blocks and one icy receptionist later, she was sitting on a black leather couch, its back cool against hers, which was covered with sweat. Outside the window behind her, Eighty-sixth Street sent traffic noises skyward from twelve stories below. Mark's office looked more like that of a shrink than a lawyer, but he considered himself an adequate practitioner of both arts. Lawyers made people crazy, he thought, and he did his best to mitigate that for his clients.

There was no desk, only a table with bony metal legs and a thick glass top in the corner opposite the one where Annie was. A baby grand sat plumply toward the middle of the long, rectangular room, before a wall of thoroughly stuffed bookcases. On the wall opposite the bookcases were a few ink drawings by the notorious Ace McGowan, a man Annie's favorite art history professor had a few years ago referred to as one of the "worst offenders." These inks were innocuous, though, no neo-Cubist misogynist twists wrenched into the female bodies portrayed. They were, in fact, quite lovely: simply done, black line on white paper. Playful, even.

Mark strode in and was across the room in three steps, planting huge kisses on each of Annie's cheeks and squeezing her shoulders with affection.

"How are you?" His voice surrounded her, its confidence warm and soothing. He sat her back down on the couch and moved to his table.

"Will he stay?" Mark asked, searching his satchel for papers that would put the Texas property in hock at the federal pawn shop. Maybe things would work out. Maybe they'd be able to keep it. Kurt had always seen the ranch as his ticket to legitimacy. They had taken the place upstate with the intention of eventually moving to Texas—when Kurt was no longer using the ranch as a warehouse and distribution center. But they'd grown to love the area; they'd established the store and Alex had arrived and house became home and then Timothy came along and the house became chaos, but even homier. Annie sat forward to let her back dry.

"I wouldn't bet the ranch on it," she answered.

"Ha," Mark said, pulling out the papers. "Well, that's exactly what you're doing, but we both know that."

"We're a family, Mark. He won't run."

"You could get a bondsman for fifty Gs cash."

"We'd better hang on to our cash," Annie said. "Got to pay the lawyer."

"Indeed you do, my dear," he said. "I'll be your best friend forever."

He signaled her to the table, ran a hand through his Einsteinian hair, and offered his pen. She guessed him at six-six; he was the tallest man she knew.

"Bound to've happened," Mark said. "I've been urging him to get out for years."

"Haven't we all. They killed our dog. Left his body in a trash bag on the front porch."

"Good God," he said. "Miserable sons of bitches." He spread his hands on the table and wilted onto his arms, then raised his head. "I'm sorry, Annie. I know what it's like to lose a dog. I'm sorry."

She thanked him. He gathered himself and again offered her the pen, arranged the papers neatly on the table, ordering them for her signature.

"Look," he said, "if I know Kurt, he did everything he possibly could to piss them off."

"He's grown out of that, Mark."

"Maybe." He sighed. "Anyway, there's nothing we can do about that. Let's just stay cool here and get him out."

"He'll go nuts."

"That's precisely why they did it."

"I can't believe this is happening."

He leaned across the table. "Annie, I'm sorry. Kurt's one of my oldest friends. I love him. But things are changing. The Colombian hoods will do more than shoot your dog if you make them angry."

"We have nothing to do with them."

He got up and walked to the window. "Yeah, yeah, yeah," he said. "Peace and love. Brotherhood. Don't forget, I was at Columbia in 'sixty-eight."

"How could I?" Annie tried a smile. "You won't let anyone forget."

"Hey, I don't claim to be Bill Kunstler."

"I'm thankful you're around to defend Kurt. If you're a sellout, at least you're a brilliant sellout."

"Thank you, I think." He came back to the table. "Are you okay?"

Things that were supposed to be thoughts were zipping around in her head, but she couldn't latch on to them. Was she okay? That was the question. She guessed she had to be and nodded.

"Good." He packed the papers in his briefcase. "Let's go get him."

As they entered the empty elevator, he put an arm around her shoulders. "I don't think they have much on him," he whispered. "And they've got nothing on you. You're lucky." For a long moment their faces were so close, she could see the tiny veins in the whites of his ice-blue eyes. "Or else you're very careful."

•

Kurt looked as if he'd been out in the woods for days—his clothes dirty and wrinkled, three days' growth on his face, his hair uncombed and spiked at odd angles, and he'd lost perhaps five pounds. When he fell against Annie in a hug, the smells coming off him wanted to push her away, but she held tight. She hadn't often sensed in him the fear that emanated from him now. There was something else, too, a recognition of danger, an edge, a wariness that she'd seen in him only rarely.

"The boys okay?" he asked. She nodded.

"You?"

"You know me," she said.

He put his lips to her ear. "I'm sorry," he whispered. "I'm so, so sorry. I didn't—"

"It's okay," she said. "Everyone's okay."

"You found Kane?"

She took a breath, wishing she knew what to say or how to say it. He looked at her, waiting for an explanation.

"Someone shot him," she said. "They left him on the front porch."

His face clenched with pain, then rage. She took his hands and held tight. He let his head roll to one side and she could see he was swallowing back tears.

Mark cleared his throat.

"Miserable motherfuckers," Kurt whispered.

"I'm sorry, Kurt." Mark said. "But he's gone and there's nothing to do about that. I'm sorry. They have thirty days to indict."

Annie felt her knees give. Mark shifted his case into his left hand and stretched out his right to Kurt.

"Think about who's gonna roll."

"They get anybody else?"

"Doesn't appear so, but I'm not sure. Make some calls. Let me know." Mark shook Annie's hand and pecked her cheeks and walked away, leaving them standing in the shadow cast by the monolithic brick tower of MCC New York. Someone had painted large neon-pink letters on the wall near the main entrance: *Carmine Persico slept here.*

Annie took Kurt's hand. "Let's go," she said.

He was dazed, sitting behind the wheel. Annie was concerned about whether he should drive.

"No," he said. "I'm okay. I just need food." He started the engine and pulled toward street level in the dank garage. "And floss," he added. He had always been meticulous about his teeth. Three nights without brushing had left his tongue coated with disgusting fur.

He sat in the idling Jeep while she got bananas and mangoes and cherries and so forth at a Korean stand on the Upper West Side before they headed north toward the George Washington Bridge.

"Where is he?" Kurt asked.

"We buried him up on the ridge. Mike helped me."

"God," Kurt said. "Are you really okay, baby, or being brave?"

"They scared the shit out of me," Annie said. "Figuratively speaking."

"Question you?" He handed her some cherries.

"I didn't give them anything," she said.

"What did you think of that Kessler guy?"

"How'd you know his—"

"He transferred me from the county lockup. Told me all about you. I think he's in love."

"Yeah, right." She snorted.

"He said you were scared."

"How would he know? And why would he care?"

"I'm just telling you what he said. I'm sorry you went through that."

"So am I."

"Which one killed—"

"I don't know. He was such a good dog." She felt tears coming on and tried to blink them back, but had to reach for a tissue. "One of them found some stash in the pantry. They could have taken me in. Kessler wouldn't let them."

"What'd he say?"

"Nothing. He pretended it was oregano and nobody called him on it."

"Wonder why."

"Who knows? They missed your stash, though. Thank goodness, or they would have had to arrest me, I'm sure."

"They were pissed, huh."

"They were pissed off long before they knocked down the door, sweetheart." She rolled down the window and popped a cherry pit out.

"Uh-oh," he said.

Annie smiled at him. "It's biodegradable."

"Not that," he said. "I know I'm in trouble when you call me sweetheart."

"No," she said. She took his hand, starting to feel sufficient distance between them and the jail. "Though one of those jerkoffs was kind enough to refer to me as that. There's a bruise on my back where another one rested his knee for half an hour."

"Assholes."

"I figure I got out light."

She saw him glance at her. He thought she was hiding something.

"I'm okay," she said. "I'm fine. They didn't really hurt me. Not really."

"You'd tell me."

"Of course."

"Don't they get it? I'm the one, not you, not my boys. They had no business whatsoever to do that while I was gone. This is so fucked."

"Kurt," Annie said, "if one of them decides to come after you, that's what they do, and they don't make an appointment to kick down your front door. You're playing their game. They get to make the rules."

"And break them."

Motherfuckers. That guy Kessler. Kurt wondered how Annie could still love him after what she'd gone through. Maybe she didn't. Maybe she was just doing what she thought right for the boys. He saw her in the garden, nurturing the plants, gathering lettuce before dinner, clipping a bit of fresh thyme for the dressing. He tried to imagine her on the floor, an agent above her with his gun pointed at her head. He had to find that one, find out somehow which one had pinned her to the floor like that. And then what, *fool?* You gonna beat him up? Do a number on a cop and get your ass locked up again? The pressure started in his temples and pushed its way across his brow and into the sinuses above his eyes. He loved her, he loved this woman truly, and the thought that harm could come to her, the thought that he might not be able to protect her from them—how dare they come to his house and terrorize his wife, what if the boys had been home, and what about Kane—he felt his fingernails biting into his palms and realized he had the steering wheel in a death grip. He took a slow deep breath and let out a long sigh, saw Annie glance at him. She put a hand on his thigh, and he felt a flood of relief. She did love him. She loved him in spite of the life he'd made for them. He had to get out of the business. If he was committed to his family, and he was, he had to get out of it. He thought back to his father suddenly, to all the times his father wasn't around, which was most of the time. What the fuck's the matter with you, you don't see you're doing the same thing he did? So you're not out playing cards, so you're not out playing golf. You're still out. You're out. And they're at home, wishing you were there. Until the motherfucking cops come and kick down the door. Maybe next time drag your wife off to jail. Put your kids in some kind of completely fucked-up place and—he heard Alex and Timothy, "Daddy, we wanna wrestle. Let's wrestle!" He felt an ache in his chest and the burn of tears in his eyes, and he didn't know what he believed in anymore. He didn't know about rights or duties or liberty or any of it. If the law was fucked up, that was the reality; to continue to break it was to risk everything he'd worked to achieve. Maybe he could do something to change it somewhere down the line. But he knew he could not ask his wife to continue living as they had been. She deserved better. His children deserved better. He loved his family and did not want to be torn from them.

"Annie."

"Are you going to prison?"

"I don't know. We'll see what they've got."

"Did you really crash a plane?"

"You could call it a rough landing, but there was no way to get the thing back out. Nobody was hurt."

"So," she said.

"Do you remember the night before we got married?" He looked over. "How I asked you what you would do if I got busted, would you stay by me while I did the time, and you said yes?"

"No," she said. "I told you I was glad you were getting out of the business, that otherwise we wouldn't be getting married. And I said if you fucked up and did something stupid and got busted, I would feel no obligation."

"But you said—"

"I said if the cops framed you, if they set you up, I'd be there for you."

"You said you'd be faithful. I remember that specifically."

"Is this a setup?"

"No."

"Anyway, that was before our children."

"So what's different?" he asked.

"Everything. Everything is different. And if it wasn't a setup, it must be a fuckup."

"Someone else's."

"Whose?"

"Pilot error."

"Detail. You were the one calling the shots. You've stayed in it, Kurt. You said you wouldn't and you did. Years now."

"Here we go," he said. "You knew what I was doing."

"I believed you every time. No more. They're about to take you away from us. We're about to lose everything. If they lock you up—"

"We don't even know what they have. Maybe nothing."

"And if they don't? You'll just get back out there and keep doing the same thing until they catch you again, won't you? Until they lock you up."

"No."

"You've been saying that all along."

"Annie, I understand now. I get it. All right?"

He exited at Ninety-sixth Street, watching in the rearview mirror, made the light, and swung left onto Riverside Drive, then right on Ninety-fifth, right on West End, making illegal right-on-red turns at each intersection. Then right on Ninety-sixth, and back onto the parkway, exactly where they'd left off. They were silent, each checking the side mirrors for tails while he maneuvered in traffic.

"We're clean," he said. He waited. Nothing. "There are choices, right? Go to trial, drop a fortune on my defense. You heard Mark."

"Or?"

"We can get new identities. Move somewhere far away and start again."

"And wait for them to find us? You're a father now, remember? Your children deserve your protection. They shouldn't have to live like that."

"I think they could handle it," he said.

"And what happens when they go to school, if they slip up somewhere and next thing you know the cops come and take Daddy away? You can't expect that of them. It isn't fair."

"Lonnie's kids know what he does," Kurt said. "And Father Francis, too, his kids. Bill told me once about some friends of his, how their six-year-old son marched into the living room one day and threatened to call the police when he smelled pot. It's this DARE program. No one knew what to say; then the kid's grandmother, right, she looks at him dead-on and says, 'What you need to consider, young man, is what will happen if you do that. If you call up the police, they will come and take your parents away and put them in jail. You need to ask yourself who will take care of you and feed you and tuck you into bed at night and give you clothes to wear. You need to think about who will read you stories while your parents are in jail. If the police take your parents away, who will love you?' The whole family was totally stunned. But the kid got it right away."

"And now the kid thinks the police are bad guys."

"Sometimes they are. You want them to split us up?"

"The only way to keep that from happening is for you, Kurt, *you,* to get out of this business. Stop breaking the law."

"It's a fucked-up law."

"I know it's a fucked-up law!" She heard her voice getting loud on her, anger flooding her tone. "I don't care! I don't care about political ramifications or religious freedom or hypocrisy or any of it. Right now I care about my family. I care about my husband and children. I care that you will stop. Just fucking stop. For your family. Remember us? We're the ones who love you."

"I told you I would."

"Time and again. I don't want to have to check the rearview to see if the cops are following us. I don't want to be part of that world. I don't want my children to grow up in it, with that fear. Okay? Do you hear me? I will not stay with you if you continue to smuggle! I will not stay."

Silence. Her heart was pounding; her face was flushed.

"I don't want to lose you," he said. Again, silence. In pain, almost in tears: "In fifteen years, baby mine, even in ten, they'll be grown up. I want to be with my kids while they're kids. It's the most important thing in the world to me."

"Really?" she said. "It's not as if you've spent much time with them lately."

He took her hand, squeezed too hard. She flinched. "Sorry," he said, letting up, patting her arm. "Annie. I mean it. I love you. I love our children. I love our family. This was gonna be my last trip."

"Kurt," she said. "The next trip is always the last one for you, until another one comes along."

"As much as I believe in what I'm doing," he said, "it's more important to me that I be with you."

For the instant he faced her, his eyes were blue and fierce. He meant it and she knew it. It scared her, the strength of his love and the feelings it pulled up in her. With Alex and Timothy it was still simple, but Kurt had so much going on, so much history. They both did: as relentless as weather. She couldn't begin to sort it all out. What she knew was that from the start they had shared the desire to create a family and to do things right this time around, to overcome their individual pasts with love for each other and their children.

And now this. The stupidity of it. She reached for his hand on the steering wheel.

"We can't let them separate us," he said. "It would kill me."

EIGHT

Kessler took a large crunchy bite out of an apple and caught the juice trickling down his chin, sucked it from his finger.

"Perfect," he said. "I have found the perfect McIntosh."

Brad Wilson, riding shotgun, nodded and stuffed a third brownie down his throat, let go a small, contented sigh before washing away chocolate with a mouthful of Jolt. Kessler turned his attention back to the road, a winding blacktop country lane.

Trowbridge. Fuck this guy. Thirty days to beef up the case or lose it. Years now on this one—when something bigger came along, it demanded immediate attention—but always the file was in the bottom right drawer of his gray metal desk, where he could put a finger on it without even looking. His desk, his chair, his file cabinet. Like all those in the office, manufactured by convicts, and there were moments Kessler wondered if they'd been made by someone he'd helped put away. When he started with the agency, he'd been on a mission. These days, he went to work. But this was what he liked about the job, this part: the hunt.

He couldn't believe that finally, at last, Trowbridge had blown it big time, crashed a plane, even, and he also couldn't believe they didn't have a solid case against the guy. Some kind of luck he had.

He eased the station wagon to a stop on the side of the road, a gravel spot obviously used for turn-arounds. It was only a hundred yards or so to where the driveway from the Trowbridge residence opened onto the road. A large weeping willow afforded good cover. The maples and oaks were beginning to tinge with color, but the willow, its leaves pale and slender, still had thick foliage. There was a cornfield directly across the road, the plants at stiff attention, like soldiers in formation. If Trowbridge came out and noticed the car, Kessler would claim engine trouble and ask to borrow the phone. But he doubted there'd be any trouble. He'd been chasing smugglers for nine years now, and knew that criminal egos sometimes confused the word "bold" with the word "careless."

He rolled down a window. The air was sweet and fresh. He breathed deeply. "They should bottle this stuff and sell it in the city."

Wilson took another swig of caffeine-enhanced soda and said nothing. Kessler turned his attention back to the woodlands. Surrounded by assholes.

"What's this guy do?" Wilson said. "Sit home in front of the tube?"

"He'll come outside and play," Kessler said. "Sooner or later."

"This is like three days now, you know?"

"Hey. Food's good. Air's fresh. You got something better to do?"

"It's Saturday, boss. I got a date tonight."

"I'll get you back in time for your date."

"I was kinda hoping to get a workout in before."

"So you need an extra hour." These guys. "We'll manage."

"Two'd be better."

Kessler appraised Wilson and rolled his eyes. Wilson was, in the vernacular, all cut up, his musculature extremely well defined, bulging beneath skin that stayed the same shade of tan—roast chicken brown—year 'round. Couldn't work undercover if his life depended on it, which undercover sometimes did. So of course Wilson wanted nothing more than to get down and dirty and do a long-term investigation. No way Kessler would put him under. He'd get killed. All Kessler wanted to do was fire him.

"Nothing happens soon, we'll head back," Kessler said. "You'll have time for your workout."

"You nervous about this guy?"

"Gotta hook him to that plane."

"They'll indict on what we got."

"Nonsense," Kessler said. "Tire tracks won't cut it. We need a real live human sitting there testifying."

"What is it about—"

Kessler waved him off.

"I almost had him on a trip he did a few years ago. Slipped right out from under me. Now it's looking like he might do it again. I can't believe they got the load out."

"If we could get back by three or so, that would be good," Wilson said. "Not to change the subject."

"We'll try."

"Someday I'll get past being a self-indulgent prick." Wilson smiled at him, uncertainly. "But not until I have to."

"Goes with being single," Kessler said. "Enjoy it."

"You're single."

"No," Kessler said. "I'm divorced."

He thought back to his last date, his first in ages. While Wilson and crew tossed the Trowbridge house, Kessler had been on a bust of his own. He hadn't called the woman since, had no intention of doing so. He felt out of it, out of the whole scene, and wasn't sure he wanted back in. Dinner had been raw vegetables, nibbled, and she drank water obsessively, if that was possible. He'd sat and watched her lips moving but was unable to fathom what she was talking about—some high-tech exercise program involving huge rubber bands, and then something about television. An assistant U.S. attorney had set the thing up, and next day when he asked how it went, Kessler said, "No hard feelings, but I owe you." At one point he'd looked up from his pasta and imagined that he saw the word *Vacancy* on her forehead, flashing in pink.

When his beeper went off, he said a silent thanks to the god of reprieve and, after apologies and cab fare, ran Code 3 all the way up from the city. And there was Annie, Mrs. Trowbridge, sitting in the one remaining upright chair in her living room. The doper's wife. He had tried, in the days and weeks since, to keep her out of his mind. He did not need any turmoil.

There'd been a brief fling with an informant a few months after his divorce—the first time in his career—and it nearly got him suspended. He still didn't know exactly how it happened, only that it had a lot to do with how lost he'd felt, how the only things inside him were emptiness and pain, competing for space in his lungs. The informant had simply reached across the table at the diner where he'd agreed to meet her and taken his hand. They were like that, the good ones, able to spot a moment of weakness even if the uncertainty was no more substantial than the blink of an eye.

It was late at night, and he would've gone home to an empty apartment. Instead, he went with her, and there was no love about it; the rest of the night was just fucking, and more fucking, and more, until sweat and daylight overtook them and Kessler pulled on his pants and staggered home. He'd sat down at his kitchen table and poured a large glass of bourbon, and he felt empty, and the pain was still there, but dulled by exhaustion. And he went back for more the next night, and the next, and her voice took on a certain lilt. When she began expecting him, he bailed, and—what to expect from a snitch—she dropped a dime on him. Called his boss and made a complaint. Kessler explained, and his boss, having dealt with this sort of thing many times in the past, suggested that a nice dinner and an apology might go a long way toward settling things. It hadn't seemed adequate to Kessler, but he'd taken her out and told her the truth and told her that he was ashamed and told her how sorry he was. She'd understood, or pretended to. You know better now, he told himself.

Movement in the garden caught his attention and he nudged Wilson.

"His old lady?" Wilson shifted in his seat.

"You should know." Kessler had chewed Wilson out good for putting Annie in handcuffs and trashing her home. Wilson was fresh out of DEA Group 27. Most of the team were currently under indictment or had taken early retirement to avoid prosecution. Wilson had been one of the lucky few to get away with a transfer. Kessler knew the guy who'd been the head of the group. Another asshole. And stupid. Just plain stupid. Enough hubris in his left pocket to supply George Custer and George Bush at once. The suits, the higher-ups, the administrators at their desks, wanted Kessler to straighten Wilson out. Kessler didn't think it possible. Maybe Wilson could come around, but he'd got off to a miserable start, and Kessler's crew was his last chance to prove he could be a decent agent.

Kessler raised his field glasses. There she was, opening the gate, entering. He watched as she knelt to clip some lettuce. He watched as she stepped carefully toward a large healthy tomato plant in one corner of the garden.

"Can I have those a minute, boss?" Wilson.

"Huh?" Kessler lowered the glasses. "I've been meaning to tell you," he said, "I don't really like being called boss." He handed over the binoculars.

"Hey." Wilson shifted in his seat, adjusted the focus. "No problem."

"Where you going tonight?" Kessler said. Trying to lighten the mood. He watched as Annie bent to pull a weed near the gate on her way out of the garden. Oh, man. Her ass was a work of art. She was in khaki cutoffs, rolled, and a delicate kind of undershirt-looking thing that left her shoulders bare. Kessler flashed on what it would be like to be standing behind her, his arms around her waist, putting tranquil kisses on the back of her neck. And those shoulders. He leaned his head back, closed his eyes. This won't do, he told himself. This will not do. But then, no harm just sitting here watching.

"You okay?" Wilson's voice held concern.

Kessler snapped back up, opened his eyes.

"I'm supposed to know?" He remembered how she'd looked that night when he and his men had trooped out of the house to return to the city. Staring out the rear window of the agency Chevy, he'd seen Annie standing on the front porch, watching them leave. He wondered what she did after they'd gone: laugh or cry.

She hadn't given him a thing. There'd been no belligerence, none of that nonsense like *if looks could kill* or anything like that. But when her eyes met his there was a defiance that unsettled him and therefore intrigued him. As if she was daring him to something. He wasn't sure whether it was her protective instinct operating, willing him and his men from her home, or whether she was challenging him. To what, he didn't know.

But he wanted to know more. Needed to. About her. About her children, her situation. About her relationship to Trowbridge.

This much he did know: she deserved better. Every time he considered her, his thoughts returned to that. He wondered, if it came down to it, whether she would go on the lam with hubby, try to keep her family tight. No sign yet that he might flee, not that Kessler had day and night to spend on this case. There was just too much shit going on. All the time and everywhere, much of it petty and nonsensical, and everybody running around as if tomorrow was about to club them from behind. He took a deep breath of air and looked around at the glorious late summer morning and realized it had been forever since he'd got out of the city. Lately he felt like Pacman, scurrying around gobbling meaningless dots while the hooded creatures that were his job attempted to surround and consume him.

And there came Trowbridge, striding out to meet his wife, slipping an arm around her shoulders and pulling her close to him. Bastard. He kissed her as the boys came running up, and she bent to give each of them a kiss before heading back into the house. Kessler watched Kurt lead the boys toward the garage.

Wilson put down the glasses.

"Here we go."

"Check these babies out," Wilson said. "They should be illegal." He held out a yellow-and-white wax-paper bag to Kessler—whiff of serious chocolate.

"Maybe later." Kessler waved it away. "I'll get some on the way home." He pictured himself sitting in front of the television, sneering at Letterman and downing one brownie after another in his miserable little apartment. He didn't know why he still lived there, aside from inertia. Columbus Avenue at 106 Street. Two bedrooms, allegedly. Two closets was more like it.

The neighborhood was mostly Dominican, with a smattering of Jamaican, and that had been fine too, a couple of years ago, after his wife of fourteen years said enough already. Barbara. He'd thought, then, as much as he'd been able to think at all, to submerge himself in an alien culture. So far, beyond trying some odd-looking vegetables from the bodega across the avenue and tuning his ear to their Spanish, he hadn't got around to it. He didn't let them know he was fluent, but he understood every word when the grocer across the street said to the customer in front of him, "For you, it's sixty-nine cents a pound. For the gringo behind you, it's eighty."

Some kind of willful torpor kept him there, walking up three flights of worn marble stairs to his apartment. Summers he sweated and bore the crushing noise of the streets, salsa music twenty-four nonstop hours a day; winters he sweated in quieter rooms because the radiators could not be controlled. He could've found another place, but it was as though, by refusing to move, he was staying one step closer to the life he'd had before, to his family. And, it had occurred to him recently, maybe he was making himself pay for losing them.

He smelled brownies and realized Wilson was holding out the bag again.

"Last call. Only one left."

"Stop trying to fatten me up," Kessler said. He chuckled. "Someone shot these people's dog. Was it you?"

"Oh, man." Wilson sighed. "I like dogs. Dog spelled backward is god."

Fuck this guy, too. He'd done it, no question. Wilson was new breed DEA, and Kessler didn't care for the changes he'd seen in the agency over the course of his years there. Wilson, like the others in Group 27, was well protected by civil service regulations, though there was nothing civil about him. It would take an act of war to dislodge him from his badge, his nine millimeter, and his pension.

From what Kessler knew, Group 27 had begun pushing the envelope soon after Wilson was assigned there, and they kept on pushing until they punched a tiny hole in one corner and the thing began falling apart. They'd been busted for everything from barroom brawls, where they pounded homosexuals for sport, to kidnapping an Israeli heroin dealer from a hotel room in Egypt and very nearly killing him in an airplane bathroom. Claimed he was trying to escape—at 37,000 feet.

Wilson slapped a hand on the dash; Kessler's eyes popped open. Down the road, a dark green Jeep was pulling out of the driveway.

"The Fates are with us," Kessler said.

Wilson moaned, sort of half-heartedly.

"Don't break my chops," Kessler said. "I'll get you there in time for your date." He wasn't sure he would. He didn't care if he did. "Driving his wife's car today." Kessler cranked the engine, but waited until the Jeep had disappeared over the hill peak before pulling onto the road from behind the camouflage of the weeping willow.

"We shoulda taken the Jag," Wilson said. "He knocks us off, he'll leave us in the dirt, this piece-a-shit ride we're in." Kessler, over Wilson's vehement, single-syllable objections, had chosen a pale yellow station wagon instead of the green Jag that had been confiscated in Queens a few weeks ago, the car Wilson was dying to try out.

"He knocks us off," Kessler replied, "we simply turn around and drive the other way. We not here looking for a hot-pursuit situation."

"I'm always looking."

They followed at a distance as the Jeep headed east on Krumville Road, winding downhill toward State 209. A chipmunk darted into the road in front of them; Kessler braked hard, the chipmunk stopped, raised up on its hind legs, darted left, darted right, darted left again. Kessler couldn't stop in time, closed his eyes, and grimaced as the chipmunk disappeared under the left front tire. He felt a crunch, thought he even heard it.

"Humans one." Wilson snorted. "Chipmunks zero."

Kessler shook off the queasiness, ignored Wilson. At the bottom of the hill the road leveled and headed straight across the cornfields that stretched across the valley. They could see the Jeep turn north on 209.

"Nice ride," Kessler said, rolling through a stop sign as he made the left after the Jeep.

"It'll be ours soon," Wilson said.

In Stone Ridge, the speed limit dropped to thirty mph, and 209 became Main Street, lined with trees and stone houses that were residences or small shops or both. The Jeep pulled into the post office parking lot; Kessler steered the wagon into a driveway across the street, the Marbletown Reformed Church, circled the small gravel parking lot behind the modest white building, and pulled back out front to park. A hand-painted sign on a wooden easel read:

PENNY SOCIAL
DOORS OPEN 6:30 P.M.
CALLING: 7:00 P.M.

"Where are we, nineteen forty-eight?" Wilson raised his blond eyebrows.

Kessler shrugged, watching through the windshield as Kurt helped his boys from the back seat of the Jeep and they bounced along the sidewalk, Kurt behind them. At the front door, the little one, the redhead, continued to bounce while the older one grabbed the door handle and gave it a yank, to no avail. He looked up, stepped aside for his father. Look at this guy. Kessler shook his head sadly, thought of his own kids. The first three or four times he'd tried to drop in, early after the divorce, they'd all been busy: Daniel off to a basketball game with his friends, Sarah headed to see *The Princess Bride* with hers, and little Justin—little, he was six then—going to a birthday party. He didn't ask Barbara her plans. She no longer spoke to him beyond what was required to maintain a façade of civility. All those activities, all that busyness. He wondered how she managed it without him, running a home, raising the kids, holding her job at the foundation, and then he realized she'd been doing it even when he still lived there. Closing in on two years now since his last visit.

He thought of that Harry Chapin song, the voice in his brain loud and strong against the quiet of a small-town Saturday morning . . . *when you comin' home, Dad, I don't know when, but we'll get together then, Son, you know we'll have a good time then.* He remembered his father telling him—on one of those rare occasions when they were speaking to each other instead of yelling—that gentlemen don't discuss their ailments.

Maybe Barbara would've stayed with him if he'd finished law school. But lawyering would've stolen his time the same way agenting had. Any job would. Because, he realized as he watched Kurt Trowbridge hold open the door of the post office for his kids, he would've buried himself in whatever work he'd chosen. That was his way. It had never occurred to him to take his kids to the office.

Or maybe it was just that he'd been afraid of smothering in all that love. Didn't matter now. His kids weren't his kids anymore. They were strangers.

And look at this guy, hanging out with his boys, enjoying doing the weekend drill.

Wilson took up the field glasses and scanned the front of the plain blue building, focused on a small plaque to the left of the front door, and read the inscription: " 'This building dedicated to public service, 1963, John F.

Kennedy, President of the United States . . .' " He handed the glasses to Kessler. "Scumbag."

"You didn't like Kennedy?"

"Never met the man. I meant Trowbridge."

"You let it get personal, best way I know to fuck up a good investigation."

"It's nothing personal. He's a scumbag, that's all."

Kessler put the glasses on the seat. He didn't need them. Any fool could see those boys loved their father.

"I was in a pool hall in the Bronx when they got him," Kessler said. "Skipped school that day. Won eleven dollars playing eight ball, and even when I got caught on the skip, everyone was so shocked by what had happened, I skated on it. Completely. Even my father."

"Lucky you." Wilson rolled his pale blue eyes, ran a hand over his almost crewcut blond hair, and bared his teeth at Kessler in something that resembled a smile. "There he is, and look at that."

They watched Kurt put a large box wrapped in brown paper, heavily taped, into the back of the Jeep.

"I gotta tell you, man, I'm looking forward to locking this motherfucker up for the rest of his life." Wilson thumbed in the direction of the post office. "The rest of his fucking life."

"What'd he ever do to you?"

"What is this, man, some kind of test?" Wilson shifted. He was big, the seat was small.

Kessler shook his head no, slowly.

"He's a fucking dope dealer," Wilson said. "I bet there's dope in that box. Let's fall on him right now and really fuck up his day."

"No," Kessler said. "Let's fall on him later and fuck up his life."

"Yeah," Wilson said, grinning now like a fifth-grader with his first copy of *Penthouse,* "and then we can fuck his wife."

Kessler bridled. "I heard a lot of shit about Group 27," he said. "And right now I'm thinking most of it must be true. You are one sick fuck, Wilson."

"Don't give me that shit, man." Wilson made a fist and pumped it into his open palm. "I saw how you were looking at her. I may be stupid, but I sure as hell ain't blind."

Kessler started the engine and put the car in gear, shaking his head back and forth. He waited until the Jeep was down the road before pulling onto Main Street.

"He's a Class A violator," he said finally. "No way he's using the U.S. Mail to move product. He does tons, and that's how I want him: with tons and completely red-handed."

"If there's dope in that box, he's red-handed right now. And we could seize the Jeep, too. I *want* that ride."

"You just want to get back to the city."

Wilson hung his arm out the window, let the air play with his hand.

"Did you shoot his dog?" Kessler gave Wilson a sidelong glance.

Wilson returned it.

"Does the Pope shit in the woods? You already asked me that and I already told you. Boss."

Fuck the suits, too. Kessler didn't want this asshole in his group.

They followed at a distance through town, past H.A.S. Beane Books, Twin Goats Gifts, Five Hand Design, past a framing shop and the public library and Bodacious Bagels. No strip malls. The businesses were housed in restored Victorians or old stone homes.

"Nice little town," Kessler mused.

"Seen a sports bar anywhere?"

Kessler sighed.

"I could never live here." Wilson flipped down the visor, checked his teeth in the mirror, looking for chocolate stains.

"The citizens of Stone Ridge are grateful, I'm sure."

The Jeep took a quick left onto 213, and Kessler found himself directly behind it. He hung back a little, but staying too far back would be as much a knock-off as following right on his tail. It worked out. Only a few miles down the road, the Jeep pulled into a private drive. Kessler continued on.

"Okay," Wilson said, scribbling the address in his notebook. "I can work with that. Let's head for the city."

"It's early yet." Kessler eased down the road until they were out of sight. He found a place to turn around, and when he passed back by the residence, he got a glimpse through the trees that lined the road in front of it. Trowbridge was talking to another man, wiry and looking pretty worried from what Kessler could see.

"I got a plate number," Wilson said. Scribbling again.

Kessler felt a wave of satisfaction flow into his gut, warming him like good cognac. But he was still pissed at Wilson for knocking him off about Annie. Life was hard enough.

He drove back to town and parked again at the church across from the post office. If Trowbridge had any more to do, he'd have to pass by here sooner or later. Wilson sat quietly, resting his eyes, seeming resigned to Kessler's schedule.

It wasn't even a half-hour wait. The Jeep rolled past, Trowbridge looking like a million other dads in his conservative haircut and baseball cap. They pulled out after him and followed him to a low wooden building, open-fronted, near the edge of town. A couple of picnic tables sat beneath an awning attached to the side of the building, the wall next to them covered with flyers of assorted colors. In front, large wooden tables held piles of watermelons and cantaloupes. *Davenports,* the hand-painted sign read. Tail end of corn season. The place was full of city slickers. Kessler pulled in and parked in the side lot, near the corner, so that he had a view of the front parking area.

Kurt and the boys came out of the building and walked across the parking lot to a pay phone near the road, laughing about something and licking ice cream cones.

Kessler watched Kurt stick the last of his cone in his mouth and pick up the receiver. The boys began dancing around their father in a circle, laughing and slapping high fives each time they made a round.

"Happy kids," Kessler said, mostly to himself. He pictured them all at home, in the kitchen Wilson had helped trash. He saw Annie at the stove, the boys nearby, dancing the way they were right now. Try as he might, he couldn't place Kurt in the picture, didn't know where he would be or what he'd be doing. "Very happy kids," he added.

"This guy is about to make a delivery," Wilson said, anger entering his voice. "We can pop whoever he leaves that box with, flip them, and check this creep in at the Crossbar Hilton."

"He may already have left it somewhere."

"Open your eyes. It's right there, in the back of the Jeep. I can see it from here." Wilson was adamant. "I'm telling you, he's about to make a delivery."

Kessler could see the process, Wilson getting pumped to make an arrest, getting pumped to kick some ass. As if he was a kid on a high school football team, standing in the locker room, listening to the coach's voice get louder and angrier and filling with fight. *Fight-fight-fight! Go-fight-win! Pound some heads! Kick some butt! WIN!* The kind of attitude that got agents killed. And sometimes civilians.

"Brad. Do you know what patience is?"

"Yeah," Wilson answered. Scornful. Belligerent. "Patience is a virtue."

"Think he'd burn me?" Kessler asked.

Wilson eyed him. Kessler had shaved his beard and cut his hair a few days earlier, revealing a strong jaw and some gray around the temples. Today he wore a hemp baseball cap and rimless shades.

"Be real. Of course he would. I'll go."

"Keep your distance," Kessler said. "And get some grapes, why don't you."

Kessler sat watching people come and go from the market, thankful that it was so busy. Trowbridge hung up the phone and led the boys across the parking lot toward the Jeep. As they approached it, Wilson came out, carrying a large bag of groceries. He wore a tight T-shirt to show off his muscles. Kessler hated that.

And then—what was this—Trowbridge homed in on Wilson and began watching his progress. Fuck. Kessler watched helplessly as Wilson led Kurt's gaze right to the station wagon. And then his eyes locked with Kurt's.

Trowbridge stood for a long moment, watching as an oblivious Wilson opened the passenger door and got in.

"Brilliant," Kessler said, cranking the engine.

Trowbridge took each boy by the hand and gave Kessler one more long, intense look. And then he raised his hand and pointed a finger at him, jabbing the air, his lips pulled into a half-smile, half-sneer. *Made you, motherfucker*. He turned his back and walked toward the Jeep with an irreverent swagger.

Kessler threw the wagon into reverse.

"You blew it," Wilson said. "We've been burned."

Kessler eased the wagon toward the exit. "I want a wire on that pay phone," he said, all business. "And I saw one by the hardware store and another near the grocery store. First thing Monday. And that house across the road from them looked vacant. If it is, rent it and get some guys in there. Twenty-four hours, cover it."

Wilson stayed shut up, folding his arms across his chest to fume silently.

"What if the magistrate won't go for the wire?" he said finally.

"Wilson." Kessler took off his hat and smoothed back his dark brown hair. "Didn't you come to me from Group 27? Surely you know what to do."

Wilson snapped his notebook shut and let out a sigh.

"Let's swing by their place on the way home," Kessler said. "It's practically on the way."

"What if we run into him again?"

"We're already burned. Time to drive him up a little. Make him good and nervous."

"I doubt that'll happen," Wilson said.

"I don't." It didn't matter to him now whether they saw Trowbridge again or not. What was done was done, and the afternoon was clear and warm. It was a beautiful day for things like bike riding and hiking and gardening, things Kessler never did. But he thought the garden was probably right where she would be.

NINE

The first snow came the day before Thanksgiving, just after Annie dropped Carol at the train station in Rhinecliff. Carol had stayed; Annie kidded her about her fear of divorce court being stronger than her fear of police raids. But Carol was quick lately to accept invitations to visit friends in the city. She was spending the next few days with an old high school friend, another transplanted Texan.

Annie watched flakes of white ice swirl toward the windshield as the Jeep cut through the beginning storm on the way to Uptown Kingston. The Rhinecliff Bridge offered a mile-long view of the Hudson River, its shores uncluttered here, the woods broken in only a few places where huge old mansions occupied vast expanses of tree-dotted lawn. She wondered what Henry Hudson had seen here. Opportunity, she supposed, with perhaps a dash of glory. He was, after all, an explorer in the service of a Dutch monopoly that had sent the British and Portuguese packing from Indonesia, Malaya, and Ceylon.

As she exited on to 9W, she shook her head at the strip shopping centers that blighted both sides of the road. The ugliest sign, she thought, belonged to Fay's Drugs: black on yellow back-lit plastic. It went perfectly with the ugly brown-painted cinderblock building to which it was attached. Annie hadn't been in, but knew anyway what the place smelled like: a putrid stench of antibiotics mixed with industrial-strength floor wax, the smell of fluorescent light, and some kind of sugar scent emanating from row upon row of artificial candies.

But Uptown Kingston was holding its own against the developers, who seemed to prefer razing trees and pouring asphalt along the highway to restoring beautiful old buildings on cobblestone and brick streets.

At Schneller's, standing in a crowd scented of wet wool, Annie stared at the large chalkboard behind a counter stocked with all manner of fowl and an impressive array of beef. The latter she didn't look at too long, finding it heavy and unnaturally red, like those who ate too much of it. When her number was called, she had to squeeze around a large and firmly planted man in a black wool full-length coat—city wear—to put her paper ticket in the bucket on the counter. She said excuse me, but he seemed not to hear. A man in various layers of cotton and wool and a fur-lined cap noticed her difficulty and stepped aside.

"I called last week," she said to the counterman. "It's Jenkins"—the name she and Kurt used when dealing with merchants who wouldn't recognize them or people with whom they'd have no further contact. It seemed strange to her the first time she'd done it—used an alias—but thrilling in a minor way too, the way a teenage girl feels while browsing her mother's closet: it was perfectly safe, but still there was the hope of finding something secret and unexpected. She kept her eyes on the chalkboard until the man returned with her order.

"Two pheasant," he said, "and a Cornish game hen?"

Annie nodded and he turned to wrap the order. The man with the cap pointed at the chalkboard and said, "They get a pretty penny for that pheasant, don't they?"

"It's enough to make me want to take up a shotgun," Annie kidded.

"God bless you." The man laughed, and she noticed his flushed cheeks and smelled beer on his breath. She wondered if she was splurging in honor of Thanksgiving or in spite of it.

She paid for her package, smiled at the man in the cap, and headed out into the cold.

She passed a snowplow in the opposite lane as she headed south on the Lucas Avenue extension, into the countryside. A few minutes out of town, there were already three or four inches on the ground, and but for the plow, Annie's was the only vehicle on the road. She passed a sign at the end of a driveway leading to a mobile home, big white stenciled letters on an irregular piece of plywood painted hot orange: DOG BITES! STAY THE HELL OUT!

She wondered what the police thought when they drove past. Did they suspect illegal activity, or was the sentiment displayed simply too out-front for that? She wondered what kind of pain made someone post the sign in front of their home. And as much as she tried not to, she found herself dwelling on what she had come to think of as Kurt's situation. She did not want to name it.

The grand jury had been postponed for some unfathomable reason, but Kurt's case would go before them next week. The date was approaching with the speed of disaster, and Annie felt helpless. It was driving her and Kurt apart. Moments she felt him reaching, other times he was cold, and she knew the same was true of her. They still touched each other, but more often when the boys were looking on than not. Instead of a reassurance, the occasional caress to a shoulder or cheek had become an attempt to assure Alex and Tim that everything was just fine. And who knew? Maybe nothing more would happen. Maybe the government's case would prove to be as thin as it seemed on the surface.

But she couldn't deny that Kurt had, in essence and in reality, played right into their hands. He'd had to test them, to push them and keep pushing until he'd got them angry enough to shoot his dog. She watched snow swirling toward the windshield and felt as if she were swimming in a cold, heavy liquid, something leaden, and she was unable to see the opposite shore. The men who worked for the DEA seemed to her to be at least as dangerous as the marauders in the employ of the Dutch East India Company, who'd managed to separate the British from a prime source of tea. And Kurt had a need to engage them in battle on a personal level. She'd heard enough stories over the years, and now she had met them firsthand, men in black masks waving guns around and screaming at her. Her home was wrecked, her dog was dead, her husband had been jailed and might be on his way to prison. Her sister was terrified. For what? A plant? Though she knew Kurt had been through his own ordeal, she could not understand his bringing all this grief down on them. When Alex and Tim began asking about Kane, where was Kane, what happened to Kane, she had lied to them. Out and out lied. First time, to them, and she felt awful. Kane had been hit by a car. Stay out of the road, little boys, the road is a dangerous place. Kurt had been angry at her, wanting to tell them the truth, but it was too late unless he was willing to expose her to their children. "Go ahead," she'd said, "rat me out." Then he seemed to understand that she was doing what she deemed best for the boys, and he backed off. But he had to know that Annie considered Kane's death largely his doing. He was the one who wasn't content just to steal the bubble gum; he had to stick his tongue out at the police as he was running away.

That one, Kessler, thank God he was in charge. Annie laughed at herself when she realized that Joseph Kessler reminded her of a high school boyfriend, the first guy who'd ever invited her to smoke a joint. It was a scant few weeks from the afternoon of the drugs-and-Communists lecture that her mother had dutifully, earnestly, delivered to her in the kitchen. Phil had fallen in next to her as they left American history class.

"It's the ultimate oxymoron, don't you think?" he'd said.

Annie looked at him, shifted her books.

"The term Civil War."

She'd laughed, agreed. The Civil War seemed to be the great divide as far as the teachers of history in Texas were concerned, though there were some who preferred to remember the Alamo.

They'd gone to the movies, *Butch Cassidy and the Sundance Kid,* and she was delighted that Phil slipped his arm around her shoulders and actually watched the movie. Afterward, they'd gone for hot fudge sundaes. On their second date, before a late showing of *2001: A Space Odyssey,* they drove to Spring Lake. It was rumored that a woman who dressed in evening gowns would sometimes approach one of the cars parked at the edge of the lake on Friday or Saturday evening to ask for a ride. On being admitted to the car, she would direct the teenage couple to a large home on the west side of the lake. When the car arrived, the couple would find that their passenger had disappeared, the only trace of her a dark wet spot on the back seat. The lights would come on in the house, and a man would come out, weeping over his long lost wife, who'd drowned in the lake in 1947.

Phil had eyed her with mock suspicion and said, "You're not the police, are you?" and brought out a joint. He dropped his voice to a confidential, slightly nervous whisper. "Maybe we'll see the Lady of the Lake," he said.

She'd been apprehensive, curious, embarrassed that she coughed so much, and then just giggly. It didn't seem such a big deal, really. It only made them giggly. But in the halls of Lake Worth High the following Monday, she noticed that people who didn't usually acknowledge her were saying hello or nodding greetings, as though for the first time they respected her. She was in.

Phil had gone on to Texas Tech and a degree in engineering, something to do with oil. She heard he'd married one of the several Tech cheerleaders who dressed in red and black and tossed each other into the air, shouting and smiling, every Saturday during the football season, and now they had a couple of kids and lived in Austin. According to Carol, the Lady of the Lake was still rumored to be around. Annie smiled, wondered if she believed in ghosts, considered that if she did, she probably saw them more as memories on a molecular level than as any kind of actuality.

She could have married Phil. And had a comfortable home in Austin, and kids, and the comfortable satisfaction of a law-abiding life. But she had fallen for an outlaw, and she had a comfortable home in New York and another in Texas and knew that it could all disappear in the next instant. It was a façade.

But her attraction to Kurt was way beyond a simple matter of chemistry. And it had grown stronger over the years, bolstered by his devotion and honesty. Yet he had to understand that it wasn't fair to keep taking the risks they'd shared early in their courtship. It wasn't fair to say I love you and put it out there on the table like a stack of red chips, waiting to see what cards the dealer would toss your way.

•

The kitchen was warm with cooking. Annie added the mushrooms to the soup and stood stirring, her hip cocked against the cabinet as she watched the others at the long oak table next to the windows. A pair of downy woodpeckers were at the bird feeder, observed by Alex, Tim, and Lacy until the kids noticed their breath clouding the windowpane and began trying to make bigger and bigger clouds on the glass. Outside was cloudy, too, the sky heavy with impending snow.

"So," Mike said, "I'm walking back to my apartment, I got a sack of groceries or whatever in my hand, and as I approach the building, I pass the service entrance and I see this guy walking out carrying a stereo. He's a young kid, maybe fifteen, sixteen. And then I realize that the stereo he's carrying is mine. That was the first time I thought about moving out."

Kurt took a sip of wine and tossed a laugh at Mike. Laura shook her head and picked up the open bottle of red, got up to join Annie near the stove.

"Can I help?"

"Thanks," Annie said. "But all we're doing is waiting."

Annie watched dark red liquid curl into a crystal goblet, a water glass really, but Kurt liked to use them for wine. Laura added a bit to her own glass and raised it to Annie. Squeals of laughter brought their attention to the windows, where their children huffed and puffed with increasing vigor.

"To hyperventilation," Laura said, and touched her glass to Annie's. Annie, seeing that Laura was uncomfortable, raised her eyebrows in a question.

"I have to stop working at the shop," Laura said.

"I understand," Annie said, turning away quickly to hide the blush of anger or embarrassment or both she felt creeping into her cheeks. Instant sunburn. She busied herself moving things around on the counter, straightening; grabbed the sugar bowl to put it in the cabinet. It slipped, her shaking hands, it slipped and fell, shattered on the floor.

"Oh," Laura said, Annie voicing it in chorus.

She was hurt, she was disappointed, but she had half-expected it.

"I've got it," she said when Laura moved for the dustpan under the sink. She knelt to pick up the pottery shards and sweep the sugar away. Not too many people were eager to be around when the cops might show any minute. And it wasn't as if Laura needed the job. She worked Saturday afternoons as a way to get herself out of her basement studio, where she threw clay. The sugar bowl had been a housewarming gift to Annie when they'd first moved to the community.

"I'm so sorry," Annie said.

"It's okay," Laura replied. "I can make you another."

Annie did understand, sort of. It was perfectly reasonable that Laura and Mike were concerned about an association with someone who might be about to get locked up.

"I'm sorry too," Laura said. "Mike's afraid they'll harass you, and that I might, you know, be working at the shop one day and they could come in with a search warrant or something."

Whatever. She would miss Laura's company. Laura spoke grownup.

"Odds are they won't," Annie said. "It'll only be in court from now on."

Mike shifted in his chair, turned his attention to them.

"I'm sure that's true," he said. "But she really should concentrate on her own work now."

"You'll always be welcome back," Annie said.

Laura smiled.

Annie had dressed the pheasants with a stuffing of leeks and pecans, and saw now, as she placed them center table, that they had come out firm and juicy. Kurt carved the pheasants while Mike refreshed the wine glasses; platters were passed and plates filled. Annie was pleased that things had come out well, but it seemed unreal to her, or maybe just extremely temporary. It was as though she were in the waiting room at the emergency wing of the hospital, thumbing through magazines, anticipating a diagnosis.

With everyone poised to begin, Mike raised a glass.

"To our friends and gracious hosts," he said. "Thank you for having us to share this meal with you, and let us be thankful this day for our health, our friendship, and those little monsters over there." He paused. "And Ronald Reagan," he added. "Let's not forget to be thankful for him."

"Oh, what does it matter?" Laura said. "They're all actors anyway. At least he's got a couple of movies under his belt. Brings something legitimate to the political arena."

Nods of agreement; polite smiles. A silence fell. That's what it was. They were all being so fucking polite. What to talk about? Kurt was about to be indicted.

"Babe," Kurt said, "this pheasant is outstanding."

Mike and Laura agreed. What to talk about?

"So," Mike said finally, directing his words at Kurt, "what are you looking at?"

•

Sunrise tinged the few remaining clouds magenta and underwater blue as Annie listened to the quiet in the house. Not a sound. Utter stillness. The tiny wooden table in the middle of the kitchen held a mess from yesterday. Alex had made several concoctions, adding salt or baking soda to water, stirring carefully but inevitably spilling. On a wide pine plank of the floor, water had pooled into the shape of a heart. Annie could not believe how perfectly drawn it was. She left it there, hoping it would evaporate before it got stepped on.

She pressed the button on the coffee maker and heard the padded thud of cat's paws landing against the wood floor in the hallway. Juju, the stealth gray mouser, had arrived upstairs from the basement, where she slept on the stone inlay that held the woodstove, baking her bones. Annie went to the cupboard for some cat food and took it to the bowl in the corner. Many was the night she would come into the darkened kitchen at two, three, or four to see Juju crouched motionless next to the refrigerator, waiting for some hapless rodent to emerge from beneath it. Neither Annie nor her husband could abide the extremists in Woodstock who would let their houses be overrun under the pretense of respect for all life. Instead, she and Kurt respected the rules—and the chaos—of nature. As the mother bear protected her cave and cub, Annie protected her home and children; her duty included keeping the rats at bay. She'd quivered the first time she saw Juju with a bloody, screeching mouse in her teeth, but soon came to see it as part of the cycle. Juju took birds, too, as effectively as she did rodents. Annie had watched the cat crouch under the big lilac tree outside the kitchen window, waiting for a titmouse or nuthatch to light on a branch. The birds had seemed brazen at first, even reckless. Annie was amazed that they would sit there, well within reach, alternately looking at the cat and digging in the bark for insects. Then she read somewhere about a visible shiver running through the skin of prey just prior to its being attacked, as though signaling the predator to come forward and take it.

The gurgle of the coffee maker brought her back to the kitchen, and she reached for cups and cream as the machine sucked and bubbled the final drops of water from its reservoir, sounding like a kid finishing a malt through a straw.

She heard Kurt stir just as she topped the stairs.

He took the cup from her and sipped carefully. The sky outside the window was dark gray now; it would still be a couple of hours before the sun cleared the tree line atop the ridge behind the house.

Annie, seeing the blackness of the trees, their limbs spindling skyward in a near-winter prayer, was thankful for the lack of clouds. Kurt had said last night how much he looked forward to a day with the boys and her, and now it looked as if they might be able to get outdoors.

She sat down next to him and rested on one arm.

He put down the cup, took her hand, pulled her toward him.

"Sit with me a while." He lifted back the covers. "I need to hold you."

She slid in beside him and he wrapped his arm around her, the bedsheets and his body warm after the cool air in the kitchen.

"I love you so much," he whispered, nuzzling her ear with his lips. "I still can't believe it when I hear them call me Daddy. Sometimes I have to shake myself." She felt the weight of his arm. "I can't believe there are these two wonderful little boys, calling me Daddy. I can't believe my good fortune."

She let her head rest on his chest; her ear against his bare skin could hear the strong and regular beating of his heart.

"I love you, too," she said. She wanted to ask him if he meant what he'd said on the drive home from the city. She wanted to extract some sort of concrete promise, but even words written in stone could not be called absolute. She thought of that game, Rock-Paper-Scissors, where you held your hand in a fist behind your back, and on *three* threw your hand out in front of you—fist for rock, flat out for paper, peace sign for scissors. Scissors cut paper, paper covered rock, rock smashed scissors. The symbolism was complete and simple. You knew right away whether you'd won or lost or had to play another round.

Kurt loved her and the boys; of that she had no doubt. He was a good father. It was Carol who'd asked her, one night after a few glasses of wine, with the kids in bed and Kurt out with Mike, "What's it like to be married?" Annie was taken aback. "Don't you know?" And Carol had shaken her head with such sadness that Annie had been moved to ask if Ron was violent.

"Oh, no," Carol had said. "Not that. No. If anything he's a wimp."

"Some wimps are cute."

"Not Ron. And he's a creep too. He goes to work and he plays golf. That's what he does. Oh, yeah, and he fucks my ex-best friend."

"Let's talk about him in past tense." Annie was always startled to see her sister without makeup. It was rare that she did, but here was Carol, with her ordinary eyes, almond-shaped and deep green, like Annie's, but with tears now, waiting to fall. Annie wanted to say something to ease Carol's pain, but did not know what would do that.

"He was never there for me," Carol continued. "He just installed me in a house and expected me to run it and give him his meals and give him sex when he wanted it and wash his clothes and that was it; those were my functions in life. It was like he didn't even live there. It was a hotel, a place for him to catch a nap and shower before going back outside to play."

"There should be a contest," Annie said. "Jerkoff of the Year. Nominees must be male and married and have distinguished themselves in the prior calendar year by some totally stupid and selfish behavior that left their spouse climbing the walls."

"What's the prize?"

"A six-month stint on *Wheel of Fortune,* you have to play every night, but you don't get to keep any of the amazing and wonderful prizes. Or maybe you have to spend a year on Dr. Tetlow's yacht, undergoing his version of analysis."

"Spare me." Carol smiled and sipped her wine, shook her head sadly.

"What?" Annie asked gently, getting up to put a new log on the fire.

"You and Kurt seem to have it all so together," Carol said. "I don't know that I'll ever find that kind of relationship."

"Stop looking. It will find you," Annie had replied. What she hadn't said was that, though their relationship was strong and good, yes, and full of love, there was the small matter of her husband's repeatedly risking his freedom. That floated under the surface, like a cold-water current running invisibly through an otherwise warm and gently flowing river.

She closed her eyes and shifted to her side, wrapped an arm across his chest, and snuggled in under the covers. He sighed with contentment.

She hoped he would be able, this time, to keep his promise.

•

There was enough snow that the sled could glide, but not enough to impede Kurt and Annie as they hiked upward. Kurt leaned into the hill, planting his boots firmly as he pulled the sled. Alex and Tim looked liked colorful, child-shaped marshmallows in their snowsuits; they gripped the handles and laughed and shouted at their father to go faster. Annie trailed along behind, searching the woods for Kane's ghost, remembering the hours they'd spent trekking here. He had been her wolf dog, and she missed him. But strong as the ache was, it did not detract from her joy at watching her husband and children, being with them as they walked through the woods on a beautifully sunny afternoon. She saw the unabashed love on Kurt's face as he turned to laugh with the boys. He caught Annie's eye, too, and this, she knew, was a day she would cherish for the rest of her life. Feeling the pull of the nameless thing that connected them, she tried to remember if her father had ever looked at her the way Kurt looked at his sons. He may have, at some point early, beyond her memory, but she doubted it. It didn't matter now. The love on Kurt's face as he looked at his children astonished her. Never had he been so handsome, his eyes ordinary blue under the winter sun, his eyes as radiant as the sky.

He ran with them all the way down the long final slope that approached the house, the one Annie ran in temperate times. The sled bounced wildly, but Kurt held the rope and bounded down the old quarry road as the boys' squeals of delight filled the woods.

"Come on, Mom!" Alex called, and more squeals, and Annie picked up her pace. There were days when she felt metamorphosed into another being. She knew she was still Annie, but to the boys—and even somewhat to Kurt—she was Mom, with all that the title did and did not encompass. Mom. Physician. Priest. Poet. Housekeeper. Homemaker. Each of them, to his own degree, expected her to make everything all right. She only wished she could.

As they rounded the final curve, Annie was hit with the shock of Lonnie McGrath's car in the drive. The outside world intruded suddenly on the afternoon, like a headache. A wave of something between disappointment and apprehension swept over her; she saw Kurt's quick glance at her, as though he could drive out her resentment with a look.

"I'm sorry," he said sadly. "I wasn't expecting this." He handed her the rope and trotted the last fifty yards to where Lonnie sat in his car. She walked slowly, towing the boys, listening to them ask where Daddy was going.

"Just right up there," she said. "To see his friend."

She liked Lonnie. She knew she should say hello, but instead, as she approached the house, she talked loudly to the boys about going inside for some hot cider.

She got them in the door and out of their boots and snowsuits and herself out of her boots and layers of warmth and they all stood around the woodstove, thawing their toes. That was it, how it was with Kurt. There you were, having a wonderful time, and as suddenly as disease strikes, somebody would walk into the afternoon and ruin everything.

Alex picked up the heavy wrought-iron poker, looking at her as though waiting to be told no, and jabbed tentatively at a log. She nodded okay. He began jabbing more forcefully, knocking loose a few cinders. He and Timothy smiled at each other, eyes bright. Annie, watching them, wondered if smuggling ran in the blood.

"What did I call those things?" he asked, stabbing at embers.

"Firestars," Annie said.

"Oh, yes," he said, nodding at Tim. "Firestars. That's right."

"Firestars," Tim parroted, nodding with great seriousness.

Kurt came in alone. He smiled, or tried to. "I've got to go into the city."

"Why?"

"Cash," he said, "I need to pay Mark."

"When will you be back?"

"Tomorrow," he said. "Early as possible." He pulled her close, wrapped her in a hug. "I'm sorry," he said. "I have to finish this. It will all be done soon."

"Daddy?" Alex stood holding the poker, his question a lament.

Kurt walked over and knelt near his sons.

"Hey, big boys," he said. "I gotta go to the city. I'll see you tomorrow, all right? We'll hang out some more. I'll miss you guys. Give me a kiss?" They hugged and he looked at Annie. This didn't count; this situation had arisen before, and he would need a little time, anyway, to dig himself out of the hole he was in. She would understand. She took a step toward him and he got to his feet and hugged her again.

"No choice," he said. "I'll be back as soon as I can." His kiss was sad and loving, and she made herself okay with his leaving. Not happy, but okay.

Darkness arrived early that afternoon, and with its presence and Kurt's absence, she found herself missing Kane more than ever, feeling more keenly the isolation of being in the country at night. Her fear was not of burglars or murderers or rapists, but of government agents.

After a dinner of Thanksgiving leftovers, she and the boys went to Kurt's office to curl up on the couch in front of the woodstove. Annie read *Go Dog Go!* She read *The Cat in the Hat*. She read *Harold and the Purple Crayon*. She told stories of lambs, of pigs, of spiders.

"Nothing to do, nothing to do, put some mustard in your shoe," and Timothy cracked up over that and had Alex going too, in great belly laughs, guffaws, when the phone rang.

"Sounds like a party."

It took her a moment to place the voice. Eric.

"Want some company?"

"Just reading bedtime stories," Annie said, trying to recall if she'd given him her number. She looked at Alex and Tim, who had regained their composure and were watching her, the book still open on Alex's lap. She mouthed the word *boring*, drawing it out, crossing her eyes, and they giggled softly. "I thought you were headed for Beirut."

"Not immediately." He laughed. "Not sure I want to hang out with war correspondents, you know."

Annie felt awkward, didn't know what to say next. The silence was stretching toward embarrassment.

"Let me photograph your boys?" he said. "I'd love to."

"I'm just not sure it's a good—"

"Annie," he said. "It's all different now. I want to be your friend." His voice was determined and sincere. "I always liked you," he said. "I'd like to meet your husband. He made bail?"

"Yes."

"I don't know many people up here yet. And we're practically neighbors. Know any single women?"

"Oh." Annie laughed, relieved. "So that's your motive."

"What, I have to come out and bang you over the head with it?"

"But, Eric," she said, "every time I ever saw you you were surrounded by, shall we say, nubile young—"

"I'm over that," he said. "These days I'm looking for substance."

"Get out of here."

"Scout's honor." He laughed.

"As in Boy Scouts or as in those guys who lead the hunting party?"

"Annie. I'm sincere here, I really am."

"Just kidding," she said. "In fact, I do know a few single—"

Car lights in the driveway brought her to her feet.

"Someone's here." An unexpected arrival would never have done this to her before. She could feel her pulse in her neck, pounding with fear. "I'll have to call you back."

"You have my number?"

She said yes and hung up, swinging Tim onto one hip and Alex onto the other and heading quickly for their room.

"Help me out," she said to Alex. "Hold on." He was getting so big that she wasn't sure how much longer she'd be able to carry both of them at once. She almost never did anymore, except when they were frightened at the same time, or, like now, when she was alarmed.

"Let's see what's in here," she said, making sure Tim had his balance before releasing him. She grabbed things from the bin in the closet and scattered them about the room. "You guys decide what we're going to play," she said to Alex, "and I'll be right back

"Mommy, who's that?" Alex called after her.

"I'm going to find out," she said. "Wait there for me."

"Mom," Alex said, "you're being bossy."

"Sorry, hon. I'll be right back."

She went downstairs and pulled on her boots, slipped into her heavy sweater, grabbed a hat from the basket next to the doorway, and stepped into the cold night. The stars astonished her; they always did.

A man sat in his car, leaning to read papers under the dome light. A tow truck was behind Kurt's GMC.

As Annie approached the car, the man got out. He was her height, heavy about the middle, and had a kind face. His hair and beard were silver, as was his modest suit.

"I'm afraid I don't have very good news," he said. Annie went tense, trying to blame it on the cold. He held out some papers. She took them without looking. "I'm from the sheriff's office. Deputy Jay Donnelly. I have to take the truck." He pointed at the GMC. "They have reason to believe it was used in the commission of a crime. I'm told to seize it by federal order."

Annie stood holding the papers, thinking it odd that he spoke with an Australian accent. And then, she was not sure why, she began silently to cry.

"I'm sure you're a very nice person," the deputy said. "I'm sorry to be the bearer of bad news."

She made no attempt to stop. It felt good, crying in front of this stranger, letting her tears carry away the pain of the past unending weeks. She nodded to acknowledge what he'd said, and continued to cry. She hadn't realized how much she needed the cleansing.

The deputy stood, alternating his attention between Annie and the tow-truck driver, who rattled chains loudly as he hooked the truck to his winch. The deputy's gaze settled on Annie, and she saw that he was extremely uncomfortable, verging on distraught.

"I really hate my job," he said. "I don't enjoy doing this at all. I'm a painter, actually. I moved up here from the city and I went broke and I had to have a job and this was all that was available. I really hate it."

Annie smiled through her tears.

"It's okay," she said.

She walked back to the house, locked the door behind her, and grabbed a couple of tissues from the downstairs bath on her way upstairs.

Tim was sitting in the lap of the giant white Teddy bear that Mark Levine had given Alex at birth, watching as Alex leaped about the room, doing his version of karate. He had made a cape from another birth gift, a crib quilt from Ace McGowan, now ragged with wear but still beautiful, and held to his chest a glow-in-the-dark star he'd bagged at Halloween.

"Tacular Man!" he shouted, and ran to jump onto his bed.

"Spectacular Man?" Annie said. "My favorite superhero?"

TEN

The car was clean but for personal stash, so no big problem there. Kurt sat back for the ride, trying to calm himself as Lonnie steered onto the thruway. He wished he were still in the woods with Annie and the boys. But at least he'd be able to pay Mark. He heard Wham inside his brain, belting out . . . *somebody tell me why I work so hard for you* and the bass voices in the background going *Got to get some money.* He should've gone on to law school with Mark. The guy was knocking down major bucks in the drug business, only he wasn't risking prison doing it. And there it was, one major reason why pot was still illegal: too many attorneys making too much money off one pathetic and stupid law. He stretched his shoulders in the big white leather bucket seat of Lonnie's 'seventy-seven Olds, a yellow 442 with a white ragtop, impeccably kept, and tried not to let memories of his last ride down this road—how long ago, several weeks?—intrude on the day. It was impossible. Joseph Kessler was part of his life now, like a sinus condition that could not be got rid of. And snooping around these days, too. Watching. Surveilling the house. It tied a knot in Kurt's guts when he thought of Kessler—lurking around, trailing him on his errands, trying to catch him at something, anything, waiting for a slip. And it pumped his paranoia to a practically unbearable level. If he thought about it too long, he would approach that state of mind where he would be driven to physical violence against his surroundings.

It hadn't happened often, and certainly not since he'd met Annie. He was changed by then. He had a grip on it. But the first time it happened? Man. His father had brought him to it, or he had achieved it on his own, when he was seventeen, hormones roiling the blood and brain. He was by then a champion wrestler, having taken the state title two years in a row, and he no longer knew the man who relentlessly drove his mother to tears.

He'd been standing on the front porch of a comfortable suburban house that was a ten-minute drive down tree-shaded streets to a quaint downtown.

He heard his father's voice, then his mother's, his angry, hers angry and hurt. A dish shattered against something; his father came out on the porch, breathing hard, car keys in hand. It had happened once too often, and Kurt was big enough now, strong enough. He ripped a board free of the railing and smashed his father with the strength of a fine athletic son coming of age in a household full of anger. He swung the board with rage and grace. He struck home.

His father ran, shirt torn, shoulder bleeding, face tight with terror. Kurt ran after him, and in the effort of running caught himself again and threw the board to the ground, disgusted and angry, but filled with awe at the realization that he was big enough now, strong enough. Things would change. He could protect his mother the way he'd always wanted to.

And things did change, but not much. His father's eyes held a wariness that hadn't been there before. His parents' arguments became more controlled. He'd finished up his senior year and got the hell off to college.

Fuck all that. The whole bloody scene. What he and Annie had was different. It had to be. He couldn't go through that again. He shook his head, trying to clear it. He remembered how methodically Kane had gone about the business of marking his territory when they'd first brought him home. He, too, had a territory, his home, his space, his land, what he'd worked for and taken risks for and made his own: a place where his wife could garden and his boys could run in the woods, a place where nobody could tell him what to do or how to live. Home. Sanctuary.

And now this motherfucking cop was trampling the boundaries. He wondered if Kessler had ever been a streetfighter, and in the same instant knew the guy hadn't. It wasn't that Kurt was proud of those years; he considered himself, gratefully, to have evolved beyond that, but it was still in him, and when he thought about Kessler's pursuit, he wanted nothing more than to meet the man—one on one, take it to the mats. He took a joint from his jacket pocket and fired it up, pressed a button to crack his window. Tune into the Jah love, man, deal with the angst, lose the violence. It was nowhere; it was not a solution.

Lonnie adjusted his own window and checked his speed at sixty.

"What are we smoking?" he asked.

"Thai," Kurt answered, toking deeply. He passed the joint. Good flavor. Nice aroma. He wondered what kind of head it would have this time of day.

Lonnie handed the joint back. Kurt flicked the ash and put the half-joint into a film canister, slipped it into his jacket pocket.

Instant paranoia. Annie and the boys had looked so comfortable when he left, sitting wrapped in a blanket on the couch, sipping mulled cider in front of the woodstove. It was entirely possible that he would never see them again.

"So," Lonnie said.

"They want twenty-two hundred a pound." Kurt turned to his friend. It was okay. Everything was okay. Face your fears, go into them, go through them. He trusted Lonnie, knew Lonnie was standup. He took a deep breath. "I may have to bail on this one," he said.

Lonnie twitched.

"I've got a family to think about."

"Jesus. Lotsa guys do, man. What's happening?"

"Grand jury," Kurt said. He sighed. "I'm the target."

"We expected as much, right? They got nothing. But they call that guy Gary, he'll break weak."

"I talked to him. He's cool. Said as far as that went, he didn't know a thing. Far as I know, I'm the only one arrested."

"He's weak, man. I'm telling you. I've seen it before. I can spot it."

Kurt didn't respond.

"Other than him," Lonnie said, "this crew is air tight. You know that."

"Yeah. I know." They caught each other's eyes; Kurt saw Nam in Lonnie's. He knew what his friend was considering. Trained to kill by the Marine Corps, Lonnie had done so skillfully. And the most effective move now would be to make Gary Smith disappear. Lonnie would do it if Kurt gave the word.

Kurt remembered himself all geared up to join the military, even in his sophomore year, just waiting for graduation, ready to kill or die for the honor of his country.

And then Mark Levine had moved to town and joined the wrestling team, and he and Kurt had fast become friends. One day after practice, a Friday, Mark had taken Kurt for a ride in his 1940 Ford convertible coupe and introduced him to pot. Right away, Kurt knew that nothing would ever be the same. He wasn't quite sure, while the radio played Dylan, the Beatles, the Stones, and Mark tooled him around town, exactly how things had changed, but he knew they had. On the practice mats, he could pin Mark two out of every three matches at least; but Mark, Kurt thought, was someone who had a larger awareness of the real world. He was glad they were friends.

Later that night, they'd sat parked at Wallace's, a drive-up burger joint, checking the scene, Kurt hoping to hook Mark up with a girlfriend. Not that Mark needed help. He was smart, really intelligent, and friendly. His hair shone like a newly minted penny, and his eyes were blue as a Maine lake in June. But he was still the new guy.

The screeching of tires had heralded the arrival of the Wellesley Red Raiders' star quarterback and his entourage. Off-season now, and Kurt would ordinarily have been with them, downing Carling Black Label and looking for fights and, later at night, for girls. He saw his buddies eyeing him, took a sip of Coke, and gave them a nod that said he was content to stay where he was. They were cool with it. They hung around long enough to grab a dozen or so burgers and were off again in a cloud of exhaust.

"Good bunch of guys?" Mark asked.

"Maniacs," Kurt said. "But, yeah. We got this idea that we'll all join the Marines together when we graduate."

"Fuck that," Mark said. "There's no Hitler in this one. This one's about money. Corporations. Viet Nam's still happening when I hit eighteen, I'm outta here. Somebody get me some snowshoes."

Kurt hadn't answered, but something stirred within him, an awareness, a consciousness at once exciting and frightening. He'd never met anyone who was opposed to fighting or who dared to question America's good intentions. He and Mark would spend many hours discussing it, the politics of war, and Kurt would look back upon that day knowing he'd been changed: for the better and forever.

Now as he sat watching Lonnie steer his big Olds down the thruway, he had no doubt that the man driving would take Gary Smith out of the picture and quite possibly wipe out the government's case as well. Lonnie saw it as a simple matter of self-defense.

"It's not just you," Lonnie said. "He can bury all of us."

"He said he would stand up. I know him, Lonnie. He's honest, hard-working. He's got a family. He's no punk."

"He wasn't there 'cause he wanted to be. He was there 'cause his old lady told him to make some dough."

"They got no dope." Kurt turned the radio on, adjusted the volume low. Pretenders. *Middle of the Road.* "They've got no evidence whatsoever."

"They got a whole fuckin' airplane. And I'll bet they got a few pounds just sweeping the floor of the thing."

Kurt never should have let Smith on board; he'd broken his own rules in hiring the man. But he'd needed help, and when Annie came to him and explained about Gary's wife being so desperate and all, Kurt had wanted to help out. Do the guy a favor. And Annie liked him. She was always saying what nice work Gary did on the property.

Kurt reached across and rested a hand firmly on Lonnie's shoulder.

"Anyway, they don't even know he exists. I hope."

"What's that mean? 'I hope'?"

"That agent, Kessler, the one popped me, searched the house?"

"Yeah."

"I knocked him off on surveillance."

"When?"

"Little over a month ago. September, I think."

"And you're just telling me?"

"If you'll recall, you bugged outta here right after you got paid and I got popped."

"What? I was supposed to hang around after that?"

"I know. But don't jump my case for not keeping you posted."

"So's he still around?" Lonnie was checking the rearview every ten seconds, just the way they'd taught him in driver's ed.

"The cop?" Kurt shook his head. "Haven't seen him, but I assume so." He tapped Lonnie's arm. "He was right on my ass. Sent some musclehead over to eavesdrop while I was on a pay phone."

"Sounds like he wanted you to see him."

"Maybe. Either way, it's weird."

"Big time."

"The thing scares me about it, aside from the obvious, is that I went to Smith's place that day."

"Oh, Jesus." Lonnie moaned.

"But that was before. I don't think he'd picked me up yet."

"Are you serious? You were at Smith's the same day this fuck was on your tail? Are you out of your mind? We gotta do something."

"Like what?" Kurt didn't want Lonnie to answer, and Lonnie knew it. But what were they supposed to do? Maybe Lonnie was right. The United States government had declared war on them. The DEA unquestionably qualified as a major enemy. Most of those guys were insane. The mere fact that they'd taken the job was adequate evidence of mental imbalance. And now it was war. Were they functioning under the rules of war? If Smith was a traitor, didn't he deserve to be killed? But Kurt couldn't get his mind wrapped around murder. No way, no how. He was at a loss for thought, as if his brain had overloaded on fear—of himself, what he was capable of—and short-circuited. Or something. He could blame it on the pot, but he knew better. Think. Just follow it through, one step at a time; the answer will come. It took him a moment to realize that the answers wouldn't formulate in his brain. The answer was dead center in his chest, where the muscle that pumped blood and kept his life going banged away mercifully.

"Brother," he said to Lonnie, "we don't kill people. Put those thoughts out of your head." He saw a hint of a smile on Lonnie's lips.

"Hey, you're the boss, Kemo Sabe. I'm just telling you, we could have a problem."

"Take the next service stop," Kurt said. "I gotta piss. And we gotta check for heat."

•

They found a garage near Cadman Plaza, just over the Brooklyn Bridge, and crisscrossed their way slowly to Congress Street, stopping at a Korean fruit stand to make sure no one was tailing them. Kurt looked for 3C on the building panel and pressed the intercom buzzer.

There was a burst of static, and then Bill's voice: "Who goes?"

"Nancy Drew," Lonnie said.

They pushed through two successive wire-reinforced glass doors of the converted warehouse while a buzzer loudly razzed them. The elevator was huge and moved very slowly, its motor grinding steadily during the climb.

Warm air and the scent of tomato sauce whooshed into the hallway when Bad Bill opened the door.

"Come in, come in," he said, leaving them to shut and lock the door as he led the way into the loft. His massive body filled the short hallway; there were mere inches of clearance between his shoulders and the gray barnboard walls. The hall gave on to one huge room with three industrial-size south-looking windows set in old red brick. A wooden sleep loft sat sturdily against the east wall, which was also of bare brick; beneath the platform was the bath. The kitchen area was against the west wall, stainless and concrete, totally high tech but for countless Mason jars lining a large open cupboard. The jars were filled with grains and beans and pastas, homemade sauces, and herbs and spices, many from Bill's rooftop garden. Kurt noticed a jar of Colombian from the last load tucked between a jar of lemon balm and one of sage, and plucked it off the shelf.

"Before I forget," Bill said, and took a jar from the other end of the shelf. "For your old lady." He held it up. "Habañeros." He smacked his lips. "These babies? Next day your asshole will be singing hallelujah. Smoked 'em myself, upstairs on the deck." He patted his chest a few times—be still my beating heart—and put the jar on the counter. "Don't forget." And then, almost to himself and surprised, "She thanked me for that sauce I sent over."

Kurt took the jar of Colombian and a wooden tray to the dinner table, on which bottles of alcohol, glistening antiseptically in halogen light from above, formed a centerpiece. Platters of mozzarella and peppers were two of many. He took out a bud and began breaking it onto the tray. There was always a demand for *cannabis sativa.*

Lonnie poured two shots of tequila, and Kurt sat sipping and watching his friend cook. Anyplace else, the effort of getting his bulk from one place to another left Bill in a constant state of breathlessness, but in the kitchen—and Kurt had seen him there many times—Bill was so absorbed in the preparation of food that he forgot how many pounds he was moving around. Now, he slipped lightly from counter to sink to refrigerator to stovetop, practically pirouetting as he sniffed and stirred and rolled his eyes in delight. He was in love with any good meal, especially one made by his own hands.

"The sauce I made in August," he said. "Had a good crop a' tomatoes upstairs, cooked 'em fuh *days,* got a freezer full of sauce." He held up an inch-thick slab of tuna and waved a hand at three others laid out on the counter. "Took the boat out this morning—yestehday too—got blue-fin both days. Fought like mothahfuckahs. *Gorgeous.* I'm gonna do us a putanesca here, with a little linguini." He began cutting the tuna into inch-square chunks—and suddenly stopped, slicing the air with the knife. "You know," he said, "four thousand pounds of that load might as well be seaweed. Moldy as hell. We'll never be able to get rid of it."

Lonnie raised his eyebrows. "Two tons?" He looked at Kurt. "The Colombians are going to love that."

The stereo was on and the music pulled suddenly at Kurt: the Police: "*. . . every step you take, I'll be watching you.*" A love song. Fuck Joe Kessler and the white horse he rode in on. Outta my life, asshole. An image of President Ronald Reagan illuminated the TV screen in the corner, the head bobbing at a friendly, octogenarian tempo as he lip-synched the silence. Bill had the volume off to accommodate the music. Next to the TV stood a life-size, full-color latex statue of Frankenstein's monster. The corner itself was plastered with monsters of every size and description, tacked to the walls in their packages or resting on shelves above the television. There was the Wolfman, there was Fin Fang Foom. And Godzilla. And Rodan. There was / were Dr. Jekyll and Mr. Hyde.

Kurt poured two shots, passed one to Lonnie, sipped slowly, and watched Bill ease the tuna into the sauce. He had known him for a solid ten years now. Completely dependable. The word "stalwart" came to mind. That was Bill Schapp. If he said two tons were bad, they were bad.

He needed few things, but those he needed he took seriously: good food, good liquor, good smoke, good sounds, good transportation (for both land and water), and fun toys. He fished and camped and once in a while permitted his girlfriend to drag him to a place in the East Village, a quasi-gallery, where he would purchase primitive art. He mixed a fine martini, using Boodles gin and fresh unpitted olives a perfect shade of green. He stirred, though he didn't for a minute believe that garbage about bruising the gin.

Kurt watched as Bill pulled the spoon from the sauce and tasted, brought his bunched fingertips to his lips and kissed them—*voilá*—back into the air, set the spoon carefully on the holder, and brought an empty shot glass to the dining table. The huge captain's chair creaked under his weight, but Bill ignored it and poured a whiskey, which he threw back in a single gulp.

"Be just a few minutes now," he said, nodding in the direction of the stove. He grabbed a remote from the table and lowered the stereo volume. Then to Lonnie, "You like putanesca?"

Lonnie grinned yes; Bill shook his head vigorously and smiled back. Kurt had asked Lonnie once why he didn't fix his mouth and Lonnie had said something about the pathetic VA dentists. But Kurt had a feeling it was because Lonnie knew that the missing teeth gave his face a somewhat maniacal cast that told a story instantly. Even if it wasn't conscious knowledge, Lonnie understood the value of being able to intimidate with a smile.

"The last of the load will be cashed out next week," Bill said, just realizing that he was out of breath from dancing in the kitchen. "I only wish we had more." He took the joint Kurt had rolled and lit it, inhaled deeply, exhaled slowly, nodded, poured another drink. Bam. Down the hatch. He slapped the glass hard against the table: a shudder ran head to toe.

"How much cash you got?" Kurt asked.

"Half a mil, six hundred K. More tomorrow."

"Good. Where's the moldy shit?" Kurt drew on the joint, passed it to Lonnie.

"Warehouse," Bill said. "Staten Island."

"So we'll give it back."

"Send it up north," Bill said. "See if the Canadians'll buy it. Never know."

Kurt sipped tequila and waved Bill off. "I'll ask my people what they want to do. Maybe we'll send it up north." He took out his books, ready to go over the figures with Bill.

"After dinner," Bill said, checking his watch. "It's almost ready." He rose from the table and soon returned, carrying three plates laden with linguine putanesca. The aroma of Bill's homemade sauce—home-grown tomatoes, garlic, olives, capers, anchovies, the tuna—awakened Kurt's hunger. Bill made another trip to the kitchen and brought out salad.

"The secret is," he whispered on approach, "you soak the anchovies in a little milk for about three minutes before you add them."

All conversation ceased as the three men dug into their food. The only sounds were occasional gentle grunts of pleasure from Bill and moans of admiration and thanks from Kurt and Lonnie.

Afterward, they sat silently for a while, smoking a joint as intently as a bunch of Brahmins with afterdinner cigars. When Kurt brought the books out and began crunching numbers with Bill, Lonnie strolled over to the TV and found a Knicks game.

After expenses—not counting lawyers' fees—Kurt's end would come out at around seven hundred and fifty K. He wanted to put away at least a million, maybe two, for Annie and the kids. Before. Before what? Jail? Going underground? He felt slightly sick and poured another shot, downed it.

"Cheers," Bill said, raising an eyebrow. Then, "Moldy dope I can deal with, but I don't wanna be getting moldy myself inside some fuckin' prison cell. Know what I mean?"

"They've already postponed the grand jury once under some bullshit pretense," Kurt said. "They may not even indict."

"The beard gonna hold up?" Bill poured another.

Lonnie came over and sat down, poured a tequila, and sipped, looking from Kurt to Bill.

"I say no." Lonnie's voice was firm. Bill's head jerked up.

"We don't do anything," Kurt said. "Don't forget, Father Francis headed for the woods, too. Nobody's flipping out about that."

"We've known him for years," Lonnie said. "He's still out on the coast, man; he's cool. I'm gonna join him soon as we're done with this."

Bill's index finger tapped a slow steady beat on the table, sounding unnaturally loud in the nervous silence. What a bitch.

"Unless Gary gives us all up," Lonnie added.

"He doesn't even know your names," Kurt said.

"So they show him pictures."

"What else they got?" Bill asked.

"He can't give us up if they don't have him," Kurt said. "I told you. I talked to him myself. They didn't pop him. I'm it."

"They might have some sweepings from the plane," Lonnie said.

"Okay, all right," Bill said, "they got what they got. Let's keep moving on this Leb." He looked to Kurt.

Kurt sat for a moment. He'd done several trips with the Lebanese; the setup there was extraordinary, almost risk-free until the hash landed stateside. But it was a major hassle doing business with them. Most important, he had promised Annie. He had promised, and he was going to live up.

"I gotta bail on this one," he said.

Bill didn't blink. "Whaddaya talking? Now's the perfect time."

"Sorry," Kurt said. "I'm out. That's all."

Bill's eyebrows shot up; his mouth fell open. "Whaddaya?" He was breathless. "We been partners for years. Years. What are you talking here?"

"I have to. That's all."

"Just put it together. We'll do it," Lonnie said. "You stay in the background."

Kurt wondered if this was what it felt like to betray someone. The trip had been in the works for months; he'd spent plenty of time and money laying the groundwork; and now he was readying himself to bail out just about the time he'd really be needed. It wasn't the right thing to do. His crew deserved better. It would be a serious payday for them all. But if he did it, he couldn't very well stay in the background. The connection in Lebanon was his.

"It's not that," he said. "I'm out, my friends. I gotta get out." He wasn't sure what he felt, but he was still seeing Annie and the boys sitting in front of the woodstove. He had to do this. It was time to make good.

Bill suddenly burst into laughter. "Hey, buddy," he said, shaking his head. "How you gonna pay for your ticket? You got family to support. You got lawyers to pay."

Bill. He had a knack; he knew how to cut right to the heart of things. Kurt didn't have an answer.

"And you got partners here who got time and money invested in you. Just keep it to yourself. You don't have to tell the old lady."

Kurt sat still, feeling slightly faint. One good trip would make all the difference. He knew his enemy now; he had sat face to face with Kessler. And he'd leave Smith out of this one. Then, if he had to, he could take Annie and the boys and leave the country. He sipped the tequila. He'd lost the catch at Kennedy, though. The guys who were grabbing his shipments before customs got to them had left; their boss was suspicious. If he did this trip, he'd have to reroute the shipment. A bitch, to be sure, but once you started having to cut in bosses, things always got complicated.

"The Leb," Bill said, taking a deep breath, as though inhaling the smoke of hashish. "It's gonna be so heavy."

Kurt looked at Bill, then at Lonnie. He owed them this. Annie wouldn't have to know. One serious payday, and he could get out for good, get out forever.

"We're gonna need a new catch. Any suggestions?" he asked Bill.

Bill flipped his hand skyward and pursed his lips. "Whaddabout that guy, Nocenti's cousin in Jersey? You could talk to him."

•

Lonnie was draped in the passenger seat, taking a nap. Kurt was at the wheel in a bluish funk, stuck in Friday night traffic on the Brooklyn Bridge, berating himself silently.

Kessler's words came back to him, hammering at a brain that glowed gold with tequila: *Think about your kids, buddy.* Buddy. Fuck him. *Smart guys get out of the business, but you can't, you're hooked on it. Think about your wife.*

How could he? He had to; that was all. And the business was changing. Kessler was right about that. He would get out. It was time.

He left Lonnie parked on Eighty-ninth with four bags of cash tucked into the stash built into the car's trunk, and walked to Mark's apartment-office three blocks south, carrying one for his lawyer.

Mark looked troubled, the north-south crease in his forehead just above his nose in full furrow. They embraced and clapped each other hard on the back before Mark led him to the living room.

They sat on facing black velvet settees; between them was a glass and iron table.

"What are you drinking?"

"Is it obvious?"

"Not terribly."

"Tequila."

Mark went to the kitchen and returned with a crackled glass bottle of Añejo Patrón and a couple of shot glasses. He removed the cork and poured while Kurt put his black cloth bag full of money on the floor next to his boot. Five more to come tomorrow. Those he would carry home to his wife. He studied the Afghani war rug beneath the table. Tanks, missiles, and helicopters, woven in blues and browns and oranges and whites. Lots of military green. Tribal weavers, their ancient art passed from one generation to the next, working with images of the twentieth century; flowers and geometry replaced by guns and destruction.

"Listen, my friend," Mark said. "We've got big trouble. This U.S. Attorney on your case, his name's Richards. Derrick Richards. Major asshole."

"In my book all prosecutors are assholes."

"I know one or two who're cool. But that's beside the point." Mark sipped his tequila. "The grand jury handed down your indictment this afternoon. We're due in court Monday. He asked for a CCE. And they gave it to him."

"Speak English."

"Continuing criminal enterprise. The Kingpin statute."

"What the fuck does that mean?"

"It gets worse. They've got an unindicted co-conspirator. Somebody's saying you brought in ten tons. If we take this to trial and lose, you're looking at life imprisonment with no parole."

Kurt took a long slow swallow from the shot glass, draining it, and reached for the bottle. He watched himself pour another.

"Whoa, pal," Mark said. "You driving?"

"It's all just illusion, right?" Kurt said. "Yeah, I was driving. I'll let my partner take over." He replaced the cork.

"Richards has got a major hard-on. They say you've been doing this for a long time, and they figure if they squeeze you, maybe you'll cooperate."

"You mean rat."

"Hey, man, I know. It's a bitch. It's a major—" Mark stopped talking and downed a shot.

Kurt poured still another, already ruing the way he'd feel in the morning. "This guy Kessler's been on my case for years," he said. "I don't even know how long. I don't know what he knows. But, I mean, he told me he thinks I'm gonna slide on this one."

"When? Was he trying to get you to cooperate? Because I'm not at all sure you're going to slide on this one. Someone is talking."

Kurt sat staring at the rug. Stunned to silence.

"He's a straightup agent," Mark said. "At least that's his reputation. But they've come up with a lot more since you were arrested."

"Life in prison? What the—" Kurt stood, began pacing.

"It's simple." Mark poured another shot. This one he sipped. "They've got a rat."

"I don't fuckin' believe this."

"Believe it. You've got to be careful. Very, very careful. If they've flipped somebody, you're fucked. And it sounds as if they have. You use your regular crew?"

"Mostly," Kurt said. "Lonnie's with me strong. Father Francis is cool too."

"Bill there?"

"Yeah. Out of the question." Kurt contemplated his boots. Dumb fuck.

When are you gonna learn to listen to yourself? "Gary Smith," he said. "Gary Smith."

"Do I know him?"

"No. He's a handyman, works at a place down the road from us. He did some work for Annie. He's not a bad guy, but he wasn't into it. His wife made him do it."

"Bingo."

"Everyone else is accounted for."

"Talked to him recently?"

"No."

"He gonna give them everybody they want?"

"He won't lie for them, if that's what you mean."

"Who all's in trouble? What does he know?"

"First names. Bill, Johnny, Lonnie, Father Francis. Where we did it. He didn't meet the pilot; I don't even know if he got a good look at him."

Life with no parole. Is this happening?

"You're in touch with them."

"Oh, yes."

"I may need their lawyers' names."

Kurt sat down and let his head rest on the couch. Fucking Gary Smith.

"How much damage can he do?"

"He can say I hired him to help unload the plane."

"That's quite a bit." Mark let out a long sigh. "Rats make the world go round."

"He won't just spill his guts. They'll have to squeeze him."

"They're good at that." Mark shifted, leaned forward. "How's Annie? How're the kids?"

"Fine," Kurt said. He pulled himself up. "Everyone's fine. Can I use your phone?"

Mark motioned at a slab of glass next to the couch. Kurt picked up a handset.

"Touch four," Mark said.

"Who's in front of me?"

"My office, the MCC, and the U.S. Attorney's office."

"Nice company."

Kurt, listening to the electronic ring through the receiver, wondered if Annie would pick up, wondered what he would tell her.

•

Annie stood watching Spectacular Man jump on the bed; his smile had brought everything right, and she hesitated to move when the phone rang. Maybe Eric again. Or maybe a courtesy call from the sheriff's office, a quality-control specialist who would ask if the deputy had been courteous and efficient when he stole the truck.

"Phone!" Tim shouted. "Phone!" Alex stopped jumping and smiled at Annie, proud that his brother had learned a new word.

Kurt's voice was gentle, apologetic.

"Hi, babe," he said quietly. "I'm at Mark's." His tone told her he wouldn't be coming home tonight.

"The sheriff's office was here," Annie said. "They seized your truck."

"Those—"

"The deputy was very nice," she said, speaking briskly, fearing that if she slowed down she might burst into tears again. "So you have to stay over?"

"Can't avoid it," he said. "I'm really sorry. I wanted to be with you."

"See you tomorrow then," she said. "Want to talk to Alex?"

"*No!*" Alex shouted. "I'm not Alex. I'm Tacular Man."

"Oh, excuse me," Annie said to him. And, into the phone, "Would you like to talk to Spectacular Man?"

She put them to sleep in their beds, though she knew that by morning they would probably both be in hers. Tim could climb out of his crib at will these days. Escape from Alcatraz. He delighted in it. She fell asleep almost instantly, her last waking thought that perhaps tears were soporific.

Sometime in the night, she awoke to Timothy's chanted cries of "Mommy . . . Mommy . . . I want my mommy . . ." and before she was even half-conscious she was at his crib, reaching for him, soothing and shushing. She tucked him against her shoulder and felt the whisper of his breath on her neck as she leaned to pull a blanket over Alex, curled in the corner of his bed.

She wandered back down the hall to the bedroom and to the side of the bed where Kurt might have been sleeping, and then back to the rocking chair in the boys' room. The short walk had put Timothy to sleep, but she sat down anyway, rocking him gently, trying to shed the sense of disquietude that lingered in the night like an unsettled argument.

She wondered where Kurt was, worried that he might get rash in the face of his burdens. Why had they done this? Why hadn't she convinced him, really pushed, until he understood that he had to get out of it or she would leave? But she didn't want to leave him. She should have found a way to make him stop. As if she could have. She thought about the sad little sheriff's deputy, how he'd said, just before leaving, "I'm a nice man. Really I am." She thought about the power they had, agents of the law, about how they could come and take your car or take your house or take your bank account. And about how they could come and take your husband or your children. Her children. She held Timothy closer, careful not to wake him, and worked to stop herself from imagining it: her children being pulled from her arms by a deputy or a social worker or whatever the hell it was they called themselves. The law could rip a family to shreds long before dragging anyone into a courtroom. She kissed her younger son's head and took him back to his crib, eased him down with his head pushed up against the pillow, just the way he liked it.

She would not sleep now. Pointless to try. It wasn't quite four, but the day had begun. She removed her gown in favor of long johns and slipped back into her robe and moccasins.

She started coffee and checked the thermometer: 20 degrees, and not yet December. Downstairs, putting a log into the stove, she caught a finger between it and the stove opening, cutting and burning her knuckle at once. She brought her hand quickly to her mouth, tasting blood and ashes as she cleaned the wound. When the fire was blazing, she sat down next to the open stove door, watching the flame dance within, awaiting its warmth to fill her.

•

It was near midnight when Kurt and Lonnie checked in at the Gramercy Park Hotel, stuffing the money bags under the beds before passing out behind a mixture of tequila, marijuana, and nervous exhaustion. Kurt found himself awake almost every hour. Unindicted co-conspirator. A snitch. A rat. Gary Smith. He raised his head, looked around the small, plainly furnished room, heard the fits and starts of traffic seven stories below. Life without parole. You'll die in a prison cell, motherfucker. His head fell back on the pillow.

He was on the street by six, pumping quarters into a pay phone. Gotta get Bill up and running, get the rest of the cash, and get the hell out of Dodge. He would not be taken from his family. He would take them with him. He didn't know how or when or where; he didn't know anything except that he wasn't about to stick around and go to prison for-fucking-ever. He thought again about Lonnie's willingness to do away with Gary. He couldn't believe he was even considering it. The guy was decent and hardworking and honest. He had kids. He was a handyman, for God's sake, and a good one. He had carefully restored a crumbling shed in back of the house; he had replaced a leaking pipe in the hand-dug well, easily two hundred years old, near the shed, and repacked and restored an old hand pump he found in the pile of junk the previous owners had left inside the shed. Annie used it to draw water for her garden. He had done storm windows and laid the stone on which sat the woodstove, replaced the thimble and hooked up the stove when Annie finished blacking it. He was patient with his work, but efficient too. He loved working with old things, using his hands to bring the discarded, the forlorn, the used-up and forgotten back to usefulness. Kurt had liked him from the start.

But Lonnie was right. Lonnie was dead-on right. If the feds had got to Gary Smith, the entire crew could be busted. Maybe it was what Lonnie said: a clear-cut case of self-defense. Shit. Kurt's brain was buzzing with confusion. It sounded like a goddamm hornets' nest in there.

•

Headlights glared down the long drive leading to Gary's house and hit the modest cabin that he had taken from ruin back to a plain and simple functioning. The place was cozy. The place was charming. It had been built in the 1930s on the banks of the Esopus Creek, enjoyed for twenty years or so, and then left to fall apart, which it had done most effectively. Gary had started with the foundation, moved to the roof, and worked his way back down. He'd washed and oiled the ceiling beams, built a fireplace of stone, gathered windows and sinks and floor planks from odd places all over the county, gathered the discarded and made it useful once again. He'd plastered the walls, tinting the plaster with coffee or blueberry juice: no toxins, please. He'd planted a Japanese maple in front, apple and pear trees on either side, blueberry bushes out back. His oldest son, now six, was learning to fish in the creek. In spring and summer, and even into fall, Gary often pulled dinner from the water. Twice a year, his wife made soap and candles, some for the family, some to sell in area shops.

Kurt liked and respected him. Kurt wanted to murder him. Why the fuck had the guy caved in? Slow down, buddy; you don't even know if he has. Yes, you do.

Lonnie killed the engine and the lights at once. The front porch light came on and Gary stepped out the door before Kurt was out of the Olds. Lonnie stayed in the car, closed his eyes. It was none of his business unless Kurt said it was.

Gary looked at Kurt directly as the two approached each other. He wasn't ducking anything. That was the thing about him Kurt most respected: the unwavering honesty.

They shook hands. Kurt looked past him; he could see Smith's wife at a window, watching them.

"I'm sorry about your troubles," Gary said.

"Did they arrest you?"

"Threatened to."

"How'd they find you?"

"I guess they know I do work for you." He shrugged. "They came and asked a bunch of questions."

"Damn, Gary, what did you say?" He wanted to ask Gary why he had talked at all, but he knew the answer was standing behind the glass, peering out at them.

"Man," Kurt said. He let loose a sigh. "I tried to do you a solid."

Gary bent his head, stubbed a toe against the dirt.

"They subpoenaed me. And her. I got three kids, man. I can't do any time."

"There's plenty of guys in prison with wives on the outside."

"I don't aim to be one of them."

"Then you shouldn't have been along, man. It's that simple. If you're in, you're in it all the way . . . You got a lawyer?"

"Court-appointed." Gary shrugged again.

"Call mine. His name's Mark Levine. In the city, East Eighties."

Gary was quiet for a long moment. "This fellow I got, he seems okay."

"Trust me, Gary. You don't want some half-ass public defender looking out for you. Call Mark."

"Like I said, he seems all right to me."

"I got kids, too, and a wife. There's some things a man just doesn't do, you know."

"I'm sorry," Gary's mind was made up. "I've got to do what I've got to do. It's not up to anybody but me, and I'm the one who'll live with it."

"Think about it long and hard, brother."

Gary stiffened, pulled his hands from his pockets, and let them fall to his sides, ready. "I have thought about it. I've thought about it a lot. I don't take well to a threat."

"Unless it's coming from the cops." Kurt's anger surged, his jaws went tight. He tried to press it back, press it down, contain it.

Gary stepped forward, hands fisted at his sides, arms taut. "I think you should go," he said.

"I thought you were standup," Kurt said. "Annie always loved your work."

"She in on your business?"

That broke it. Kurt shoved Gary in the chest, hard. "Fuckin' rat." Almost whispered. The blow knocked Gary back, but he recovered his balance and came at Kurt, his lips pulled into a snarl, fists raised, looking for an opening.

"You want it that way," he said, quiet and slow; "that's all right too."

Kurt stood, his fists positioned, rocking his weight from foot to foot, ready to circle, ready to pound this motherfucker.

And then he heard Lonnie step from the Olds and shut the door. Gently.

"No," Kurt said. "No." He stepped back from Gary, out of range, dropped his fists. "Not going that way." He stepped farther back and slowed down, slowed everything down, getting his breath, letting his anger float into the dark night sky. He looked past Gary to the woman peeking out from behind the curtains. "Shit," he said.

Gary dropped his fists, too, and tucked his hands back in his pockets.

"She's got no way to make it without me," he said. "They said they'd put me away for twenty years."

"That's a cop-out," Kurt said. "If you testify, you're a rat."

"Plain and simple." It was Lonnie, who'd silently come up beside Kurt.

Gary raised his eyes to the stars, glittering hard against night, and then back to Kurt.

"I'll think things over," he said. "Don't come around here threatening me."

"I didn't come here to threaten you," Kurt said. "I came to tell you I think you're making a bad mistake. I came to hook you up with my lawyer."

"I already got my own," Gary said. "We'll be in touch."

He turned and walked toward the front porch. Kurt watched the curtain fall closed behind the window.

ELEVEN

The air in the living room had cooled. Annie went upstairs and checked on the boys before slipping down to Kurt's basement office. The woodstove was a black Viking that Gary Smith had found heaped in one corner of an old shed near the big Dutch barn behind the house. Horribly rusted, its stubby legs piled inside its belly, the thing had looked to Annie unusable, but Gary assured her it would give off blessed good heat. He would fix it himself, but couldn't get to it until close to Christmas. She used a wire brush to take off the rust and applied a coat of stove black, rubbing it to a deep sheen over the course of a week, and the stove had since helped them through two of the brittlest winters she could recall.

The wood supply was thin. She wondered why Gary hadn't brought in more. Always by Thanksgiving he and Kurt would have laid in enough for winter, stacking it fat and dry under the shingled roof of the woodshed, next to the barn. Maybe Kurt had told him to lie low since the bust. Whatever it was, she would have to remind Kurt that the matter needed his attention.

She took the poker and jabbed at the glowing remains of a log, breaking it into orange embers on a bed of gray ash. Firestars. She fed three new logs into the stove's small front opening, placing them to draft before checking the damper and adjusting the vent, scanning the floor for cinders.

Silence. The boys asleep for almost three hours now. Carol would be back from the city tonight, via train and taxi. Kurt, she hoped, was still on his way back from seeing Mark. Gone a day and night longer than he'd planned, he had phoned earlier to say he was on the way. Almost eleven now; even if he'd hit the worst of traffic, he should have been home by nine-thirty. They had feared eavesdroppers on the phone, but she knew from his tone that something was wrong.

She went upstairs to her chair in the living room, pulled a black wool throw, a wedding gift, over her lap. The carpets were clean, the upholstery repaired. The front door had a new, stronger lock. Surfaces were repaired, but Annie had begun to date things from Kurt's arrest. "A few days before the bust," she would think, or, "Since the bust happened . . ."

What needed mending now was the bond between husband and wife. She supposed her part of it was her fierce desire to make sure the boys weren't hurt. Someday they would go away, move out of her orbit and into the world. It would begin happening sooner than she wanted, though a small part of her looked forward to the time when she would have her own life again, time to attend to her needs without feeling that she was slighting her family. But now, while they were so small, so helpless, they came first—they simply had to. Kurt claimed he understood, claimed he agreed, but he had grown steadily more dour over the past few weeks.

They came in together, Carol and Kurt, she pleasant with wine and a long weekend with friends, he taut with news he did not want to deliver. Carol saw how Kurt looked at Annie and how Annie didn't look back.

"Why don't you two take a drive?" she suggested. "I'll be here with the boys. Go have a drink or something."

They didn't say much on the ride over. The bar at the Krumville Inn was dark and fully occupied. Leather heavies from the city sat shoulder to shoulder with locals: electricians, carpenters, well drillers, truckers. A couple of guys played eight ball while another leaned on the pinball machine in the corner, listening to Morticia Adams dare him to play, watching a friend get taken to the cleaners. The juke box held *Spirit in the Night* and plenty of Van Morrison. It was said that you couldn't get directions to the Krumville Inn; you had to drive around lost in Ulster County until you were drawn to it.

Kurt ordered Stoli straight up for himself and with soda for Annie. They sat gazing past each other. Another round. Wondering what to say, how to say it. He took her hand; his felt weighted with fatigue.

"Don't touch me unless you really want to," she said.

He rolled his eyes and went to the jukebox. A short time later she heard Mick Jagger sing *I'm just waiting on a friend.*

"So tell me," she said finally. "Just tell me."

He was silent for a long moment, and she realized what it must have been like for Carol the time Ron took her out to lunch and said, "I filed for divorce this morning." *I did the paperwork that will officially undo our love. Negate us, what we were. I filed the documents with the proper authority.*

Kurt's eyes warned her; and then his voice, which had soothed so many times, said, "If I go to trial and get convicted, I'm facing life with no parole."

She heard words coming out of her mouth but did not know who'd said them.

"Life?"

"With no parole. I will die in prison. I could commit murder and get less time."

He didn't know this new law. None of his friends did, either. Somewhere along the line a politician had drawn up some papers and got his cronies to vote yea, and now the feds could lock you in a cage until you stopped breathing.

"For marijuana?" She felt stupid. Not uninformed, not miseducated. Stupid. How could they not have known this? Life with no parole.

Their eyes connected, and everything they had worked for and hoped for and dreamed of shattered and fell on the table between them. A mound of salt. Dust.

"You said they don't have a good case."

"Gary Smith might cooperate."

His words didn't register. There was a mistake. There must be a mistake here, somewhere.

"He says he's got no choice." Kurt shook his head slowly, shifted his gaze past her to a huge blue-fin tuna hanging on the wall behind their table. "He says he's got a family to think about."

She wanted to scream, "A FAMILY MAN! HOW REFRESHING!"

"The question is whether to even show up," he said.

Her husband was talking.

"That's what I've got to decide. I show up to face charges, it's not even up to the judge, the sentence. Mandatory minimums, and the minimum on this case is life without parole. There won't be any bail."

Betrayal was the word that came to Annie's mind. Just that. Betrayal. He had gambled their future. The boys' childhood. Their house, their home, their love. Because he needed to lose it?

But she'd known. And done nothing to stop it, or nothing beyond talking about it. She'd known but didn't want to. And therefore hadn't.

"What did Mark say?"

"He's worried."

"How can they . . ." she started, but let the sentence fall into the empty air.

"You got five or more employees working for you, you make a few hundred grand a year, you do it by bringing in illegal foliage, these days it's CCE, continuing criminal enterprise."

His words came out angry, and she took the fury as directed at her, as though it were her fault for mentioning to him in the first place that Gary's wife was pressuring him to make some serious cash. Annie was the one who kept everything running smoothly; she was the one who dispensed love, who nurtured, who gave sustenance. Kurt's arrest had thrown everything awry. Agent Kessler had tossed some kind of psychic hand grenade into their living room and blown their connections to smithereens. Nothing was right anymore. Nothing could be. The tether was stretched to the limit, to the point where it would either snap them back together or break apart and send them reeling into the darkness, free-falling, unconnected, despairing of love.

What could he have been thinking? What could she have been thinking? That they'd get away with it, year after year? She looked down at her drink—confusion on the rocks with a twist, and lemme have a shot of despair with that.

"He's going to testify?"

"He's been subpoenaed by the grand jury. Says they'll lock him up for twenty years unless he cooperates."

"And you?"

He shook his head. "You know I can't do that."

"I know you don't want to."

"Babe, I go to the source. You know? It gets serious at that level. And it's wrong, anyway. It's just plain wrong."

"It's right for you to go to prison and leave your little boys out here with no father? Leave me? Is that right?"

He didn't answer.

"I'm supposed to bring them to visit you in some hellhole?"

More silence.

"We're almost out of firewood," she said. "We'll have to find someone else."

"No problem," Kurt said.

"I'm too tired to think," she said. "Let's get out of here."

He drove with his right hand heavy on the wheel, his weight shifted against the door. Well after one, and rain splattered rudely against the Jeep's wide windshield before getting sloshed to one side or the other by the wiper blades. The last of autumn's plumage was being torn from the trees by a whipping November wind and thrown to the blacktop road in the form of wet, slippery leaves.

"You're doing another trip," she said.

"We have a decision to make." His voice was flat, businesslike. "I want to know that you'll go with me."

"On the run."

"If I can get ID, I can get us out of the country."

"And then what?"

"And then we'll settle down somewhere and make a life for ourselves."

"I thought that's what we were doing here."

"I'll get out. It'll be different."

"Tell me you're not doing another trip, working on one right now."

"I have no choice." His jaw so tight the muscles in front of his ears were bulging, pulsing with anger.

"You and Gary both. Nobody has any choice. I don't want to live this way."

"You were happy to live this way as long as there was no heat."

"That's not true. Every time you do a trip, it's always 'This is the last time.' Always."

"It just hasn't worked out. But it will."

"Why? How? When? Can we be more specific here?"

He glared at her. She glared back. They turned their attention to the roadway. He was alone, and she was alone; they drove through the night.

"So you want us just to pack up, leave house and home, and take the boys on the run. How can you ask me to do that?"

"Life with no parole," he said. "That's how." He pulled even farther from her, shifted in his seat. She couldn't stand this. She couldn't stand that somehow he expected her to make everything all right. He expected her to be his mother. He expected her to understand even when she couldn't. *Understanding at all cost is injurious to both parties.* Where had that come from? Didn't matter; she wouldn't. More, she couldn't stand that Kurt had taken his love away, closed himself off, removed himself from her. He was sitting two feet away, and he might as well have been in Asia. It had happened before and she had hated it then, too. And it was all the worse now; she could reach over and touch him, but she couldn't reach him.

The boys had felt it. This week, all week long, even more than last, they had been bickering, picking on each other over a hundred little nothings. Tim would walk up to Alex and shove him in the chest—just to hear him scream. He'd even managed to knock Alex down once or twice when he caught him daydreaming. When they woke in the mornings, it was with angry howls instead of their usual laughter.

Maybe it was that—the knowledge that Kurt's hostility toward her was filling their children with fear and anger. Maybe it was that. Maybe it was that mixed with three vodkas, or maybe it was just something awful in her.

"It's all fine and good for you to sit there and say you don't want to live like this," he said angrily. "You think I want to live like this?"

"Then don't."

"I don't have a choice right now!" He shouted, and she heard her father, bellowing at her mother, and it was all too much the same: men raising their voices, men banging on tables, men exerting their superior heart-lung capacity, intimidating on a physical level, *music is the highest art,* let's make noise. Music gives pleasure, noise gives pain, listen to my baritone, listen to my bass, my basso profundo I can crush your body I can rip your eardrums like they were a virgin's hymen. I can yell until you cower. Fuck me or die, bitch.

She heard rattlesnake warnings in her head, the sound so dry it was liquid. She did not want to fight. She did not. They were doing what her parents had done and his parents had done and how many parents before them. What were they doing and why were they doing it? He screamed, and she was cornered, in a cave, backed up against an ancient stone wall, snarling at an enemy who was bigger and stronger and more experienced. She was fighting for her life and the lives of her children, and her only weapon was ferocity. Something rushed up, swelling against her skin until she thought she would explode, and she lurched across the seat and was on him, smashing his face with her fist, using her left hand to brace herself against the seat back and strengthen the force of her blows. She was on him without fear. On his terms. On male terms. Her fist struck his cheek, his nose, his eye; he raised an arm, she felt her knuckles hit the hard knot of muscle in his biceps, she felt weak, she felt monstrous, she was screaming, and his eyes were wild with the surprise of her attack.

"You said you wanted children!" She heard the ugliness of her voice. "You said you wanted a family!" She threw her body weight into her shoulder and down her arm and into her fist; she rose in the seat, faked a punch, landed another blow to his eye, hard this time; she felt it in the bones of her hand.

She wished she were hitting herself.

She pulled back. Kurt was ducked down behind his arm, stunned. She couldn't see him through the glaze of rage that choked her sight; he was over there somewhere, and she had to get out.

"Stop the car! Stop!"

"FUCK YOU!" he bellowed, and his words hit her physically. He stepped on the accelerator.

She grabbed the wheel, wrenched it down hard. The Jeep veered into the ditch and jolted to a stop, its front wheel stuck in the mud. He stared at her, unseeing, unable to recognize, and she knew he was right. She found the door handle and heard him screaming something and then she lunged back at him and landed an open-handed slap on his cheek.

"ASSHOLE!"

The ditch was thick with mud, and she almost fell before pulling herself up onto the road. She waited for the car to screech away, waited for mud to sling at her from the back tires, but heard only a low grind as he put the vehicle into four-wheel drive and eased out of the ditch.

She did not know the man driving away.

Their blood had mingled, but she did not know him and he didn't know her. She watched the taillights glow red rounding a curve in the road.

She thought back to their meeting, that awful party, at how Eric had straightened up. She would have too, probably, even without Kurt. She would have found someone else and had a family and it wouldn't have been like this. Looking at prison. She would have found someone without Kurt's need to gamble his freedom. Someone whose love of family was sufficient to get him through another day at the office or wherever, just not anyplace where the cops would come. She thought back to all those evenings, when she'd first started dealing mutual funds, before the partying, when she'd gone home after work to a glass of milk and a volume of Jung, looking for enlightenment or at least a small peace of mind. She could not put a name to her emotional state; funk was the closest she could come.

She had tried to shake it all through the final year at NYU, first on her own, and then with the help of a shrink in the university's health program. When Dr. Wulf steered the discussion toward her father, she found herself saying words like "distant" and "absent" and "liar," but couldn't take herself into it any deeper than that. And then graduation had come along, and the job at the Calvani Group, and the phone calls to Eric.

And her friend Kathy insisted she had found Annie's Mr. Right, and when Mr. Right didn't show, here came Kurt.

She thought about the time, after she'd locked herself in her apartment to get past the cocaine spiders and the shakes and all the rest of that nastiness, when she'd called him to say she was fine now, thanks. And they'd gone to a reading and they'd gone to dinner and they'd gone for coffee and talked into the small hours of morning.

"At the risk of speaking in psychobabble," she'd told him, "I seem to have a pattern of getting involved with men who are hurtful."

He bent over the small marble table, surprised at her words. "I don't know that we have much of a future then," he said. "I'm just not into hurting women. Or hurting anybody, for that matter. Not into putting that kind of energy out there."

He'd walked her home and kissed her good night, but it hadn't been a very good kiss; it was like a courtesy. She didn't think he would call, and he didn't, and then she realized that he probably *was* a nice guy and that she'd frightened him. She picked up the phone and dialed.

She didn't remember exactly when, but not very long after that, they began seeing each other in earnest, he sharing his dreams about family, talking about how it was the most important thing in the world to him. She wasn't sure at first, about the stirrings his words created in her. She had never given much thought to any of that, still running as she was from her childhood.

There was that Sunday morning when they'd gone, sleepy-eyed and reeking of sex, to a funky little Ukrainian place on Second Avenue and spread the *Times* on the table. An item that started small on the front page, one of those predictable periodic brouhahas where experts said drug use was on the rise again, had taken his attention from her and prompted her to ask, finally, though by now she thought she knew. "What is it you do for a living, besides make phone calls?"

He put the paper down, took a sip of coffee, and whispered in her ear, "I'm a smuggler."

They'd carried the paper back to her apartment and undressed again and scattered it all over the bed, reading, drinking coffee, massaging, touching, enjoying skin against skin as the springtime sun slanted through the window, heading toward noon. He placed a hand on her belly, rubbed ever so gently, smiled, and said, "We could put a baby in there."

She had never before felt so loved and so loving. So free.

And when they boarded the flight to Austin, Annie had looked out the window at the ugliness of La Guardia and wondered how the view had changed since her mother boarded a flight with her father, who'd come north to West Point to catch success and instead had caught a Yankee wife.

"This is different," she kept telling herself. "He's not like your father, and you're not like your mother, and you've never been this happy before. Ever." She heard the captain say, "Sit back, relax, and enjoy the flight."

There had been that craziness with Father Francis in Texas, when the state narcs had chased them down, expecting to find a van full of pot but instead had found only their little black transmitter. And then quiet time, she and Kurt alone together at the ranch, and water seeking its level.

They had gone into the desert to be with fire, to be human and small, naked together on a blanket beneath a vast Texas midnight, calling out to the stars. And later, still wrapped in each other, they listened to the howling of wolves.

She had known the next morning, before doctors or tests or the weakness of those first months. She had known in her belly and in her heart, and in the way Kurt looked at her, too. He sensed what neither of them had the courage to speak, and it filled his eyes with a wonder as innocent as any Sunday morning.

They followed on Father Francis's heels, back to the city, away from the wrath of the Texas authorities, and Annie found herself sitting in Dr. Wulf's office, terrified of the future but as content in the moment as ever she had been. He sat as though she'd never been away, waiting for her to begin the session.

"I don't know what's happened, how it's happened, forget about why, but I am, as they say, *en famille.*"

His face broke into the first grin Annie had seen on it, and it was, no question, completely genuine. He was happy. For her. He said *mazel tov* and meant it.

"And the . . . ?" Sniff-sniff.

"Not a factor," she said.

"You'll need to be careful."

She could not recall that he had ever before uttered a single word of advice to her. It was as though, because there was life in her belly, he had transmogrified overnight from psychiatrist to father. Good father. Kind father. Gentle and caring.

"Will you marry?"

"Probably," she said. "We think so."

She wondered how she would have felt if he'd asked, "So who's the father?"

"What would prevent it?"

"Nothing, I guess, except that we both dread becoming yet another dysfunctional family."

"Awareness helps," he said. "What does he do?"

"He's in antiques," she lied, already cognizant that to tell anyone, *anyone,* what her fiancé did for a living was to risk sending him to prison. Besides, he would be out of it soon, and it wouldn't be a lie when she said he sold antiques.

"I'm happy for you," Dr. Wulf said.

Annie thanked him and said she probably wouldn't be coming in anymore.

"There's no reason you need to stop right now," he said.

"We think we'll be moving upstate," she explained.

"Think about it," he said. "Call me when you decide where you'll be. I can give you some names."

She hadn't.

And now it was dark and rainy and windy, and she was alone on a country road and crying for tomorrow, scared more of herself and what she had done than of anything she might run into out there in the night.

·

She quietly ducked in the door, praying not to have to face Carol, confusion buzzing in her skull like a swarm of yellow jackets. She pulled off boots thick with mud and hung her rain-beaded sweater on the rack next to the kitchen door. The house was quiet, the kitchen lit only by the nightlight that burned next to the stove.

He was not in their bed, but on the couch in his office, lying as though asleep, though she couldn't tell in the dark. She stood in the door for who knew how long, wanting to do or say something that would make it all go away or else finish the fight and get it the hell over with. She did not see how there could be any making up this time.

They had argued before, like all couples, but they'd always fought fair, or else one of them had managed to step back until tempers cooled enough to talk the trouble away. She wanted to wake him but was afraid. He had stood honorable in the face of her assault. He had been a man. Better, even.

She was rounding the corner to the stairs when she heard him say, "You can't hit worth a shit," and then the rustle of the blanket as he turned his back to her.

She paused, fearing to turn around. She climbed weakly up the stairs, groggy with vodka and spent rage, disgusted with herself and sick that he was still in the house. She forced herself to walk through the living room and up the flight to the boys' room.

Alex was sprawled beneath the covers, arms above his head, feet resting at either side of his bed. His form was athletic and beautiful; Annie wondered at it, and at what he would become. Tim was curled in a ball, resting on his knees, butt in the air, his head pressed against the mattress as though he wanted to burrow beneath the pillow. She pulled the covers to his shoulders and stepped back, terrified by the depth of her love.

It was always true, and each time it amazed her: the sleeping child as angel, or the closest thing to one on earth. The bees went away, driven by love back to their harmful nest somewhere deep in her brain.

It occurred to her that the right thing would be to leave the boys with Kurt and go, disappear, spare them the violence of her heartache. He would teach them to wrestle and play baseball.

He could not teach them from inside a prison. She heard Kessler: "I'm always reassured when I encounter yet another faithful wife." She had thought him kind when he removed the handcuffs.

Whoever it might be best for, she could not leave them. Kurt was a man she had met and fallen in love with, one who no longer seemed capable of accepting her love or of offering love to her. But her children were of her blood.

Alex's birth had been difficult; he'd presented shoulder first, and her uterus had to work long and hard to right his position. And the cord had been around his neck—not once, but twice. The doctor had mentioned Cesarean, but Annie beseeched him with her eyes and he'd stuck with her.

On the table during the violent, pitocin-induced final contractions, she had blurted out to him, "Okay, okay. I'm convinced. God is a man."

But when, at last, she held Alex curled on her belly and felt his skin against hers, when finally he was out of her and in the world with the light of ages still shining in his eyes, when she felt a flood of love pour toward him and saw tears of joy streaming down Kurt's face, she knew that she was forever different in the world, *femina;* that the three of them were connected finally and always.

She'd worked just as hard with Timothy, though his birth had been much easier. She'd stayed on her feet through most of the night as Kurt walked her about the halls of the hospital, stopping to let her hang from his shoulders when the contractions came. There had been no doctor; the midwife had worked with her, quietly supportive, listening, helping, letting nature be the guide. And when Timothy arrived he went right to her breast, Kurt enfolding both of them in his sturdy arms, and tears, again of joy.

Now she stood, frightened of their future, fearing the pain they would endure without Daddy in their lives. She thought about Carol, about what Carol would be going through if she had children. A faithless husband, a divorce. And how do you tell the children? Kurt was faithful. Kurt was—until this—loving. Kurt might be about to disappear forever.

She tucked covers to her sons' shoulders and gave each a kiss and walked back downstairs. She couldn't bear this. It had to be done now, tonight.

He was in the same position, his back to the room, curled beneath the blanket he'd taken from the living room couch. The wedding gift.

"You wanted me to hit you," he said. "I'm not going to hit you."

"I don't know what happened. Something just happened. I don't know."

"You wanted me to hit you."

"I did not."

"Yes, you did. Then you could take the boys and leave me."

"If that's what I wanted, I would have done it the night the cops came." Anger rose in her again; she tried to press it back, keep it from her voice.

"It's what you expected. Your father. You wanted it."

"What I wanted," she said, her voice too level, too even, to hide anything, "was to knock you on your ass so you would open up and talk to me. I'm going crazy here, do you know? I've been trying to talk to you for close to a month now. You haven't been available."

He sat, tossed aside the blanket, got up, and began pacing. "What if things had happened the other way?" His voice was rising. "What if I'd hit you? Would you have called the police? Would you have left me, kicked me out? What if it'd been the other way?"

"It's not the same," she said.

"What do you mean, it's not the same? It's exactly the same. What's not the same?"

"You said it. You said I didn't hurt you."

"I was trying to be mean," he said. "You hurt me. I've got spots in my left eye. I'm seeing spots. I don't know what it is. You hurt me."

"I know I hurt you. I'm sorry."

"What if I'd—? What would you be doing right now, talking to the cops?"

"Did I talk to them when they had me in handcuffs? No. I don't talk to the cops; why do you keep bringing them into it?"

"You might as well. Fucking Gary Smith."

"I'm not him."

"You made me bring him in."

"Made you?" She was astonished. "Made you?"

"Fuck."

"Oh. There's an answer."

"If you hadn't told me—"

"Well, I did! I told you he wanted to make some money. I told you his wife was really on his case for him to make them some motherfucking money. I don't recall forcing you to do anything. Most of all bring in another load of pot, which is why you were arrested. Not because I asked you to hire Gary Smith." She caught herself short with a gasp. Whoa. Slow down here. Don't wake the boys. "If you hit me," she added quietly, "it would most likely put me in the hospital. You know that."

"I was lying down here thinking, wondering if you were gonna come down here with a butcher knife and kill me."

"I was upstairs wondering if you might do exactly the same thing."

He sat down on the couch; she leaned against the wall. She did not even know how to be in the room with him, how to stand, how to hold herself.

"I don't know what happened to me," she started. "You know I'm not like that; I would never—" But she had.

He looked at her in the firelit room, and for an instant, just an instant, she saw the flash of fear in his eyes, she saw how scared he really was. And then it was gone, replaced by hostility.

"I don't know what's going to happen," he said. "I don't know if they can . . ." He pulled his hair, kneaded his temples. "I didn't intend this to happen."

"I know," she said. If he was at fault, she was too, and that was what she could not abide. She wanted it to be all his doing, but it wasn't. He wasn't the only one sucking up to risk. By staying with him, she had. And by having his children, she had brought two innocents into a frightening and maybe deadly situation. She'd had some hard moments, during her second pregnancy, when the realization came that, as a vessel of life, she was also a pinnace for death, and the apprehension had hung over her like the relentless snow clouds of February in the Catskills.

"You won't go," he said. "They won't put you in jail." She knew he wanted to believe what he was saying, but neither of them was sure.

"I'm sorry," she said.

"I feel I don't know you." He got up, opened the stove, knelt to poke at logs that needed no pushing, hung the poker on its hook, and turned toward her. "I didn't know you were capable of this."

She understood. She understood his side, saw herself through his eyes. And then she understood more, and she began to cry. She saw her father, walking into a house full of strangers: his. He stopped just inside the kitchen doorway, loosening his tie, his face damp with sweat from the blistering Texas sun, his wallet empty again and the scent of whiskey on his breath. The house was air-conditioned and had a dishwasher, but his wife was angry, as usual. He guessed that was why his children seemed like noisy visitors to his home. Maybe he should sell it, move them all somewhere else. Things could only get better. All he needed was a good solid sale, and things *would* get better.

"Something snapped," Annie said. "Are you going to tell me that's never happened to you?"

He didn't have to answer.

"We are all capable of it," she said. She tried to make out his face in the light from the fire in the stove. "I'm sorry, Kurt, for hitting you. I am very sorry." Her face contorted, and she worked not to gasp with the tears. "But I think," she managed, "that you should ask yourself if you were trying to drive me to it, to push me over the edge, because I've been trying to talk to you, I've been *desperate* to reach you, for weeks now. I love you. I love our children. When you took your love away, I couldn't bear it. And you know what your situation, what all this is doing to me."

"Annie," he said. He reached out and pulled her to him, wrapped his arms around her, and held her against his chest, and the anger went, and the ache, and the cold hard thing that for weeks—forever, it seemed—had filled the space where her heart should be.

His fingers traced gently down her neck; he leaned to kiss her and took her hands. His lips, warm and gentle, brought her to him, healing, chasing away the fear, and they stayed in the firewarmed darkness, hands joined, strength-held, the kiss on and on and into each other, and then they were naked together on the blanket before the stove, the room good with orange-yellow light. He traced the curve of her breasts and cupped them in his hands, leaned to caress with his tongue. He slipped his hands beneath her and raised her to him, a tiny moan escaping as he entered, and they were together and one and they kissed, and kissed, and kissed.

TWELVE

She heard the 5:52 rumble into the station below, took a sip of Guinness, and watched the bartender slice limes. She felt as if she were a truant, skipping out on motherhood like a seventh-grader avoiding Monday morning math class. But this was where Eric suggested they meet.

At one end of the bar, a guy with spiky black locks who looked about twelve worked at a crossword and sipped beer. Other than that, the place was empty. She wasn't sure why she'd agreed to meet Eric, except that when he called yet again, with the new generosity in his familiar voice, she had blurted to him about the charges against Kurt and life with no parole and how confused she was, and he'd insisted that they talk. In person. "I can help," he'd said. "No strings." She wondered why he would want to, but considered herself in no position to decline the offer. Something had to be done. She dreamed lately of strangers sitting in a room, frowning as they listened to a prosecutor tell them what an awful human being her husband was.

The Rhinecliff Hotel was a plain white wood rectangle stood on end; Annie wasn't even sure if they rented rooms. Inside were bare wooden floors untouched by anything but shuffling feet and an occasional broom, for centuries, it looked like, and the long wooden bar; there were wooden tables and dark corners. On Fridays and Saturdays, precociously jaded young musicians in up-and-coming bands with names like Dog Puke came to do heroin and make music. Cutting edge.

The place was perched on a bluff overlooking the Hudson River and the train tracks that ran along it and the train station a few hundred yards up the tracks. Beyond that was the Rhinecliff Bridge, and, farther up still, out of sight but never sufficiently out of mind, was the spot in the Hudson that General Electric had for years used as its corporate toilet. The PCBs had settled to the bottom and sat now, an underwater boil on the riverbed, giving fish who swam past complimentary nervous breakdowns. Rhinecliff itself was not much more than the train station and the hotel and a deli and a small, excellent Chinese restaurant. A smattering of quiet and faded homes, their owners presumably immune to the rumbling and blowing of the trains.

Eric had said he had a shoot in the city and would arrive around six, and here he came, khakis and turtleneck under a navy car coat; must've dropped his equipment in his car before walking over. Hands free but for a small satchel. He squinted when he stepped in from the evening light, looking for Annie in the gloom; smiled when he saw her. Hung his overcoat next to hers on the wall rack; paused to give a brief kiss to her cheek before taking a barstool.

"Just like the not-so-good old days," he said. He took her hand, his skin cool from the outdoors. "How are you? I'm glad you showed."

"Me too," she said, not sure what she meant.

He caught the bartender's eye and ordered a beer. He and Annie sat quietly, neither quite sure what to do next. Annie suggested they move to a table.

They settled in a corner as a few more commuters straggled in and took what looked to be their regular spots at the bar. Eric frowned. "Are you okay?"

"Under the circumstances," she replied.

"Which are?"

She told him. He took a long sip of beer and sat back in his chair. "So you're rolling along singing Variations on Better Homes and Gardens, and now it's all about to disappear. Must be, I don't know—"

"Lost," Annie said. "Lost is a good description of where I am right now."

"What's your husband say? He must feel like a total ass."

"We had this huge fight." She looked around the room, at people tucked into their places, comfortable, at ease, or seeming to be. She didn't know what to say, how much to reveal. She thought she could trust him. He'd been in that world. But still. "It's okay now," she added. "That part anyway."

He tapped his temple with his fingers, as though he were trying to decide something. "If I was looking at life in prison," he said quietly, "I'll tell you exactly what I'd do. I'd turn into someone else and get the hell out of the country."

"We have children to think about."

"I'm out of my depth in that department," he said. "But it seems to me that if you guys are happy together, you should try to stay that way."

"Easy for you to say."

"You could do it."

"Become someone else? I don't know."

"You don't become someone else. You're still yourself. You just take on a new name and birthday, that's all. You go somewhere decent and you make a life."

"Presto chango."

He laughed. "Something like that, yeah."

"So's that why you asked me here? To tell me it's that simple? It doesn't seem that simple."

He shook his head. "But when you get right down to it," he said, "it is pretty simple. Life and all that. Eat, drink, breathe and be merry, or eat, drink, breathe and be miserable." He gave her a long and steady appraisal, as though she was to understand something that, so far, she did not.

"I'm scared," she said, and felt a flood of relief at the admission.

"You should be, right now. Of the possibility that your husband might be sitting in prison for the rest of his life. I mean, try to imagine it. Day after day, after hour after hour, after minute after minute. Until he dies."

"I can't. I don't want to." She didn't know why they were talking or why he had asked her here or why she had come. They'd almost been together, once or twice, but both had realized it was a dead-end, that if they got under the covers it would only be because there had been the opportunity, and they would get out feeling sad and defeated. "We were smart, you and I," she said.

"One of the rare times in my life." He smiled. "Even messed up as we both were. I'm glad. But I'm still lonely, and I still expect you to set me up with your sister."

"You could've told me that over the phone."

"I wanted to see you. It's been too long. Ridiculously. But I couldn't have told you that I can help you with this, ah, situation."

"You know a judge or something?"

He laughed softly. "I wish." Then he was businesslike. "Have you considered it? Seriously? Has Kurt?"

"What. Running?" She looked at him. He wasn't joking.

"I'm asking for a reason," he said.

She thought about the time in Texas, Frenetic Fred, the rat, the snitch, the informant. How he seemed so friendly while he was trying to set them up with the cops. Kurt had a sense about these things, usually, but Annie wasn't sure she did.

"If you're going to run," Eric said quietly, "you'll need ID."

They didn't have it. Kurt hadn't been able to connect with his usual source. The guy was somewhere in Afghanistan, last anyone heard. But she couldn't come up with a single reason in the world why Eric would want to stick his neck out for them, risk prison for old times' sake.

"I'm not cheap." Eric sat back, one finger tracing the initials cut long ago into the table top.

"What are you talking about?"

"ID. I can make you into anyone you want to be. Driver's license. Passport. Whatever."

"Why?"

"Because it's what I do, and because we were close once, sort of, and I'd like to help. I do good work. Very good work. In fact, not to brag, but, next to the government, I'm probably the best there is."

"Why?"

"I just told you."

"No. Why do you do it? Why do you—"

"Break the rules? Kiss the girls and make them cry? Why did I sell dope? Why do I—"

"You get the picture. Why?"

"Because otherwise life is intolerably and utterly boring. That's why."

"You just said it was simple. Not two minutes ago."

"Simple. Boring. What's the difference?"

"And because you want me to set you up with my sister?"

"Not my primary motivation," he said, "but I would like to meet her. I've had more flings than a competition Frisbee. I'm tired of that shit. I mean it. I'm looking for a relationship. Like a real, substantial, genuine relationship."

"I don't know if she's ready for that. She's coming through a horrid divorce."

"Then she probably needs a friend. Anyway, that's for her to decide."

"I think she needs someone who's a little more—"

"That's not up to you. That's not fair."

"Is it fair that I know you are less than law-abiding and I still let her get involved with you? That's not right."

"I'm not the kind of guy who gets caught. I'm careful. Meticulous. You don't have to worry about that."

"Funny," Annie mused. "My husband always said the same thing."

"It's different. He's into a whole 'nother thing. I could pay a fine and be on my way."

"Don't call her yet. Please."

He was suddenly quiet, seeming hurt at the thought that he might not be right for Carol. Annie was touched by his vulnerability. She'd always thought him impervious.

"Say she does, and yes, I think she would. But what does she do when you get hauled off to jail?"

"Been there, done that. It won't happen again."

"When? What for?"

"For that nasty white powder, and it was only an interminable weekend at Rikers Island. I made bail and beat the case."

"How?"

"They lost the evidence. I think the cops probably took it. Gave it to some snitch or something, or used it themselves. Who knows, who cares. They didn't have it when it came time to up it in court."

"So you didn't beat the case. You lucked out."

"Annie, please. You're shattering my carefully constructed alternative reality."

She was tired suddenly, tired and missing her children. She shouldn't be here. But he was offering to help.

His eyes were full of concern.

"Maybe it's a chance for me to make something up to you." He looked past her, at the bar, remembering something. "You know," he said, "if you hadn't run off with that cowboy . . ."

"Eric." Annie laughed softly. "Kurt is not a cowboy."

"Of course he is. He wouldn't be in this trouble if he weren't. Anyway. I always thought that we might have got together."

"I thought we almost did. Or is my memory the faulty one?"

"I'm not talking about that. I'm talking really. Together."

"Back when you were dating all those long-legged beauties? Is that when?"

"I was so bored. I can't tell you."

She didn't say anything.

"I was always very attracted to you."

"You were always very attracted to everyone."

He laughed.

"Okay," he said. "Okay. The shields are up, I can see that. We were all pretty messed up back then, no? But I'm not coming on to you. I just wanted you to know."

"Thank you."

"I fell in love," he crooned. "In the poultry barn at the Dutchess County Fair." He folded his hands over his heart. "So Carol, her name is. Your sister?"

Annie laughed, nodded yes, slowly enough that it meant no.

"Oh, come on," Eric said. "She's a grownup. Let her decide."

"This is too weird."

"No, it's not. It's not weird at all. What you're going through: that's weird. And I can help. Talk to Kurt." He took her hand, gave it a friendly squeeze, put a bill on the table, and got up, offering his arm.

"Tell her about me." He went for their coats and helped Annie into hers. "I mean, tell her I'd like to meet her."

He walked her to her car. It was dark and the stars were out, hovering in airlessness. She started the engine; Eric stood at her window until she rolled it down.

"Tell her I'm a nice guy," he said.

"Are you?"

He turned and walked back toward the bar, shot over his shoulder, "Talk to Kurt. Call me."

•

The Gotham Hotel was tucked away in the Fifties, just off Fifth Avenue, a sanctuary for the chronically hip. True to its name, it was Batmanish but small (and knowing that small was clever), unable and unwilling to compete with the big chains. Yet there were big rooms, big comfortable chairs, and a big atmosphere, somewhat casual, that strolled arm in arm with the nonchalant security of the place. Kurt and Annie flowed through the plush carpeted lobby with the rest of the foot traffic and were taken to the eighth floor by an elevator that was slow, steady, and comfortable, like an old Cadillac. If there were any agents around, they were blending.

Kurt led the way down the hall, which was lined with the same carpeting, thick and quiet.

"I hope this guy's for real," he said, taking Annie's hand.

"He's got no reason to lie to me," Annie said. They found the room, knocked, and waited. Kurt was nervous still, though no longer angry. When Annie had told him about meeting Eric in Rhinecliff and showed him Eric's card, Kurt nearly had a paranoid seizure. The Wizard of ID was an underground legend. Best in the business. Best ID man in the world. Or so word had it. So Annie had known this guy from the time he was a two-bit coke dealer. Kurt had mused about that brief meeting at the party where he'd met her. Did it qualify as synchronicity? Or was it all part of some elaborate trap? There were days when all life seemed a setup; just when you were in position to score, just when you thought you finally had it together, something would rip through the curtain and scream *Surprise!*—and everything would fall apart.

But this guy had to be cool, whether or not he was an asshole. Kurt had heard of him well over a year ago, and the word now was that the Wizard of ID wrote the book on fake identification.

He had a rep, he was cool, on the streets after all these years, and Annie had assured Kurt that Eric was long out of the coke business and all that. Still, this was a nervous-making situation, not the same as dealing with scammers he'd known and worked with for years. He wished his regular guy hadn't disappeared. Annie said she trusted this guy. He wondered if they'd slept together, was angry at even the possibility, jealous anyway, at the thought of it. She hadn't come out and said they never did, and Kurt hadn't exactly asked. He just wondered, was all, why she seemed so ready to trust the guy. She'd trusted Gary Smith, too. But if this would help get her out into the world, if she was comfortable to use this guy's ID, hey, whatever. Kurt would arrange a new set of papers as soon as he located his man. In the meantime, this would do. What was important was that she come with him. She was bringing the boys and coming with him. That was all that mattered.

The door opened and Kurt ushered Annie in, quickly and quietly, as though hushing the activity would obviate the need for secrecy.

Door closed and locked behind them, Annie received a peck on each cheek from Eric and watched as he extended a hand to Kurt. She knew that Kurt thought of Eric as her ex, but if there was something antagonistic between them, she did not see it.

The room was well lit, and Eric, she noticed, was beginning to bald on top; he would eventually have one of those fringes of brown around his skull, just above the ears. Brown eyes, too; odd she didn't recall how the outer corners drooped so that his eyes formed a kind of sad smile beneath slender eyebrows, also downturned. He'd begun a beard since their meeting a week or so ago. It was coming in quickly, trimmed carefully on his square jaw. Straight out of the prep world again: khakis, navy blue turtleneck, loafers. A black wool sport jacket was draped across the bed. The rest of the room was filled with five or six large, empty cases, standing open. A backdrop and stool were pressed tight into one corner, facing an industrial-type camera and laminating equipment. Next to that, receiver, amplifier, tape deck, CD changer, speakers, a microphone. To the casual observer, he was set up as a sound man.

"I guess you can be a new person every day if you want," Annie said, and felt stupid for saying it, but didn't know what else to do. *Socially Inept.* Still. After all these years. She had read recently that shyness as a character trait resided in the genes, and she was pretty sure she had that: chronic shyness. Hereditary shyness. She wondered if Alex or Tim had inherited it. She wondered if, by the time they were grownups, all life would have been reduced to chemistry, all spirit dismissed by science. But, then again, scientists were the breed who once swore that Earth was flat and thought that removing your thyroid gland was good for you.

Eric seemed not to notice her discomfort; he was busy with his equipment. She remembered when she'd first met him, how he'd shown himself to be one of those guys who thought to intrigue every woman he met by ignoring each of them in turn. But he was changed now. Maybe she should introduce Carol. Maybe a wizard was just what Carol needed. Yeah, right. Just what she needed: an introduction to the criminal element. What are you thinking? Moron. You're about to go underground. With children. And you're going to encourage your sister to date your ID man? Forget it. Just forget it.

She looked at Eric bending to his equipment, and suddenly it was as if she wasn't there. She was watching a movie or was in some strange holographic reality that was simple illusion. Complex illusion. What is real, what is not? She didn't know. Except the fear. The fear was real. You have to do this, she reminded herself. You have to do this.

"Not to rush you," Eric said, "but I'm in a bit of a hurry." He stepped to the camera, his manner that of a prep school headmaster: if only I can keep everything orderly enough, I will be fine. Chaos is terror. She'd never seen him so efficient and focused.

"So are we," Kurt said.

"My inventory's low right now. I can make you Mr. White from Florida." More adjusting. "That cool with you?"

"That's fine," Kurt said.

"Have any final destination in mind?"

"Not yet." Kurt didn't want to go into anything. He didn't know this guy. And already he didn't like him. He didn't like him from the first time he'd met him. Six years? That party. Awful. Annie strung out. Man. Six years, and here they were, kids at home with a sitter while Mommy and Daddy go out for the day. Shopping? No. Movies? No.

"These are quickies," Eric said. "They won't make it through a computer check." He looked at Kurt, waiting for a response. There was none. "I can meet you in Florida with some *very* clean paper," he added. "I'll need two weeks. Passports, too."

Kurt had expected as much. It was always something with these guys. But all they needed right now were drivers' licenses.

"Look this way and smile as if you've been working fourteen years on an assembly line and this is your first trip to Europe." Eric adjusted something and then flashed both a grin and a burst of light at Kurt.

Annie took her place on the stool facing the camera and thought she knew what it must be like to pose in the nude that first time, before it became a job. Who was this guy, except someone who had aided her desperation; she didn't know him *at all* and he was going to have a picture of her and know what her alias was. What was she doing? Not true. She did know him. She'd known him for years and it was all okay; it was just that she didn't know this world but was in the big middle of it, scared to death that she was going to wind up in prison, unable to care for her children. The thought made her dizzy.

Sitting on the stool and watching Eric put something into something else and fiddle with knobs and levers, she pulled her lips into a smile and stared at the camera. The room went slightly out of focus, and all she could see were the tear-streaked faces of her boys, looking up at her, and then eye to eye, because she was down on one knee, trying to figure out what to say to ease their pain, which she understood was as terrible to them as any turmoil she might be facing. When they cried like that, it pulled at her in a way she'd never before experienced, at a place deep enough to make her understand that the birth connection could be severed only by death.

". . . color hair?" Eric was speaking to her.

"Brunette," she said. "I'm going darker."

"All the rage." He produced a shoulder-length wig, wavy, curly, and big enough to attract attention away from her face.

She put it on, reminded of the time she'd tried on a football helmet that belonged to one of her boyfriends when she was six or so. It was completely uncomfortable, and she didn't much care for the idea of slamming her head into things. She'd liked playing football, though, as long as there were no uniforms involved. And then, around seventh, eighth grade, the boys got bigger and stronger and began expecting her to stand on the sidelines and cheer them on. She had signed up to run cross-country and track instead. See Annie run. Run, Annie, run.

A burst of light, a mechanical whine. He had her on film. The skin on her back itched; she rolled her shoulders to rub cashmere against it.

"You all right?" Kurt said softly.

"Fine," she said. She had to be. See Annie run. There was no other option.

Eric went to work at his machines, cutting and laminating and stamping. When he was through, they would have drivers' licenses, birth certificates, and a couple of credit cards, for emergency use only, please.

"You know," Eric said to Annie, "it doesn't look to me so bad, living on the lam. I see people every day, and they do fine, just fine."

Annie nodded. Eric handed her a license, the photo appropriately awful.

"You're right," she joked; "you do good work."

"It's just that you look so—"

"Totally scared?" She laughed nervously. Kurt gave Eric a slim stack of Ben Franklins.

"Fifteen hundred," he said. "The rest when we get the briefs. Two weeks?"

"That's the ticket," said Eric. "Pleasure to do business with you." "You'll be fine," he assured Annie again. "You'll be just fine." As they made ready to leave, he touched Kurt on the sleeve. "Annie has my card," Eric said. "Call when you're put down in Florida. I'll either meet you myself or send a messenger with the paper."

"I'd prefer not to meet anyone," Kurt said.

"I expect I'll be able to make it," Eric said. "Just on the outside chance, though. He's been with me for years."

"I'll call," Kurt said.

In the hall outside the room, Annie took her arm from Kurt's. She thought she might faint, and leaned against the wall.

He slipped an arm around her, concern lining his face.

"What is it?"

What was it? He had to ask? His eyes went soft and he pulled her to him, pulled her head to his chest.

"Baby," he said, "it'll be all right. I promise." He stepped back and took her by the shoulders. His eyes were blue and honest. "We belong together. I just want to be with you and the boys."

She wanted to speak, to tell him how she still didn't know if she'd be able to go through with it. She couldn't.

"I'm sorry," he said, and pulled her close again. "I'm sorry things have got so weird. I'm doing everything I can to straighten it all out. I love you."

The arrival of the elevator caught them in a kiss. Annie, still numb, rode down unable to talk.

"You know," Kurt said, his voice adjusted to elevator volume, "if he was really your friend, he'd have given us a discount."

Annie smiled, more politely than conspiratorially, and wished she were enough at ease to enjoy being alone with him. She'd almost forgotten what it was like, to be out with him and no munchkins around. But even the clear blue sky hanging over Manhattan felt clandestine, the stone and glass towers beneath it oppressive. Fear. Fear did this. The latest ubiquitous window sticker, now showing in a car window near you, had jagged blue or red lettering: NO FEAR.

Yeah. Right. You gotta paste it in the window, you might as well put one up there that says SCARED SHITLESS. Maybe if she could tell him, confess to Kurt how frightened she was, maybe that would make things easier. Or maybe it would only diminish his respect. She wondered what he feared, wondered if he would ever tell her.

•

Tim balled up his fists and tucked them next to his belly.

"Hi-yah!" he shouted, and hurled his body at Kurt, slamming his head into his father's chest, screeching with delight and scrambling to escape almost before he landed. Kurt grabbed him and in a single move flipped himself onto his knees and pinned his squirming son to the mattress.

"No, Daddy, no!" Tim yelled, his laugh first guttural, then becoming a real belly laugh. Annie moved farther toward the edge of the bed to give them room. Alex stood on the bed next to her, one hand braced against the window frame behind him, laughing with total abandon and slapping his thigh with delight.

"Pinned him, pinned him, Daddy wins!" Alex shouted. "My turn!"

Kurt released Tim, who squealed loudly, his body quivering with excitement as he scurried onto Annie's lap. He knocked her book to the floor with his head as he snuggled his way up her torso, nestling into a position where he could rest his head against her shoulder but still see what was happening with Kurt and Alex. He rested happily, flexing his feet against her legs. He had kicked every time he was awake in her womb. He had kicked right up until labor. And within hours of his birth, he began moving his legs every waking moment. He got a rhythm going and worked at it, watching his older brother walk around, kicking, kicking, working those legs. And one day, when he was about ten months old, he'd stood purposefully next to the bookcase and walked across his bedroom floor to the window, where he looked out for a moment, then turned to glance at Annie with the nonchalance of a Parisian diplomat.

Alex was taking it very seriously, moving carefully around the perimeter of the bed, searching for the proper angle of attack. Wondering if this would be the time he might really beat Dad. The boys' version of wrestling included several karate-type moves that would certainly be illegal on the mats. He crouched, glowering at Kurt.

"Heee-YAH!" he shouted, leaping, throwing a foot into Kurt's chest, collapsing on the mattress in a fit of giggles.

"Oooh!" Kurt cried. "He got me!" He lifted Alex above him, swooshed him through the air, back and forth, back and forth; Alex held his arms and legs out as though he were skydiving. The two of them laughed and laughed. Timothy couldn't stand it; he scurried from Annie's arms and jumped in the middle of Kurt's chest, screaming happily as he flew through the air.

"Oooh!" Kurt cried. "No fair, now it's two against one!" The three of them became a tangle of arms and legs and laughter. Annie was aware that the grin on her face, large and silly as it was, could not possibly express her happiness.

She stepped into her moccasins and went down the hall, still smiling at the music of their laughter.

Four walls, the color of desert sand at sunrise. She sat on Alex's bed. White-trimmed windows, one facing south, the other east. The room caught shade in the summertime, full sun on a cold winter's afternoon.

Timothy would want his stuffed animals. Mr. Whale. The shaggy white dog he called Baby Bubba. And his favorite rubber frog, large and light green, who lived in a swimming pool in France. Fwance, he said. A fwimming pool in Fwance.

The boys would keep their first names. They didn't really know their last name yet, so that was not a problem. She and Kurt had their new Florida drivers' licenses and Social Security cards, credit cards. Some weeks ago, Annie had taken the boys' birth certificates from the safe in the closet under the staircase and gone to work on them.

"You can do it," Kurt had said. "You are, after all, an artist."

"Yes, dear," she'd answered.

He'd returned her look and led the way to his office, where he clicked on the IBM Selectric and the Xerox machine and pulled a bottle of Wite-out from the desk drawer.

When she'd finished, Alex and Timothy had new last names. All she needed was a notary seal for the Xerox copies, and that she would get when she took care of Laura and Mike's dog next week. She thought Laura would probably have done it knowingly, but better to leave her friend innocent. She would miss them. She wondered if they would understand; thought probably so.

She let the fresh paperwork tumble for a moment in the clothes dryer, glad that she'd never got around to getting Social Security numbers or passports for the boys. Now they would be registered as Alex and Timothy White, sons of Elizabeth and John.

She took them to the ugly black-and-gray-checked six-story oblong box that sat across the corner from a seventeenth-century Dutch Reform church made of stone and served the government's needs in Ulster County. The employees inside took money and handed out the various licenses that were necessary under penalty of fine or imprisonment if you wanted to purchase or operate vehicles or machinery or cross borders or get married, own property or have a pet.

Annie chose a miserably cold but beautifully sunny afternoon when the boys had been cooped up for a couple of days while December snows fell. In the clerk's office, she presented their birth certificates and silently gave thanks that her children were going nuts on her, Alex laughing maniacally and pushing a screaming Timothy in circles in the stroller while Annie dug in her purse for the fee. There were three women in the office, coifed, made up, and manicured, wearing heels and smoking cigarettes while a country music station played quietly from a small portable radio on someone's desk. The woman who was helping Annie worked quickly, sympathetic with the mother whose children were misbehaving.

"They'll arrive in the mail in about ten days," she said. She pursed her lips and wrinkled her nose. "You've got your hands full there." She smiled, tilting her head at the boys. Annie smiled back. Ten days would do very nicely.

Out the east window of her home were the stone walls Annie had come to love, light gray against the night, dusted with yesterday's snow. She would miss them. European immigrants had cleared the fields here as their ancestors had there—picking rocks out of Earth and balancing the stones into walls, making a field for livestock or garden rows and fencing it at once.

Eric hadn't seemed to think it was so bad, living on the run. But he wasn't doing it. He was only providing identities. Dr. Tetlow apparently liked the fugitive life, though. And there were others she'd met. They floated into the area and called from pay phones to invite Kurt and her for coffee; they chatted, talked politics, talked movies, talked travel. And they floated out again and might not be seen or heard from for a couple of years or more. Arrest was always a possibility.

She would tell the boys that they were going on a long trip and suggest they pick two or three favorite things to bring. No. Low-key this one. She went to the book case. *The Cat in the Hat.* Definitely. *Goodnight Moon.*

Harold and the Purple Crayon. And their newest: *The True Story of the Big Bad Wolf.* Alex loved it.

She drifted and got lost at the bookcase until she noticed that the house had grown quiet. Before walking back down the hall, she took the stack of favorites and put them on the bed to be packed.

They were all three sprawled, Kurt on his back with a son on either side, their heads resting against his chest. Annie felt a surge of love swelling in her; she tried to let the fear that lately slipped in just beneath it flow on through, out of her. Tried to let it go. Often she could.

•

Steam rose, filled the upstairs bathroom; hot water flowed through her hair and over her scalp. Its warmth brought to mind a midsummer evening, up on the hill, fire and stars the only light. Air scented with pine and the musk of last autumn's leaves, now a soft carpet of brown on the forest floor. Water rinsed over her; she let herself enjoy its caress. Cicadas arrived in late July, early August. The geese came back in March to summer on the pond across the road. They were clamorous visitors, putting up a fuss if they heard so much as a door slam within a quarter mile of their château.

Tomorrow she would slice oranges in half, press the halves onto the ream of the juicer. Set Spiderman cups before Alex and Timothy at the small wooden table they had helped her build and paint. Heat syrup and butter and make sure to put some in each little square of Alex's waffle, because he gave her a smile of appreciation when she served it that way. She would be able to look out the large kitchen windows and see woodpeckers perched in the winter-bare lilac tree and, behind them, stone walls.

She would have to be sure to pack Tim's favorite red sneakers, his purple cotton cap, and those neon-blue sunglasses Carol had bought for him. Lately he would wake in the middle of the night, no longer demanding to nurse; rather, wanting his shoes or hat or the sunglasses—sometimes all three. He'd lie there screaming until Annie brought whatever it was and dressed him in it. If she tried to remove anything, he would wake immediately and begin yelling again. She supposed it was a harmless way to take power, but it was a nuisance, and she hoped he would get over it soon. Alex slept through it all. So did Kurt.

She put out a hand to catch some water. Soft. She wondered how the water would be wherever they wound up.

She thought of her mother, still there in Austin. And of her mother's most recent visit; it must have been last Christmas. It had not been their best. Alex had an early evening swim class at the Y, and Grandma had accompanied them. On the way out to the car afterward, Annie took Tim's hand to cross the parking lot, and was happy when Alex took Grandma's offered hand with a smile. Between two rows of cars, their bumpers glinting in the glare of vapor lights, Annie had seen a man approaching. He was black.

She thought he must have lived for a time in the city, for she could see he was as nervous as she about eye contact. That was how you spotted city dwellers: they wouldn't dream of looking a stranger in the eye on purpose. But Annie and this man were both in the habit, apparently; her eyes met his as they approached.

"Good evening," he said. "How're you?"

"Fine, thanks," Annie said. "You?"

"Doing fine," he said, "just fine."

"Hi," Timothy said. She smiled down at him, at his face open with friendship; he was willing to give it to the world at large.

"Hi, there," the man said; and they passed.

She noticed then that her mother had pulled Alex to give wide berth to the stranger, and was looking at Annie with both fear and disgust. How many times had she seen that look. It was serious. Annie watched as her mother, glancing behind herself, dug in her purse for a cigarette, seeking nicotine to calm her nerves and missing the dignity that the man had carried with him as he passed in the dark, scary night.

Everything about the visit had been dismal, from the weather to Annie's realization that her mother was molding the son-in-law relationship into an old, familiar shape: men are bad, men are horrid, men can't be trusted. Kurt was aware of what was happening and did his best to stay out of the rain, but it saddened Annie.

They had spoken last week, but not really. Annie had barely said hello before passing the phone to Alex and then to Timothy. She'd been afraid that something would break, that she would burst forth with the whole story and end up choking on inadequate tears.

She caught herself, let the water run against her back. Let it go. Just—let it go.

He had promised: *I will protect you.*

At the reading, that first real date, he'd picked up their tickets and they were ushered to ninth row center. People to the left, people to the right. Knees to traverse. She'd confessed to being nervous when she felt she couldn't escape.

Don't worry. I'll protect you. She thought of the deer she'd startled that day in the woods, how it lived as the hunted. And how, to the hunted, the pledge of protection was nothing short of a promise of salvation. Jesus on the Cross. Trust in me; I will protect you. Kurt had put an arm around her shoulders, given her a light, reassuring squeeze. She had twined her fingers into his and squeezed back.

Such an absurd gesture.

"Protect me from what," she whispered in the shower. Warm water rinsed her lips, dripped from her chin. "*Your* enemies?"

She could persuade him to stay and work things out. Mark was good; Mark might be able to make a deal for a small sentence, something they could live with. Agent Kessler seemed reasonable. He'd said he could help. Annie wondered for a moment if she should call him, but immediately knew she couldn't. Not now. Not yet. Kurt would see it as betrayal. She would go with him. She would do everything she could to make things work. See Annie run.

She hoped to squeeze in one last walk in the woods. Before they left. Before they left their home. Say good-bye to Kane.

Carol would return from the city tomorrow to stay and try to sell the house. Or maybe the government would seize it. Carol was being oddly cool, or maybe understandably cool, about the situation. When Annie had first approached her, she said of course she would do all she could to help.

"That includes praying for you," she'd added.

Annie got out of the shower and toweled herself dry. She picked up the box of Herbatint. Tomorrow morning, she would go from dark blond to brunette. Kurt had already started a beard. Carol would take the boys somewhere while Annie packed.

She listened to the silence of the house. Her children were sleeping. Her husband was sleeping. They planned to leave after sundown, as close to bedtime as possible.

She looked in the mirror above the sink, wondering who she would become.

THIRTEEN

Well after midnight: thump/da-dump/thump/da-dump/thump/da-dump. And here came the horns. Again. What. What was this. It is winter outside you people are supposed to be hibernating don't these assholes ever sleep. Loudspeakers, da art of da noise, crashing the gates of his sleep like storm troopers on acid, doing—was it flamenco? Doing what, doing what, God please let me sleep. Please. Let. Me. Sleep. Thump/da-dump/thump/da-dump/no chance/da-dump. Groggy consciousness. Yanked outta there again, from his first decent sleep in weeks. Or was it years?

Kessler sat up and grabbed a cigarette from the pack on the nightstand, angrily flicked the match into an ashtray he'd picked up at an airport during a rare vacation with Barbara.

Barbara. There it was again. He heard Neil Young, his near-falsetto overriding the salsa banging against the windowpanes, slipping in through the two-inch crack because if he left the windows closed he would roast slowly as he slept, awaken done medium rare. There was no controlling the radiators; in winter his apartment was an oven. Neil Young. Outlaw and proud of it . . . *'cause we're already one, our little son won't let us forget* . . . Daniel. Sarah. Justin. He wanted to see them. Hold them. Simple. He loved them. Missed them every day.

He took a drag and let it go: the smoke floated out like a sigh.

"These fucking things," he said, frowning at the Gauloise in his fingers. He rested the cigarette in the ashtray and picked up his pistol. Stepped over to the window. The noise. Pounding. Thumping. Brass and bass.

"You are making me insane," he said, addressing the populace at large. To himself: "Lighten up already."

But it was constant. Constant. Salsa music spilling out of open windows and ricocheting off stone and brick walls. Getting to him big time. The week before Christmas, Hanukkah on its heels, and lately some guy in the neighborhood was dressing as Santa and strolling around the streets holding a bucket and ringing a bell, seeking donations, but Kessler was onto him: the guy was selling crack cocaine, dealing that rock. Dope dealer imitating a Salvation Army chump imitating Santa Claus. Merry Christmas, boys and girls. Make that Merry Xmas. No doubt Santa had Ecstacy, too—the latest in designer drugs.

Top it off, the city was in a heat wave, the afternoon high fifty-five that very day, tomorrow supposed to stretch toward seventy, and he still hadn't got any gifts for his kids. Didn't know what they wanted. Didn't know how to ask. He was wrung out, that's all.

He stared out the window, dazed, looked for the speakers. He would find them, take them out. Bah-boom. *Lucy, I'm home!* He'd come out of the Air Force an expert marksman and still was. Practiced regularly, but not zealously, viewing the weapon as part of the job, not part of his life. He would prefer to function without it. But marksmanship came naturally to him.

Two in the morning, said the clock on the wall. Where was Santa Claus when you needed him? I only want one thing, Mr. Claus. Sleep. I want one solid week of silent, blissful, REM-loaded, totally and completely uninterrupted s-l-e-e-p. I want to sleep right through New Year's Eve. Forget Santa Claus. I need Mother Nature. Send a blizzard, would you? An eight-foot snowfall that will put a blanket of blessed silence over this whole astonishing mess and make it—shhhhh—quiet. If not peaceful, at least quiet. Ah. There.

He wondered if he had converted to insomnia by choice or if it was simply the noise. He used to sleep, before moving to this, this, whatever-it-was. Home? Barbara and the kids were still in the place on West Eighty-third. He could stroll over any time, any time at all.

He wasn't sure how long since he had. More than a year maybe, not since a few months after the divorce. He didn't know what his children looked like, what they ate for dinner, what they did after school. He didn't know what gifts to get, and he loathed the thought of having to ask his former wife what they wanted.

He spotted the speakers, resting on a window ledge directly across the street, pumping out the sounds, a regiment of horns chopping the air above the hip-swishing beat laid out by drums. Inside the apartment, the lights were on; people danced in the living room. Partytime, the sidewalks were crawling. Hey, why not? Got no job? Strung out on the government teat and tomorrow looks just like yesterday? Let's dance.

Most of the neighborhood was unemployed, and there was enough crack to go around for everybody. If you couldn't find Santa, there was always the drive-through up on 109th Street. It's illegal, folks, must be something good, so come and get it. Whoever wants it. Lots of Jersey license plates. Suburban white boys taking some home to their girlfriends in Secaucus, hoping to get some of that other in exchange. When Kessler had first moved in, right after the divorce, he couldn't make it from the curb to the front door of his crumbling building without getting offered the latest name brand. He'd considered it once or twice—thought to try it out instead of making an arrest. Life had been black-and-white to him then, depression manifesting itself by turning the world into a poorly lit B movie with a soundtrack from Santo Domingo.

These days he was doing better, though there were times he thought he was the only remaining adult in America who wasn't on Xanax or, what was that new stuff, Prozac, whatever the scrip of the moment happened to be, and wondered why he was holding out. But even the best-intentioned could easily cross the line. He'd done it early on, when he was fresh at the agency—full of belief and the desire to be a frontline fighter in the war. He raised his hand and said *I do* and they put him undercover in a long-term street-level investigation. He grew his hair and beard and took a new name, and after a while when he looked in the mirror it wasn't Joseph Kessler who looked back at him. But it was all right; he was in it for the cause.

And then the suits told him it was time to pull up, make some arrests. He remembered lying in bed for a few days, the flu-like reality of withdrawal not so dramatic as when you watched some actor writhing in agony on the screen, but a bitch all the same. Every time he awoke from the toss-and-turn nap-sleep, the radio played Supertramp, *When I was young it seemed that life was so wonderful . . .* and he couldn't stand their whining teenage voices.

And then it was over. He was himself again, or maybe.

When he felt all right, when he felt physically good for the first time in months, that was when the danger started. When he began thinking oh, hey, yeah, I can deal with it. I can handle it. Been there and back, I can chip with the best of them. Lots of agents did.

But every time he joined them, he felt the deadening begin, his soul going so soft, so close to home that it wound up hard and cold, a stranger under his skin. It had been years now.

He'd stayed clean and liked it that way. Let the new guys go through it, though he knew the effort was futile, nothing but a show for the politicians. He remembered how Barbara had looked at him during those times, remembered the same voice that had said so sincerely, "I love you," saying—in a tone that sounded like ice cracking—"There's no point trying to discuss it." He had looked at her through pinpoint pupils and wished, even fucked up as he was, that she cared enough to talk to him. That she wanted to. Thought he was worth the effort. Or felt that she could. Whatever.

He wished. He might not be alone now, staring out the window at two A.M., looking for Santa Claus.

Movement near the phone booth in front of the corner bodega caught his gaze: he watched a drug deal go down. Where was the Partnership for a Drug-Free America when you needed them? Drug-free America. Yeah, right. Self-righteous fucks.

He watched the hand-off and tried to ignore that he no longer believed in the effort. Nine years down, eleven to go, and it was a sham, a scam, and a farce. His own agency's statistics told the story. He was tempted, sometimes, when someone asked what he did for a living, to explain that he was a night janitor, sweeping the Kafka-esque corridors of H.Q. for a multibillion-dollar, worldwide, international conglomerate: Nirvana & Death, Incorporated.

"Stop romanticizing," he said to himself, and laughed out loud, and remembered the gun in his hand. He was at home with it and disliked it intensely, like his ex-wife. But the opposite of love was not hate; the opposite of love was indifference. He hadn't quite got there yet, not as far as Barbara went. Not that he held hope of reunion. He missed his kids. The speakers thumped away on the fire escape. Here came John Lennon, the voice piercing his brain above all the racket . . . *although I'm so tired, my mind is set on you* . . . He shook his head, trying to clear it. Gonna blow nine years and a pension because some assholes across the street are having a good time? He put down his pistol and stepped around the bed to retrieve what was left of his cigarette. An inch of ash. He took another drag, felt the mild rush of nicotine and God-knew-what-else surge into his blood, relaxing and energizing at once. He'd read somewhere that they radiated tobacco leaves to keep mold from taking them, wondered if that was part of the buzz.

The smoke tasted like shit. He'd been at it this last time around since his marriage went AWOL. Time to quit. Time to pull up. Coughing like nobody's business, and lately when he lit up in public, the nasty looks made him feel criminal. But he had to prepare himself, get ready to give it a serious effort, and knew he wasn't quite ready.

He'd quit before, several times. He had always quit when a baby came into the house: first Daniel, then Sarah, then Justin. And even when they weren't babies anymore, he never went back to smoking in the apartment. Now he wondered if they were all home safe and in bed, thought about maybe going by one day this week. Try to reconnect. Barbara made it difficult. She hated his guts, or at least acted that way. He thought sometimes to take it as a compliment; she was anything but indifferent to him. But she made sure he was uncomfortable when he came around, as if it were all his fault, as if he had driven her to the comfort of another man's arms.

End of December, and January and February still to get through. April might be cruel, but at least there was daylight and the promise of warmth. He despised winter. Nothing personal. It was what it was and he couldn't stand it. He didn't need any additional depression factors in the equation that was his life; things were unbalanced enough. Greater than. Less than.

Is not equal to. When winter added dark and cold, things just got more skewed.

The light changed, here came traffic. Where were all these fools going at two o'clock in the morning? And then—what was this—there was this kid. A *kid.* Three years old, four at the most, and riding one of those Big Wheels, an oversize bright red plastic tricycle, right down the middle of Columbus Avenue. *Take me to the river. Rock me on the water.* What. Was. This.

He unfastened the grate, stepped onto the fire escape.

"Hey!"

Five faces tilted up at him. He pointed to the child in traffic. One of them bolted, skidding around moving vehicles to grab the child and his tricycle, skipped back to the curb, and delivered them to safety. He looked up fiercely at Kessler, the outsider. *Fuck you, man; we got it under control down here.*

No problem. Kessler climbed back into his miserable bedroom.

Children. Children. Where were his; what were they doing? It was all right. They had a good mother. He tried not to send mothers to jail. Or almost never, depending on what was best for the children. As if he knew. But he thought he did, most of the time. You could tell, and it was all in how you worded the report. A lot of the new guys didn't care; they did their best to send away anyone they could. Women were buying it major league these days. He'd never seen so many of them being shipped off to the slammer. Mules, mostly. Girlfriends, mostly. Fools for love, mostly.

Fools for love. He pictured her in the garden, the way he'd seen her that day, with Wilson bleating at him to come on, we got what we need, let's go. And Wilson was right; they had what they needed. They had Gary Smith and they'd put him in front of the grand jury, much against his will, but he had nonetheless testified. The indictment should come down this week. Wilson would be thrilled, happy to get off surveillance. Kessler called him at least twice a day, making sure there was no sign of departure. He would go back himself tomorrow and sit in the house across the road, stare through the field glasses and maybe catch a glimpse. He would wait for a call from Mr. Prosecutor Derrick Richards, and when it came, he, Kessler, would go personally to make the arrest. He would accompany Richards to the arraignment, where the prosecutor, he was sure, would ask for no bail. And, Eighth Amendment notwithstanding, Richards would most likely get it. He wasn't asking for excessive bail; he was asking for no bail. Trowbridge was an escape risk; keep him locked up until trial. They'd take Kurt back to MCC, where he would stay until the formal proceedings began, guilty until proven guilty.

Kessler wondered if Annie would stick by her husband, wondered what were the limits of her tolerance. He felt an odd piece of sadness, regretting that he was part of such a trauma in her life. He wished she was the one he'd met for a date that night instead of Mz. Bimbette of the Universe for 1987. But it was Trowbridge, really, Trowbridge who'd refused to pull up and who'd brought the heat down on himself and his family. He thought again of her in that garden, thought of the gorgeous day it had been. Thought how he'd like to spend a single afternoon with her, talking. Sitting under a big tree, maybe, with a good loaf of bread and some cheese and a bottle of St. Émilion. On a blanket under a tree on a day just like the one they'd missed. He thought these things and knew the urge was trouble, but it was fine, just fine, to sit thinking.

He wondered how long the junkie who'd just scored would live. Get a fucking life, man. These days he could only feel bad for them, the way he did for the beat cops, the guys on the street dealing with all that crap; and then he turned off feeling anything, because he was tired, and all he could feel lately was bad.

He lay down in bed, closed his eyes.

Thump/da-dump/thump/da-dump.

"Paging passenger Kessler," he whispered. "Flight 107 to Happiness is ready for departure. Paging passenger Kessler. Please proceed to Gate Three immediately."

•

They didn't dare put a fire in the woodstove. Wilson, wearing three sweatshirts, sat on his cold, sculpted buns in a folding metal chair, keeping watch out the living room window with a nightscope atop a tripod, lamenting a lack of flannel drawers. The world was various shades of green: leaf green, caterpillar green, forest green gone to black in most places. Ghost green.

"I can't see shit," he complained.

"You'll see it if there's movement." Kessler's voice almost echoed in the empty stone cottage. He spoke to Wilson from the bare kitchen, where he stood waiting for Mr. Coffee. Wilson had insisted on bringing the thing, and Kessler was glad of that, sort of. More coffee; just what they needed. It's seven P.M.; bring on those long-night-ahead java jitters. At least it would warm the belly.

He carried the two cups carefully, steam rising from them in the cold, dark living room. A small candle burned in a rusted jar lid in one corner. Wilson had discovered it in a kitchen cabinet.

The young agent took the coffee and sipped noisily. "Colder than a witch's teat in December out there."

"Whadja expect?" Kessler, at the window, studied the darkness. Clouds obscured stars and what there might be of a moon. It really was dark out there. Leaves fully down now, still fairly crisp, what with the lack of snow, covering the yard with a thick coat of brown. He liked the comings and goings from this cottage, shuffling through the leaves. Remembered afternoons as a child spent raking huge piles of them and jumping in, tumbling and wrestling with his brother and a bunch of neighborhood kids. Eons ago.

"Yeah," Kessler mused. "What we should do is every September make sure we're on a case that'll take us somewhere tropical by this time of year. Forget this cold weather stuff. You ski?"

"Hot damn." Wilson bent to put his cup on the floor, clapped loudly, and stood up. "Here we go," he announced, glancing around the empty room as though there was something to look for, as though he could see more than two feet in front of his face.

Kessler also put down his coffee and followed Wilson through the house to the back entry, licking Styrofoam taint from his lips. The black BMW he'd grabbed from the agency garage was parked right outside the kitchen entrance, on the drive that looped around back of the cottage.

"Another piece-a-shit ride," Wilson said, getting behind the wheel.

"All they had left," Kessler replied. Lately the agency garage was full of them, nothing available but black Beemers, seized from would-be hotshot drug dealers. Kessler knew the value of less stylish rides. "Stay put," he said, "until they're well down the road."

"You da man," Wilson said, peering out the windshield at nothing.

•

Not even out of New Paltz via snow-covered Mohonk Mountain, and they sat at a stoplight, Annie staring into the back window of an Ulster County sheriff's car. Her knuckles were hot; she tried to relax her grip on the wheel. She prayed in her head, chanted, *Mother of God please don't let him notice us. Please don't let him please don't let him.*

Ease up.

No fear? She had fear. Real and strong and despised. Suddenly there are cops everywhere. This is how it would be. She would be afraid to stand next to one in line at the post office. She would be terrified to come upon one directing traffic. She would come to scorn and despise them for the fear they brought to her existence.

Surely they wouldn't be this blatant. He couldn't possibly—this young deputy in front of her—be part of some kind of surveillance.

Be still my beating heart. Hah. This wouldn't do. Cops were the ones you called for help. She didn't want to be afraid of them, resent them. But there it was, right in front of her, in a squad car: her worst fear wore a uniform. She was terrified that he would hang back, fall in behind her, pull her over. ID, please, ma'am. Pretty please with sugar on top, right before I take you in. She thought she might melt onto the floorboard. She gripped the wheel tighter, because if she let go, the shakes in her fingers would make things seem worse than they undoubtedly were. If this was what it would be like, she was not long for this life, this version of life that Kurt seemed to think she would adapt to so easily.

Again she tried to see through the rear window of the deputy's car. There was a kid in the back seat, leaning forward because his hands were cuffed behind his back. Okay. It was only an arrest. Some poor schmuck got caught. *Only*. An arrest. Everything is okay. Slow down now. Try to take it easy. Her pulse was in her ears, that loud and hollow pounding, the sound of her own blood rushing.

She glanced over at Kurt. Eyes closed, resting before his turn at the wheel. The boys had fallen asleep almost before they pulled out of the drive.

The prisoner in the cop car was maybe twenty years old. A skinhead. Probably a student at the community college. The deputy, from what Annie could see, had the same haircut and looked about the same age. Maybe they'd gone to the same elementary school. Yo, wanna play kickball?

"There's a cop car in front of us," she said quietly.

Kurt didn't open his eyes.

"Just act normal," he said.

"Act normal."

"Like we're a family, headed for vacation in Florida, right?"

Okay. What's normal.

You know. Normal. Without a care in the world.

That's not normal.

The light changed; the sheriff's cruiser eased away. She felt sorry for the kid in the back seat, wondered what he'd done and whether the punishment would fit his crime. But maybe he was a rapist. Maybe he was a serial killer. Maybe he'd sold a few joints to an undercover narcotics agent. Who knew? She wondered who cared.

She cleared the toll booth and looped onto the southbound entry ramp, glancing again at Kurt, and then at the rearview. Here came two more cars behind her on the ramp, accelerating, keeping pace.

Kurt was sleeping like a babe. Sleeping the way she wished her babes would sleep. Soundly. The way she couldn't; lately, waiting for the law and disaster. Look at them now, their innocence shining in the quiet. Everyone asleep; no one tugging at her. Peace. She wished she were in the woods. Only a few months ago, midsummer, well before the bust, there had been that day. She was running, on the uphill part, pushing herself and out of herself, and there came out of a hemlock just front of her—a great horned owl. Massive and dignified. Swooping before her path, arching into the air and through the forest; amazing how such a large creature could thread its way through the ordinary and magnificent trees. She had stopped in her tracks, breathless, captivated by its majesty and grace. And that was where she should be now, instead of here on the highway, steering a tons-heavy piece of metal down the road at sixty-something miles an hour. The car that was immediately behind her passed as soon as they were on the thruway proper. She thought about falling in behind it. But it was low-slung and red, moving, flying, its driver begging for a ticket.

"There they go," she read to the boys in the evenings. *"Look at those dogs go! Why are they going fast in those cars? What are they going to do? Where are those dogs going?"*

That's where she should be. Sitting in front of the woodstove, Alex to the right and Tim to the left, reading stories. She checked the mirrors again. That one car was still behind her, three car lengths or so, settled in for the ride. She couldn't see what it was, only that it was a sedan, and dark. It was nothing. It was cops. It was nothing. Traffic was light. Why didn't they pass her and go on?

She set the cruise control at sixty-two and adjusted herself in the seat, straightened her back, checked the mirrors again, carefully; tried not to let herself ponder the various possible outcomes.

"They will not catch you," she whispered. Everyone stayed asleep. But another voice, from a less confident section of her brain, replied, *You can't say that. Maybe they've been watching your house. Listening on your telephone. You don't know what they're going to do.*

It doesn't matter. The only people who get caught are ignorant, belligerent, arrogant, or messy. Was that Ms. Watkins talking? Ms. Watkins, the pseudo track coach? The only ones who get caught are those who want to get caught. Coach Smith never got caught. Annie could have done him in. But she was chicken. Thinking, in her wisdom, that no one would believe her. Okay. That was then. Now. You simply will not let it happen. You won't get caught. That's all.

Ah, Sweet Denial.

A string of cars came up on the right, the lead doing close to eighty easily, followed by three or four hangers-on. They zipped past, zigging one by one back into the right lane as they did. Yeeeeha, folks, here we go. Fast. You, too, can pretend it's the Indy 500. Still, the car behind her didn't move. It stayed steady, stayed a constant distance from her. So what? They're just driving. It's not a crime to obey the speed limit.

What are you going to say if it happens? This isn't happening? *They can lock you up for this, stupid.* But I'm not stupid. And I'm being careful. I have to do this. I'm not stupid. *Ask someone who's crazy if they think they're crazy.*

She slowly decelerated, letting the Jeep's speed fall to just around fifty, just barely over fifty. The car behind her slowed too, and then slowed more, letting distance open up, and that's when Annie woke Kurt.

She accelerated again, back to fifty-five, just exactly the speed limit, and reset the cruise control, took her foot off the pedal, and straightened in the seat again.

"I think someone's following us," she said.

He pulled himself up, blinked hard a few times.

"You sure?"

"Not sure. But I think so."

Kurt glanced in his sideview.

"The first one back," she said.

"BMW," he said.

"How can you see?"

"The headlights," he said. "You can tell by the shape, the configuration."

The car had let more distance open up, and now, as Annie and Kurt both watched mirrors, another car passed it and pulled behind them, stayed for a while before pulling out into the passing lane and easing by them.

"There's a rest stop up here not far," he said. "Let's take it."

She speeded up to sixty-five.

Kurt eyed the mirror steadily as she cruised down the highway. Annie did too, until he chuckled and said, "Better watch where you're going, Annie Oakley."

She drove the car. She knew how to drive. She could even drive fast if she had to, and she could drive well. Her grandmother had taught her, not how to drive fast, but how to drive. The fast part she'd learned herself, later, on roads that wound through the hill country. Granny had taught her on the vast flatlands of west Texas, where blacktop highways stretched straight and level forever, and it didn't much matter if you went off the road because there was only flat and level and endless blue sky for as far as you could see in any direction you looked. She'd got behind the wheel when she was fourteen, and Granny's Oldsmobile had seemed more like a boat than a car, but Annie had got the hang of it quickly.

She drove on. She pulled into the rest stop, one huge building that housed assorted fast-food outlets and rip-off tourist shops; she parked toward the back of the lot.

"Take a few minutes," Kurt said. "I'll stay here." The boys slept on.

She entered the tile and stainless steel labyrinth of the ladies room, listened to the roar of industrial flushes while she washed her hands at a dirty sink. She got coffee and cookies at a small red-and-white Mrs. Field's franchise near the building exit.

When she returned, he had moved to the driver's seat. She got in, folded sip-tops into place, put the coffee cups in the console holders.

Kurt accelerated back onto the thruway and immediately pushed the speed up to seventy, seventy-five, seventy-eight.

"You're going to get stopped," she said.

"I can afford a ticket. At this point." He held the speed for close to three miles, eyeing the mirror, and then began slowing.

"You're right," he said finally. "They're on us."

She felt her stomach bottom out, as if they'd topped a rise in the road and dipped suddenly on the other side.

"I expected as much," he said quietly. "We'll have to split up."

"Let me guess," she said. "I'll take the boys."

"I'll take them."

"No," she said. "It's okay. I'll take them."

They left the thruway at Newburgh and crossed the Hudson to Beacon, where there was a train station.

•

Wilson parked in the lower lot, at track level. They could see the stairway from where they were.

"We're burned," Wilson said. "I should get on that train."

"No arrest yet," Kessler said.

"He's a fugitive."

"Not yet, he's not. We don't have a warrant. We don't even have an indictment. He's still free to move."

"God bless America."

They sat, the two of them, surveying, through the windshield and a chain-link fence and across the tracks, out to the wide dark waters of the Hudson.

"I'm telling you," Wilson said finally, "she's in the half-hour lot, she's dropping him off. He's going."

"We don't know who's going—"

"Right now, right here, right in front of our eyes. Why would they drive all the way here for him to catch a train? There's three stops closer to their house. They burned us and he's splitting and if we don't stick with him, he'll get away. For-fucking-ever. There goes our case."

"Nonsense." Kessler's voice was so loaded with patience it sounded ready to explode.

"Down the tubes."

"It's a simple matter of we call the office."

"Like excrement."

"We'll have someone there at Grand Central. They'll pick up surveillance. Patience. We need an indictment."

"Yeah. Okay then. Look how patient I'm being here. I don't fuckin' believe you."

Kessler considered Wilson. Creep. Bad judgment. This guy had to go, long and short of it.

•

In the short-term parking lot, across from the station door, Kurt woke the boys, his voice gentle, bringing them out of their dreams.

They were groggy and disoriented, but as soon as they heard the word "train," they pulled themselves to full consciousness and looked around eagerly. Annie zipped their coats and pulled up their hoods and braced herself for the cold.

She took their hands, and Kurt led the way hurriedly to the station and down the interminable stairs to the platform, where wind came firm off the river, scraping at exposed skin. He put his bag on a bench and turned to embrace Annie, kissed her, and pulled her close. She pressed herself against him, took the moment for all she could. His strength was there, unwavering, and his love. The station lights bathed everything in shades of the surreal. The rails seemed unnaturally solid. And the spikes holding them in place. Even the rust seemed heavy and consequential.

"We'll all be warm and safe soon," Kurt said, managing a smile, but Annie wasn't sure of the bravery behind it.

He pulled her close. *I will protect you.* Then he bent to hug the boys, and the train came rumbling in, bellowing and blowing its horn, shaking the earth beneath them.

•

"He's getting away," Wilson said. "We are sitting here watching him get away."

"No, we're not," Kessler said. "There's only one bag. She's not going. He's not getting away. This is a business trip."

"Bullshit! Like I said. She's gonna drive him to Beacon to get the train? Get off it, boss; you're blowin' this one big time."

"He won't leave her."

"What the fuck are you talking? She's not the one we're after!" Wilson slammed a hand against the dashboard. "He's getting away."

"He won't go without her. Not far."

"Who gives a fuck? He's splitting; he's not going to show for court. He's splitting! Don't you get it?"

Kessler shifted sideways in the seat. "Yeah, you're right," he said to Wilson, his voice dripping with sarcasm. "You're absolutely right. We should jump the fence and shoot the bastard, right there. Put a little blood on the tracks."

"Fuck you," Wilson said. "You're letting him slide."

"We got nothing to arrest him for right now. I'm not gonna let your bonehead attitude fuck up a perfectly good case. We arrest him before we have paper, and his lawyer will walk him for sure."

"You don't give a shit about him anymore. You care about her. That's what's happening here."

Kessler watched the platform, where she was wrapped in her husband's arms. It had to be freezing out there. The train's headlight cut around the curve in the tracks just north of the station.

"I care about her," he said, "because she will lead us to him, and probably when he's holding heavy."

Wilson clammed up and paid attention as the train came in.

When it pulled out, there she was, standing on the platform, her little rugrats waving at the train long after it was gone, until she took their hands and led them toward the stairway.

"Back to the city," Wilson said morosely.

"Stay with her," Kessler said. "Let's see where she goes."

•

It's simple. She told herself. *Just drive the car.*

No problem. Just drive the car.

She took 9W north for a while and pulled into the vacant lot of a lumber supply place, looped through the parking lot, and headed back south. In the rearview, she saw a set of headlights, those same headlights. They performed a similar maneuver, only in a different parking lot, and that's when she knew for sure. She had expected them to follow. Kurt had too.

Okay.

Fine.

She got back onto the highway and drove to the bridge and crossed the river and hit the thruway. Back the way she'd come, north on the thruway, as though she were indeed returning home, but she would skip the New Paltz exit and take the one to Kingston. She maintained nine miles an hour above the speed limit. She did not want to get stopped.

She turned on the radio. Oh, God. The Woodstock talkshow motormouth, his guest list a who's who of the Most Boring People in the World, but they all had lots to yap about, and he was ready to listen and comment. And comment. And comment.

She hit the Seek button. Wished it controlled more than just the radio.

•

The train was No Smoking, but you could still smell from when it hadn't been that way. Kurt found a window seat and turned to the darkness. Already missed them. Already worried for them. But Annie could be a cool customer when she needed to.

•

Annie approached Stone Ridge from the north, pulling off 209 onto the tiny road that ran behind the firehouse and along the edge of the woods.

The headlights followed.

Fuck it, then. She turned onto Fording Place Road, dirt and rutted, and shifted to four-wheel drive, eased along beneath trees. And there it was, under the dim light of moon behind breaking clouds, water. Flowing ever so slowly. Fording Place Road disappeared into it, ran right into the creek, emerging on the other side and winding again into the dark woods. The water looked to be almost two feet deep tonight. Perfect.

Here came the headlights, behind her.

She watched them approach, and she drove into the water.

Slowly, carefully, she drove through the water, easing out on the other side, and there was the car that had followed her, most likely Kessler, or maybe some guys he was in charge of. There it was, stuck on the opposite bank, the headlights glaring angrily into the night.

Annie couldn't help it. She was scared and she shouldn't have done it, but she tapped her brakes a couple of times, just to say *So long.*

•

"Damn!" Wilson said. "Damn damn damn. I don't fuckin' believe it."

Kessler watched the Jeep's taillights disappear around a curve in the road.

"The creek flowed gently under soft moonlight," he said. "Annie Trowbridge drove toward her destiny."

"Un-fuckin'-believable." Wilson threw the car into reverse, did what started as a by-the-book three-point turn, but the road was too narrow and trees edged either side, so he wound up going back and forth half a dozen times, muttering.

"So, *boss,* where to now? Back to the city?"

"No," Kessler said. "Back to their place. I'll wager she's going home." He hoped she was going home. If she wasn't, he was fucked. He should have been angry at losing her, pissed off that she'd tricked them this way, but he wasn't. First off, he wasn't sure she was leaving. He was banking she'd go home. Second, he'd always been a man who admired resourcefulness. He was almost proud that she'd ditched them, and so smoothly.

"Stop at a pay phone," he said. "Let's get someone from the office over to Grand Central."

Wilson drove fast down the dirt lane, screeched onto the blacktop, and gunned it, heading for Stone Ridge. He skidded to a stop in the hardware store parking lot. Kessler got out, pulling up the hood of his parka as he approached the pay phone. Man, it was cold.

Wilson stayed in the car, heat blasting, watching Kessler impatiently pump quarters into the phone. And then Kessler started waving an arm around angrily, practically jumping up and down before slamming the receiver onto the cradle and stomping back to the car.

He got in with a blast of cold air.

"Head south," he said.

"What about—"

"Grand Central," Kessler ordered. "Now."

"I thought—"

"Everyone's busy," Kessler said. "Not a soul available to assist."

"The whole office?"

"Yeah. The whole office. Busy or off-duty and unreachable."

Wilson sat, unbelieving.

"Come on, move it then," Kessler said. "We gotta beat that train."

FOURTEEN

Annie stood on the beach and watched the sun rise and tried to recall her joy on waking in the morning as a small child, the thrill of knowing that the sun was out. Two days before Christmas. All she wanted was to get away clean, get away safe. It would be at least two days before the boat arrived. Santa Claus, where are you?

A chunky German tourist took deep audible breaths, pounding a beer-barrel chest as he stretched, bikini-clad, ankle deep in the surf, facing a lazy Fort Lauderdale morning.

Annie, waiting for full sunrise on the nearly deserted sand, wondered whether this new life would turn her into a perpetual tourist. The idea had its appeal, but she knew that she had long been after something to hold on to, to cling to the way her babies had clung to her neck during their months-long struggle to gain the most rudimentary control: desperate with love.

And one day the cling became a hug, given by choice, and she began to understand that her battle against impermanence was not only difficult but futile. She had been a tourist all along, even when she was Mrs. Kurt Trowbridge, wife and mother, purveyor of two-hundred-year-old book-shelves and the like, living in a house built by settlers on a piece of land at the edge of the Catskill Mountains. Maybe that's what the settlers had been after as they stacked rocks—big, heavy rocks—thousands upon thousands of them, forming fences and houses and chimneys and barns: the illusion of permanence. More likely they were just trying to clear a spot in the rocky land, grow some crops, get out of the weather.

She attempted now to relax, let the colors of morning flow in, and the breeze, and the occasional cry from a gull. Tried to let her surroundings prevent thoughts of Joseph Kessler and what he might be doing, what methodology he might be using to track down Kurt, and track down her, as well.

She tried to swallow but couldn't. She wasn't choking, exactly; it was more like a localized paralysis. Kurt said no one had followed him. She was sure she had lost them. No one had given a second look as she and the boys boarded a plane in Newark that night. Nor when she rented a car at the airport, nor when she checked in, joining her husband at the hotel. No one had followed. But maybe they were both wrong; maybe they were deluded. The cops were out there, Kessler was out there, and he had to be looking for them. Waiting to pounce. She stood there on the beach, in the gentle morning air, trying to breathe. Tried again. She couldn't. Calm down. Just calm down. It will be okay. It. Will. Be. O.K. Will. Willpower. Will it. Control it.

Close your eyes.

Okay.

Swallow.

She gulped at the knot in her throat.

She gulped again.

Swallow.

Air.

She gulped air.

•

Later that day, and for a considerable portion of the next, Alex and Tim paddled for their lives in the pool, blocky, bright orange jackets keeping them afloat as they fought the water. Kurt took Timothy and tossed him high into the air, catching him just enough to ease his entry, bringing squeals of delight. Annie tried to get Alex to stop battling and simply float, get to know the substance, but he was eager to conquer it. When Timothy's happy screeches caught his attention, he stopped struggling and hung off Annie's neck to watch.

"I wanna do that," he said, suddenly excited, kicking again, trying to make his way to his father. Annie floated him over, and he jumped from her to Kurt. She opened her arms to Timothy, and Kurt handed him over. As she floated Tim toward a shallower part of the pool, he began squirming against her.

"Uhn-do-dat," he said, twisting his shoulder to point back at Kurt and Alex.

"You can take turns."

He started to pout; Annie swirled around slowly in the water, floating him at arm's length. He smiled at her and said, "Again."

She stretched, she took whirlpools and saunas, but always the tension returned within an hour of exiting, lodging itself right between her shoulderblades.

And then the message light on the phone was blinking, and Kurt left to go to whatever pay phone it was he had scoped out on his arrival. Annie phoned room service and watched the boys jump on the beds, Alex leaping the abyss between them while Tim stood at the edge of one bed, crouched to jump, and waiting, staying himself, instinct overriding desire.

Dinner arrived: nouveaux riches pizzas. The Cuban who delivered the tray tugged at his black vest while she signed the check—Mrs. White—and said, "Thank you very much, Mrs. White; have a pleasant evening." She started to correct him, caught herself, wondered if he noticed. Maybe he was a cop. Maybe he was a snitch. The waiter shut the door gently behind him.

The boys hung at the edge of the table, so eager to grab a slice that their fingers wiggled involuntarily, but afraid that if they touched they would get burned.

She watched the closing door, hit by the loss of her name. It was different from the name change of marriage. Then, the name was attached to her identity. It was real, she existed in the world, she was becoming a wife and mother. Mrs. White, though; this was nothing but a dirty little secret. How would she hang on to enough of herself while becoming someone she didn't know? Say good-bye to yourself, sweetheart, forget you ever knew me, shape Mrs. White from scratch. You have no history now; you have to invent your past.

What was she talking about? Mrs. White. It was a name, and temporary at that. Mrs. White belonged to Eric; she would get another identity when Kurt hooked up with his regular ID man overseas. It was a name, that was all. She knew what she believed. She knew what she had to do. That was all. Sticks and stones.

Take a breath, sweetheart. Take a long deep breath. You're in a hotel room in Florida in the middle of winter. There's room service. Soon the boat will come and you'll get out of here. Ever wonder what real freedom tastes like?

•

Kurt parked the rental in the garage and sat, psyched and freaked at once. Hadn't they given Kessler the real live slip but good? Divide and conquer. Catch me if you can, motherfucker. If you do, that makes me one, too.

He'd got off the train at Grand Central wondering first if Kessler's men would be there to pounce, and when they weren't, wondering if Annie would have second thoughts and simply return home instead of coming with him. But no one had arrested him and no one had followed him, and he grabbed a flight out of La Guardia. Annie and the boys had showed the next day, completely exhausted, but there they were.

They were coming with him. They would escape. Start over. Begin again, with the advantage of experience.

It was sticky outside, seventy-something and sea breeze humid. It felt great. He reached for his briefcase, thought better of it. No sense dragging the thing around with him when it didn't have anything in it. Only his phone book, and he wouldn't need that here. He got out and locked the car. The parking garage wasn't even half full.

Sick of bars and sick of hotels, he walked into the lobby bar at the Holiday Inn. December tourists, whitewashed or sunburned and sipping tropical cocktails, filled the air with the hum and murmur of relief as they talked about what fun it was to escape the vagaries of the northeast winter. Christmas? Forget the pines and snowdrifts. Give me palm trees and piña coladas.

He'd just sat down when Eric arrived, right on time, revolving through the front door and wearing his Fort Lauderdale variation on the theme: khaki shorts and sport shirt, trim brown hair, trim brown beard, carrying a camera bag. Who was he today?

He spotted Kurt, shook hands.

"Joe Tourister," he said. "Boise, Idaho. Thanks for coming." Trying to be friendly this time. He smiled and handed Kurt a package: the briefs. Passports. Good ones. Flawless. Kurt slipped him an envelope that contained payment. The waitress approached and Eric ordered Scotch rocks, raised a brow at Kurt.

"Espresso," Kurt said.

Eric asked about Annie and the boys, how everyone was, were they enjoying Florida. The last question seemed odd, coming from someone of Eric's experience; Kurt nodded yes without knowing whether he meant it. The waitress came and left; Eric sipped his drink and studied Kurt.

"So these people I know," he said, "they're looking for a connect in Lebanon. They've got cash, they're serious. Ready to move."

"Sorry." Kurt shook his head. "I've retired. I'm out of the business."

"Just like that?"

"I almost blew it, you know? Almost lost them."

"You're not out of the water yet."

What was this. Kurt tapped the envelope, raised a brow at Eric.

"These'll hold up?"

"Indeed they will. All the more reason to hook me up."

"That puts me right in the middle of whatever you do."

"Not at all."

"Nothing personal. You get popped, your friends get popped. Somebody mentions my name. I'm in it."

"I get popped, I make bail, and I turn into a new person. Same for my friends." He leaned forward, spoke quietly. "Hey, man, you're already on the lam. What does it matter?"

"I promised my wife. That's what matters."

"They have plenty of cash. You could make a couple of hundred grand just for arranging things. More if the trip goes successfully. Don't tell me you don't need the money."

A serious chunk of change. All he'd have to do was introduce Eric. And lie to Annie.

"I'm sorry," he said. "I appreciate what you've done for us. But I'm out of it. I've got to say no."

Eric took a sip of Scotch and sat back. "My people will be disappointed."

Kurt tried to decide whether there was a threat behind the words. It didn't seem so, but he didn't know this guy. He wished Annie had come along. But she'd already said just get the passports and get out of there. He assessed Eric for a long moment.

"I'll make some calls," he said finally. Better to leave the guy happy until Annie and the boys and he were safely out of the country. "What's your end?"

"Enough to make it worthwhile. Who you dealing with over there?"

"Muslims," Kurt said.

"Trustworthy, I hear."

"So far."

Eric reached for his camera bag. "I have ten Gs these people gave me," he said, "to assure you we're serious. A retainer of sorts."

Kurt waved a hand at him.

"Hang on to it. Until we're sure I'll be able to do something for them."

"No problem," Eric said, surprised but amenable.

"It may be a few weeks." Kurt downed the last of his espresso. "You're reachable through that same number?"

"Just give a jingle," Eric said. "The service will know where to reach me."

Kurt left the windows down for the short drive back to the Hilton, enjoying the warm salty air. Maybe they should head somewhere south. Some island. Hard to believe there were folks up north battling against all that bitterness. Ice and snow, man. Enough already.

When he pulled under the porte-cochère, a bellman approached immediately. Kurt left the engine idling and reached for his briefcase.

It wasn't there.

The bellman opened the driver's door with a smile, and the interior light revealed an empty passenger side. Kurt checked the back seat. Nothing. The car was empty but for him. He turned off the ignition, grabbed the keys, and got out. Maybe he'd locked it in the trunk.

Nothing there but a miniature spare tire. Fuck. Why was he looking? He knew right where he'd left it, on the floorboard of the front passenger seat.

He handed the bellman the keys and took the receipt.

Just gone. Not a scratch on the car anywhere. Who was better at breaking into cars than the cops? He wondered if Eric's talents ran in that direction. Could he have snatched it before he came in? He almost hoped it *was* Eric. Because if it wasn't, it was very likely the heat, and that meant they were close by, probably waiting to see what he was up to before falling on him big time.

"I'll need it in an hour or so," he told the bellman, and headed for the bank of pay phones down the hall from the lobby. Time to adjust the plan.

Godzilla was at the head of the table when Kurt blew into the room. The sight of his family sitting at dinner shocked him into a vague sense of incongruity. Oh, yes, this is my family. The criminals, nice guys, actually, are out there in the ocean somewhere, floating in a boat, heading our way. He hoped they were going fast, hadn't hit any weather.

"Hey," he said, dropping his arms as he took up a Popeye stance. He pointed at Godzilla's green plastic hide.

"Is that guy eating my pizza?"

"Yeah!" The boys shouted in unison and began ripping at their half-eaten slices in an entirely uncivilized manner.

"You pizza-heads."

They giggled and stuffed their mouths. Kurt grabbed a slice and carried it with him to the closet. He pulled out the suitcases, soft canvas bags that would convert to backpacks, though large and unwieldy ones.

"You gaga head!" Alex shouted.

"Gaga head?" Kurt turned to him. "You . . . you . . . you squid head."

"What's a squid?" Alex shouted.

"Lives in the ocean," Kurt said. "Not so intelligent but it tastes good."

They giggled, slowed down on their dinner. Kurt used one hand to pull things out of the closet and place them on the bed, the other to feed himself pizza. Timothy let a dangerous smile creep onto his lips and said, quietly, "Daddy. Let's wrestle."

"We'll have to do that later, pal. Right now we got places to go." Kurt looked at Annie, sitting between them, her dinner barely touched, and a wave of guilt swept over him. He had no right to ask her to do this. No right except that he loved her, he loved them.

"Someone broke into the car," he said.

Annie said nothing as he stuffed the last of his slice into his mouth and chewed furiously.

"Oh, no," Alex said. "Our car's broken?"

"Nope," Kurt said. "They stole my briefcase."

"What's *stoll?*" Alex asked.

"It means somebody took it," Kurt said. "Like, when somebody takes something that doesn't belong to them, they *steal* it." To Annie: "All it had in it was my phone book, really. I'm sure that's what they wanted." He pressed his palms hard on his temples, as though trying to squeeze his mind back into place. "Whoever it was knew how to pick a lock. I couldn't even tell the thing had been touched."

"Are you sure you didn't just leave it somewhere?" She didn't want to ask in front of Alex whether he suspected a particular person. He would probably say, "The cops." Which would mean they weren't getting out of the country after all. Which would mean they were hours, maybe minutes, from getting busted. She shuddered from head to toe. What was she doing? She had to be crazy. She flashed on the night the cops came through the door, and the terror was with her again, sitting next to her and grinning, like a demented dinner guest demanding to be fed and fed and fed some more while she dug in the pantry and put things in pots and cooked and sweated and laid plate after plate of food in front of him and he just kept eating and smiling and ordering more, more, more. She felt as if she didn't know Kurt anymore, as if she had never known him. Who was he and what was he doing there and why were they going with him?

She sat quietly, managing not to scream.

Kurt gave up on his self-inflicted massage and resigned himself to a headache. "Are you okay?" he asked.

"I'm fine," she said. Breathe in. Breathe out. "I'm fine."

He shook his head, recognizing the tone. "We have to go."

"When?"

"Now."

She took a long drink of water, found some cartoons on the television, and began packing.

There wasn't much, but it was scattered all over the room. They wreaked chaos wherever they went, these two. She put Godzilla into the large black canvas bag that Kurt lugged with him everywhere these days, as though carrying his religion in a suitcase. All you had to do was look at the root of the *-ism* to know what was being worshipped. Communal values, social values, this guy Marx. And don't forget capital, fast replacing all the others. Money. Let's worship money. Yeah-yeah-yeah. Capitalism. That sounds good. And if we want to make something really expensive, all we have to do is make it illegal. So Kurt carried around a big bag of money. Some cops could be bought. Some places, it was expected.

But she didn't want to be around it. Didn't want to be part of it. Growing your own, maybe handling a few pounds for friends, that kind of thing, sure. And that time making fools of the Texas narcs, that was fun. But kick it up to the point where you were talking millions, and things got nasty fast. There was always some creepy arms dealer or petty despot looking to make a fast buck. Stay away from me, she thought. Keep your war to yourself, thanks very much. She stuffed things into the cases and despised her own hypocrisy and realized there was still time to say no. Still time to bail out on this, to regain some equilibrium and go home. Sanity might be out of the question, but it wasn't too late to tell Kurt that he'd pushed it too far, expected too much in exchange for "I do."

He got down on his hands and knees to check under the beds, and the boys were on him in an instant, pummeling him, clambering onto his back, shouting, "C'mon, Daddy, let's wrestle!"

He stood upright, laughing and pulling them with him, shaking his head no. "There's no time," he said. "Know what we're gonna do?"

"What?" cried Alex.

Kurt bent to let them climb off him and onto the bed, pulled them close, and whispered. "It's a surprise. But you're gonna love it. Now quick, let's get your shoes on." He glanced over at Annie, standing near a half-packed suitcase, watching them. She smiled at him. Weak. He went over and wrapped her in a hug.

"It'll be okay," he whispered. "It'll all be okay."

She checked the boys; they were back in TV land.

"I'm scared," she said quietly. "I'm thinking this is a mistake."

"Oh, baby, don't," he said. "Please don't. Look. If it doesn't work out, you'll go home, that's all. If at some point it doesn't feel right, I'll get you back to New York. Or wherever. I promise. But give it a chance. Please. I need you. Give us a chance."

•

The night sky looked bare and deep blue. The moon was hangnail thin, a night away from being new, but the glow from Fort Lauderdale obliterated many of the stars Annie was used to. The boys were at the edge of the dock, tense with excitement, leaning forward to peer into dark water.

"Guys," Annie said, "not too close, please." Two steps back, a quick glance at Mom, one step forward, Timothy following Alex's every move. They couldn't stand still; they couldn't get close enough to the water.

"They know not to fall in," Kurt said quietly.

"It's only a question of how much fun they could have versus how much trouble it would get them in."

He smiled at her and stepped onto the dock to take the boys' hands.

"Are there sharks?" Alex looked up at Kurt, his eyes wide with a fear that was mostly mock.

"There are," Kurt said, "but we'll be in a boat, where they can't get us."

A real boat. Oh, joy. Oh, rapture. Annie looked around in the darkness and tried not to let her fear show. She was exhausted from the travel, wrung out from the waiting, afraid of what she was about to do. Now she was, officially, part of it. She wondered what the charge would be if they caught her. The phrase *aiding and abetting* came to mind, as did *flight to avoid prosecution.* She wondered where she'd heard them or read them. They were not part of her world.

But now they could lock her up, too. She heard the announcer's voice from an aspirin commercial burned into her brain when she was a kid by some TV advertiser practicing saturation bombing: *What's a mother to do?*

What's a mother to do? Simple. Step onto a boat on a nearly moonless night and sail away from life as you know it.

". . . in the shark water, Mommy," Alex was saying.

With two children. Okay. What was sanity but a willingness to conform to certain standards. What was mental health but a psychiatric establishment concept.

"Mommy," Alex said, "what's that boat song?"

She reached down and stroked his hair, thinking back to his struggle in the swimming pool. She hadn't liked floating either, until she was in her teens. The best time was at night, when the moon was out, shining silver on the surface of Spring Lake, and she rested there, in and on water, feeling her body sink or rise with the taking of air. It had taken her years to learn not to fight the water.

"The boat song," she said. She knelt, sitting on one leg and looking into his eyes, and sang softly:

Row, row, row your boat,
Gently down the stream,
Merrily, merrily, merrily, merrily,
Life is but a dream.

Alex joined in, and they did two more rounds before they were interrupted by the low rumbling of an engine. A boat eased slowly out of the darkness and nudged the dock.

It was not a rowboat.

She recognized it as a Cigarette, one of those slender-nosed craft that zipped across the water at just under the speed of light. Rich, powerful cocaine smugglers used them because they could outrun anything the Coast Guard had. She imagined the Coast Guard guys saying to their bosses, "Hey, how can we catch them if we don't have a boat that can keep up?" She hoped the boat hadn't been purchased with money from cocaine. Even thinking about it made her feel poisoned, her body's way of saying, "Hello. Me again. Please don't forget: that stuff is toxic."

She could not picture Dr. Tetlow involved in that, though she knew he had always been free and easy with his prescription pad. Trying to ease people's pain, she was sure. Annie had done the Valium thing when it was happening, but came away from the chemical worse for the experience. Even so, she'd always had the sense that Dr. Tetlow was essentially kind beneath his particular brand of insanity, making the condition benign.

The man at the helm obviously knew Kurt. Annie could feel the tremor of adrenaline in her fingertips. She saw them exchange greetings. Alex was on her right and Tim on her left, her arms around their shoulders. It surprised her somehow, but maybe only because she wanted it to: her husband was in charge here.

What was she doing? What had she done? More than that—what would she have to do?

"Let's go, babe; we've only got a minute." Kurt was stepping aboard, getting his balance, reaching to help her. She was stiff with numbness. *What would she have to do?* Get on the boat, the Cigarette. Ride with it out to Dr. Tetlow's yacht, *The Final Analysis,* somewhere offshore in the dark. Floating out there in the shark water. Dr. Tetlow. She barely knew him. If she went, she could never come back, unless she was willing to face prison. If she stayed, she would shatter her family as she had the sugar bowl when it slipped from her hands to the kitchen floor.

"Annie?" His hand was out, reaching.

She'd promised. *Don't make promises that you can't keep.* And what had he promised her? *I will protect you.* If she went, what kind of life for the boys, for her? Cut off from everything and everyone they knew except each other. And how would Kurt support them?

"Annie!" His voice was not angry. It was desperation she heard. It hit her then, full on, the vastness of her self-deception. She had married a smuggler, and what smugglers did was risk their freedom, sometimes their lives, to bring in the booty, the stuff lots of people wanted but this or that government said they couldn't have. Kurt had been a smuggler long before he met her. He was a smuggler now, still, after all the time she'd spent waiting for him to become something else. He would, in all probability, always be a smuggler. He was a gambler. He liked the life because it made his heart pound and his blood rush the way it used to just before a wrestling match—so far into fight or flight that he had to battle with his own stomach not to puke—and like those opening seconds on the mats, when he had someone in a grip and was about to put him on his back and pin him. He liked beating the government at their own game. Forget his father's golf course, forget his father's bridge table. Kurt loved high stakes.

"Mom!" It was Alex, tugging at her hand, pulling her toward the water. "Let's go!"

"Annie, come on." Stern now, his voice commanding, trying to give her strength.

She stood fast, stood on the dock holding her children firmly, shaking her head.

The man in the boat looked at Kurt and said, "We're hot, man. I can't stay."

For a moment it looked as though Kurt would get out, climb back on to the dock, and pull them into the boat by force.

"Annie, please!" Pleading.

She was unable to move.

"I'm sorry," she said. She felt Alex tugging at her. "I love you," she said.

The engine revved; the boat made its turn. She saw Kurt looking, she saw him looking at her, and her heart turned to dust right there inside her chest, surrounded by soggy lungs, mixing to mud. He cried out to Alex and Tim, "I love you!" and they pulled against her, trying to force her after their father. And they watched helplessly as the boat roared away into the dark.

Again they pulled, trying to jump into the water, Alex wailing, "Daddy, Daddy, please, don't go!" and yanking his arm hard, trying to free himself from her grip, and Timothy, too, struggling against her, enraged, screaming, "NO-NO-NO, Mommy, NO I want Daddy I want Daddy!" Screaming, tears pouring down their cheeks, and her own tears falling on their helpless and vengeful heads as she yanked them away from the dock, struggling not to slap them into submission and despising her desperation.

She held them by their wrists and began to drag them to the garage, where the rental sat indifferently. The huge heavy backpack strapped to her shoulders tried to pull her to the ground. She dragged them, against their will.

"I hate you!" Alex screamed. "You are not in my heart anymore!"

She walked, pulling them through the night, all those blocks. Alex called her stupid and mean and bossy. He raised his face to the sky and screamed.

In the garage, people stared at them dumbly. She thought one or two would intervene. Her frown, or maybe her tears, kept the strangers at bay. Timothy had lost what language he had to rage, was dependent on screeches to convey his terror. His loss. His anger. His utter unwillingness to surrender to her decision.

The cars in the garage glittered under fluorescent light, seemed made of colored glass. She forced her children into the rental, strong-arming them, climbing in after them. Strapping them down with seatbelts, locking the doors. It looked like a kidnapping. She got into the driver's seat, expecting the car to shatter when she slammed shut the door.

All the way out of town, headlights glared at her, accusing her of betrayal. Her children screamed. They hated her. They were right. At long last, they were right and she was wrong and everyone knew it. Their enmity was pure.

"And you deserve it," she said, out loud, to herself. She glanced into the shadows of the rearview. Their noise was such that they missed her words. "I meant no offense," she added, babbling. "But it's true. You're a wreck." She drove into the night, headed north on some road, some highway or other.

"You're a wreck," she said again. She turned on the radio. Loud, trying to drown out the venom-filled screams of her children. The music made it worse, turning the car's interior into some weird postnuclear-war circus. She turned it off.

Didn't they know? She loved them. Couldn't they understand, just this once?

They screamed. She drove. They kept screaming. She thought about joining them.

And then, as suddenly as their wails started, they stopped. Glancing behind her, she saw them slumped in their seats, eyes shut, swollen from crying. Silence. Blessed silence. She remembered an August morning, when Kurt had been away and she'd awakened at three in the morning to find them both in her bed, snuggled against her, and the windows cracked just right to let in a cool breeze, and it was raining. Gentle and steady, perfect rain, beautiful rain, whispering from the sky, lulling her back into sleep, and her babies safe there with her.

She drove on. In silence. She did not know where she was going. She drove.

And then, red lights. Behind her. Right behind her. Oh, shit. Oh, no. Red lights. The gleaming chrome grin of a cop car. Gotcha! A state trooper's vehicle, on her tail as if he's ready to bump her, push her down in the road. Pull over, bitch. Pull over now. Her face got hot; she thought the cop would be able to hear her heartbeat even before she rolled down the window and handed him her license, and what the hell name was it in, Eric's brand-new ID. He was a jerk. She looked at the cop's face and immediately saw him in a strip joint, drinking intolerably cheap beer and resting a fist on his crotch, and the only thing he could think was *I'd like to get me some of that*. Because that's what guys were supposed to think when they went to the strip joint instead of home to whatever. He shone his flashlight into the car, saw sleeping children. His tight little smart-ass smile eased up.

"Are you aware why I stopped you?" He looked nineteen.

Answers flooded her synapses: because I married an outlaw, because I know where he's going, because I helped him get fake ID, because I'm a terrible worthless human and a lousy mother, because I forgot to turn off the toaster before I went for groceries last week last month last year, because I can't match colors, because I fight with my sister, because you can. Just because you can. Is that the right answer? Stop me and get away with it? Is that why? No, officer, if I knew why you stopped me, I assure you I wouldn't have been doing it in the first place. I obey the law. I am a law-abiding citizen. I can even, under duress, be persuaded to say the Pledge of Allegiance.

"No," she said quietly, "I don't."

"You didn't see those big orange signs back there? Reduce speed to forty-five?"

It was only a few weeks after the bust—she and the boys had been at the Hudson Valley Garlic Festival—the first time she told Alex and Tim that if they got lost or got hurt and needed help, they should look for a policeman. She'd pointed one out so they'd know what the uniform looked like. Timothy nodded, but Alex had looked intently for a long moment before turning his frightened face to her. "Police arrested Daddy," he said.

"That was a different kind of policeman," she'd said. "The policemen here will always help children. They like children a lot."

Alex had nodded approval, stuck a knuckle between his teeth, and started a rhythmic twisting at the waist until he sighted the kids' section and shot his finger out suddenly in that direction, as though his body were a compass and had found magnetic north. Discussion over. Time for fun.

"I guess I didn't," Annie said.

"Where are you headed this late at night, ma'am? Are you in some kind of trouble?"

"I'm going home," Annie said. "I was in Florida visiting friends. I'm on my way back to winter."

He smiled at that, and handed back her license.

"You should consider a hotel for the night," he said. "It's almost three in the morning."

"You're right," she said. "I'll do that."

"There's a Motel 6 about three exits north of here. Right on the road. Can't miss it."

"Thank you," she said.

He touched a hand to his hat, the way that man in the gas station ads used to when she was little. Service with a smile.

The Motel 6 was made of painted cinderblock . . . *and the third little pig built his house out of brick* . . . She carried the boys into the room one by one. Out cold. Their bodies weighted with exhaustion. She got them into pajamas and tucked them in, the scent of sunshine, sweat, and tears floating up to her from their faces.

"You're mean," Alex whispered, and his eyelids closed.

Annie brushed her teeth and got into bed. She heard Goldilocks: *Oh, my. This bed is toooooo hard.* A sound came out that was part laugh and part cry. Comfortable was not an option. The best she could do was lie there, let her body try to rest. She thought she could discern the scent of concrete, rising up through the marine blue carpeting that smelled of a plastic she was sure had been developed for NASA.

Last thing, before exhaustion overrode anxiety, she saw Kurt gliding away on the boat, gliding and gliding, gliding across the ocean, 'neath the light of the risible moon.

•

Dr. Tetlow approached the railing where Kurt leaned, looking for morning behind the overcast sky. The air was gray, the sky was gray, the sea was gray. Doc seemed taller than Kurt remembered, and had put on a few pounds. The skin around his eyes was crinkled into a permanent smile.

"Found your sea legs?" Doc asked. "I have meds if you're in need."

"I have the remedy right here." Kurt pulled a joint from his shirt pocket and ducked his head to light it. They smoked and watched the water roll and swell gently, solid here, a single thing, a living skin on the earth's surface.

"Heavenly," the doctor said, exhaling. "I dropped something similar in the Bahamas. Any of this around?"

"I'll let you know," Kurt said.

"I'm sorry she didn't come with you." Doc clapped a large hand on Kurt's back. "It was more than a last-minute quarrel?"

"There was no quarrel. I don't know what it was. She freaked. I don't know."

"She wouldn't, you know—"

"It's okay, you can say it. No. She wouldn't rat."

"I didn't mean—"

"It's all right. You don't know her. But she wouldn't do it." He began doubting the words even as he spoke them. How the fuck could he say what she would do? She had betrayed him. She had promised to come with him, and she had bailed at the last second, when it was too late, when he was powerless to change it. Well, fuck her and her self-righteous bullshit. He could still hear the boys, hear their cries. How could she do that to them? To him? She had broken up the family. She had failed her wedding vows. Fuck her.

"The Coast Guard is full of thieves," Doc said, "and they can board at will."

"Modern-day pirates." Kurt wanted to be alone, but feared to offend Doc, who had just risked his freedom to bring Kurt from danger. Man. What was this? What was happening? He kept seeing his father, kept seeing his mother and the way they looked at each other and how he'd known they hated each other's guts. But it wasn't like that with him. He loved Annie. She was just messed up these days. Or maybe it was him. Maybe he was like his old man, afraid that if he got too close to his kids, they would turn on him and disappear. But that point was moot now. Annie had taken them. She had taken his children away. She had failed him. Couldn't deal with the thought of freedom. Couldn't get past her fears. She wasn't herself anymore, anyway. She was someone he couldn't know. The boys weren't even in school yet, but every night was like a school night. The house was full of rules, full of discipline; Annie was nothing but a drag.

He wondered where they were, what they were doing. Her refusal to come with him was unconscionable.

He flicked the glowing tip from the joint into the water.

"You probably just spawned a tornado in Kansas," Dr. Tetlow mused. He sighed. "I am taken back to an incident of youth." He laughed, a harmless but unsettling laugh. Probably similar to the one he gave just before he started screaming, with foam flying from his lips, at the end of an hour-long presentencing statement to an irate judge in Seattle. ". . . and so I say, give me Lithium or give me death!" and diving headlong through a second-story window onto a first-story rooftop, rolling, falling, stumbling with the grace of a rhinoceros onto the clipped green lawn of the courthouse and running for his life.

He had been a fugitive for the seven years since.

"But I've listened to too many tales of sad childhoods," he continued.

"I began to think happiness was a pathology." He laughed again. "Cause to celebrate: we should soon be crossing out of U.S. territorial waters."

"Thank you, doctor," Kurt said, "for coming to our rescue."

"Your rescue."

"Would you go in again? If she changes her mind?"

Dr. Tetlow fingered his wedding band and was silent.

"How long's it been?" Kurt said.

"Three years now I guess." Doc shook his head sadly, his egg-shaped face creased by a frown. "I told her some time ago that I would understand if she filed for divorce."

Kurt hung on the rail. He felt gutted, plain gutted.

"How long does this go on for you?"

Doc gave a rueful smile in the direction of the vast and distant horizon.

"James Lowell, I think it was. 'There is nothing so desperately monotonous as the sea, and I no longer wonder at the cruelty of pirates.' " He chuckled. "There is no statute of limitations once you've been indicted. They can pursue me for the rest of my life. You too, now, I guess."

"It sucks."

"They'll come after you strong in the coming several weeks. Best we just float around out here a while, stay away from land. No record of your leaving the country; that's helpful."

"I've got to get my head clear."

"A month or two, things will cool down. The marshals, you know, the Fugitive Unit will get the case. They're swamped. Can't begin to keep up. Your paperwork will wind up in a stack on somebody's desk."

"Let's hope."

"Count on it."

"Glenda hasn't left you."

"She will eventually, unless it turns out she's seriously into long-distance marriages. That wasn't our original plan."

"Maybe she'll join you. Go somewhere else."

"She doesn't want to uproot the kids."

"Even if it meant you would all be together?"

"They'll be in high school soon. Maybe after that. We're awaiting repeal of prohibition."

"You and me both."

"Maybe she just freaked," Doc said. "Give her some time. Then get in touch."

"It's not like her," Kurt said. "She told me she'd give it a try. She bailed on me. She's never done that before. It's not like her."

"Know what Glenda told me when she refused to come with me?"

Kurt shook his head.

"She said I should understand. She said she seemed to be the only one available to take proper care of our children."

•

The deck was empty; Kurt took a place fore and sat, eyes closed, facing the sun. He wanted to get pure. He wanted to get clean. His brain had been clouded with the minutiae of business and the pressure of trying to keep everything from Annie; that's what had consumed his life since the bust. He thought back to those months before he met her when he'd been in the area of the Teotihuacan ruins, not far from Mexico City. He had gone nearly two weeks ingesting nothing but fresh fruit and juices, meditating daily. He had climbed among the ruins, sat studying the Pyramids of the Sun and Moon, wondering if, should he hit eighty or ninety, he would be a wise old man or a doddering old fool.

There were temples, palaces, dwellings of a people whose community had flourished there for over five hundred years but who lost it around A.D. 750. Five hundred years, down the tubes. He wondered if the good old U.S. of A. would last that long. He had his doubts.

But he knew what he should do now. What he had to do. What was right. Get pure. Slow down and remember who he was and where he wanted to go. It was so easy to lose track of things; he felt buried beneath a mountain of insignificant details, the rubbish of daily existence. He had to move carefully. And he had to recover his family. He had to find a way to make her understand that nothing and no one else meant anything to him. Only her. Only the boys.

He opened his eyes and saw whales, a hundred or so yards out; three of them, he thought. One was a baby. He tried not to let the hurt overtake him. In spite of himself, his attention again turned inward; he was searching his interior for signs of life.

And then knowledge crept in, sitting next to him and slipping its arm around his shoulders like an old friend. Annie had not betrayed him. She never had and she never would. The pain was replaced by something so huge as to verge on the unendurable. The realization of what he had done left him completely, perfectly, utterly numb. Empty. If he let himself feel, just at that moment, he might leap over the rail into the unforgiving sea, reject Doc's attempts to pull him back on board. If he let himself feel, he might drown.

He would absorb this emptiness inside himself, rattling around like dice in a crap table cup, and he would focus with all his strength on one goal. He would find a way to reunite his family. Somehow. They would be together again. He would find a way. Annie. Alex. Timothy. That was all. He needed their love. He needed to give them his love. He would not go through life without them. It would be criminal, unconscionable.

He sat, perfectly empty, and when tears came, he let them. *Old enough to know better. Cry, baby, cry.*

FIFTEEN

Joseph Kessler dragged into the office, weak-muscled and bleary-eyed. Followed the stink of chemically processed coffee to the lounge, as euphemism had it, at the end of the hall. The room was small and unventilated, smelled of industrial floor wax and the coffee, too long on the burner. He could not believe how tired he was. It's seven A.M. Do you know where your brain is?

Bright shining packages of artificially flavored, artificially colored, preservative-loaded, and highly caloric substances hung from hooks behind smudged Plexiglas in two large brown metal vending machines against the wall. Kessler's sleep-deprived brain decided to have him on: the packages came alive, dancing, swinging from their hooks, and singing in chorus: *Food, glorious food, hot sausage and mustard . . .* He rubbed his eyes, turned away, found his mug—I HEART NEW YORK logo on the side—from among those in the dish rack next to the sink. Pour some coffee. Inside the refrigerator: half a jar of pickles and no milk. Again. A bachelor's cooler. He hated Coffeemate, not just the powder—whatever that was—but the name. Coffeemate, inmate; every time he looked at the label he saw prisoners standing in a circle in some big yard, sipping from steaming Styrofoam cups and grimacing at the film it left on their criminal tongues. Waiting for the morning score. Get stoned in jail and you're free—even if there's razor wire on the chain link.

He'd almost got locked up once himself, would have, except that he was too young when he and Joey Diaz jumped into a brand-new shining black 1966 Malibu one night and went for a serious ride. A seriously fun ride. But, ah, sweet sixteen: the charges disappeared when he achieved majority. At eighteen—magic—Kessler was squeaky clean on his job applications: a/k/a Lucky.

He did not want to go to his desk. The paperwork there, stacked and stacked and stacked, was daunting. *Whadya expect,* said a voice in his head; *yer a bureaucrat.* It was J. Edgar himself, Hoover with a Brooklyn accent. He pictured the Head Fed wearing one of those housewifely aprons from the fifties, the kind with the ruffled shoulder straps, over his pinstriped suit. In a kitchen. Making pie. *Can she bake a cherry pie, Billy Boy, Billy Boy. Can she . . . Charming Billy.* Maybe he'd seen it on a postcard somewhere. He liked postcards, the funny ones, anyway, the unintentionally funny ones best. If he were young and in love he might collect them. Send them to friends who'd scattered themselves across the face of the earth.

But what a whacko that guy Hoover was, and somehow got himself into a place where he could help shape history. The power. The power.

Thank God he was gone, that's all. Well before Kessler joined up. Six years with the bureau, right after the Air Force. Sarah and Daniel born while Daddy was out chasing bank robbers. Foolish Daddy. Barbara had demanded a change after that, and he convinced her that DEA would be different. He'd go in as a supervisor, spend more regular hours in the office, less time on the streets. He would choose his investigations, have control over his time. Yeah. Right.

He walked back to his desk in the empty, silent, oppressive, and carpeted office. Someone—bonded and with the proper security clearance—had come during the night and emptied all the wastebaskets and vacuumed the carpet and dusted the desks. He sat down in his chair, with that comfortably familiar squeak he had not, in nine years, been able to locate and oil, and opened the bottom right drawer of his desk. File upon file. Life upon life. Trowbridge. At last. Today was most likely the day. He took a sip of awful coffee and felt it melting the walls of his stomach; he opened the file and saw a photo of Kurt Trowbridge, handsome enough even in a mug shot, and thought yet again about Annie.

"Fool," he said quietly, talking to the picture. "I'll find you." Wondered if he was kidding himself. Maybe he shouldn't even try. Maybe he should just leave Kurt to the marshals, let the Fugitive Unit deal with him.

Maybe Wilson was right: it wasn't about Kurt anymore. But look at that attitude, the upward tilt of the jaw. The challenge. He closed the folder and placed it on his desk next to the out tray. They would indict. Derrick Richards was sure of it. He'd called Kessler to say, *Yes yes yes, you do know how to testify. Devastating. Simply devastating.* And Gary Smith, though visibly reluctant, had said what had to be said. Continuing criminal enterprise. Kessler sat staring at the file. Continuing criminal enterprise. How did one distinguish that from what went on in the vicinity of Wall Street, or from tankers spewing oil into the seas? How did one distinguish that from art? How did they choose whom to indict?

He killed the coffee with a grimace and sat back in his chair, waiting for the caffeine to kick in. A photo of his brother, a snapshot image of Andy holding on to a pair of skis and smiling into a bright sun, greeted him from the desktop. Andy. Wearing sunglasses and a knit cap pulled low on his forehead. You couldn't see much of him except for his tentative smile.

Four years younger and even more the daredevil, planning to spend the summer after grad school—philosophy, poor sucker—traveling in Alaska. Kessler figured Andy would get his feet back on the ground that summer. But the last semester, when he was finishing his dissertation and preparing to defend it, he'd lost it completely. Nothing—*nothing*—could stop him from getting what he wanted. Kessler had tried. His mother had tried. His father had tried. Andy's girlfriend had tried. Andy pushed them all out of his life, went way downtown. What he wanted, in the end, was his next pathetic little fix.

And, as happens every so often, somehow some shit made it to the streets without getting stepped on the customary number of times, and it was good stuff. It was really, really good stuff.

It was killer.

Kessler could still let himself get angry about it, when he felt like it. But he didn't want to. He didn't want to feel all that just here, just now.

Addicts had dropped dead all over the city. That batch even killed a couple of investment bankers right in their financial prime. Kessler went numb and sat *shiva* for his brother at his parents' apartment on lower Fifth, a place he rarely went to, because he and his father always wound up shouting at each other. Always. Except that night. His father the lawyer, his father the gentleman, his father whose hobby was writing plays in Yiddish, much to the amusement of family friends, sat quietly that night. There was a bust of his father on the baby grand in the corner of the modestly spacious living room. It was a generational thing, Kessler assumed. Many of his father's friends had busts of themselves, as though by having their likenesses carved in stone they could get their mitts on a level of immortality that would supersede the faulty and all too human memories of family and friends.

His father sat stoically that evening in the chair where he always sat during Kessler's visits, his watery blue eyes remembering the past, his hand absently waving away smoke from Kessler's cigarettes, until Joseph realized he was chain smoking and took the pack to the kitchen, out of easy reach. When he returned, his father's narrow, bald head was tilted back, eyes blinking rapidly to fight the tears. His father still carried a handkerchief; he used it then to dab at his eyes. That was the extent of his visible grief, and it seemed inadequate to the remaining son.

Kessler had answered his mother's questions with as much delicacy as he could muster. *I don't know, Ma. I think it was probably just an accident,* and on like that, until his father said, "Enough, Nora," and his mother thumbed her nose at him, her usually ice-breaking gesture absurd in the somber air of the apartment. But she stopped asking questions and let her tears fall in silence, while Kessler wished she would tell the old man to shove it up his ass.

They buried Andy in a huge cemetery across the river in New Jersey on a day without clouds. The sun was so bright that their shadows seemed cut into the earth. Barbara had held his hand and rested her other on Kessler's tensed biceps. He'd not been ashamed to cry.

There was a splash in the *Times* about all the heroin users who had died, and then life went on; not much need to mourn dead junkies.

Kessler went quietly crazy, got himself assigned to a task force, Feds + NYPD = Love, turned himself into a one-man street sweep. Set a new record for arrests in a single month, bent on locking up enough dealers to be reasonably sure he'd got at least one who'd sold to Andy. It was stupid, he knew, but he did it anyway.

Now he grabbed his coffee cup and headed back down the hall, refilled, and went slowly back to his desk, sipping the muddy stuff, thinking, still, that it was during those months that he'd lost Barbara for good, and how the fuck could he have blown something so basic, so simple, as love?

He picked up a report, looked at it unseeing, put it down. There were too many of them, there were too many cases, there was too much paperwork, too much everything. Growing all the time. The paperwork and cases. He remembered the morning, some six weeks down the road from Andy's funeral, when he had a dealer flattened against a graffiti-covered wall, the puke-stained pavement beneath them, and he was working hard to restrain himself when the guy broke and ran. Kessler gave chase, nearly pulling a hamstring as he sprinted the littered sidewalk and careened into a burned-out tenement on Avenue C. The guy leaped to hurdle a couch sitting in the middle of the ruins, misjudged his depth, and Kessler, his lungs sliced with pain, jumped on him. He wanted to pound the dealer, wanted to beat his memories of Andy into the guy's head, blow by blow. But he didn't; he held back. He had one cuff on when the guy jerked his arm loose and sprang to his feet. The two stood, estimating each other, Kessler's handcuffs dangling from the dealer's left wrist.

"I ain't runnin'," the guy said, gasping. "I am not running from you." Gulping air, desperate for it. At the end. At the point where nothing mattered. "But tell me this," he said. "You're Kessler, right? Go ahead and tell me. What the *fuck* is your problem, man?"

It stunned him. He stood, vulnerable while time took off on him. The dealer stepped toward him, Kessler reached to the small of his back, pulling his gun. Shoulda done it before, but these days he had rage at his side.

"You stupid fuck," the dealer said. "How does it feel to be famous? We all heard a' you by now." Stood there, daring him. Like go ahead and shoot me, man, but if you do, you're a stupid motherfucker and doomed. "The heroin didn't kill him." Eyes hard with honesty. "He killed himself." In his face, not backing down, this guy was pissed-off and arrogant and right. "He just used brown to do it."

The handcuff dangled threateningly. Kessler felt it in his nuts, like when he was in an elevator that moved too fast for comfort. He'd get away with it. No question. Just him and the dealer here, and him alone when it came time to file the reports. He felt the gun in his hand, shifted his grip.

Fuck it. This guy and Andy and fuck the DEA, too. Ain't gonna die for any of them. There had to be something, somewhere, worth living for, but this wasn't it. He holstered the gun and took out his keys. Held up the one that would unlock the cuff.

"Get the hell out of here," he said.

He spent the rest of his shift in a faceless bar on Avenue A, and then he started over to visit his mother, planning to tell her what the scumbag had told him. He walked, and through the haze of alcohol that bathed the afternoon in a bluish pink light the color of halogen, he remembered, just in time, that she knew. She'd known when she asked her questions, and so had he. But he was glad he hadn't said it to her, and he was glad she hadn't said it to him.

He wound up going to her anyway, and sitting next to her on the couch, and crying for his brother, while she held him and cried for both her sons.

The telephone on his desk jarred him from memory. Thank you, God. He picked up the receiver.

"Joseph." Proud. Excited. It's not just a job; it's an adventure. The prosecutor.

"Derrick."

"Sic 'im, boy. Go get 'im."

Jesus. You couldn't find jerks like this anymore. The rest of the human race had evolved and left poor Derrick behind, sitting at the edge of a muddy pond, twiddling his opposable thumbs.

"You got the indictment, I guess?"

"The grand jury charges . . . blah blah blah . . . did engage in a continuing criminal enterprise . . . blah blah blah. Oh, yeah, I got the indictment. Let's get his ass in front of Judge Fingerhood. You know where he is?"

"Pretty sure," Kessler said. "I'll keep you posted."

He hung up. Didn't have a fucking first clue where Kurt was. He grabbed the phone again and punched in Wilson's home number.

The hello was beyond groggy.

"Hey," Kessler said. "Sleeping Beauty. Your presence is requested at an arrest party."

Something fell off a table on the other end of the line.

•

"What?" Wilson said. "Like you thought they'd actually be here?" He looked around the room, eyeing lamps, eyeing a blue vase on the mantel.

"Don't," Kessler said.

Wilson broke into a hard laugh, a series of barking guffaws that filled the room with spite.

"Why not?" He laughed. "Like what? You think they're coming back?"

"Who knows? You know?" Kessler knew. He could feel it. Annie was smart. Annie would wise up. He was only surprised that she wasn't back already. Or maybe he didn't know at all. Maybe she was gone forever. At any rate, fuck Wilson.

"Oh," Wilson said. "Uh-scuse me. Right, boss. We'll find them. No prob."

There were ashes in the woodstove. The house was cold and smelled abandoned. Nothing had been cooked there for a while. Kessler picked up a note near the kitchen phone. To Annie. From the sister. *If and when you get this, I'm at Liz's in the city. Sorry. Call me.*

"I got a question, man."

"What, Wilson. What is it?" Kessler stood at the kitchen window, noticing the garden fence, which protruded through the foot or so of snow that looked as if it had fallen just last night. The late December sun was sleepy-eyed and lethargic.

"What the fuck we doing here?"

"Two things," Kessler said, turning to face him. "Looking for clues, which at the moment seem to be sparse. And, far more important—you of all people should know this—covering our asses. Far as we're concerned, Friday didn't happen. We saw no signs he was leaving and we pulled up on the surveillance. We came here expecting to find him. Got it? Dude?" This last with unrepentant, unabashed sarcasm.

"Oh," Wilson said, mocking. "Yeah. I got it."

"Hey." Kessler again. "It should be easy for you. Remember your days with Group 27. Remember tearing that defendant—heroin-dealer-fuck-him—a new asshole in the airplane potty at seriously high altitude. If that doesn't work, recall that you were sent to me for a thorough evaluation, to determine whether or not you should be fired and disgraced. Or maybe prosecuted. Get the picture, *dude?*"

"I hear you," Wilson said. Attitude disappeared. Tone gone.

Kessler walked upstairs, found himself in the children's room. Surfaces bare. A toy here and there, but a glance revealed that things were missing. Toys and books. He opened a dresser drawer. Empty, or almost.

He stood in the doorway to their room. Their room.

Her room. He'd had to persuade Richards not to include her in the grand jury proceedings, though even Richards knew there wasn't a good case against her. At the time of the hearing, anyway. Things were different now.

He went downstairs and found Wilson in front of the refrigerator, scanning the almost bare shelves. Wilson opened the freezer side.

"All right!" he grunted. "Café fudge swirl."

It occurred to Kessler that Wilson was the kind of guy who would do just fine with Olivia Newton-John. He could be her hero. He could be the One. They could wear tight black leather pants and dance together. Work out, now, let's work it out.

Wilson grabbed the container and held it out to Kessler. "Ever had this?"

Kessler shook his head. Wilson began opening drawers, located a spoon, and dug in.

"Where you figure they are?" He slurped. Trying to make friends again.

"At large," Kessler said. He wondered how often Annie had stood here at the window, wondered what she had been thinking when last she was here, readying herself, he supposed, to walk away from the home she had made. For her husband. For her children.

He wished she hadn't gone.

•

She drove and drove and drove, onward, pulling her personal wagon train, headed for Texas, she thought, she assumed, listening to the boys bicker in the back seat as they took their anger at her out on each other. She ignored them. She ignored them until they were screaming; then she began screaming herself, drowning their child voices with her grownup one.

"Stop it!" she screamed. "Just stop." She hated herself for doing it, but she could not bear to hear them fight anymore. Could not bear it. Each time one of them tried to speak, she countered with "Stop!" Over and over. "Stop!"

"But, Mom—"

"Stop."

"Ma—"

"Stop! Stop. Stop. Stop." Pause, listen.

"I—"

"Stop-stop-stop-stop-stop."

A sigh. They did not know her. Frustration all around.

And finally there was silence again, and they were on a back road somewhere, she didn't know where, somewhere between Savannah and Macon, on blacktop, two lanes, rickety pickups rattling past and the sky hanging over them like a huge blue blanket that was too heavy, pressing your toes to numbness as you slept, unaware, on your back. There were trees out there somewhere, she was sure; there were trees and birds and deer and, in another season, wildflowers. She was driving past trees—couldn't see them. It'd been years since she'd seen a magnolia, with its magnificent leaves and cream-colored, syrupy sweet blossoms. In an uncle's yard, in Dallas. Her father's brother. Her father's brother whose wife had caught polio and was confined to a wheelchair and couldn't hold her head up; it bobbed on the end of her bent neck like a giant sunflower at the end of its season. And her voice was a croak when she spoke to Annie and Carol. But Aunt Beverly loved to smile and she loved to see children playing in her yard, running around under the shade of the magnolia; she enjoyed her nieces' astonishment at the size of the flowers. She appreciated the wonderment of children as only the childless can. Every day, for more than forty years, Aunt Beverly's husband picked her up from their bed and dressed her and put her in her wheel chair and wheeled her into their kitchen and made breakfast. And wheeled her to the bathroom and brushed her teeth and helped her with her morning toilet. Then someone came to stay with her while he drove off to work with numbers in an office, forgetting himself in other people's accounts. And at the end of the day he drove home and kissed his wife and made dinner for the two of them. And he bathed her again and he put her in their bed and they slept. Even though Annie was only a child—only a child—she recognized extraordinary love when she saw it.

She drove past trees, sure there were magnolias out there somewhere. She drove, the road and everything else unfolding on the windshield like a movie on a screen. She couldn't see anything. She watched the stripes go past on the blacktop, not allowing them to hypnotize her.

And then Alex said, slowly, quietly, waiting for her to stop him but she couldn't because there was such sadness in his voice, "Mommy?"

And everything was in that word, that voice, that sentence which was a question. *Hush little darlin', now, don't you cry,* but it wasn't some sweet lullabye; it was Chrissie Hynde singing about getting the hell out of Dodge with her baby sleeping on the seat next to her.

Annie reached behind her and touched Alex's knee, and he took her hand immediately. She saw a rest stop ahead and pulled over. There was a lone picnic table. She got out and took Alex ever so gently from the car, trying not to cry, but it was no use. He melted against her when she lifted him, wrapped his arms around her weakly, afraid of her anger, and she hugged him to her and kissed his ear and said, "I'm sorry. I'm so, so sorry. I love you." His strength came back to him, and he hugged her and pulled back his head to smile: a trembly, uncertain, beautiful little smile.

"I'm sorry too," he said.

She carried him to the picnic table and seated him on it, went to get Timothy. He snuggled against her and sighed, and did not want to be put down. Mommy was Mommy again. The world was right.

They sat there in seventy degrees and sunshine, in December, and smelled the green of the trees and watched the cars go past.

"I'm sorry Daddy had to go," Annie said finally. Alex sighed and rested his chin in his fists. Tim wriggled against her.

"Where are we going?" Alex reached for her hand, began playing with it. She smiled at him and began to thumb-wrestle.

She had thought to drive to her mother's house, two or three days west, to Austin, with its rolling hills and gentle winters and music. But sitting there in the afternoon, she knew what her mother would not say. Her mother would not say, "I told you so."

"Home," she said. She took Alex's hand; shifted Timothy against her. "We are going home."

•

It was still there, as it had been for well over two hundred years. Their house, solid and silent, like winter. The front porch welcomed her until she flashed on the image of Kane, but she let it go and the welcome returned. Let it go. The boys leaped from the car and began running in wide circles around the front yard, jumping and kicking the snow, falling, tumbling, playing extra hard to make sure it was still fun without Daddy. Annie grabbed the bag of groceries they'd stopped to get and headed for the door.

"C'mon, guys," she called, as if they were just returning from the market. "Let's get snowsuits before you're all soggy."

Alex whooped and led Timothy in wide circles around the pear tree, its limbs bare now, reaching for the winter sun. Darkness came so early.

Annie keyed open the front door and turned to call them again. No use. They were into it sincerely. Ecstatic. She would have to put down the groceries and go get them. She pushed open the door and stepped in.

The room was warm—how could that be? She hadn't noticed any smoke from the chimney. But she hadn't been looking. There was a fire. In the fireplace. There was a fire.

There was a man standing next to it.

Her arms went limp; the grocery sack fell to the floor. A can of tuna fish rolled out and clattered to a stop at the edge of the rug.

He stood next to the fireplace. She gasped and stifled it at once, her body electric. She was deaf, his lips were moving, but all she could hear was the roar of apprehension. The boys, outside, she had to . . . *On the floor, bitch, now!* What? What was he saying. He wasn't saying that. Voices screamed in her head. What was he saying? He moved to the couch, sat down.

He sat down.

It was okay.

He was sitting down.

She stood, trying to get air to her lungs.

Like an invited guest, he sat down. On the couch, like someone who'd come for the weekend and was beginning to feel at home. She hadn't recognized him, at first, without the beard.

"I knew you'd be back," he said. She remembered the kindness in his tone. His ability to soothe with his voice even in the strangest of circumstances. Even that night, it had been that way.

"I'm sorry I startled you."

"Startled me," she said. "Startled me. Yes."

"Are you okay?"

"Excuse me," she said. "I have to get the boys." She walked out into the fading afternoon, trying to slow her pulse. Thinking maybe she could get them into the car and drive away from here, just go and keep going until it was safe to stop. But if she did that, they would never be safe. There would never be anyplace safe, ever again. She watched Alex chase Timothy around the yard, the two of them delirious at being freed from the confines of the car and happy to be back on familiar territory. Neurons were firing too fast to allow her any decipherable train of thought; everything moved in slow motion.

"Alex!" she called. "Tim! Come inside now. You're getting all wet. You'll get chilled."

They came, giggling and tumbling, cheeks flushed, all out of breath. She herded them in and took them straight to the tub to remove their snow-soaked clothes. He smiled at them as they hurried past.

"Mommy," Alex said as Annie closed the bathroom door behind him, "who's that man?"

"His name is Mr. Kessler," she said. "Come on now."

When she brought them out of the bathroom, they stopped short in the doorway, ducked behind her legs, and peeked out.

"Hi," Agent Kessler said. "My name is Joseph."

"My name is Alex."

"Hi, Alex. Is that your brother?"

Alex nodded yes proudly. "His name is Timothy. He turns two—" He looked to Annie.

"In another month," she said.

"In another month," Alex said. "I'm already four. I'm *older.*"

"Excuse us a moment," Annie said, urging them upstairs. He watched them go up; she saw him watching, and he had a look on his face, a tiny smile. An appreciation. It put her at ease, a little.

They rushed to their closet to find toys they'd missed. She got them into sweats and left them to play. Play and play and play, little boys, while Mommy remains composed, no matter what the circumstances.

She seated herself in the club chair across from him. It was so comfortable, that chair.

"History repeats itself." What a stupid thing to say. She wondered if there was a smile on her face. She couldn't tell what her lips were doing.

"Are you okay?"

"No," she said.

"Where is he?"

She heard Alex Trebek: . . . *aaaand, today's Final Jeopardy answer is* . . .

"I don't know."

"That's a lie," Kessler said, "but it's one you should stick with."

This was not happening. She was not having this conversation. His voice was pleasant. Gentle and mellow. And his eyes the opposite, intense. Searching and keen.

"It's not a lie," she said.

"It's all in the question, isn't it?" he said. "Where did you last see him?"

"Getting onto a boat."

"Where?"

"Floating," she said, " 'cross the wide testosterone sea."

"Let me guess." He smiled. "Fort Lauderdale."

Annie shrugged, thankful she had on a rollneck sweater so he couldn't see the pulse pounding on the side of her neck. She wondered if he'd seen them, if he'd watched Kurt get on the boat. How could he know this? He was guessing. Surely he would have arrested them. How could he have guessed it, just like that?

"I'd like to work something out," he said. "I want to close this case." He was as she remembered him, though the crease between his eyebrows seemed to have got deeper since he'd shaved his beard. His jaw was strong and cleft. He was in jeans and a dark turtleneck, a thick wool sweater draped on the arm of the couch next to him. And resting on it, a shoulder holster with a gun. He had taken his boots off and left them on the mat by the front door.

He saw her take in the weapon.

"Regulations," he said.

"Regulations." She pictured a book on his desk, or somewhere near it, a book chock full of regulations, everything spelled out, everything placed in order and numbered for easy index. What to say, how to say it, what to wear, when you could eat, and when you could have days off, and how to bring grievances. Procedures. How to handle prisoners. "Thank you for building a fire," she said.

"I was hoping you would come home. You shouldn't come home to a cold house." He nodded toward the kitchen. "Your sister left a note. Said she was in the city. At Liz's. Who's Liz?"

"A friend of hers."

"Nothing else?"

Annie shook her head.

"I can talk to the prosecutor."

"She's only a friend."

"I meant I could ask him to lighten up."

She pictured Kessler at his desk, papers everywhere, cases, people's lives, stacks and stacks of reports detailing illegal activities and the suspected whereabouts of criminals and expense reports listing how much it cost to try to catch them.

"I had—have—a family myself, Mrs. Trowbridge. I'm not a homewrecker. You can talk to me."

"Call me Annie." Mrs. Trowbridge. Mrs. This. Mrs. That. There'd been that movie she and Carol went to see, *Mrs. Soffel,* about the wife of a warden in nineteenth-century Philadelphia, City of Brotherly Love, a dedicated and scrupulously religious woman who, of course, fell in love with one of the prisoners and eventually, of course, helped him escape, and in the end, of course, was scorned by him, but for her own good. The prisoner was Mel Gibson. Mrs. Soffel was Diane Keaton. They were both excellent in their roles. The film itself, as Annie recalled, had been a good one, based on a true story. She remembered Miss Watkins, in one of her many asides during warmups: *Mrs. is a contraction for Mistress.* Annie, afraid of both words, or their connotations, had looked it up. Miss Watkins had been telling the truth. She wondered if Carol was still a Mrs. or was now going by Ms.

". . . I don't want to see anyone get hurt," Kessler was saying.

"Neither do I," she said.

"He should come in."

She sat there.

"You must have some idea. Some feeling."

"Intuition? I wish I did."

"Ask me," Kessler said, "he's being a fool."

"Wouldn't you run? I think I would."

"You almost did, didn't you?"

She didn't answer. She realized, suddenly, that she should not be having this conversation. She should be telling him her lawyer's name, telling him to talk to her lawyer if he had any further questions.

"He was a fool ever to risk you, those boys upstairs, what you must have had together. He was a fool. I would never have done that."

"Oh," she said. "Is that the voice of wisdom I hear?" That is what she should do. Get up. Walk into the kitchen. Pick up the phone and call Mark Levine. She sat there.

"No," he said, "it is the voice of someone who's been there and knows better. Do you think he can live the rest of his life without seeing them?" Nodding upstairs, toward the boys. "Without you?"

"Men do it all the time," she said. "Day in, day out."

"You married him."

"I don't know what he'll do."

"He's your husband."

"Some men are single, or bachelors, I guess, some men are gay, some men are married men, and some men are husbands. Married men are a dime a dozen. Husbands are rare."

"You forgot divorced." He smiled to himself, shook his head. "Some men are divorced." There was a sadness on his face that surprised and moved her. "I don't see how anybody could walk away from you," he said.

"Did you leave your wife? Your kids?"

"She sent me away."

"Why?"

"I guess because I was never there to start with. Not enough, anyway."

"And now you wish you had been?"

"Now I don't know, except that I miss my children. I miss having children in my life. I am child-deprived. And my children grew up father-deprived. It's an awful thing. You see it in them. I hope yours don't have to." He got up and reached for the poker. Began adjusting logs, tending the fire, paying close attention to the task. "I saw him with your boys, you know, out doing errands. I can't believe he left you."

"He didn't, exactly, by choice." She thought again she should shut up and call Mark. And what, build a wall between herself and this man, who did not at the moment seem at all an enemy? That was how she'd been looking at him, in terms of friend or foe, yet here he was, saying he wanted to help her and seeming to tell the truth. But that was how they worked, wasn't it? Good cop, bad cop? So where was the bad cop?

"I swear to you," she said finally, "I don't know where he is."

"You will. At some point."

"Why did you come here?"

"Because I want to talk to you." He put the poker back and leaned on the mantel. "The man he buys hashish from also sells heroin. Were you aware of that?"

"I don't know anything about any of it."

"That's a lie, too," he said, "but again, if I were you I'd stick with it." He wasn't as large a man as she'd thought the night of the bust. Her fear had made him bigger then. "Look," he said, "I don't want to see him locked up forever; that's horseshit; that's not what I'm about. Though personally, I think he's a bastard to have put you and your kids in this mess." He sat down and shifted forward on the couch, leaned toward her, and she was embarrassed at what she felt and should not have felt. His green eyes were keen and sincere, looking straight into hers now, his jaw strong, his demeanor intelligent and kind. "You deserve better, you and those boys."

She deserved better? They deserved better? As in, you've all played by the rules and you got this guy in your lives who doesn't, and you deserve better. Who in the world got what they deserved?

"Persuade him to come in, help me get his source. I'll make sure he does less than five years in a minimum security federal camp. With good time, he'll be out sooner. You can visit. Lots of people hold it together that long."

She wasn't sure she could hold it together for the next ten minutes, forget five years. But the offer was a good one; she understood that.

"If I hear from him," she said, "I will tell him."

"Tell his lawyer, too. Maybe he can talk some sense into him."

She wondered if there was the slimmest chance that Kurt would go for it. And she wondered if she wanted him to. There were moments, these brief and fleeting moments, when she felt betrayed. Utterly and totally betrayed, and she thought it might be best if he stayed gone forever. And then this little voice would come and say, *They want him to die in prison,* and suddenly it wasn't betrayal. It was survival.

"Why are you doing this?"

"I know you're only trying to keep your family together." He nodded again toward upstairs and shook his head. "I lost mine and I wouldn't wish that on anyone."

"I don't even know if I'll hear from him."

"You will," he said. "And look, not to admit anything here, but you could help out too. You're not completely in the dark."

She shook her head no, firmly.

"I could get you in witness protection. New identities, new home, new jobs. The works."

She'd read about it, witness protection, and from what she could see, it left you somewhere between being a sequestered juror and a prisoner doing life without parole. In a velvet cell, but prison nonetheless.

"I know, I know. You want to talk to him first." Kessler frowned. "Take care of yourself, Annie. He's a big boy. Take care of yourself and your children."

"I'm not part of it," Annie said. "You can guarantee five years? In writing? On paper?"

"I see this all the time, you know. Listen to me. Take care of yourself."

She said nothing.

"You know he's doing another load."

"No," she said. And it was true; she didn't know anything about it except that she suspected Kessler was right.

"Lie number three, but who's keeping track? What are you gonna do? Your sister gonna raise these boys? As it is, at best you're looking to join the ranks of single parents. At worst you're looking at a piece of time yourself. Don't you think they'd miss their mom?"

Where had this come from? There was a steel marble rolling around inside her skull, pressed to the bone by centrifugal force, making a noise like a roller rink full of skaters, and huge.

"I'm not in the business," she said finally. "I'm not part of it."

"You ran with him." A smile played at his lips. "Off the record now, not that it matters because the statute has run on this one, but. How'd you guys steal that load from the DPS? In Texas that time?"

Annie couldn't believe he knew about it, but he was obviously amused. Or maybe it was a trap. But how could it be if the statute was up?

"It would seem to me," she said, "that if a person knew there was a transmitter in a load and knew the cops were following at a distance, there might be time to pull into the woods somewhere and unload the bales and find the transmitter and put it back in the van and continue on until the cops decided to fall on them."

"So that when the cops did fall on them," he said, "there'd be nothing but a transmitter." He grinned. "I bet they were royally pissed."

She smiled back, and it was a weird twist on the comrades-in-arms sort of thing, though she could tell he thought it was really funny. But then his face changed.

"You helped him escape," he said. "That much I know." He looked at her for a long moment; suddenly snapped his fingers. "And now, just like that?" Again. Snap. "Just go away and leave me alone? You know what conspiracy is? I could arrest you right now."

Right to the gut and ringing in her ears at once. Snap. He could. She'd thought for a while that he was her friend. But here he was, rearing his ugly head. Bad cop. Who needed a partner? Kessler could be both at once.

"Do you like your job?" Change the subject, yes, and get a little offensive, yes, but she wanted to know. She wasn't sure why.

"Government gig, you know." He didn't miss a beat. "You go in all starry-eyed, get slapped around, most folks come out the other end just wanting to play golf or sit on the beach."

"What fun."

"I'll be out with my pension at forty-two. Still time to get some living done."

"What does it feel like, putting people in jail?"

His head jerked ever so slightly left and he glanced away, then straight at her again.

"I've put some real scum away. And some, like your husband, not so awful. But they were in the game, same way he is. And they knew the stakes, same way. And I caught them fair and square."

"By whose terms?"

"The only ones we have."

She thought she heard sympathy in his voice, but maybe she was only hearing what she wanted to.

"I'm not doing anything wrong."

"Annie," he said, suddenly cold but low-voiced, aware of the children upstairs. "Let me introduce myself. Special Agent Joseph Kessler, United

States Drug Enforcement Administration. Know what I can do? I can take your house, your cars, your bank accounts, I can take you and put you into the system, and you won't see your children again until you come out, *if* you come out at all."

The skin of her back and face flooded with heat; she was opposite a stranger, a stranger in the woods, stronger, bigger, more powerful, beating his chest and roaring; the tips of her fingers stung, as if pricked with a thousand needles.

"Who the fuck do you think you are?" she said, anger raising her voice. Fighting, fighting, fighting against panic. Again. She was tired of fighting these, these, *things* inside her trying to drop her to her knees, these things inside her saying *On the floor now, bitch.* "I don't know what I'm doing," she said. "Okay?" Was she pleading? Was she praying? "I'm just trying to get to the next day, Special Agent Kessler. But if you're going to put me in jail, do it and get it over with. At the risk of sounding self-righteous, I know right from wrong, and I am not doing anything wrong."

He rose and began pacing in front of the fire. "Look," he said. "I'll arrest him eventually, whether you help me or not. You don't do nine years in this business without developing several sets of eyes and ears, you know? I'll get Kurt with or without you, and his supplier as well. Better you should get some benefit from it, and him too. I'm trying to help you. I'm willing to talk to the prosecutor."

"The one who wants life."

"Hey." A shrug. "It's nothing personal. Kurt is a Class A violator and the guy wants a merit badge so they'll look at him come promotion time. He'll negotiate. Here's the deal. I want Kurt's supplier, and I want him to surrender. In return, he'll do five, you'll walk. Your kids will be safe—with you."

He stopped pacing. Waited.

"What choice do I have?" she said. *Lie number four,* she thought, but felt nothing. This one came out smoothly, easily, driven by the instinct for self-preservation. She was ripping at the cuticle on her thumb. It was bleeding. Kessler saw too, and walked back to the couch. Let's all just relax a little bit here.

"I'm sorry," he said, sighing. "I didn't mean it to go that way. I didn't intend to threaten you. I just—" He shrugged, gave a weak smile. "I fell back on habit."

"Hell of a habit," she said.

"I'm sorry. I've been in this business too long. It changes you. I want out. Soon. I'm looking for something new. He shifted sideways, resting an arm on the back of the couch. "I'll help you," he continued. "Let me help you. We'll work something out. Things will be better," he said. "I mean, are you happy with this? How could you be? Who knows where he is or when he'll be back or even *if* he'll be back?"

"Just like any businessman."

"Yeah, well, that's how it goes, right? Women do the work of the world and men conduct the busyness. He's making money by breaking the law. Who cares whether it's right or wrong? It's illegal. You don't need this shit." He stroked his chin, contemplating. "I gotta tell you something. Kurt is part of a world that I know well. I know he works in Lebanon, and I know the first thing the Lebanese ask any arriving businessman is if they want to get laid." He got up once again, walked as far as the kitchen doorway, and turned to her.

"I'll wager he's using you. You watch. You'll have his babies and raise his kids and run his household, and then the kids'll be in college or maybe even in high school, and he'll decide life isn't as exciting as it used to be and the way to get some excitement is to take up with a young woman. You watch."

"Not pulling any punches, are you?"

He shrugged. "You and I have to be able to trust each other. If this thing's gonna work, it's important that we be honest."

"Did you cheat? On your wife?"

"I was faithful," he said. "And I was faithful to my job, and it cost me my family." He walked back, slipped into his holster, and pulled on the sweater. Went to the door and laced on his boots.

"I think he's going to come home soon," he said. "I think you'll hear from him before too long."

She sat there in her comfortable chair, her favorite chair.

"Tell him I want to work something out. Let me give you my straight-line so you don't go through the switchboard. I have a pager, too."

She took the card he offered.

"The best thing for all of you is if he comes in." His voice had softened.

"There's got to be a compromise."

"We'll work that out," he said. "Now, straight up, do you know where he is?"

She stared past him at the living room wall and had a perfectly clear picture, suddenly, of the frogs she and her classmates had been forced to dissect in ninth-grade biology. Stick a large pin through the brain to numb sensation, and then slice right up the middle and lay the belly wide open; stab through the skin with straight pins, jab them into the black wax of the dissecting tray beneath a wee creature who only wanted to eat bugs and make more frogs. "Don't worry," the biology teacher had assured. "They don't feel a thing."

"Annie?" His voice pulled her back. She waited.

"Maybe at some point you'll feel like doing us both a favor. This is important. The prosecutor will listen to me. I can help Kurt."

She said nothing. Perhaps all he wanted was what he'd said in the first place: to close the case. He reached suddenly and took both her hands in his own. They were strong, the touch gentle. She should pull away, she didn't dare pull away, she didn't want to pull away. She wanted to pull away and run upstairs to the safety of her children. His hands were strong. His hands were trustworthy and honest. Steady. His hands felt good, holding hers; "I want to help you."

When he'd gone, she went to the kitchen to check for messages. Don't think about it. Don't do anything right now except get your house in order. Fix everything the way it was before, only different.

No messages. Surprise surprise. There was the note from Carol. She picked up and dialed, got Liz's machine. Left word she was home, please call back. She felt a pang for her sister, the different worlds they lived in. She wondered if her mother thought one of them luckier than the other, or pitied them both. Carol had what Annie saw as cultivated looks, and those would go in a few years; then what? All that combing and brushing and application of makeup took up space in the brain that could be put to better use. She thought her sister probably found it frustrating never to have tried her intellect. Or who was she to say?

Carol had left out of fear. Good for her. Not for the fear, but for having the smarts to pick up and walk away from a bad scene. Good for her. It made perfect sense not to want to be around. Annie had thought that her return home would be a return to some kind of normality, even more than that. With Kurt and his wheeling-and-dealing far away, she could begin to build a real home, a real family. Make something substantial, something the government couldn't pop in and confiscate.

"Mommy!" Alex called. She heard the boys bumping down the stairs. "We wanna go back outside!"

She watched through the kitchen window as Alex and Tim chased each other around the perimeter of the garden and rolled in the snow, with the blessing of the late December sun just at dusk; they were rolling and playing as though they'd never left.

She put away the groceries, catching a hint of their laughter. She was at the pantry arranging jars when Alex burst through the kitchen door, breathless, his cheeks red with cold.

"Hey, Mom!" he shouted. "Is Dad coming home tonight?"

"Not tonight, hon," she said, hoping a smile would ease the blow, but he'd hardly seen her. His face fell and he slammed the door behind him and she heard him shouting at Timothy, "No! Not tonight he's not coming. I'm a monster eagle and I'm dangerous. Better run."

She folded the grocery bag carefully so it that would take up less space. She wondered where Kurt was and what he was doing. She wanted him to be sitting in a room somewhere, crying over their loss.

She burned dinner and yelled at the boys when they made faces and refused to eat it. She didn't know why she had tried to cook and hoped Kessler was wrong about Kurt doing another trip and wished he seemed more like an enemy. She grabbed a package of something frozen, shoved it into the microwave, and—*Presto! Look how easy life is!*—put it in front of her children. Sat down herself and poked at the brown and lumpy thing that was supposed to be vegetable lasagna. Picked it up and took it to the sink. Looked out at the darkness. Listened to her children, at their little table in the middle of the kitchen, threatening to throw macaroni and cheese at each other.

"Don't you dare," she said. Silence as they began eating again.

She could not go on like this. Would not go on like this. Life was simple. Life was easy. Air. Water. Food. Sleep. Love.

She would reopen the shop, herself this time, without Kurt or Laura or Carol or any other turncoats. She would do it. *It's just another day.* She would make a life for herself and her children. She was not without resources. Not without spirit. It was a matter of digging it out, sorting through her feelings even as she would sort through the mess in the attic of the shop, and in the attic of the barn, and in the attic of this house. No telling what she would find, once she started looking.

SIXTEEN

Winter arrived in earnest, and with it the heavy snows. Some years the cold wasn't so bad; some years the snow was bearable. This winter, though, promised early on to be unforgiving. There was no word from Kurt. She refused to let herself be aware, on a daily basis, of her anger. She knew it was in there somewhere, but she would not give in to it. What good would it do to sit around mouthing the words *How could he do this?* None at all. She shut herself down and bent to the tasks of daily existence. Air. Water. Food. I love you, Alex. I love you, Timothy. She made soups and stews and breads. She fed them. *Just wait until spring. We'll plant the best garden ever.* Her back grew strong from shoveling snow, keeping open a path to the garage. When he came to mind, she forced him out.

Six days a week, she took them to the shop with her. She helped them make a place under the staircase in the corner: they brought toys and crayons and books and stuffed animals. It was their boat. By day, they sailed the high seas in search of sharks and whales and whatever else was in the mysterious deep. Annie found a recording of *H.M.S. Pinafore* and played it for them and soon they were singing. *He polished up the handle so carefullee that now he is the ruler of the Queen's Navee.* Tim was still able and willing to laugh his belly laugh. Sometimes Alex would join in, and then Annie could smile too.

How could he do this to them? Joseph Kessler called almost every week just to stay in touch and to ask if she'd heard from Kurt. At first she was terrified by the ringing of the phone, wondering if it was Kurt, or if it was Kessler calling to say he'd made the arrest. But then a pattern developed:

the phone rang every Friday between seven and eight, when the boys were in the tub. And his voice grew friendlier even as it grew more familiar. For some time, she wasn't sure that she should talk to him, but decided it was probably safer to do so than not. And then it became easy. And soon it became something she let herself look forward to, just a little. It was pleasant to talk to someone who wasn't a customer or a child. And eventually, she wasn't sure when, he stopped asking about Kurt. He called just to see how she was doing.

"How are you?" he would ask.

Fine became okay, and then turned into things like *well-adjusted* or *I'm not quite sure.*

"Oh," he said one evening, "so we're being honest. Does this mean I can admit insecurity and tell you that I'd like to stop by sometime?"

"I'm not sure about that either," she said. He let it drop but continued to call.

January edged and scraped its way into her bones like a glacier carving the Hudson River Valley. She began to look forward to Fridays, to the warmth in his voice. She did not know what they shared, beyond solitude and Kurt, and when Kessler said, "Please, call me Joseph," she was both happy and apprehensive. But he was kind, asking after Alex and Timothy, asking if there was anything she needed, anything he could do to help.

"Why?" she said one evening, the phone pressed to her ear as she rinsed dishes and cleared counters.

"Why?"

"Yes," she said. "Why are you doing this?"

"Doing what?"

"Being so nice to me."

"Do you want me to stop calling?"

"No," she said. "I want you to tell me why."

"Does there have to be a reason?"

"Is there one?"

"I care about you," he said. "I think you're a good person, a kind and decent person. I know what it's like. My wife, my ex-wife . . ." He paused. "I care about you."

"But you're supposed to hate me. I'm one of the bad guys."

"No," he said. "It doesn't work like that."

•

Once February's bitterness arrived, even the snow ached with cold, cracking and popping late at night as subzero air attempted to squeeze white crystals to implosion.

Mondays she left the store closed and took Alex to a gymnastics class while Tim climbed all over her and whined that he wanted to play, too. Afterward, they would go to the grocery store. Sometimes they stopped at the library or the mall. Sometimes they baked cookies or breads or cakes. She cooked their meals. No one called, except Joseph and her mother. Since the arrest, friends had disappeared. Even Carol had disappeared. And when her mother ventured to phone, always the undertone was there: I told you so.

"I haven't heard from him," Annie would say. And, "No, I don't need any money."

"How are you living?"

"It's the stock market, Mom. It's churning out all these rich youngsters who can't wait to drive a few hours north of Wall Street to try out their new skis and search for the perfect dining table. The money's new. The table has to be old. Really old."

"Like me?"

"You're not old, Mom," Annie said. "You're just prematurely grumpy." Sometimes they would laugh.

The shop verged on turning a profit. And there was still money in the safe. Kurt had overnighted a package from somewhere in the Bahamas not long after Annie arrived home; the last she had heard from him. No message, just a small slip of paper with a penciled heart, Cupid's arrow piercing it, slipped into one of many stacks of hundred-dollar bills. Enough to live for a year, at least, even if the shop failed. But it would only be a matter of time before the asset seizures began, before the government moved in to take the house, the car, the shop, the ranch. Everything but her first-born male child. Unless Kurt came back and threw himself on the mercy of Mark's ability to negotiate deals. Unless he was willing to do time.

Lately, the boys asked less often about Dad. Where he was. When he was coming home. They'd grown tired, she supposed, of hearing their mother say, "I don't know."

She read them, and herself, to sleep almost every night, through book after book. They would listen until Annie's voice became a drone and they each went unconscious.

Alex grew more surly as winter progressed, directing most of his anger at Tim. He would walk past and knock his little brother in the back with his forearm, leaving Tim stunned and furious, lying on the floor, screaming. It was as if he thought Daddy would show up to straighten things out if Alex hit Tim hard enough. When Annie tried to talk to him about it, he would pick up a toy and try to interest her in it. He looked at her differently now. Something was hardening in him, and it showed in his eyes.

She was up often in the darkness, no longer nursing Timothy, but wandering about the house in the small hours, the tiny morning hours when her neighbors were fast asleep. She would tiptoe into her children's room and pull up the covers they had invariably kicked off.

Winter. Interminable winter. Mother Nature down for the count. Let's all be very, very quiet.

One or the other, Alex or Tim—Kurt had named them—would wake and stagger into her room almost every night. She would hold the boy as close and gently as she possibly could, remembering him in her belly, amazed at the wellspring of tenderness inside her, and whisper, *It's okay, sweetheart, everything is okay. It was only a bad dream.*

This night, like so many others, they had dinner early and fell asleep on the couch, Annie in the middle, holding a copy of *The True Story of the Big Bad Wolf* against her chest, Alex and Tim with their heads on her lap.

She awoke near midnight to find the house cold, and herself cold and groggy. She carried the boys upstairs, feeling keenly the difference in their weights. She soothed in whispers as she changed them for bed, put blankets over their shoulders, fought back tears, and tried not to blame herself for having to do this alone. As if she should have known better. She wondered if, wherever Kurt was and whatever he was doing, he remembered what it was like to tuck his sleeping boys in for the night. *It doesn't matter,* she told herself. *I don't care.*

Back downstairs, she sipped at a glass of cabernet and knelt on stone and placed kindling in the fireplace, crisscrossing it over pieces of newspaper that deserved their collective fate. Stories of war and famine, greed, criminality, and disease. Turn the page: there's a sale at Macy's.

Strike a match. Watch it burn. When the kindling was aflame, she added the larger logs and sat back cross-legged on the floor, waiting for them to catch. The house was the same; the house was infinitely different. No husband lived here, no father. Not even a married man. She missed him, this night. That was all. She was home with her children and she could be angry at him, she *was* angry at him, but she had loved him, their blood had mingled, and now she missed him. She missed his scent. The wind was angry too, a howling midnight scourge straight out of Canada, and it was almost Saint Patrick's day. This one sounded like more snow. She was tired of shoveling snow.

When the fire was going, she sat, thankful to be in front of it. Thankful the hellions had surrendered to sleep. To think about raising them by herself, without Kurt, to think about it too much was to invite a sense of interminable helplessness. She sat quietly, as she had every night since the boat carried Kurt into the darkness and she had pulled her screaming, crying children away from the dock and brought them—against their will—home. She sat, waiting for the police to break down the front door. And then she would remind herself that Joseph Kessler was in charge. He would not let it happen again. It was memory, awful memory, intruding on her life. She knew she could not continue this way. She did not know how not to. It seemed to be a matter of control, of self-discipline, a matter of something she did not have a handle on.

Outside in the dark, snow began, a new storm coming on, promising to get heavier before morning, promising to bury everything in white. She thought she should leave the comfort of the fire and go out, begin the task. It was easier if she did it from the start and kept at it while the snow fell, checking every hour or so for accumulation, shoveling again before it got too deep. Almost midnight. She was not going out there. Deal with it in the morning.

She stared at the fire. How long had it been. One night and everything's changed. She didn't want to remember. Her muscles brought themselves to her attention with pain; they were a solid chunk of tension, knotted and taut with fear as she sat on the floor in the living room.

Alex cried out in his sleep. She slipped upstairs quickly, was at his side and rubbing his back before he was wholly awake.

"I love you, Mommy," he whispered, and then his breathing went steady. Asleep again. She leaned to whisper in his ear, hoping her words would enter his dreams, "I love you too, precious."

She wandered down the hall to her room. Her room now. Her room. It was a good room, still, with fine sunshine in the morning and a view of the stars at night. She turned to leave and started at the sight of the tiny red light on the answering machine, blinking.

What trouble was this? Telemarketers didn't usually leave messages. She had taught herself how to play *Mary Had a Little Lamb* on the phone buttons and did this whenever a falsely friendly voice said, "Good evening, Mrs. Trow——" *That's Miz to you, asshole.*

She went over and pressed the button.

"It's me." Kurt's voice. She almost sank to the floor. Kurt's voice. Choking. "I'm still here and I love you all and I miss you desperately. I hope you're okay. I'll call again when I can." He sounded miserable. He sounded in trouble.

She went back downstairs and watched the flames caress wood even as they were eating it, and she was as confused as she ever had been in her entire life. Where was he and what did he plan to do? She wondered why the sound of his voice could do this to her, rattle her as though someone had taken her by the shoulders and shaken her. Home was not home anymore. This place had become strange to her. She wanted her home back. She wanted things to be okay. She wanted someone to tell her she could start over, do things right this time. Erase the bust. Erase the search. She thought about Kessler's offer. He seemed so kind—and so sad; somewhere under his skin was a huge sadness. But he was quick to smile in spite of it. And he seemed to understand that for her to break the bond prematurely, before the boys broke it naturally, would leave scars and unhappiness all around. She was not just obligated, but driven, to keep them all together. It was instinct. It was female. Ergo, it was right. He didn't blame her for trying.

It didn't matter now. Kurt had broken it. Kurt had broken up the family. But he was running for his life and she thought she would probably do the same, in his situation. She was not innocent; would not dare claim to be.

He sounded as if he was in trouble.

Her eye caught the telephone on the table by the couch. He had sounded so bad. She thought for a moment about calling Kessler, but what could he do? What would he do? She counted time with him by the week, by the Friday evening calls. With Kurt it had slipped to the month. She wondered how long it would be until she began measuring his absence in years or stopped measuring it altogether.

What could anybody do? The massive stone wheels of justice were rolling, creaking, and groaning under their ancient weight. They were playing the game; she was on the sidelines now, rooting for nobody.

When the big logs caught some fire and the heat began burning her knees, she took up the poker and shifted the logs until the flame established itself, burning deep orange and yellow. Alex, fascinated with fire, had lately begun wanting to strike matches and light candles. Sweet danger. She moved to the couch, pulled a blanket about her. She thought about how Kurt used to sit next to her here and put his arm around her shoulders, pulling her to him with a smile. She missed his touch. She missed the way he whispered, yes, baby, yes, and his back arched above her, the way they connected, and how he held her so close for a long time after, caressing.

She listened to the wind, rumbling against night, abolishing the fair weather that had cradled the sun that afternoon. It was strong; might even take down a tree back in the woods. Bitter winter, the overstayed guest, throwing his last party of the season in someone else's house.

It was late. She had to anyway. Do something. She picked up the phone, dialed Mark. Several rings; he answered sleepily.

"Sorry," she said, bit her lip. Keep control.

"What?" he said. "What is it? Are you okay?"

"There was a message, from Kurt. He didn't sound good and he didn't say where he was or what was going on. I'm scared for him."

"Jesus God, Annie, I'd—" He was waking himself, anger creeping into his voice. "I don't know what to tell you, how to help. He's doing whatever he's doing—"

"I know. I just, I don't know. Are they saying anything?"

He sighed. "This fucking guy, this prosecutor, he's bipolar or something. One day he's willing to deal, the next he's an intransigent fuck."

"He sounded really bad."

"Look, Annie, try to get some sleep. Call me tomorrow. We'll figure something out."

"Sorry I woke you."

"Anytime. I love you both."

She hung up the phone and pulled the blanket about her. She wasn't sure how long it had been since Joseph had called. Three or four weeks now, at least. She didn't know why he'd stopped, but refused to dial him to find out. She wished she could sleep. She wondered if she ever would again. Just walk into her room and lie down and put her head on the pillow and close her eyes and feel the blessed descent of unconsciousness and then not a thing until daylight opened her eyes.

On the floor. Now. She could still hear that voice, that angry, hate-filled guttural growl, echoing in her living room. And always, since that night, once darkness came she found herself hearing things that daylight obscured from her ears: the cat's paws hitting the wooden floor as it jumped from its perch on a windowsill upstairs, a mere twig of a branch brushing against the roof near the kitchen window, and sometimes the silence so deep she could hear the pulse of her blood in her ears, the dead quiet silence of winter in the Catskills.

She pulled the blanket close and let drop a few tired tears, missing her husband, missing the touch of his lips, and missing most of all the love he brought home to his family whenever he came through the door.

A blast of cold air shook the house.

"I know," she said, out loud, to herself and whatever ghosts were in the room, ghosts of settlers, ghosts of people who stacked rocks until their backs gave out. "He's gone."

•

Razor, scraping whiskers. Fingernails, scraping skin. Scratch. Scrape. Scratch.

No. She was asleep, she was in slumber; it was a blessed, peaceful, desperately beautiful sleep. No dreams would be recalled, though she could not remember the last time she'd had anything but mediocre nightmares. This night, the maimed and helpless, the wandering, the unconscious and confused, they would all stay away from her bed.

Sploosh. Scrape. Sploosh. Snow onto snow. Late snow. Spring snow. Loose and wet. The quiet splat of it. What was this. Metal against stone. Scrape.

Timothy's head pressed into her armpit. Alex's leg draped over her calf as he sprawled over most of the bed. She felt them, their loving dependence, dreaming maybe of the place before, and the thundering of their mother's heart coming to them through liquid, through warmth. Blessed sleep, please stay.

Scrape. Sploosh.

Again. Someone was shoveling the steps, the huge bluestone steps that led to the front porch. Stacked, one by one, how many years ago, by settlers.

Scrape. Sploosh.

Okay. She was awake. Again. Whoever was there, fine. Burglar, thief, come on in. Just, please, be quiet. I'm trying to sleep.

She lay there, eyes closed, feeling her children next to her, their breath warm and innocent. Angels. Resting so they could bring fresh love to the world when they woke. Devils. Lying in wait to terrorize her.

Scrape.

Scrape.

Tap-tap-tap.

Okay. Okay. I'm up. I'm awake.

Why wasn't she afraid? She should be afraid. She opened her eyes.

The light was up. The sky was blue. Morning. Relief. How long since she'd slept into a blue sky?

She put on her robe, from their honeymoon, heavy and white, soft. Wrapped it around her, found slippers, went downstairs. Coffee-coffee-coffee. On automatic, she ground and poured and hit the switch. Blue skies. She was forcing herself not to go to the door. Not to be concerned. But wouldn't it be amazing? If he were out there, doing what he'd always used to do?

A silence followed by the sound of footsteps on the wood of the porch and the careful placement of the snow shovel against the wall.

She knew Kurt's steps; these weren't his.

The walkway, the steps, all shoveled, clean of snow. The morning sun, an orange fireball burning off the last wisp of pink-blue cloud below it, made the wet stone shine gray and blue amid the fresh white blanket draped about it. The day was cold and stunning.

Joseph Kessler stepped back as she opened the door, stamped his feet. "Good morning," he said.

She stood in the door and they looked at each other, comparing memories, Annie supposed.

She stepped aside.

He took off his boots, that same sweater. There was no holster beneath, no gun. "Off duty," he explained.

"If you're looking—"

"I've been away on a case," he said. "In Asia. I should have phoned. I was concerned for you."

She was going to say she thought Kurt was never coming back, even though she'd hoped only moments earlier that it was he making all that noise. She was going to say he'd left a message and she thought he was in trouble.

Somewhere.

She poured coffee while Juju sat on the windowsill, eyeing chickadees and nuthatches in the lilac tree outside, licking her paws, sharpening her knives. Cats were what they were, unabashed predators. There was no sorrow or shame in the killing. Juju considered her regular offerings of dead mice, laid delicately in the middle of the kitchen floor, to be her contribution to the orderly running of the household. Annie scooped the bodies up and took them out to a far corner of the yard, where it met the woods, and tossed them back to the earth.

In spite of the late snow, the buds on the tree seemed unharmed. Soon they would flower, offering delicate petals with their fleeting lives and their sweet, sweet scent, clean as sunshine, to the world outside the window.

Joseph Kessler sat at the kitchen table, sipping coffee and watching the birds. His presence was comforting. He looked at her as though he couldn't believe they were both in the same room.

"What are those called?" he said, nodding out the window. "The yellow ones."

Goldfinches. The yellow ones.

"By July," she said, "they practically glow in the dark."

He reached for her hand.

She thought of the hundred million simple easy ways that Kurt had betrayed her, the promises. Broken. She thought of the nights spent aching for him, worrying about him, wondering where he was and if he was all right.

Kessler brought her hand to his lips and kissed it. Her fingers then, each one; and looked at her, and folded her hand into both of his, and sat looking, for the longest time.

"I'm scared," he said. "I can't stop thinking about you." He laughed softly and shook his head. "This shouldn't be happening."

She watched his hands on hers, watched him examine her fingers, feeling what she hadn't for such a long time, and feeling she should tell him to let go of her hand. She should let go herself.

"That's not true," he said. "This should be happening; it's just frightening, is all."

"You're used to being alone."

"Maybe I am, but that doesn't mean I like it."

"I'm flattered," she said. "Really you have no idea how." She pulled back her hand. "But I am still a married woman. And a faithful one."

"Aye." He sighed. "There's the rub."

He took her hand again and looked at her, and his eyes were open, vulnerable, seeking only a moment's kindness. She thought perhaps she understood his sadness. And perhaps he understood hers.

"But you're not," he said suddenly. "You can't still consider yourself married. He's gone. He's abandoned you."

"He would say I abandoned him."

"He would be wrong."

"Who's to say?"

"Is this your home? Are you here? Where is he?"

"He had no choice. I had a choice."

"You made the right decision. And anyway, he did have a choice. He had lots of choices, and every single time, he chose to jump out there and risk everything. His freedom. His family. Even, sometimes, his life. I see it all the time. I know the type."

"What are you saying?"

"I'm saying I'm not the kind of man who would walk away from his family. I understand the difference between husband and married man."

He stood up and pulled her to him, pressed her head to his shoulder.

"You deserve better," he whispered. "Probably you deserve better than me." He put his lips next to her ear. "But I am here and I want to stay here, with you. I want to care for you."

It was forever since she had been held. Forever since anyone had let her be like this, the small one, the one cherished. She didn't want him to leave and she felt guilty about it and she berated herself for feeling guilty all at once. Why should she feel guilty, except that she still knew how to be a good little Catholic girl, how to be seriously and fundamentally guilty, how to suck it into her psyche, like a sponge soaking up vinegar?

Her husband had abandoned her, abandoned their children, and here was a man who wanted to be here with her, a man who knew how precious her children were to her and who knew and perhaps wanted—did he?—to cherish them as she did. She felt him patting her back, rubbing gently, massaging away the loneliness, pushing away the pain. She put her arms around him, afraid though she was; she put her arms around him and they were close, so close, and it was forever since she'd been held this way.

She did not know how long they stood like that. She opened her eyes to see Juju sitting in the windowsill, licking her paws. She heard Alex, sleepily, calling for Mommy, and felt Joseph tense. They stepped apart, embarrassed, maybe. Or was it just awkwardness?

"You should go," she said, glancing at the kitchen doorway.

"I'll call you." With that, he was out the door, closing it quietly behind him. She heard Alex, stumbling sleepily down the stairs, and went to meet him.

SEVENTEEN

As they headed into the gaping mouth of the Holland Tunnel, Johnny gave Kurt a nod and said, "We got trouble, bro." Kurt, still solidly jetlagged, let his head fall back against the seat.

What. What kind of trouble.

"Got a call from customs. They want to escort the containers to the warehouse and do an on-site inspection as we unload."

"I don't believe this."

"Maybe it's nothing."

"What does your uncle say?"

"He says it's unusual."

They drove in silence through the peach-colored glow of vapor lights posted along the Jersey Turnpike. On either side of the wide, pale roadway, industry made known its presence with huge rectangular buildings of ugly brown or beige steel. Smokestacks spewed poison filtered to government standards. Kurt watched as it leaked dark gray and white against the weird orange-gray glow of the manmade sky.

"Lawyers and politicians," he said to Johnny. "Yeah, let's let those guys run the country."

"Usually," Johnny said, "they just open the containers, look inside, maybe open a couple of boxes near the back, and wave you through. He thinks it's 'cause the shipment's from Beirut."

"They're trashing the entire planet."

"Hey, Kurt," Johnny said, "you with me here?"

"Yeah," Kurt mumbled. "Source country."

"We don't get shipments from Beirut, usually. Not these days."

"It's fucked, man," he said, as much to himself as Johnny. "The whole thing. But at this point it's like *who cares.*"

Johnny raised his eyebrows.

"Hey, it's not that bad. We gotta be careful."

"Not that." Kurt slumped in his seat. "I miss my kids. Big time. And her."

"I could go see her," Johnny said. "Or Father could."

"No," Kurt said, and added quietly, "It would only upset her."

"What—" Johnny started.

"It's not like that," Kurt said. "It's just, she doesn't want to be around it."

"So what are you gonna do?"

"Like I said before. This is it."

"She gonna take you back?"

Kurt shrugged, the gesture seeming absurd to him even as he did.

"Yeah," Johnny said. He sighed. "Family. That's some heavy shit. I plan on staying single as long as I possibly can."

"You can't believe how much you love them," Kurt said. "It's like—it's scary. I've got to see them. See her."

"That's what they're counting on," Johnny said. "I'm tellin' you, let me go get her. Or Father. She likes Father."

"Never do," Kurt said. "She's already pretty freaked out."

"She trusts us."

"It's not that. I don't want to upset her. Any more than I already have." His stomach was in knots again, tight with apprehension, but the rest of his body was simply numb. He felt as if he were in a maze, like the corn maze he'd taken the boys to last fall. They'd run through the rows, laughing when they hit dead ends, surrounded by leafy green stalks that stood eight, even nine feet high. But he couldn't even manage a smile at the memory. He was scared; that was the long and short of it. Scared that he'd lost them for good.

He closed his eyes. Press on, brother. Save it. Get it back. Find a place, somewhere on the planet, where you can watch them grow, maybe even grow a little with them, learn what they have to teach you. Forget about the rest of it. Just live. He had always loved farms. He knew guys who'd made their stake and used it to buy land. Got out before they got caught. Went back to the land. That was what he'd been trying to do; that had been his intention when he moved the family out of the city. But he'd been too enamored of the idea of beating a system that could not be beaten because it was absolutely corrupt; he'd been too caught up with the cat-and-mouse of it to notice that his dreams were slipping between his fingers like money.

Half an hour later Johnny eased his green Econoline—*Nocenti Brothers Trucking* in dark blue script on either panel—into the moderately well-lighted parking lot of a glowing chrome diner on the edge of Bayonne. Johnny's Uncle Dominic, who could be seen at his booth from the parking lot, dabbed at his mouth with a napkin, paid his check, and came out to the van, walking with the streetwise swagger of a man with lots of practical knowledge and a pocketful of cash.

His designer sweats were shiny and blue. His Nikes glowed white and unscarred against the new blacktop of the parking lot. His silver hair was clipped and combed straight back, every single strand knowing its place and staying there. Johnny got out and slid back the door; Dominic clapped him on the back as he stepped into the van and settled himself on the rear bench. He offered a hand as Kurt climbed back to sit beside him.

"What's going on?" Kurt said. "Are we hot?"

"I don't think so," Dominic answered, his voice as scratchy as a sore throat. "Sometimes when something's coming from a place like Beirut . . ."

It sounded to Kurt like *Babe Ruth.*

"They wanna take a closer look," Dominic continued. "Don't mean they think there's goods in it."

"But our profile is good."

"Yeah." Dominic nodded solemnly. "Hey, customs knows this company we lined up. They buy shitloads of dates and we do business with them all the time. So what's the problem. Now, we say, because of Ayatollah Ko-what's-his-face, it's coming through Beirut this time and it's no big deal. The question I got for you is can we hold up to an on-site inspection?"

Kurt reached in his pocket and grabbed a scrap of paper with numbers. What was he doing? Where was he? The containers. Okay. Focus on the task at hand. Don't think about anything else. Focus. He handed the paper to Dominic.

"There are seven of them," he said. "These three have hash. The drivers should get the clean ones first."

"That's gonna be hairy." Dominic clasped his hands. It occurred to Kurt that the guy was about to ask for a bigger cut.

"Hairy was Beirut," Kurt said. "Fucking bombs. Fighter jets, guns everywhere. They're blowing the place to smithereens. *That* was hairy."

Dominic placed a hand on one knee, nodded acknowledgment.

"But anyway," Kurt said, "if we don't pick up at least a few of these containers, customs will know something's wrong."

Johnny turned to them from the driver's seat. "Maybe they already know."

"Either way," Kurt said, "you guys are just the truckers. They gotta prove you knew the stuff was in there."

·

Another room; another prison cell. The telephone was on the bed, next to his thigh. He had one hand on the receiver.

Sit tight. Sit tight. See it through.

He wanted to hear her voice. He wanted to talk to Alex and Timothy. They were so close—and what he'd gone through to get here.

Afternoon reruns. *Get Smart* cluttered the small pixelated TV screen. He stood it as long as he could, then went out to make calls. He told the answering service to have Eric leave a number and time where Kurt could reach him next day. What the fuck. The guy wanted hash, the guy had cash, Kurt could move maybe the whole load and be done with it. Get everyone out of here, for good. Paris would work. Or somewhere smaller. South. A quiet place. A village surrounded by farms. Did they still exist, or had the Burger King and his tribes of Dunkin Donuts invaded even Provence?

He killed an hour at a small basement bookstore—used, rare, and out of print—watching the windows, looking for heat. Then he walked, aching for her, wanting to call her, knowing he shouldn't. This wasn't fair. Maybe he should skip it, skip out, split, and be the outlaw he'd thought he wanted to be. What if she didn't want to come with him? What if his children had forgotten him? They probably all hated him by now.

Walking the streets of Manhattan made him remember her even more vividly. A pay phone at Twenty-third beckoned, *Call her now.* He reached for the receiver but saw it was slimy to the point of being unusable; keep walking, keep walking, stop to look in a window, pretend to be browsing but your eyes are on the streets, looking for agents. He missed his family. That was all.

He zigzagged his way to the bar next door to the hotel, took a wooden stool near the pay phone, and ordered a beer. He sat, wondering. How could he have fucked it up so totally, so completely?

•

Laura's face was pale and her eyes tight with concern. She and Annie stood on the porch, watching the boys run around the greening front yard, chasing each other, knocking each other around, alternately screaming and roaring. They were lions, they were eagles, they were nice monsters. Bad guys, beware. They were here to save the world.

"He said call from outside." Annie looked at the paper Laura handed her: 212, a New York number. The handwriting was elegant, genteel, like Laura and Mike's new gift shop in the historic district. Annie had driven past once, afraid to go in. "I'll watch the boys," Laura said. "If you like."

Annie said nothing.

"I'm sorry," Laura said. "I heard you were back, but I just didn't know . . ."

"It's not that," Annie said. "I wanted to stop in. I should have called. I wasn't sure—" She looked at the note. "I hope this didn't—"

"Go," Laura said. "I'll watch them."

Annie drove slowly, the sunset glaring the colors of ripe peaches, threatening another long dark night. The landscape was familiar and it was unreal—stone houses, stone walls, fields waiting for the springtime plow, pastures dotted with black-and-white cows. What was all that out there? Was that real life?

And then here it came, the voice she'd tried to quash, attempting to bury it beneath marriage and children and home and a proper little shop full of old treasures, full of other people's discards. *If you didn't want the outlaw life, why'd you marry an outlaw? What is it in you, sweetheart? What are you afraid of?*

Maybe you're the one who's scared of it all; maybe it's you who can't fathom it. Maybe you hate the whole thing, the bills and the play dates and the television screaming bad news and the going to the dentist and the taking the boys to the doctor to get those goddamn vaccinations that scare the shit out of you but you sign on the line saying you understand that some kids have died from these things and you hope it won't happen this time, to your baby. Maybe you just wanna know who's in charge here, got a few things to discuss at the next board meeting, but you know, *you know, sweetheart,* that ain't nobody in charge. Ain't nobody keeping score except William Bennett. And the fools in D.C. don't give a shit about anything but what table they'll be shown to at the next luncheon, who's zooming who. Maybe you *admire* Kurt's unwillingness to submit. Maybe you *respect* his renegade spirit. Maybe you like the idea of living free in the land of the free. Maybe the phrase *There's safety in numbers* means that you like the odds on whether or not he'll stick around. Seven come eleven: you get another chance, Polly Pureheart.

She pulled up to the pay phone and leaned out the car window. But the boys had changed all that. Everything. Every single aspect, every single moment. Every single breath was different since their arrival and would be different again when they left. But now, right now, her first obligation was to them, to their safety, to their spirits. Right after Alex's birth, Kurt had continued to play music he loved, the music he and Annie had loved together—rock, blues, jazz—only now, with a baby days old, Annie couldn't seem to get through to him that the music made her insane. There was something going on with her body, something she had no control over. The music they'd loved wasn't music anymore; it was noise; and he had to understand but he didn't. It went, went right to her gut, scraped the still raw walls of her healing womb; it made her shudder. It made her want to scream.

It was several months before she was able to handle the sounds, but in the meantime Kurt just didn't get it. He couldn't fathom that it was not a matter of choice on Annie's part, a matter of suddenly changed taste. It was the nature of the postpartum female body: we need peace and quiet for the newborn, for our child who is new to this world. Peace.

For our child. For our children, who are wholly, utterly, completely—for this short time only—dependent upon us. Joseph Kessler's wife had sent him packing. He'd come around too late. And who knew what else had gone on?

"Annie."

She tried to speak.

"Annie?"

"Yes."

"I have to see you."

"Are you okay?"

"Bring them to me. Please."

She didn't know. She didn't know but she was aware that if she didn't honor his request, none of them would ever forgive her. She owed it to each of them. But it would hurt them if they saw him. It would make them deliriously happy and he would leave again and they would be devastated. She and Kurt would each go into it knowing he would leave, knowing he wouldn't stay. But the boys, they were helpless with love for him. They could prepare themselves for Daddy's next good-bye, but they could never be fully ready for it, for the pain that would come after.

"Please," Kurt was saying. "I have to see you. I have to."

"Where have you been?" As if it mattered, like the *where* of it was more important than the *why* or the *how*. "I won't let you break their hearts. Again. Not ever again."

"Annie, please."

"You can come in. You can do five years."

"Says who?"

"We can visit; we'll stand by you."

"What are you talking about?" Incredulous. "Are you talking about prison?"

"Call Mark. He's trying to work out the details."

"Annie, I'm not ready to give up. I want us to—"

"No." She could hang up. Just hang up and leave it at that. "Call Mark."

"Just bring them. Please, Annie, bring them to me."

"I won't call you again, Kurt. I won't let you hurt them."

"I'm not trying to hurt them. Or you. Or anybody."

"But you are. Don't you see? You are."

"Don't you think it would hurt them to see me in prison?"

"Not as much as if you disappeared again. Not if they knew you'd be coming home someday."

There was a long silence, and she heard him say "I love you," and she heard herself say the words to him, and she watched people coming and going at the market: mothers and fathers, husbands and wives, children, uncles and aunts. Families. A woman in jodhpurs, toothpick-anorexic skinny, clinging to the arm of a much younger man. Up from Manhattan to look for antiques and the promise of springtime, desperation in her gait.

The dial tone, rude and flat, brought her back to the phone. She leaned out the car window and replaced the receiver.

I love you. He'd said it. She had said it. And she did, still, but differently. It was up to him, now, to come to terms with what he'd done. It was his decision. She was sad for him, for all that he'd wagered and lost, but she would not let him hurt them. Or her. Anymore.

She wondered why she had suddenly felt strong enough to refuse him, where the strength had come from, and then she got scared all over again. Wasn't that her way? It had taken graduation and three thousand miles to break the thing with Coach Smith. It had taken Kurt to break the thing with Eric and his magic powder, platonic, yeah, but it probably would have been only a matter of time. It had always taken someone or something new before she could say good-bye to trouble: an awful present was preferable to an uncertain future, and she couldn't be sure of the future if there was no one there to say I love you, no one there to tell her she was an acceptable human being, even maybe okay to hang out with. She feared being left out, alone, scorned. And if there wasn't a man in her life to tell her she was lovable, then she most certainly could not be. But there was, now, wasn't there, someone ready willing and able to replace Kurt? It struck her that what Carol was doing was brave, one giant leap for a little girl from Texas. Carol had walked away from everything she knew when there was nothing on the horizon but another scenic sunset. She had said, "I've had quite enough, thank you." Because little girls from Texas were nothing if not polite.

Annie sat, unable to turn the key in the ignition. Unable to move. She sat, feeling tainted and pathetic. *Look, Ma, somebody loves me.*

•

Kurt's body was hopelessly mired in another time zone; trying to adapt was pointless. He dozed in the front seat of the van on the way to the warehouse, half awake, dreaming of Annie, of that time in the desert with her, dreaming of her touch and remembering the miracle of Alex, and how she had clung to his neck when laboring with Timothy's birth. It was all jumbled up somehow, the melting sunset, the wolves howling, how she had looked at him in that moment before they made the baby, next to the fire he'd made inside a ring of stones. And now she was trying to force him to come in. She could not do this. She could not take their children away. This hurt too much. He folded his arms across his chest as though to shield himself from the pain.

It was almost seven when Johnny nudged his shoulder and said, "Kurt, we're here."

The smell hit him as soon as he walked in. He inhaled deeply, unsure of his senses. Concrete, cardboard, motor oil, and—unmistakably—competing with the sweet scent of the dates, hashish. Scene of the crime. He would have cash again, the ability to maneuver. But this was it. Last rush. Last money. Last motherfucking time ever. Ever. Do it and get the hell out of here and go to them.

Bill clumped over from the office in the southwest corner of the building, grabbed Kurt in a hug, and responded, "Whaddaya mean, you smell hash? You can't possibly be smelling hash; there's no hash here." He turned to Johnny and wrapped him in a grip, pounded his back.

"Hey, bro," Johnny said to him. And then to Kurt, "It's dates, man, that's the dates."

"Bullshit. I smell hash." Kurt breathed deeply again, slowly, paying attention. "I know what dates smell like. I smell hash." He walked out onto the loading docks: three containers, open, were backed up to the doors. Boxes were stacked along the packing tables near the docks, more than half of them open.

"They had a dope dog in here," Bill said. "Walked him all over the place. Didn't find a thing. Problem is, the hash is still at the pier."

Kurt spotted a box coded with red straps among the other colors, took out a knife, and slit the thing open. Why was he here? Why was he doing this? For money, asshole. That's why you're doing it. Get yours and get the hell out. He pried up the flaps, lifted a layer of wax, and scooped out a big handful of dates. He rapped his knife handle against the tin box inside.

"What's this?"

Johnny and Bill looked at each other. Boxes on either side of the one in front of Kurt had been opened and looked at, closely. Inspected by agents of U.S. Customs.

Kurt walked to the containers and pulled the huge orange doors shut to display the numbers.

"Got your list?" he said to Johnny.

"Dominic's got 'em," Johnny said.

"You got the wrong containers." He pointed to the one in the middle. "That one. How did that happen? I told you guys not to pick up that one."

"Hey," Johnny said, "we didn't get to choose which ones we wanted. They pointed them out and said take those."

"So you just did it?" Kurt shook his head. And here that prosecutor thought he was the head of an organization.

"What choice did we have?" Johnny raised his arms skyward, angry. "We brought the ones they said, and then they showed up with the dog. Fuck. I didn't even get a chance to check the numbers before they were searching." He shrugged. "When they left, we figured it was okay."

"How could they have missed it?" Kurt looked them up and down. His buddies. His pals. His co-conspirators. "They bring a heroin dog or something?" Everyone laughed.

"Who cares? They missed it," Bill said. "How much is here?"

"A hundred and twenty boxes in this container," Kurt said.

"Let's get the shit out of here." Bill stepped into the container and grabbed a box. "We're looking for red straps?"

"Yeah," Kurt said. He looked over the packing tables. "They brought out four of them for us already."

"They come in here tomorrow," Johnny said, "and decide to count boxes again, we're fucked."

"They come in now and open one of these, we're butt-fucked," Kurt said. "Let's get to work."

They unstacked and carried out and moved and rearranged boxes, putting those with red straps into Johnny's van. They reloaded the containers, taking boxes from the two that were clean and building false walls in all three to make it look as if the only boxes missing were those out on the packing tables.

When they finished, drenched with sweat, they slumped into chairs in the office.

"What now?" Johnny said.

"Get that van out of here," Kurt said. "At least get the stuff we've got into the stash house. Even if they keep everything else, we'll have five million." Enough to get well out of town and take his family with him. Enough to make him hopeful that he would actually pull this off. He was physically exhausted; his mind beyond fatigue, pushed to the point of lucid panic. "They expect you to pick up the other containers tomorrow?"

Johnny nodded.

"Friday. Wait until midafternoon. Try to time it so you don't get back here with everything until close to five. By then they'll be looking to go home."

•

Another jaw-clenching day in his room at the hotel. The muscles in the back of his neck would snap at the slightest human touch. Just wait. Sit around and wait. He paced. He tried to read. Watched TV. Kept hearing Roger Miller's twang . . . *smokin' cigarettes and watching Captain Kangaroo, now don't tell me, I've nothing to do . . .*" Absurd.

He went downstairs and out to the street and down the block, grabbed a slice, and walked back to the room, putting food in his mouth, chewing, swallowing. Tension pulled the muscles of his shoulders and back toward a nexus of stress just above his tailbone. He paced the room, bent to the floor to try to stretch free of the pain. He went to the bathroom and puked.

When the afternoon grew pleasant, he opened the windows and let the diesel-scented breeze flow in. Twenty-third Street was relatively quiet: the hum of traffic and the head-knocking percussion of car horns, electronic siren blooping *woo-woo-woo* down the street, losing its wits to a scream when it hit an intersection: Faust's orchestra tunes up.

He turned on the radio—*Heart of Gold*—lay back on the bed. At least the jetlag was easing up. His eyes had stopped burning. It did in fact feel like midafternoon to him . . . *I been to Redwood, I crossed the ocean for a* . . . what? For what did you cross the ocean? This? Sitting in a hotel room breathing bus fumes while your children chant, "Where's Daddy"? Your wife wants you to go to prison, but only for five years or so. Only five. Sit here, think about all the money you're going to lose if customs pops the rest of the load. At least you've got five mil in safekeeping. Your end could keep you with your family for some time, but you gotta get the rest of the load out; that would be a real payday. Except that your wife wants you in prison. She wants to play by the rules. Try as he might, he could not understand where she was coming from. He should call Mark.

He was afraid to call Mark. Afraid Mark would back Annie up. Fuck 'em both. What could they know?

Great day for a hike. Maybe they were in the woods this afternoon. Maybe there right now. Sunday. He would go to them. The thought of doing that brought something alive in him.

He locked his room and went to the next-door bar and parked himself next to the pay phone. Same bartender, onto him but cool, like go for it pal, I dream about it myself. The answering service told Kurt he could reach Eric all day today and gave him a number.

He hung up and sipped his beer and thought about how close he was to them. He could get in the car and be there in two hours, holding his children, holding his wife.

He finished the beer and had another, walked back to the hotel. Still no message from Johnny. Or Dominic. Or Bill. Anybody. Somebody pick up a phone and let me know what the fuck's going on.

•

It was dark when Johnny pulled around to the chain-link-fenced yard adjacent to the warehouse. Kurt got out of the van and appraised the four remaining containers deposited that afternoon. Johnny keyed open a serious padlock on the gate, and Kurt followed him in.

"You were right; guy said they'll be back Monday morning." Johnny went to a container and grabbed the lock, which was looped through the hasp on the bolt holding the doors shut. It was plugged with a soft lead amalgam bearing the U.S. Customs Service seal. "Check these out," he said. "Open the lock, and you break the seal. Pretty much tinker-proof."

They walked around the container, looking for a way inside. Bill stepped over to inspect the hinges that held the huge steel doors on the rear of the container.

"Wait a minute," Kurt said. Bill was looking at the same thing he was. "Let's get this thing inside."

"I'll go get my torches," Bill said.

A few hours later Bill was back with a tow truck and welding equipment. He cut the hinges off and hooked the doors to the tow truck winch. Johnny worked it carefully, lifting huge, heavy doors off the back of the container and easing them toward the floor.

He had them a solid foot off the concrete when the hook slipped.

"Mothafuckah!" Bill yelled, jumping back and grabbing his ears. Steel on concrete. Big, heavy steel crashing against concrete. Loud. Loud as if your eardrums have been hit with their absolute maximum load. Drop a pin now and they'll shatter.

Kurt stepped over to inspect the seals.

Intact.

Beautiful.

They moved to the mouth of the container. Scattered among the several hundred boxes within were a hundred and ten with red straps and hash. Kurt pulled one out and handed it to Johnny.

Johnny stacked it on a hand cart. One down.

One hundred and nine to go. Monday morning and customs' promised return hung there near the ceiling, metallic and structured, waiting. Move one piece, and it will fall in and crush you.

They restacked the boxes inside the looted container, borrowing from the others, careful to make the number of boxes match the manifest. If customs did a total count on this part of the shipment, the numbers would work.

Kurt used a crowbar to raise the doors, and he and Bill and Johnny, once they lifted it high enough for them to get beneath, fought it to a vertical position.

"Okay," Kurt grunted. "Let's walk it over." They took it corner by corner until they had the hinges back in place so that Bill could reweld them to the container.

"Man," Kurt said. He positioned his back against the steel, pressing his weight against it. Just think about this, nothing else. Don't get distracted. "Man," he said, "this is hard work." Stupid. This is stupid work. No. This is a way out, a way back to them.

"Yeah," Bill said, "and only worth fifteen million." He fired the torch and went to work while the others laughed giddily. "We finish this, we still gotta paint the thing."

Late Saturday, Johnny locked the front doors of the warehouse. Everything looked like business as usual. Now all they had to do was sweat it out until Monday morning, when customs would arrive. And then they'd sweat some more.

Johnny and his men drove off in a rented box van, en route to the stash house, where they would weigh and do inventory. Kurt took a rental Johnny had arranged for him. North, through the wilds of New Jersey.

He was tired and his muscles ached from labor, but he could not wait any longer. He would take it slowly, no matter how difficult it was. Take it slowly.

He looked in the rearview, not checking for heat, looking at himself. He needed a shave. *What if she tells me to go away?* Don't think like some paranoid jerk. *What if she tells me never come back here again?* She won't say that. She loves me. *She loves me not.* He drove through the night, wondering where the cops were, where Kessler was, and how in God's name he could persuade Annie to come with him and should he even try. What was right? He wanted to do what was right for them. Did that mean prison? Could it possibly mean prison? He thought of an old partner, Dan, who'd chosen to go down rather than leave his wife and kids. He would be out soon, and his family was waiting. Dan, whose weekly calls from prison made Annie both sad and scared. He could hear the operator's voice, as though the tape loop had been surgically implanted in his brain, and where had they found someone with such a flat voice, such a prim and proper tone: *A T & T has a collect call from—Caller, state your name.* "Dan"*—a prisoner at a federal correctional institution. Press One to accept this call. If you accept this call, do not use call forwarding or three-way calling or you* will *be disconnected.* Disconnected.

You *will* be disconnected. Cut off. But Dan's family had waited. They'd visited. They'd stayed faithful. And Rosie. Someday they'd have to let him out. Someday his sentence would be finished. Maybe a couple of years now. But they'd fucked him. Completely fucked him up. He'd been down so long now that any direction he went was up. His family had gone and found a new father. Twelve years. Since his early twenties. Look what they took from him. Pointless.

But Annie had said five. Annie said Mark could work out the details. Mark said that Kessler was a straightup cop. Five. It was do-able. And after, he could be there for them. He could be with them.

All he could do now was go to them. Tell them how he felt, listen to what they said. They would decide together, and things would go how things should go. He rubbed his face. Needed a shave. Couldn't remember when he hadn't, lately.

•

He could have assigned this surveillance to Wilson or one of the others, but it was another chance to be near her, and he needed to see her. Go to her and see if there was a chance in the world. It was probably crazy. Hadn't she sent him away when Alex woke up, and wasn't that a good indication of how she felt? But he'd thought this way before, only this was different, this was better, and if he didn't go and put it on the table, he'd probably spend a good portion of the rest of his life calling himself coward, calling himself fool. And, ah, yes, insomnia. It wasn't as if he could sleep anyway, even when all was calm.

And Kurt Trowbridge was in the country. He had just landed a load of Lebanese hash. He was close, and Kessler would find him, fall on him, catch him just the way he told Wilson he would: red-handed, with tons.

He left the thruway in New Paltz and took back roads from there, his headlights cutting through a darkness never seen in the city. Past deer feeding in meadows, and there went a skunk, wearing black tie and scurrying across the road. He could understand why she liked it up here, even with the winters so fierce. He checked his pager, made sure its little green screen was glowing with the hour. After midnight already. He was wagering Trowbridge wouldn't be able to stay away from them. He'd pick him up at the house, tail him to the load. Call in the troops.

Maybe he should have brought Wilson. But the thought of spending any more time with that guy was unbearable. Or maybe he was thinking in terms of what to do if Trowbridge didn't show.

He would spend the night driving, easing around the back roads, cruising the Trowbridge house, and hoping to catch Kurt there.

•

Tires on gravel, and Annie slipped out of bed, heart pounding, into jeans and a sweatshirt, digging for socks in the dark and for God's sake it was nearly five in the morning and scrambling to get downstairs. She needed a dog. She had to get another dog. Springtime was coming; it was a good time for training. She would do it herself, with love that would make the attachment solid. She would teach him to warn her of intruders. Teach him to guard her children.

She was downstairs just as a light tap came on the front door. Scared, heart wouldn't slow, banging in her chest like kettledrums. She pulled back a curtain.

Joseph Kessler.

"I woke you," he said. "I'm sorry."

He sat at the kitchen table, absently examining a tiny garbage truck that Alex had left there when Annie had carried him and Timothy up to bed. She brought coffee to the table and sat silently, watching him finger the toy. He was remembering something. Perhaps a time with his own children.

"Did you arrest him? Is that why you're here?"

"No." He smiled weakly, took a sip of coffee. "It's not about that anymore."

She could tell Kurt to go away and never call again, never call any of them. Tell him she thought it best if she and the boys went through the pain of losing him and got it over with and went on with their lives. He wanted to be an outlaw, now and forever, so go be one, be heroic, be sexy, be the man of someone's dreams, but you cannot be our husband and father anymore. You are hereby released from your wedding vows. You don't even have to be a married man.

"I didn't give you much time . . ." he started. "I was just in the neighborhood . . ." he started again. Smiled to himself. "It's been a while since I've really talked to anyone. Except myself."

"My mother always told me to steer clear of people who talked to themselves."

"I don't do it out loud. Except in my own apartment."

"I guess as long as you can still hear yourself, it's okay." Another awkward moment, stretching, stretching. Socially inept. Maybe she should just admit it to him, make things easier. "All those times we talked on the phone," she said. "I don't know why it's so hard now."

"I want us to be together," he said. "That's as simple as I can put it. That's why I'm scared and that's why I came back here. I blew it the first time, and now somehow we've met and I want us to be together. I love you. I think your kids are wonderful and in time we could be a family."

"You're divorced and totally fucked up about it."

"It's a process. I'm going through it."

"It's one I haven't yet gone through."

"Will you? I mean, how long are you supposed to put up with—" He stopped himself. "He's out of the picture, don't you think?"

"I don't know," she said. "I don't know about that at all."

"This is not about him. He's gone. It isn't, anymore, about him."

"Then what is it about?"

"It's about you and me. It's about family."

He stood and reached for her, pulled her to him and wrapped his arms around her, and again, there it was, comfort, compassion, and desire all right there, right there between them. He held her to him as if otherwise they might not survive.

"I've done the infatuation thing," he whispered. "I know where all that's at. You're special to me; you and those boys are what's missing in my life. And I know I could be what you need, I could be what they need. If you'll let me." He touched her face, ran a finger down her cheek and across her neck and to her breasts, which had given milk to someone else's babies, and he said, "I've dreamed of this moment."

He touched her cheek again, pulled her closer, and she felt need and desire, long dormant, rising in her against her will.

"Dreamed of it," he whispered, so close, strong with her, and careful of his strength, understanding in his fingertips how fragile the moment was.

She thought, for that long moment, that interminably long moment, that his arms were strong enough to contain her fear, that his arms were strong enough to protect her children. She recognized his sincerity, she recognized the goodness in his sad, tired heart, recognized what he was seeking—sanctuary, the giving and taking of it—and then he touched her chin and brought her lips to his, and they kissed.

•

There was the house, solid and sure. His house. Their home.

And there was a car, pulled up in the driveway. A cop car. Unmarked, but definitely heat. Blackwall tires, and in the light of the driveway Kurt could make out the stubby antenna on the left rear fender. A cop car. Parked next to the house, just as if it belonged there.

Mother.

Fucker.

Kurt parked on the side of the road, slumped down in the seat. What was this? He saw the light in the kitchen, burning, but that was all; the rest of the house was dark. Smoke curled gray against the still dark sky, a half-moon setting, and stars fading toward dawn. He'd missed the stars, too, but they could not calm him, could not distract his thoughts from the rushing of his blood, the pounding in his ears.

Kessler. He slammed a hand against the steering wheel so hard that a shock of pain flared up his arm. It had to be. He cursed quietly and gripped the wheel. Hold on. Hold on tight so you don't bolt and kick down the door and pound the bastard who's in there. *With your wife.*

He got nervous, suddenly; he was at a disadvantage, parked on the road that way. He started the engine, cringing at its noise in the night, and drove past the house. Down the road a few hundred yards, well out of sight. Parked again and took a flashlight from the glove box, headed into the woods.

He knew his way around, even in the dark. How many times had he walked these woods? With Kane. With Alex and Tim. With Annie. Dreaming of the life they would build. He walked. He would not let himself imagine. He would not go that way. Maybe it wasn't Kessler. How could he know what was happening? But it had to be a cop in there, so to walk in the door of his home was to walk into a prison cell. He heard an owl, a great horned one, from the sound of it: a cool and dark *who-who, who-who-who.*

He found a dry spot up close against a tree trunk. Wait. Wait and watch and wait some more. No comings. No goings. Smoke rising in the night. He could see the house from here, see the light in the kitchen, not much else. He wanted to go in there raging, go in there like a threatened bear and tear the place to righteous pieces, put Kessler on the floor on his belly. Not on his back, not a clean sportsmanlike pin on the mats. He wanted the motherfucker's face against the floor, the way they'd put Annie on the floor. He wanted to murder them both.

He closed his eyes. Slow down. Slow way down now. This is nowhere. His eyes fought him, fluttering, trying to open. He forced them closed again and made himself remember. Walking in the woods with them. Sunshine on snow. Their laughter, ringing through crisp, silent air. Calm now. Calm. Rest. Gather your strength.

·

It was a tender kiss, a kiss that could open a new world. She wanted to believe in it, wanted to know deep inside that this kiss was a beginning, a change, a chance for things to be right, that this kiss was a promise, one that would be kept.

When it ended, she rested her forehead against his chest and felt the pounding of his heart; heard her own beating away inside her, and tried to listen.

She tried to listen, and she listened, and leaned against him, and listened. And she heard them saying, "Daddy!" All those times, with all that love. She remembered Kurt pressing an ear to her belly, Kurt whispering to his unborn sons, Kurt telling her loyalty was his strong suit.

And she heard her own history, and all she could think to say was "I'm sorry."

He stepped back, looked at her. Touched her cheek, finger to her chin, raised her eyes to his. Questioning.

He stepped back farther, took a deep breath. She was thinking what could be or what could never be. Who knew what he had in mind now? Maybe what she saw in him as sadness was menacing desperation. He'd blown it once and hadn't recovered; he was a knight in tarnished armor, looking for a replacement princess, and here she was, the model mother, scorned and abandoned by her worthless, criminal husband. Bring on the violins.

"Sorry," he said. "I am too. You and I, Annie, we could make a good life. For us. And for your boys."

She nodded, and at that moment it was as if she'd spent most of her life doing that, nodding yes when she didn't know, nodding yes when she wasn't sure, nodding yes when she had no idea whether she meant it or not: Yes, Daddy, I'm your good little girl and grateful that you've trained me how to be just that. Yes, Coach Smith, I don't even know what you're doing but I know you shouldn't be doing it but please please yes yes yes. Yes, Eric, I need more of that stuff, give me lots and lots of it, and then give me some more. Yes, Kurt, I will marry you and have your children and stand by you even when you flee. And now, yes. Yes yes yes, Joe Kessler, let's throw caution to the wind. I will persuade Kurt to hold out his wrists to you. I will persuade him to let you put him in a cage, and then you and I and his children can live happily ever after. Maybe she should make an Annie Oakley doll, one of those contraptions with a hollow head stuck on the end of a spring that rode in the rear window of an automobile, bobbing *yes yes yes* each time the car hit a bump.

"Maybe I am a fool," she said. "Maybe I am blind. Maybe I can't see him for who he is or see you for who you are. I don't know."

He took a step forward.

"I think you'd better go."

He stood still.

"Now."

And he went out the front door, without looking back.

"Mom?" Alex called from the top of the stairs. She hadn't heard him get up. "Is that Daddy?"

"Daddy?" Timothy's voice was a whine. Their footsteps thumped uncertainly, sleepily, down the stairs.

"No, honey," she called. "It's not."

She heard their footsteps coming closer, and then they stumbled into the kitchen, rubbing their eyes, half asleep, still thinking they'd heard Daddy's voice.

She opened her arms to them, remembering his words from that first night. *I am always reassured to encounter yet another faithful wife.* He had misjudged her.

She knelt, pulling them close to her. Closer.

·

A car door slammed; an engine turned over. Kurt started awake, banged the back of his head against the tree he was huddled near. Shit. His clothes were damp with night. He heard tires on gravel and saw Kessler's car ease down the drive and pull onto the road, accelerating rapidly, headed toward town.

The sun was still below the tree line, but Kurt's eyes burned at the light. You could tell it would be strong when it rose; morning was coming up warm. How could he have slept? He listened as the car's sound grew fainter. He would wait. He would not walk into a trap. He sat back, staring at his house. His used-to-be home. Ten minutes. Twenty. Half an hour. No one drove past. No one was around.

He bent to get the flashlight and picked his way through the brush toward the back yard.

There was the swing set. And there was the pear tree, the buds on its limbs waiting to burst into the pale green leaf of springtime. He could smell the soil, coming alive, breathing, readying itself for the seeds within to burst forth into the sunshine. The last of the snow was running off into roadside streams, splashing and tumbling downhill.

He walked toward his house. The place where he could no longer live.

The back door was unlocked.

She was at the stove, scrambling eggs. Alex and Tim were edging their way along the windowsills, clinging like desperadoes to the wall of a building, going tiptoe along an imaginary ledge twenty stories in the air while firemen below held nets so they could land unharmed. Then Alex looked up.

"DADDY!" he shouted, and jumped from the windowsill to the dining table and from there into Kurt's arms in what seemed one swift movement. Timothy turned one way, then the other, frozen with indecision, so excited that he couldn't get the word out, uttering instead a series of short, ear-splitting squeals as he clambered behind, slipping and catching himself and making the jump right after his brother. And they were in his arms, quivering.

Annie turned, gasped, dropped a fork to the floor.

"Whoa!" Kurt said. "You guys got stronger!" He pulled them against his shoulders and threw his head back, eyes closed in bliss. "Man, did I miss you two." He opened his eyes and glared at her.

She found the strength to remain standing. His eyes accused her and found her guilty with one icy glance. He turned his attention back to his children, and she stood watching the three of them, a jumble of hugs and kisses and laughter. Timothy twisted an arm beneath Alex's, trying to pry him loose from Kurt. Kurt grabbed one boy in each arm and started toward the living room.

"How about it? Anybody wanna wrestle?"

They squealed with pleasure.

"Race you!" he shouted. He put them down and they took off. And he turned again to Annie. "What the fuck is going on here? Who was that?"

"DADDY DADDY DADDY! Come on! Hurry up!"

"You tell me," she said. "It was Kessler." He followed the boys, and she went back to her cooking, hands shaking so badly that she could barely stir the eggs, listening as the boys and Kurt thumped and rolled on the floor, straining and shouting and laughing uncontrollably. She was barely able to breathe. He would go again soon; he would have to. He would break their hearts again. Alex and Tim were laughing and shouting. They were happy. Truly. For the first time in months. They were whole. She pushed back tears, grabbed a towel to wipe her eyes. She would be happy with them. She would pretend—just for these few hours—that everything was fine.

She wondered if Kessler had really left or if this was the preliminary stage of a well-laid trap.

She took the pan from the burner, heard them pulling the cushions off the couch, scattering them on the floor, and walked in to see Kurt sitting in the middle of the living room, smiling hugely as he watched Alex and Tim jump up and down, singing so loudly they were already hoarse.

Alex stopped jumping and looked fiercely at Kurt. "Daddy," he said, "you better not ever-ever-ever-ever-EVER leave again." Kurt said nothing.

"And, Daddy," Alex added, "I'm HUNGRY!"

Kurt looked angrily at Annie, and then his glare softened. She thought he didn't want the boys to notice. But he must have seen. Surely he'd seen. Kessler leaving.

"Breakfast is ready," she said.

She filled plates and put them on the table. Forks against porcelain; blueberry muffins because Alex had asked for them and she happened to have the makings; orange juice. She wrote an A with ketchup on Alex's eggs, a T for Timothy. They were so keyed up they couldn't sit still, stuffing food into their mouths with abandon. She saw Kurt across the table, as he'd been so many times before. He was tan, unnaturally so for this early in spring. He was a stranger. She did not know the hostile man behind his eyes. He handed Tim a piece of toast. They were all in one room. Together.

Kurt saw the boys looking from him to Annie, and he reached for her hand and slipped his fingers through hers and squeezed. A little too hard. He knew. He knew. Blessed relief and unfamiliar distance at once. He caught her eye and held the look intently, for a long moment. She returned his look. And then they watched their children, who began bouncing again, smiling with ketchup on their faces and fingers. Alex hummed a little tune, and Timothy joined in. Their joy came back to them. Whatever was going on with Mom and Dad would work out; it always had before. Their happiness was filling the kitchen, growing by the minute, growing until it would fill the entire house and spill out onto the lawn.

"Have you spoken to Mark?" His voice was level. Controlled.

"Have you? Where were you?"

"In Beirut."

"You sounded so bad."

"It's done," he said. "It's all done with and over."

She tilted her head. "Just like last time. And the time before."

"No," Kurt said. "Like this time. Now. For real." To the boys: "Man, did I miss you guys." He opened his arms and they scrambled from their chairs and onto his lap, smearing ketchup across one cheek and his shirt.

Love? Was that what? She let the pain flood into her until it reached the tips of her fingers and toes, and there she was, open to it, vulnerable.

"Daddy," Alex said, "tell us the story of the big bad pig and the three little wolves."

Kurt stroked the boy's hair. "After breakfast," he said. "I'll tell you as many stories as you like." He pulled their plates over and they dug in again. "Daddy was so silly ever to go away for such a long time."

"Silly Daddy," Alex agreed happily. Timothy ate quietly, paying close attention to the balancing act required to shovel eggs from plate to mouth with a fork. They were determined to be on good behavior so that Kurt would stick around.

After breakfast, Annie coaxed the boys into a bath, telling them all they had to do was rinse off and then they could play with Daddy some more.

She and Kurt sat on the couch until he got up and began pacing. "I came here intending to talk you into trying it again. Coming with me."

Annie sat, waiting.

"Who was it? Who was here? I saw the car. I heard him leave." Kurt drew in a sharp breath. "What the fuck's going on?"

"I told you. It was Joe Kessler, and I don't know when he'll be back."

"So why was he here? What's going on?" His voice was low but full of rage, barely in check.

"Nothing's going on," she said. "Nothing. I don't know. I didn't expect him. I don't know what he's doing."

"I wanted you to come with me."

"Why did you tell them you were staying? Do you think you can just waltz in and out of our lives at will?" Now her voice, too, was angry. "I won't let you do that."

He sat down again, took her hand. It was there, between them, still, the connection stronger now for his absence and what they were facing.

"I don't know what I'm doing," he said. "Why was he here? Was he expecting me to be here?" He let go of her hand and stood up again, disgusted. Looked at her the way he had that night, the night they'd fought. That look. Betrayal.

"He showed up," she said. "He's been calling, regularly, since you left. Trying to track you down, I suppose. And then he just showed up." She didn't know whether to tell him.

"How long was he here? Was he here all night?"

"I am your wife," she said. "I have been faithful to you, even when you were faithful to something else. You left, Kurt, you abandoned us—"

"I never abandoned you. I had to go. I didn't want to. I had to. And you said you'd come with me—"

"I tried—"

"I won't let you take them from me. You can go with him if you want—"

"I don't."

"He's using you to catch me. You know that."

"I don't know anything. I don't know one single thing in the world, except that I will not let you continue to break our boys' hearts."

"I have no intention of doing that."

"Really?" She could not keep the sarcasm from her voice, though she knew it went nowhere.

He made no reply. Then, "I was thinking about talking to Mark. Maybe taking a deal. Before I came here. Saw what was going on."

"Nothing is going on. Nothing."

"You owe me something, too, you know. It's not all one way."

"Kurt," Annie said, "what exactly do I owe you?"

"How about some loyalty?" he said. "How about you don't cooperate with the man who's trying to lock my ass up for the rest of my life? Can you handle that? Or would you prefer to sleep with him? Did you sleep with him? Did you let him fuck you?"

She stood up, pushed to her feet by anger, by all the nights of wondering where he was and if he was alive, and why he had made a family if he didn't want to have a family, and how on earth she was going to raise two children by herself. Women lived so much closer to death than men. Women—childbearing, those years—had death as a guest every month, and the memory of it for life. It was there in the gut, the forlorn egg, the life force, aging, waiting hopefully, and then, if not fertilized in a matter of hours, dead. And its death brought sadness and blood. Men did not know that, could not know that. Men's bodies knew the activity of the germ, producing and producing and producing, seeking release, and if not released, reabsorbed, recycled, made fresh again, made alive. Death was not intimate with men's bodies as it was with women. Maybe that was what drove them to make war.

"How dare you," she said. "You're out there playing your stupid little games, playing with fire, playing with guns, playing with fast boats, out there playing cops and robbers, and I'm the one who's caught in the crossfire. Your children are the ones who are left orphaned. No, I did not sleep with him. No, I did not let him fuck me. Don't you get it? Can't you understand?"

Her knees began to give, but she made it back to the couch, managed to sit for an instant before her body folded up on her. Her head was on her knees and she was weeping, trying not to let the sounds out, sounds that would frighten her children, her children, who were splashing in the bathtub and were overjoyed because, at last, at long long last, Daddy had come home.

She felt his hand on her back, and his other, and he was lifting her, bringing her to him, her head on his shoulder, and he was rocking so gently, so gently back and forth, rocking.

"I'm sorry," he said. "I'm sorry."

She did not know how long they sat like that. They sat, together, resting.

"I'll talk to Mark. Work something out. I can take five years," he said quietly. "If you'd promise to stay with me, to visit and bring them to visit."

"Just like that," she said, regaining herself. "You've disappeared for months, and now here you are and it's supposed to be as if you'd never left. I can't believe we're talking about this," she added. "We're talking about prison and I'm relieved."

And then the boys were shouting for their father, and he went to give them towels and clean clothes.

Later, they built with colored blocks on the living room floor while outside the sun shone and spring crept in for a visit. When they tired of the blocks, Kurt urged them outdoors. "I'll be there in a minute," he said.

"You shouldn't go out there," Annie said. "There might be surveillance."

"They'll come back inside soon."

"They love you so much."

"And I love them. And you." He went toward the kitchen. "Would you like a cup of tea?"

How many times had he said that, over the course of their years together? "Would you like a cup of tea, dear?"

He stood waiting for the kettle to boil. "I was caught up in it," he said. "It was foolish. I want my family back, Annie. I want you back. I'll go to jail if I have to." He held out a hand, asking her to come to him.

She had missed the color of his eyes, that blue somewhere between sky and tropical sea. She had missed his scent. She had missed his touch.

"I still have some cards to play," he said. "I'm a fugitive; they'll get points if I come in. And I can offer the ranch and some cash. I can bargain with them."

"And what will I tell Alex and Tim to prepare for your leaving?"

"The truth," he said. "We'll tell them the truth."

"They're so little," she said.

"Yes," Kurt said. "They're still little enough. They haven't yet lost their wisdom."

EIGHTEEN

"I'm sorry," she had said.

Kessler didn't blame her. He didn't blame anyone for anything. It was a waste of time. Leave it to the prosecutors; leave it to the judges. He sized himself up in the rearview, his clean eyes, his established eyes, his hunter's eyes. He was close now, he could feel it: electricity humming in his bones, neurons popping, the delicate thrill of the hunt. Why would she stick by him? Go-figure and who-cares all wrapped up in one neat package, an emotional letter bomb waiting to explode.

Now Kessler could retreat to the safe place, go into his work fully. It was good to feel nothing, to know he was the good guy about to do the right thing. Track him down. Do his job and be done with it, done with him, done with her, done with the whole sorry lot of them. Move on to the next case. Dopers. Lock 'em up and throw away the key and God bless America. What the fuck. Someday he would retire and start life over again. Maybe become a PI, spend nights taking dirty pictures of cheating husbands for rich, jealous women who dressed their poodles in cashmere.

He drove through Stone Ridge, and north to the bridge that crossed the Hudson, and across it into the village of Rhinebeck. The land was gentler over here, rolling pastures, orchards, not so rocky and steep as west of the river. *I'm sorry,* she'd said after he kissed her. That was okay. He'd expected it, he supposed. He would have wanted his wife to do the same, in those circumstances. Would have loved her all the more for it if she had.

Anyway, who knew what she would do once her old man was locked up. Not so many could be faithful to a cage.

He spotted a café, open and advertising cappuccino. Parked and hit a pay phone before going in.

"Meet me at the Daily Grind," he said into the receiver. He hung up and went in. There were scones and quiches and various chocolate things in a display case. He ordered a large coffee, black, took up a paper, and went to a small table near the back of the narrow space.

There was a police blotter section on page two of the slender paper. A bicycle had been stolen. Two men, early twenties, were arrested Saturday for possession of marijuana and public intoxication. A barn had been set on fire. Arson was suspected. A woman reported seeing a large, cigar-shaped object hovering in the sky at around midnight Saturday. Two teenage girls were picked up for attempting to shoplift cigarettes at the grocery store; their names were withheld.

High crimes and misdemeanors. Kessler looked up to see Eric, cool Eric, slick Eric, terrified Eric. Watched him order coffee and carry it to the table. His hands were trembling so much that he spilled it and had to return to the counter for extra napkins.

"Take it easy," Kessler said quietly.

Eric gave him a look, but Kessler's glare withered it.

"What is it?" Kessler said. "Why you so nervous?"

"I'm trying to start over up here," Eric said. "I don't exactly think being seen with you is—"

Kessler stood up abruptly. "My car's outside." They got lids for their cups on the way out.

Kessler drove leisurely, winding down country lanes, letting the morning air flow in through the windows, liking the scent of spring. Here and there, in shady spots beneath trees, the last white puddles of snow were going to water, shrinking into the earth.

Eric kept looking at Kessler, as though trying to gauge his mood.

"Out with it," Kessler said finally.

Eric dug in his bag and handed Kessler a slab of hashish, wrapped in foil. "Here's the sample."

"All of it?"

"Enough of it."

"I'm glad to see you getting into your work," Kessler said. "You're doing great."

"I just—" Eric took a long slow sip of coffee, choked on it. When he'd recovered himself, he said, "She's a friend. She's an old friend."

"Get over that," Kessler said. "You haven't seen her twice in the last five years."

"She's still a friend."

"Hey, what are you gonna do? You've been down, you've been strung out."

Eric sighed and didn't reply.

"Eric," Kessler said, "you're doing the right thing." He said it, but it sounded like a cop-out. Hey. You had to keep them motivated.

"Yeah," Eric said.

"How're you doing? Still clean?"

"As the proverbial whistle."

"Hey," Kessler said, "you're this close to freedom. I'll leave you alone after this one, unless you run across something you think I'd be interested in, or unless you fuck up again and I catch you again. After this, it's up to you."

"Where's your partner?" Eric asked.

"He's not my partner," Kessler said. "And that's none of your business. Now. What are we doing here, besides burning fuel?" He saw a wide place in the road and did a quick three-point turn, heading back toward town.

"I don't see how to do this without getting burned," Eric said. "I'm meeting him tomorrow. Don't know where yet. He'll call my service at three. We go from there."

"There we go then," Kessler said. "We'll hang together tomorrow. I'll have a team ready."

"We're even, after this."

"You walk, my friend. If that's what you decide you want to do."

He dropped Eric at a corner, not too far from the coffee shop, and headed back toward the bridge. Yeah, we're even. Scumbag. He didn't think Eric would ever get out of it. Eric had tasted cash money in exchange for his favors. Eric liked the rush. Gary Smith had been a wimp, too. Kessler found it impossible not to despise informants, but he used them all the time, depended on them the way every effective agent did. Wholly. They brought the cases, they made the cases, they did the dirty work, often killing themselves in the process, collecting their bounty when a case came through. No honor. No loyalty. No nothing except give someone over to the other side and get freedom and money and drugs in exchange. It sucked. The whole thing sucked big time. He hated this part, when the details were all down and the arrest was imminent. It was a weird kind of push-me-pull-you trip he did on himself when he knew the one he was letting go was worse than the ones he got in exchange. But they were cases. They were numbers. And that's what the agency demanded. He knew a sorry-ass when he met one, usually, and he didn't think Kurt met all the criteria. But anyway, who was he to say? Who was some fucked-up skirt-chasing alcoholic judge to say? Who was some self-righteous-can't-wait-to-go-to-work-for-a-top-flight-money-spitting-defense-team prosecutor to say? We're all just out there, out there and bouncing off each other like the shiny silver orbs of a pinball machine. Bing. You get a million points. Tilt. You lose them.

He drove south, toward the city, toward his anonymous apartment, which he wouldn't go to now because he couldn't bear it, couldn't stand it, couldn't fathom its squalor. At the moment. He drove toward the office and the telephone on his desk.

He remembered that one morning, early morning, driving down this highway and Kurt Trowbridge sitting right there next to him. Captured. Cuffed. Kessler had him. After all those years, he had the man in custody. It should have been satisfying.

But he'd kind of liked him, that morning. He still liked him, though he was completely confused about Annie. He wouldn't have minded sitting over a beer or two with Kurt, shooting the breeze, getting to know his better side.

He had to get out of this job. It was killing him. It had stolen his wife and children. It had sent him to visit prostitutes. It had very nearly killed him a number of times. He had to get out. And now he'd lost even his judgment, his ability to calculate. How could he have thought she would come to him? How could he have thought?

"You're in love, asshole," he said out loud. "You're in love."

Fuck. He drove on, the needle on the speedometer pushing eighty-five. Get over it. He didn't often speed, but today deserved it. Circumstances merited a serious push. And if he got stopped, he had a badge in his pocket. Official business, he would say. Fucking Brad Wilson did it all the time. Wilson never went anywhere at less than twenty over the limit.

Yeah, well, so the deal was going down—*mañana.* He'd need most of the office for this one, including Wilson. So give the guy a chance. But blow this one, asshole, you're out for good. He'd assign Wilson to arrest Eric. Only way not to burn him was to take him into custody. But he'd get him out the back door quickly enough, and Trowbridge would be none the wiser. Eric could maintain his friendship with Annie. She sure could pick 'em. Who knew? The whole thing might bring them closer.

•

Alone again, after the worst kind of tearful farewell, his children left in agony, and Kurt bawling halfway to the city, their cries ringing in his ears. I'll be back soon, he'd promised, but he could tell they didn't believe him. Please, he'd said. I can't stay here right now. Please trust me on this.

He'd given Annie a beeper number and said call for anything at all. He was going to get together with Mark. He was going to work it out. He would come home again before he turned himself in. He would arrange for them to have some time together before his sentence began. And he'd told her the truth. He'd told her he planned to meet with Eric the next day. At the Marriott in Long Island City. At three o'clock. And then it would be over. He would be out of it forever, and his partners would have their end and not be hurt and she would have enough cash to get by while he was locked up.

As he walked up Second Avenue he kept hearing Hank Williams—*I'm so lonesome, I could die*—as if it was coming out of a tabletop jukebox in the Blue Ridge Café a few miles down the road from his ranch. He remembered hill country sunsets washing over them as he and Annie trailed horseback along ridges and through sparse stands of low oak and mesquite. The boys would have loved it.

But he would give it up; he would cut a deal with the prosecutor; he would, as they said, disgorge assets in exchange for a reduced charge and a lighter sentence. He could see the guy, sitting at a desk, chuckling and rubbing his palms together in the name of the federal government. They didn't give a shit about right or wrong; if they did, they wouldn't be letting murderers and rapists walk in order to clear cell space for potheads. It was all just business to them, purée of crime.

He walked, trying to clear his head as the city hummed around him, buzzing under the sun, millions of worker bees doing their tasks. With zest. With bravado.

Already he missed them desperately; tried to shake it off but couldn't. It was getting hot. Unusually hot for so early in spring. Maybe record-breaking hot, the weatherman said. Kurt rolled up his sleeves and kept walking, sweat beading on his forehead. It felt okay, actually. He spotted a phone and pushed appropriate buttons.

"Unbelievable." Johnny sounded pissed off and highly amused at the same time. "The fucking food police. Do you believe these guys? Lazy-ass government agents inspect our food and say this is okay and this isn't. Meantime, they're all takin' fuckin' payoffs and we're all gettin' poisoned but this guy shows up and says our dates have—let me get it right—*an unacceptable level of infestation.*"

"If we had 'em on the payroll, they'd call it extra protein." Kurt laughed. "Fuck it. We'll sell them in Canada or the U.K. They've got a higher limit."

"Man, I had no idea I eat a piece of cake there's gonna be dead bugs in there."

"What about customs?" Kurt said. Then, "Hold on." He waited while a fire truck blew past, horns blaring, headed south on Second. Almost three, and traffic close to becoming one solid mass of hot, steaming metal, evaporating carbon monoxide. Whoever was driving the truck seemed to think that noise would make drivers pull out of the way and let him through.

"Yeah."

"They haven't showed," Johnny said.

"Where the fuck are they? Call them."

"What?"

"Call them. Tell them they're holding us up, we got people waiting, when are they coming to finish the inspection." He gave Johnny the pay phone number and stood watching the stress-ridden and the happily indifferent parade through the doors of the Big Cheese Deli until the phone rang.

Johnny was laughing. "They're not coming."

"What?" Alarm hit, washed away by relief. What was this?

"They say, get this, I call 'em up they say, 'Oh, yeah-yeah-yeah, well, we were gonna get around to that, but you know, just go ahead and break the seals. We're satisfied. Just break the seals.' Do you believe it?"

"Johnny!" Kurt shouted. Here came another one; there might be a real fire. He wished Alex and Tim were with him. They would be flipping out over all this. Firemen, in their book, were totally cool. The little holes in the mouthpiece of the pay phone were packed with grit. He watched an unwizened but wrinkled little Hispanic man sitting on a park bench in front of the bank at the corner. Public space, as the tax-break parks were called, each with its requisite vagrants, fallout from the equal opportunity bomb. Traffic opened suddenly and the fire truck disappeared up the avenue.

"You there?"

"Yeah," Kurt said.

"We worked our asses off, didn't we?" Johnny laughed.

The Hispanic man leaned over the back of the park bench and puked. Kurt turned back to the phone booth. Junkie. Disconnect me from life; I can't take the pain. Man.

"So, listen, pal," Kurt said. "I should tell you. I'm gonna try to work something out on this case I caught. If I can get five and give them some assets, I'm going for it."

"What?" Johnny's voice squeaked with astonishment. "You can't—"

"It's cool, it's cool. I'm not giving anybody up. Just property. If my lawyer can work it out. So, just, if you see something in the papers or whatever, you know, just lay back."

"You're out of your fuckin' mind, man. They ain't got nothing on you."

"Johnny," Kurt said, "I don't want this anymore. I want my family. This is the only way to get them. Good time, I'll be out in thirty-six months. I'll call you in a day or so to let you know where to send the dates. Right now, just get Bill and move that out of there."

"You're crazy. I thought they wanted life. Don't do anything. Let's get together, talk."

"Let me start this process, man, and see what develops. They know they won't ever find me. They'll deal. But I'm not going in until my lawyer has something on paper. Okay? So don't freak. But tell Bill I'll need my end A.S.A.P. if I'm gonna try to buy these motherfuckers out."

He heard a long, soulful sigh through the phone.

"Johnny?"

"No problem, man. When you come back, we'll have a big bag of money for you. But think about this. Really."

"Get some rest soon as you can, my friend."

•

The boys were on the porch, finger-painting. Annie could see them from the garden. She dug easily, turning compost into the soil, working methodically. Some people liked to use rototillers, churning the dirt mechanically, but she preferred a shovel. It gave the worms time to get out of the way, and there were no gas fumes. The soil in the garden was loose and friable already, easy to work; adding the compost made it even more so.

She didn't know what else to do with these hours except try to maintain some kind of normal schedule. Kurt said he would call when he'd met with Mark, so when the phone rang, she dropped her shovel and ran for it eagerly, clomping dirt across the kitchen floor.

"Annie?" She recognized the voice but couldn't place it at first.

"Listen, I'm in a bind here. Tell Kurt not to show. Tell him it's a bust."

She stood at the kitchen door, looking out at her half-turned garden, unable to speak.

"He's not here," she managed, and heard Eric curse and hang up.

This could not be happening. She dialed Mark's number. Learned that Kurt wasn't due there until later in the day. Found the number, dialed Kurt's beeper, punched in her number, and hung up.

She grabbed Kessler's card and dialed the straightline, missing keys, having to start over. It rang and rang and rang. How could he do this? How could he have said? Maybe there was more to it. She tried his office number.

The woman who answered the phone informed her that Agent Kessler wasn't in.

"I have to talk to him," Annie said.

"I'm afraid he's out of the office," the woman said. Bored. "He's expected back later today."

"Can't you get him on the radio or something?" Annie pleaded.

"Ma'am," the voice said, "if this is an emergency, you should call your police department."

"I—"

She calmed herself, tried to bring her voice back to normal, wound up cutting the connection without saying anything, dialed his pager, and then hung up and dialed Laura. "I have to go somewhere," she said. "No time to explain. Can I drop the boys?"

Of course," Laura said.

Bring them right over. She tried Kessler's beeper again. She tried Kurt's beeper again. She called the boys and grabbed the car keys and led them, running, to the Jeep.

Left the engine running while she herded them toward Laura's door, and then Laura was there, smiling at them, and her eyes were scared at the same time.

"I'll explain later," Annie said, and kissed them. They started crying but she had to go, and in the mirror she saw Laura take their hands and lead them inside.

She went up over Mohonk, tires screeching on every curve, and please all you deer and squirrels and chipmunks stay out of the road because I can't brake today, and through New Paltz it was amazing she didn't get stopped or run over the wannabe hippies languidly crossing Main Street.

And then she was on 87 south, southbound and down, that was what the truckers used to say, back in Texas, on their CB radios, *southbound and down, pedal to the metal,* and that's what she was, not driving, flying, staying in the right lane until the last minute and zipping around the law-abiders, out into the passing lane and back over in the hopes of avoiding radar. Here came Bear Mountain and there went Bear Mountain. Here came the shopping outlets at Woodbury Commons and just think of all the happy campers in there spending all the extra money they were saving by shopping manufacturers' outlets. The thruway opened up to four lanes and she was really moving, weaving in heavy traffic at close to eighty, then close to ninety, she had to get there, had to find him and warn him.

•

Eric sat at Kessler's desk, eyeing his beeper, black and plastic amid the stacks of paperwork. Kessler was sitting sideways, eyes closed, resting after yet another sleepless night.

"You're righteous on this?" Kessler said, not bothering to open his eyes.

"He told me he would call," Eric said. He pushed up his sleeves, wished he'd worn something lighter. Just being in the room was making him sweat. Agents were everywhere, most of them fiddling with paperwork at their desks, but you could tell they were ready to move at the drop of a pin. The room was thick with anticipation, coated with eagerness.

Kessler bolted upright and all eyes went to Eric when the little black box said *beepbeepbeep.* He grabbed it, scribbled down the number. Kessler shoved a phone at him and he dialed. Wrote down an address and said into the phone, "See you there at three." Hung up and looked at Kessler.

"All right," Kessler said. "We're pushing it. Wilson! Get the cars."

"Fuckin' A." Wilson grinned and headed for the door. Agents slipped on holsters and jackets and followed as Kessler led Eric down the hall to the elevator.

•

Long Island. Flat and sandy. The Marriott Hotel and Convention Center was huge and gleaming. Kurt drove around it a few times, not entirely sure why, going with his gut. No sign of surveillance. No one following him. The parking lot was aglitter with cars, plush little ovens parked side by side under the midday sun. It was hot outside, not the kind of weather a person wanted to rush around in.

He walked slowly toward the glass-and-steel hotel entrance, trying to slow his pulse by reminding himself that he'd been careful. He'd given Eric explicit instructions.

He scanned the front of the building. Things should be fine. He thought of the boys. He thought of Annie. He tried to recall his own name and couldn't; he forgot, for an instant, what ID he was using. Who am I? Fuck if I know. I used to be a husband and father. I was looking forward to watching my sons' wrestling matches. Might never see one. Not if you keep thinking like this. Or maybe it's the business, or maybe it's the law. *Fool.* Or maybe some perverse combination of the two. 1 + 1 = CASH.

He brought his attention to the door and walked into the lobby. Cool air. He was sweating, but it gave no relief. He'd rather suffer heat than air forced around metal coils full of toxin, anyway. He went left, upstairs to the mezzanine level. The table he took held a view: the entire bar, the entry, and a good portion of the lobby.

He breathed deep and tried to exhale the tension from his muscles. Much of it went, but his effort attracted the attention of a man sitting two tables down on the rail. Sport jacket over a navy Izod. Drinking martinis. Kurt flashed that he'd been made, but the guy was unable to focus. If he was a cop, he was too far gone to be on a stakeout. Somebody would have pulled him by now.

Check the entrance. A wannabe producer, all in black on a scorcher like this, and his girlfriend, her cocaine-faded complexion stark against something red and dry-clean-only that confined her breasts inside cones. They entered. They took a table downstairs. The man ordered something while watching his tablemate look around the bar until she, too, found somebody to look at; anything was preferable to verbal exchange with her partner. Jerks, yes. Cops, no.

Just take the money and run, Kurt told himself. Forget the rest of it. It's over. You're out of it. Take the money, get with Mark, and then it's

Let's Make a Deal with the feds. Someday you'll go home to your wife and children.

Not yet Happy Hour, but the bar was doing a brisk business already. A few who'd slipped away from the office early sat at one end, razzing the boss and getting a head start on tomorrow's headache.

He had checked the layout of the building carefully, and planned to meet Eric as soon as he entered the bar, take a briefcase full of cash from him, and give him a set of keys in return. He would make his way out through the lobby, past the cashier's desk to a short hallway, and through a small glass door exit to the rental he'd left parked illegally outside. Unless Eric came up with something about I didn't bring the money we have to go get it. If that happened, Kurt would bail. Grab a taxi and split. Go back on the lam until he could move this stuff and get the cash. But Eric had to know: *To live outside the law you must be honest.*

True. Kurt sipped at the beer he'd ordered a couple of eons ago. Otherwise, sooner or later, you wind up dead. The weekend at MCC came rushing into his head from the place it now permanently occupied in his brain: 9 North. Six tiers, A through F; he couldn't make out how many cells per tier. Maybe twenty. Utter and total fucking cruelty. To nobody's benefit, least of all society's. Five years. But it wouldn't be at MCC. Dan said the joint he was in wasn't so terrible. Just crowded and noisy and shit for food and hope you don't need a doctor or a dentist 'cause that was some scary stuff.

There he was. Scanning the bar with the kind of put-on cool that betrayed sautéed nerve endings. Not good. Kurt waited until Eric's gaze passed him unseeing, put a bill on the table, and clipped down the stairs slowly enough not to attract attention.

He met Eric at the end of the bar.

Eric set the briefcase down. Kurt gave him the keys and picked up the case. The weight felt right. Anyway, he was sure Eric knew not to fuck with him on something like this.

"Hey." Eric tried a smile but it didn't go. "What are we doing?"

"White box van," Kurt said. "Almost right in the middle of the lot. Jersey plates." He gripped the briefcase and walked. Walked away from it, across the lobby and toward the hallway. There it was. He could see down the hall and outside the glass doors. Right where he'd left it, he could see it. No sign of heat. Stay with it now. Press on.

•

She'd've sworn she'd take the paint off the Acura in the lane next to her but she slid past without touching it, or if she did scrape it the encounter was so slight as to be unnoticeable. She was *moving*. Hadn't driven like this since losing those Texas narcs so long ago, so many lifetimes ago. Fuck it. It was all or nothing now. Get there or lose him for life. A setup. A motherfucking setup. Sleazebag Eric. And Kessler. What was there to say? Cars and scenery flew past in a blur. Annie focused intensely on traffic, on not crashing the Jeep or winding up in a ditch. She would get there. She would get there in time. The Long Island Expressway stretched in front of her; scattered traffic, not as bad as it could have been, but she had to thread the needle all the same, easing the Jeep from lane to lane, behind this car, in front of that one, past that one and that one and that one, and drivers yelling after her, she was sure, pissed off at the maniac doing ninety on the freeway. She thought of that day, running, that day when all she could think was Kurt is in jail, Kurt is in jail. If they got him now, it would be life. It would be die-in-a-cage, bastard.

She'd thought Joe Kessler meant it. She'd let him kiss her; she had kissed him and let him hold her and she thought he held a promise. She had believed him.

A Volvo came into the lane in front of her and she had to swerve hard not to hit it. The Jeep went up on its two left wheels and Annie steered into it, almost hitting a Volkswagen in the process. Back on all fours, and gunning away from the angry blare of horns.

•

As he reached the front desk, a clerk vaulted over the counter, pulled a gun, landed in a combat stance, aimed dead-on at Kurt. Fuck. Kurt stopped, stunned; the gunman swung left. Kurt turned to see Eric running toward them, and that guy, the drunk, he was on his feet too and moving quickly. The gunman swung back to Kurt, back to Eric, back and forth, level, ready. What the—

"Freeze!" Kurt did. "Federal agents!" The gunman held a badge out now, his automatic in the other hand. Ready to shoot. And Kurt recognized him, saw the eyes, the guy who'd been with Kessler that day, that Saturday morning. The musclehead. Aiming and ready to shoot. Primed for it. Freaking. Shit.

And, then, Annie? Annie running in the front door, her eyes desperate, knocking stunned bystanders out of the way, screaming, "No, Kurt, no!" And someone grabbed her and threw her down and Kurt moved to help her and then there were agents everywhere, pulling out badges and sticking them on their civvies: DEA, U.S. Marshals Fugitive Unit, local police, everywhere, twenty, no, thirty, waving guns and closing in, and one of them tried to grab Eric, and Eric went into a crouch and began making noises, the weirdest fucking noises . . .

Kurt moved toward Annie, rage blinding him to the guns. They'd thrown her to the ground. "Wait!" His word evaporated, and two of the cops jumped. Kurt heard the thud of flesh on flesh, and there were four of them on Eric and one moving toward him. Then, weird as shit, Kessler was in his face, and Kurt couldn't stop himself; he reared back and punched, and it all came out in one solid swing. He caught Kessler on the jaw, a solid slam, a good punch; he hit his target with all the rage and grace he knew from all the times before.

Kessler went down, spiraling to the floor; the musclehead lunged; Kurt sidestepped him to move toward Annie, to help Annie.

"Hey, man," he said, "let's all just—"

Someone shouted, "GUN!" and Kurt raised his hands high, to show them *No, no gun,* and how had everything gotten so crazy so fast, *let's all just—*

And now he heard a blast, the explosion of it, and the roar of the bullet toward him. *Cool down here,* he'd been going to say. *Let's all just cool down.* Metal entered his chest. Dead on. He looked down. There was a hole in his sternum. He stared at it. He looked up to see them pulling Kessler to his feet, and Kessler, something in his eyes, as if he'd seen this kind of thing before, and Kessler moving toward Annie, and a ring of men surrounding him and he couldn't see anything but them. He looked again at his chest. At the hole. It blurred. There wasn't much blood; he didn't see much blood. Maybe that came after. Was he falling to the ground?

His eyes closed and he saw their faces and he thought he heard a whisper.

Daddy. Let's wrestle.

NINETEEN

"BASTARD!" She could feel Kessler's arms trying to hold her, trying to contain her, trying to stop her. She hit, she punched, she pounded and pummeled and fought hard enough to send him straight to hell, where he belonged, "YOU LYING MOTHERFUCKER! Kiss me! Bastard." She broke his grip, pushed past him and through the ring of men, and there was Kurt, on the floor, and there was his blood. So much blood, and more coming, pouring from the hole in his chest, spilling onto the floor.

She knew she was crying, but she didn't feel a thing.

She didn't feel a godforsaken thing.

She touched his face. She went down on her knees and she leaned over him and she kissed his warm lips, which had kissed her pain away such a long long time ago. She kissed his warm lips, which had spoken the name Alexander and spoken the name Timothy before they were either of them born.

Then she stood up and looked around at the ring of men watching her. And past them, at Joseph Kessler. And past him, and past the sparkling glass doorway behind him, all the way out to the sunny day glittering so clearly, so cleanly, outside.

She did not feel a godforsaken thing.

TWENTY

She put away the shovel. She latched the garden gate. She went to the porch and helped them finish their paintings, and she put away the paints.

"Mommy," Alex said, "are you okay?"

"I'm fine, sweetie," she said. "Shall we have fish sticks for dinner?"

"And ketchup? With French fries?"

"In that order, I'm sure." She tried to laugh, but it came out choking. "Goodness," she said, "I need a drink of water." Water. And air. She needed air. She breathed, kept breathing. Led them to the kitchen to begin preparing their dinner. The telephone hung in its place on the wall, hung there dumbly, refusing to stir.

She turned knobs on the oven, opened boxes, opened packages. Put this here, put that there, put it all in the oven and hope for the best. She'd never had any of those Suzy Homemaker things, the ovens and dolls and accoutrements that taught good little girls how to be good big girls. Carol had done that stuff. Annie had preferred the outdoors, where she could bang tom-toms and roam imaginary prairies, clothed in animal skins, running swift as the wind.

She had never imagined the joy that would come from children. And here they were, waiting for dinner. With ketchup. Lots of it.

She looked at the oven. And the sink. And the dishwasher. And the refrigerator. She looked at her children. There they sat, in child-size chairs at their child-size table, drawing on paper with crayons while they waited for their mother to bring dinner. Safe and sound. The kitchen was warm with cooking. They were all safe and sound.

•

She read to them, after dinner and bathtime. She put her pajamas on and they all got in her bed and she read and read and read.

They slept, finally, and she turned out the light and sat there, staring out the window at the stars. It was warm enough for her to leave the windows open. The air was gentle and fresh.

Morning came up sunny and clean. She did not know what to do. She would try to make the morning normal for her children. Normal. Okay.

After breakfast, she knelt on the freshly turned soil, her hand out to the boys: coriander seeds on the flat of her palm, miniature brown planets, their surfaces dry and bumpy. Morning sun rested just above the tree line, and a pair of black-throated blue warblers circled high above the garden. She closed her hand around the seeds and made a bench of her leg for her children. They sat, wriggling toward comfort.

"Real still." She pulled them to her and pointed skyward. They looked up; trying desperately not to fidget. First Alex and then Timothy spotted the birds and sat still.

The male did three large, looping horizontal circles and fell into a nose dive toward Earth, heading right for the garden. Annie thought he would smash himself, but at the last possible instant he pulled to a stop with a flutter of wings and lighted on a corner post. Alex and Tim sat watching, transfixed.

The warbler's back shone brilliant blue in the sunlight; his chest was white; his face and neck black. He cocked his head and looked at the plain cedar birdhouse Annie had attached to the post two down from where he sat. He flitted to the perch beneath the circular door. Paused, peeked in, and disappeared through the hole. The female did the same kamikaze dive to the same post and hopped over to the house. She said something. From inside, he replied.

"I think they're going to move in," Annie said.

Alex and Tim giggled softly. The birds had a short discussion and flew off. The boys stood up and trotted across the loamy black soil of the garden to gaze up at the birdhouse.

"When will they be back?" Alex asked.

"Soon, I think. Are you ready to plant?"

They came back to her, and each took a seed between thumb and forefinger.

"Just put it in the dirt?" Alex looked straight into her eyes, blue meeting green, and Timothy too, earnest and full of promise. Both of them had Kurt's eyes. She smiled to remember the first time she and Kurt had swum together, at that swimming hole outside Austin, and how he had to work so hard to stay afloat because his body was dense with muscle.

When she was a little girl and growing, men had brought bulldozers to the fields of Texas and cut streets into them, spreading suburbia across the landscape. Boys and their toys, building cities and making war, arrived to change the world. But there were little pockets of woods left here and there by developers intent on spoiling the countryside, and the children always found them, drawn to nature by the promise of shade and water on a blistering summer day. Word would spread, and a swimming hole was born. There were still some to be found, tucked away up here. She would take the boys soon. They could learn how to float.

She had laughed that afternoon, and followed Kurt as he climbed onto a rock. They lay there naked in the sunshine, fingertips touching on an afternoon in June that promised summer forever. He'd turned and whispered in her ear, *You're the one, Annie Oakley. You're the one.*

"Mommy?" Alex stood, his eyes a question she couldn't answer. She held out her hand and they took some seeds and went to work carefully, placing them gently in the tiny holes she'd made with a twig. Coriander seemed unsuited to rows, somehow. These would grow in bunches.

"We can make some rows over there for beans."

"With this?" Alex asked, holding a thick, sturdy twig out to her.

"That's fine," Annie said. "This will be our best garden ever."

ABOUT THE AUTHOR

The author of *Rush* and *Notes from the Country Club,* **KIM WOZENCRAFT** is a former undercover narcotics officer and a graduate of Columbia University. Her work has been anthologized in *Best American Essays.* She was executive editor at *Prison Life* magazine and is Vice President of Creative Affairs at Off Line Entertainment. She lives in New York with her husband and two children.